THE HOLLOW PLANE

BOOK ONE OF THE AETHEREALS DUOLOGY

ALLISON CARR WAECHTER

for the babes who are relearning who they are.
this is brave work.
cry if you need to.

Copyright © 2023 by Allison Carr Waechter

All rights reserved.

No part of this publication may be reproduced, distributed, or transmitted in any form or by any means, including photocopying, recording, or other electronic or mechanical methods, without the prior written permission of the publisher, except as permitted by U.S. copyright law. For permission requests, contact Allison Carr Waechter.

The story, all names, characters, and incidents portrayed in this production are fictitious. No identification with actual persons (living or deceased), places, buildings, and products is intended or should be inferred.

Paperback: 978-1-963134-00-1

Ebook: 979-8-9860604-9-1

Hardcover: 978-1-963134-01-8

Book Cover by Christin Engelberth

Editing by Kenna Kettrick

Interior Illustrations and Map by Rachael Ward of Cartography Bird

First edition 2023

CONTENT GUIDELINES

Dearest Reader,

This book deals with a lot of heavy emotions. Unlike other books I've written, the MCs in this book do not have loving families of origin or happy childhoods. They are damaged from ill treatment and are, above all else, searching for belonging.

This is an ode to found family, and learning to trust when you have every reason not to. It is not a miserable tale; it's a romance, a mystery, a story of evaluating ambition and our reasons for revenge. It's a book about all the beautiful ways we love, even when we've been hurt.

But like all my books, it does contain references to some pretty heavy topics. As always, I write these depictions from a survivor's perspective, in that I try to give you (as the reader) enough information to know what harm was done, without using those events for shock value. I try to save more detailed descriptions of violence for action sequences and moments of catharsis.

However, I would be remiss if I did not warn you about the following, and remind you that if mention of these things will be upsetting for you, please protect your heart, first and foremost.

What to look out for:

- Some descriptions of parental and sibling child abuse.
- References to torture. Some more vivid descriptions, but very short.
- Use of coercive magic related to memory.
- Descriptions of sensory overload/dissociation, anxiety, and fear.
- Very brief mention of a child's death, not graphically described.
- More vivid descriptions of dealing with chronic pain (you will **not** find a fantasy/magical "fix" in this series for chronic fatigue and/or pain).
- Brief descriptions of drowning.
- Brief descriptions of claustrophobia.

THE PEOPLE OF SIRIN

INDIGENOUS PEOPLES OF SIRIN:

The Oscarovi: Witches.

Elemental Spirits: Incorporeal creatures who align closely with the six elements: earth, air, water, fire, empyrae, and aether. Elemental spirits sometimes choose to pair with the Oscarovi as their familiars.

NON-NATIVE PEOPLES OF SIRIN:

The Vilhari:

The Vilhari are a multi-racial group of fey people who came to Sirin nearly 4000 years prior to the present day of the book. They traveled the stars in a starcraft called the Avalonne that had to make an emergency landing. When the ship could not be repaired, the entire population of the enormous ship was forced to make their home on Sirin.

Vilhar/Vilhari: This term most commonly refers to humanoid fey in the present-day of the book. These fey have pointed ears, and some have feathered wings.

Strix: The Strix have humanoid bodies and the heads (visages) of various owls. They also have taloned hands that they often cover with gloves.

Corvidae: The Corvidae have humanoid bodies and the heads (visages) of ravens and crows. Like the Strix, they have taloned hands that they cover with gloves.

Sirens/Sybils: The sirens and sybils are people with bird and animal bodies that have humanoid faces/heads.

The Ventyr:

The Ventyr were an invading force of humanoid people that came to Sirin approximately 2000 years before the present day of the book. At that time, all the fey people from the Avalonne, the elemental spirits, and the Oscarovi aligned to defeat them and drive them out. This invasion changed the course of magic on Sirin forever.

A gift for you

Thank you for participating in The Hollow Plane Tour! From Allison Carr Waechter

CHAPTER 1

MINA

The punishment for remembering had been forgetting again—and, of course, the oubliette. Water kissed my ankles, a whispered threat. It was difficult to remember if it had done so before. But then, it was difficult to remember anything.

There was no reliable way to tell how long I'd been at the bottom of this damp, stone hole. I'd been without food or water for long enough that it should worry me, but I felt no hunger. No gnawing emptiness in my belly, only a curious void in my mind.

The cold water filling the bottom of the oubliette numbed my feet. Had water ever touched me before? I should think I would know if it had. Though, there were many things I should know that I didn't. Perhaps this was another. That was the trouble with the oubliette; time moved oddly. And not because time itself was odd. It moved in strange ways because I could not remember one moment to the next.

I am Wilhelmina Sofya Wildfang, I reminded myself, for either the first time, or the thousandth. Was that even my true name? I might never know. It was difficult to discern between memory, dream, and hallucination as they flitted in and out of my mind's eye. Here one moment, gone another. This, of course, was the purpose of the oubliette. The oubliette was made for forgetting.

The water rose higher, covering my ankles. Ice cold, it stung as angry little waves whipped my calves. So small, but fierce. Was it time to be worried now? Was any of this real? I gazed upward at the churning water high above me. The smooth, circular stone of the oubliette was dizzying in its sameness. The water was the only thing that changed.

When I could move again, I looked down. Water wasn't leaking in from above, it was rising from below. There was a struggle inside me to recognize what that meant, what the consequences might be for this change. I was frustratingly slow to catch on.

Water hissed at the underside of my ribcage now, rising faster by the moment. Could water hiss? If it could not, what made that noise? Now was probably not the best time to consider the sonic possibilities of water, but I struggled to attach myself to my present reality. Was it some part of the oubliette's magic that made me still when I should move, or was this a new unknown in the forgotten catalogue of things gone wrong?

Saltwater hit me square in the face, flooding in from above now, forcing me to focus. The sheer frigidity of the water should have been enough to knock me out of my senses, but I stayed frighteningly present. Freezing water buffeted my body about, pushing its way inside my nostrils and mouth, threatening to fill my lungs—to keep me here, on the floor of the oubliette.

Why hadn't I moved?

My feet were fixed to the stone floor.

My arms could move though, as could the rest of me.

This was a new revelation, perhaps, but probably not the time to consider the implications of time moving in a linear fashion again.

What was true was all that mattered now. The oubliette had trapped me in this position for Fate knew how long, frozen in a perpetual state of forgetting anything I managed to remember. Now whatever magic governed this place failed, and I would drown.

The thought was a peaceful one at first. Whatever happened here, however long I had been here, it was too long. There was a kind of relief in this all being over. I closed my eyes against the saltwater, preparing to inhale as much water in as I could, and hurry things along. That much I remembered, I remembered how to die.

How to die, yes. But not if I *could*.

I can drown, but I will not die. The thought slammed into me, just as my mouth fell open, filling with water. I clamped it shut directly, trying to make sense of that thought. The chill in the water would dull my senses soon, but now it served to clarify things, if only a little.

I will drown, again and again, stuck to the bottom of the oubliette. Forever. It was as though the voice in my head was someone else, or at least speaking *about* someone else. I wanted to argue with the voice. The things it said couldn't possibly be true. Little bits of recent memory crept back in, haunting me. The days I'd managed to count. Weeks, even months, piling up without food or water. This was just another part of the torture: finding out I could not die, as any living creature, even an immortal, might.

For even an immortal required sustenance to survive, and I did not. While I had eaten food every day of my nearly twenty-eight years, in the oubliette, it became apparent I did not actually need to do so. And that was a terrifying thought, because what living thing could exist without food?

3

I knew its name, though I wished I did not: *fetch*.

Knowing did nothing for my current problems. I no longer had a choice about whether or not I drowned. Water pushed past my lips, filling my throat, and then my lungs. The sensation differed from what I'd imagined, a raging fire inside me, rather than cool suffocation. I could give into an eternity of endless drowning, or *do something*.

I tried to pull my feet free, but they were still stuck fast, though my arms flailed with the effort of trying to move my legs. Sudden panic shot into me, unfamiliar and painful after so long in numbness. The panic was unfamiliar, but the pain was an old friend—a lifelong companion—and with it, I pulled a piece of myself from the icy depths of the sea.

A self that existed before the fetch, before this place.

A self that need not stay anywhere I did not desire to be.

A self I had too long forgotten.

The shapeless memory of who I'd been before moved me. Even the essence of my true self was enough to remind me that I needed no jewel, no spirit, no magical aid to access the power the cosmos gave freely. My eyes shut in concentration, as my feet slowly loosened from the rock. There was no need to struggle upward or fight the water in my lungs. My body lifted, gliding of its own accord through the bubbling sapphire water. There was a snap of energy as I broke the seal that still topped the oubliette.

Water rolled off me in beads as I crested the rolling waves like a newborn goddess, drawing both aether and empyrae at the same time to push the sea back. Lightning crashed towards me, attracted by my pull on empyrae, the sweet smell of ozone filling my nostrils. This is what Maman and Helene had always feared. Unlike *them*, I could wield celestial fire, as well as shadowy aether. What I had remembered before the oubliette hardly mattered; this was the truth of me, and I would never deny it again.

Back and back the water went until it revealed a stone path that led back to shore. The water would have receded on its own eventually, revealing the stones for a brief window of time. I did not need to wait for such things as the tide. Wind whipped my soaked hair around me as my eyes adjusted slowly to the dim glow of the raging storm. Despite the low-hanging clouds, and the tempest brewing further out at sea, I had to squint in the pre-dawn air. Even the moon's weak light through the clouds was too much for me. The oubliette had been dark, even in the daylight hours.

I walked forward, my bare feet sensitive as they moved over the slick rock. Each step was painful after being trapped for so long, but from the memory traveling back to me now, this did not differ from how it had always been. The past twenty-eight years were marked by constant pain.

Rain lashed my body, the last pieces of my ragged chemise plastering to my skin. I scanned the rocky shoreline for people, but the beach was as desolate as my shattered mind. With each step onto shore, stones sliced into my tender feet, too damp for too long at the bottom of the oubliette.

As I stumbled towards the cliffs and the sea stairs, each step was an ode to pain that clarified my purpose. The hot spears of agony were not only the result of the oubliette. All of this was Maman's fault—the fault of this unnatural body she'd forced me into—the fetch. She would answer for all she'd done. First, my questions, and then she would take her punishment, as I had always taken mine. The woman was an expert at divvying consequences out, and now we would find out if she could reap what she'd sown. Aether swirled around my fingers as I mounted the sea-stairs. The fury rising in me must have set my eyes alight with a telltale glow that would infuriate Maman.

Good. Let her be angry. Let Helene try to calm me. I would not be calmed now. First there would be truth, and then they would pay. No one should wield the power to craft a person as they would a machine. Each step on the stairs was unbearable. My muscles screamed, both from disuse and the cuts on the bottoms of my feet. The fetch heated, the skin flushing as I took each stair a little quicker than the last.

My skin. *My* body. My mind spoke to me as though it were bargaining. For more time, more memories, for all I'd lost of myself. All that was futile, but to survive this, I agreed with the voice in my head.

"This body is mine," I spat out as I pulled myself upward. One step and then the next, over and over, up the face of the cliff. "And forevermore, it will do as *I* say."

Never again would I be another's pawn. Never. Again. Hot tears streamed down my face. Once I reached the top of the stairs, there would be no more tears. No more frivolous anger. As I dragged my body upwards, I promised I would become a tool for truth, a weapon for so much destruction there would be nothing left of my little family.

I might not remember why I was sent to the oubliette, but with each step closer to the manor house, memories of my dark childhood flooded back. Maman's obsession with perfection. Her constant need for more attention, more money, more status, and calling it love. The oubliette was the end of any illusions I had of ever being loved.

Love was for the weak.

The words were a memory, the breaking of a spell, cutting through the obfuscation in my mind. They were an ancient sentiment, one I'd carried for much longer than the twenty-eight years this body had carried my soul. A last tear rolled down the curve of my cheek, chilled by the fell wind tearing at my hair. Roughly, I wiped my eyes, steeling myself to meet Maman and Helene with dignity. Only three more steps. Just moments more and Somerhaven would appear—

imposing and grand, decrepit and fearsome—an appropriately isolated stage for Maman's infinite cruelty.

The barest hint of warmth hit my back. My shoulder blades drew together, aching with phantom memory. My throat closed with some forgotten loss. All that I had been waited just beyond a frustrating wall in my mind. The warmth intensified; I turned as the sun crept above the horizon, sending weak rays across the roiling sea. The break in the clouds did not last long, and soon dawn was gray as a dove's feathers.

My eyes fell as I turned, resting on the dried skeletons of summer achillea swaying the wind. I had not bothered to wonder what season it was, and if Maman and Helene would even be in residence at Somerhaven.

I paused, thoughts racing for the first time in longer than I could remember. Keeping up would be an adjustment, but I latched onto the simplest of those rushing by me and let it manifest fully. *It must be well into autumn for the achillea to have dried so.*

That was helpful. I leaned against the cliff side for a moment. Rushing into this was foolish. What if my family was not alone? These were the days of endless country holidays and hunts in the lower range of the Dianthic Mountains, but not here. Not so far north as Somerhaven. The return of such mundane knowledge was a comfort. Until winter came, Maman and Helene would be in residence. They never joined the season early, as others did, preferring to move to town only when the manor house was too costly to heat.

I wavered, balking at the inevitable. There would be no autumnal holiday at Somerhaven, no house parties or hunts. Maman allowed no such gatherings here—we would be alone. Dallying longer only prolonged what must be. I spun back towards the upward slope. My resolve hardened as I took the last three steps at an excruciating pace.

At the top of the sea stairs, I stumbled, crumpling onto the ground, unable to fathom the sight before me. My heart, which had just pounded with the exertion of climbing, stopped. The stillness crushed me as much as the charred manor house. Somerhaven was gone.

CHAPTER 2

MINA

I curled into myself, staring at the hem of my chemise rather than the burned husk of the manor house. Everything dimmed for a moment, my vision black around the edges, darkness creeping in as my mouth went dry. Was I screaming? Or was that sound coming from elsewhere?

I shook, though if I shivered or convulsed, I could not say. Somerhaven was gone, and though I would not miss it, could not miss it even if I tried, there was despair in its destruction. My head swam with dizzying confusion. Memories mixed with lies, and there was no way to discern what was real. I focused on the wet lace of my chemise, a faraway afternoon filling my mind's eye.

A sun-drenched field high in the mountains replaced the charred manor house, along with the sound of laughter. Dark shadows lurked just at the edge of the merry scene, threatening to break it apart. Something about this was wrong, but I refused to know what it was.

Helene's laughter rang out as we hung laundry, night dresses with lacy edges, just like that of my chemise. Then the sound of her crystalline soprano singing folk songs. The shadows flickered at the edge of the scene, blurring it for a moment—this couldn't be a memory. Helene's hair was not red, but icy blonde, and though my sister could carry a tune, she would never sing a folk song.

I pushed my consciousness back down, deep into the impossibly sunny day. There had never been a day so clear on Sirin, but it was possible this was something more than a phantasm. It certainly could not be a genuine memory, though. If I had been on a mountainside hanging laundry, it was not with my haughty sister. The vision slipped away, leaving me bereft, to confront what was real.

Keeping my eyes down, I hauled myself off the ground with a determination I could not wholly feel. Each breath that came through my lungs was sharp with the pain of being denied the opportunity to confront Maman. If she and Helene were dead—no, I wouldn't think of that now. The first thing to do was search the house. No need to get ahead of myself.

I took stock of what lay ahead of me. The house had taken the most damage in the south wing, where the sleeping quarters were located. There was not much of the structure left, only charred stone and shattered glass. Tempted as I was to rush in and search, I knew better than to enter ruins without careful observation. My feet crushed bits of burnt wood as I circled the house, peering into the blackened remains of windows, trying to make sense out of devastation. All the furniture had been destroyed. Or, at the very least, someone had carted away anything of value after the fire, because the house was utterly empty.

When did it happen? Why hadn't I smelled the smoke? Even deep within the oubliette, a blaze this large would have been noticeable. Only a shell of the house remained, heavy stone, charred, but not destroyed. Another gust of wind sent leaves into a tailspin, and the faint scent of rotten eggs hit my nostrils. Sulphur. The odor was an unmistakable remnant of empyraen power. Someone with command of empyrae had burned the house down.

My mind churned as I rounded the east corner of the house, looking for a point of entry that might be safe. The fire had warped the glass in the dining room doors, leaving just enough room for me to squeeze through, a path free of shattered glass ahead of me.

Inside, the rooms reconstituted themselves in my mind, filling me to the brim with memories. Some good, many bad, but most somewhere in the murky between of an unhappy childhood. Unlike the confusing mountain scene, these played out before me with painful accuracy, ghoulish and real. There was no doubt in my mind that Helene had twisted my arm 'til it broke, there by where the buffet used to stand, just to see if I'd scream. Or that Maman had struck my palms with a tassel of sharp reeds until blood beaded through tiny cuts, over there by the butler's pantry.

None of this did me any good, so I forced myself to focus only on my surroundings as I slipped further into the house. I did not think, "that is the place where Maman slapped me so hard my face swelled for a week," but "the floor in the back hall is safe to walk on." I replaced each memory that threatened to break me with careful observation. The systematic dismissal of unwanted thoughts was one way I'd learned to exert control over my life as a child, and it came back to me easily.

In what had been the main entrance hall, the grand staircase had been destroyed. Searching what was left of the second and third floors would be impossible. It had been a longshot, given the state of the house. That confirmed, I picked my way through the rubble to the library, which sat directly beneath the wing where Maman and Helene's rooms had been. It was possible some clue to what had happened might have fallen through the floors. I had little hope for that, but it was necessary to be thorough.

As I climbed over fallen walls and charred pieces of the manor, the chill of the stone bothered me. To make things worse, the northern autumn air sank into my bones with each passing moment. Though the ferocious wind had nearly dried me, the chemise alone would not be enough for much longer. My teeth chattered, and the sound was more than I could bear, let alone the feeling of them touching one another.

Focus on survival first, silly—leave all these feelings *for later.* Helene's words crept into my mind, insidious and unwanted.

"I don't need your help," I muttered, uselessly. Even the mere memory of Helene had to give her superior input. Maman was cruel, but Helene had made it her life's purpose to outdo me in all ways.

And I had let her. Wanting them to love me had been my first mistake. Thinking it was possible for my family to love *anyone* had been my second. Loving them had been my third. There would not be a fourth such mistake.

When I found them, there could be no forgiveness. No reconciliation. After the oubliette, there was no doubt in my mind that it was time for us to clear the air and part ways for good. One way or another, this was the end for us.

Still, the whisper of Helene left in my memory wasn't wrong. I did need to focus on survival first. While I could not die, my pain and discomfort were all too real. I almost turned and left the house, but my need to complete the task at hand was too pressing.

When I reached the library, the crumbling, empty shelves were not a shock. There hadn't been books in Somerhaven's library for nearly a decade. Maman had sold Papa's collection of fiction long ago to fund outfitting herself and Helene for a social season. I was asked to stay at Orchid House alone while they masqueraded about Pravhna as the wealthy family we'd once been, but were no longer. Most of Somerhaven's valuables had been discreetly sold off.

The only beautiful thing left in the library was the enormous mirror above the fireplace. It was too heavy and fragile to move—a fact I resented now as I avoided my ragged, soot stained appearance. When I caught sight of myself head-on, I recoiled. I looked like a haunt, wild-eyed and vengeful, my dark heavy hair hanging in long hanks around my shoulders. I appeared as a thing more than a woman, which was a little too close to the truth for my comfort.

A weak ray of sunlight broke through the clouds. It was only for the briefest of moments, but the pinprick of light hit something on the floor that shone. A tiny prism of light spun out around the room, a hum of power emanating from its center.

Every muscle in my body froze, my heart thumping wildly against my ribcage, a wild thing trying to escape its prison. I didn't have to see the stone up close to know exactly what it was. The massive round emerald, set in a bouquet of golden oleander, was utterly familiar. Maman had never taken the ring off—would *never* have taken it off voluntarily. My body moved as though treading nearly frozen water, thick with mounting emotion.

When I reached the jewel, my ears rang with the fury building inside me. Aether and empyrae flowed off me in alternating waves of light and shadow. Inside my mind, a keening death knell screamed out from the center of the ring. The elemental spirit within had been trapped, and now wailed with some unidentifiable emotion.

It could not be sadness, for Maman's familiar bore no love for her—only the power they wielded together. The elemental's screams stoked my desperation into a fever pitch, my body heating to an unnatural temperature. It was not possible for Maman to have left her familiar behind, trapped in such a way, even if she'd wanted to. The inspirited were bound until death parted them.

Maman was dead.

Someone had used empyrae to burn Somerhaven.

There were no answers here.

These three thoughts repeated in my mind, echoing with a frustrating lack of nuance. I tried to stop the spin of them as they gained traction, but to no avail. My fingers closed around the ring, empyrae emanating from my clenched fist in a molten glow. I had to let her familiar out. If I wanted answers, this was the only place I would find them.

My knuckles turned white, gold dripping from between my fingers on to the sooty floor. Gold was nothing to the heat of empyrae. The emerald, however, was nearly impenetrable, as all elemental portals are. Oscarovi jewelers perfected the method nearly two thousand years ago, giving our kind access to as much power as the fey, and even my power could not break the jewel open so easily. My anger mounted. I would have answers, even if I had to wring them from stone. If Maman was not here, her familiar Demophon must answer for her.

The ground shook beneath my feet as I refocused my attention. My ears rang as my empyrae built, the pressure building steadily. In the distance, something fell and shattered, but I stayed focused on the emerald, on breaking its surface open. All sense disappeared in the effort, so I was surprised to find a compact figure pulling at the hem of my chemise, bidding for my attention amongst the chaos.

My vision would not focus though, as channeling the powers of limen and the cosmos at once was no small feat. *Demophon!* I cried out, within the confines of my mind. *Answer me! Demophon!*

Near my feet, something pulled on my chemise again. It

spoke, though it was not the elemental spirit trapped within the jewel. *Demophon is gone, girl. Disappeared the moment you cracked the stone.*

Impossible. I only meant to release the mountain elemental, not destroy the stone. My fingers unfurled as I looked down. There was nothing but emerald dust and a pool of molten gold marring my palm. Demophon was gone. I fell to my knees, narrowly missing whatever had spoken to me, nothing more than a blur as my eyes squeezed shut.

Screams, ripped from deep inside my soul, ravaged my throat as I sobbed. Rage took over as what remained of the house shook. Again, something tugged at my chemise. I nearly lashed out with my power, but something stopped me. The thing at my feet was a rangy, lean hare, aether swirling off it in billowing clouds. As it moved, scratching at me with sharp claws, it came into focus. The hare was larger than a mundane beast, with harrowing eyes that swirled with the light of stars in deep space. Its sleek fur was an unsettling shade of indigo—the color of pure aether.

You'll bring the rest of the house down on yourself, it cautioned.

The floor shook harder now, as a slow creaking noise swelled into an anguished groan. The house was coming apart. What the hare said might make sense. My vision expanded to take in the room. Around me, there was a halo of safety, generated not by my magic, but by the nebula of power curling off the hare. Its body had been slightly incorporeal before, and now was dissolving before my eyes.

It was protecting me. But why? "Who are you? Are you related to Demophon?" I shouted above the cacophonous wind swirling around us.

The thing was obviously a wild elemental. All familiars started off as elemental spirits who desired more of an effect on the corporeal world, but mountain elementals rarely wished for such relationships with us. The hare did not answer, but loped away, toward the doors to the garden, the orb of howling winds breaking apart as it went.

Move! the hare shouted.

I did as bidden, running through the lush grass of the garden, until the forest loomed dark ahead. As I turned to look back, the remaining husk of the manor house crumbled. I winced—destruction hadn't been my intention—as my body gave out. The pain was finally too much, and my knees buckled, slamming into the ground. Only the long, soft grass kept me from further damage.

Movement in my peripheral vision caught my attention. Another hare crept down the rocky hillside behind the manor, through the dense forest of evergreens. Its movements were both erratic and far too smooth, as the edges of its form blurred and sharpened in turns.

As the second hare joined the first, I felt dozens, if not hundreds, of eyes on me from the depths of the shadowed forest. My stomach flipped in response, heart skipping a beat —my body recognizing what my mind could not catch up to. Elementals surrounded me, a band of spirits. My breath snagged on the gravity of the danger I was in, threatening to pull me down entirely.

Mountain elementals were not curious about the corporeal world. They did not pair with Oscarovi without dangerous bargains, and they were not our friends as their kin in cities and towns might be. Mountain elementals were more likely to lure souls into the forest to feed their nameless, eldritch gods, never to be seen again. Carefully, I scooted away from the pair of hares, trying my best not to appear hurried or afraid.

They could be vicious if not treated with perfect respect. They were medial creatures, striding the line between this reality and that which was between, but they *could* touch me. Those long claws and powerful legs were not wholly incorporeal. To be safer, I struggled to my feet, though there was nothing I could do against them if they attacked. Even with my power, even with empyrae, I would stand little chance against a drove of mountain elementals.

There was no use in running or trying to evade them if they wanted something from me. They could use the spirit paths, the limen, to find me. I'd accepted their help in escaping the crumbling manor, and now I was beholden to them. The first rule of dealing with mountain elementals was to accept no aid, no bargain, without first understanding the parameters. There had been no help for it though; I'd lost my grip on reality, letting my rage get the better of me.

All I could do was take a deep breath as they entered the garden, making a small bow in the hopes it might please them. "Greetings fair ones. I am honored by your presence."

As a child of Somershire, I knew the old ways, the old lore. I knew better than to believe that because the first hare had saved me, the drove wouldn't kill me for slighting them. Thanking them would be a mistake, as one must never imply indebtedness to an elemental. However, greeting them was essential, especially as they had addressed me directly. They did not respond to my greeting—not even an ear twitched in my direction, reminding me they were not common hares.

She of the Dark Vale has a message for you.

Hastily, I bowed again, every tendon, muscle, and joint in my body screaming for rest. I wasn't sure which of the hares had spoken, nor exactly to whom they referred. As a failsafe, I bowed lower to show that I would receive the message, without verbal acknowledgement. The less I said, the better. Mountain elementals had a habit of twisting words to fit their aims, and I was wise enough not to give them anything more to work with.

Your mother and sister were killed in the fire.

Maman's ring had led me to the same conclusion—about

her, anyway. But Helene? It wasn't possible that Helene... "That cannot be," I gasped, immediately forgetting to stay silent.

We saw the bodies taken. The voice was one and many. The entire drove spoke at once, in my mind. *If they were not deceased, then we do not understand mortality.*

I sucked air into my lungs to stay grounded. Oscarovi lived long lives, but indeed, we were mortal. Or *they* were. I was not truly Oscarovi, nor mortal, I reminded myself. I was not real and too real.

That way lies danger. I looked down. One hare pulled at my chemise again. I could not be certain, but it seemed to be the one that helped me previously. *It is not time to travel in that direction. You must go forward to go back.*

Its eyes swirled with the light of forgotten stars, and I remembered another time I had seen into such depths, but vaguely. "Forward?"

The hare nodded, pulling at my chemise with its claws, so gently it did not so much as snag the fragile, damaged fabric. I bent down to be on eye level with it. I knew not to ask for more information, but perhaps appearing more willing to receive it might speed things along.

The longer I stayed here with them, the more tempted I would be to follow them into the forest and never return. Maman had often mused that elementals snatching children was mere lore, but I knew it to be true. I'd been lured before. Even now, I felt the pull to follow them and never return. Something deep in the forest, far in the mountains, called to me.

The hare placed its paw on my knee, steadying me in my painful crouch. *It is not yet time for you to follow us. You must see your end before you can return to the beginning.*

The message was cryptic, and behind the gentle touch in the creature's paw was a threat. Not to me, specifically, but a menace. I nodded, knowing that if the hare did not say more, there was nothing I could do. Creatures of the limen saw more than we, making their words heavy with meaning, but difficult to parse out. I would not know what the hare meant until it was time.

Deep in the woods, and further down the mountain, a horn sounded, long and mournful. Every hare on the mountain materialized for one brief, terrifying moment, their ears turned in the same direction—toward the horn.

There is no more time, the hare touching my knee warned.

The hunt approaches, the drove said at once, their collective voice a mass of whispers and screams. *You must hide.*

I struggled to rise, but my hands slipped on the damp grass. The hare who'd helped me escape the house pushed its head under my arm as I stumbled. *Run, Mina*, it cried as it helped me to my feet. *Hide!*

There was only one place on the property left for me to go and the hare nosed me in its direction: the carriage house.

We will draw them off, the hare that helped me said. Something in its manner was gentler than the rest of the drove, which faded from sight, their terrible eyes the last thing to dissolve. *Go!*

Sounds of the hunt came closer. Dogs braying, carried by the wind. The hare nosed the back of my legs again as fear gripped me. The only estate close enough to ours to host a hunt that might come so close was House Montclair.

Was Viridian with them? My heart raced at the thought. I pushed myself into motion. The thought of Helene's fiancé catching me again was enough to set my feet running. My legs pumped harder, my arms churning, as though grasping for some hope to hold on to. Frigid wind cut through me as I ran through the overgrown remains of the garden, hoofbeats vibrating through my bare feet.

The hunt neared. Pain laced through me, every step

forward agony. The carriage house came into view, just down the hill from the house. It was unfortunately placed near the path the hunt would have to take, but the only cover left on the property. My body slammed into the door, unable as I was to slow down of my own accord. I could hardly clasp onto the iron handle of the door, my hands were shaking so hard.

She of the Still Places watches and waits. The drove's collective voice echoed in my head as the door sprang open under my touch.

I fell into the carriage house. Desperate as I was to hide, I shut the door softly behind me, dropping the heavy wooden bolt lock with as much care as I could. Sound carried strangely in these hills, and if House Montclair was hunting, I could not afford a single mistake. Through the windows at the back of the carriage house, crimson and gold jackets flashed in the woods. The colors of House Montclair. My enemy was upon me.

CHAPTER 3

ASHBOURNE

Dawn crept through Pravhna's undercity, slow and gray. Mist curled around my feet as I trudged home, down one steep cobblestone street after another, from a card game I'd never wanted to attend. I rolled my neck as I walked, stretching my arms out above me after so many seated hours. It had been a long night, but at least it was over.

It was hard to regret helping my partner build our business. There were only a few private investigators in the undercity that weren't completely in the Syndicate's pockets, and we walked a fine line. If we didn't socialize with the Syndicate crews a little, we wouldn't get clients who paid them for protection. And that was almost everyone.

But I wasn't the socializing sort. I'd rather have been in bed with a novel. Fate be damned, I'd have preferred to spend the evening training in the shop basement, rather than playing cards with Syndicate goons. But Skye had asked that I at least try to expand our network a bit, and I hadn't wanted to let her down. Playing cards with some of Karnon Archambeau's crew was the least I could do, and now my head ached from too much ale.

I needed a pot of strongly brewed black tea, a pastry, and a good nap and all would be right with the world. I just had to get home first, and in my drunken haze I'd taken a wrong turn. It was easy to do in this area of the undercity, which was a maze of streets that often dead-ended with no warning, or looped back on one another. The White Lady was the odd pub in a four-block radius of warehouses and small factories that were mostly operational during the day. It made the public house perfect for a quiet, late night card game among criminals.

I should not have had that third ale; my head pounded with a vengeance. I stumbled over a loose cobblestone, bracing myself against the brick wall of a glass factory that I was sure I'd passed at least twice already. I stared at the brick for several moments, appreciating the color of it for some reason unknown to my addled mind. This was why I didn't drink. Still, the glass factory *was* lovely. It was the only brick structure in a sea of clapboard buildings, which made it distinct.

I closed my eyes, breathing through the nausea that threatened to overtake me. What smelled so wretched?

Rubber. Rubber was burning and close by. But there was another smell, something sulphuric and acrid, mixing with the rubber. My head swam, but I pushed myself off the wall. If something was on fire, it wouldn't be long until the entire undercity was ablaze. Drunk or not, I had to help before the trees that canopied the undercity caught flame. The last thing we needed was the elemental spirits in revolt over such destruction.

I groaned as I followed my nose toward the horrific smell. A few blocks away, I found the source of the flames. They shot into the sky at the rubber factory. I was back where I started, across the street from The White Lady. I picked up my pace, my head clearing as my heart beat faster. Urgency took the edge of my stupor off, clearing my mind as I approached.

A dozen or so people had already arrived at the scene and appeared to be fighting the fire. I could take a moment to gather myself. I was sobering up, and quickly, but I'd be no help if I got sick on one of these good folk. Since they already had things well in hand, I braced myself internally, letting the turmoil in my belly calm down.

Assessing the scene brought me back to myself, my nausea receding. Broken glass covered the street, and flames jumped out of the rubber factory, raging and white hot. There was a touch of blue flame that receded by the moment, and was likely the source of the sulphuric scent. Someone had used empyrae here, celestial flame. My gut roiled once more, but this time not from my third ale. This was no ordinary fire, it was another of *those*.

Strange fires had plagued the city of spires for months. They went out so quickly that no one had investigated their origins, but there were rumors they didn't behave naturally. The fires seemed to have no inception point, and no reason for stopping. Nor did they ever spread, according to the rumors. Neither Skye nor Morpheus nor I had ever witnessed one, and the conclusion we'd reached was that they were likely just that: rumors.

Now, I wasn't so sure. Something wasn't right here.

I scanned the people at the scene, identifying the bartenders from The White Lady, and a few overnight guards from some of the surrounding warehouses. They'd opened the block's access to emergency water, something Pravhna was in no shortage of, and were operating the hose. Their movements were odd, stilted somehow.

I recognized Mac, the Oscarovi bartender at The White Lady, by their bright cerise brocade waistcoat. They had a loose hold on the fire hose, but didn't appear to be paying much attention to what was happening. I strode over to them, clapping my hand on their narrow shoulder. "Mac, what happened here?"

The bartender didn't turn to look at me. I moved closer to them, until I caught sight of their face. Their eyes were glazed over and black, the light from the fire reflecting in their glassy depths. It wasn't just their irises having blown out; their *eyes* had gone black entirely.

I stepped away from them, trying not to recoil at the sight. "What's wrong with you?" I asked, though now I did not expect an answer.

Mac didn't respond, but continued to move forward with the hose. I walked around the others, keeping a fair distance from them. Bespelled individuals were worth being wary of. Every single one had the same black eyes. What was worse, they were all completely silent. Only the sounds of their shuffled movements amongst the broken glass and the burning factory filled the street.

They didn't speak to one another, or even move their heads. All were breathing, but there was a stiltedness in their breathing that appeared labored, as though someone else forced air in and out of them. The amount of power it would take to do such a thing wasn't something I could rightly conceive of. Fear slithered under my skin. Only a monster could manage something like this. Controlling others so wholly wasn't just difficult, it was evil. But they weren't doing anything bad—in fact, they were fighting the fire.

Could someone have used their power to make sure the fire went out?

I swallowed hard, watching the dozen or so entranced people operate the hose, their bodies moving like puppets on strings. After a few moments of observation, the truth became clear. They weren't truly fighting the fire. They weren't even pointing the hose anywhere in particular. It was a parody of fire-fighting. And yet, the fire *was* dying. Or perhaps it simply wasn't spreading. Only the rubber factory burned.

A small, animalic part of me knew the best thing to do would be to run, to hide. Anyone who could wield empyrae and keep a dozen people in a trance was more powerful than I should even think of confronting. But I'd never been one to heed my better instincts. I swallowed my fear whole, slowing my pounding heart with a few long, deep breaths.

As unsettling as the entire scene was, I needed to find a way to help these people. The fire was contained, and whoever controlled the trance was nowhere to be seen. I let my eyes fall shut to send my senses of smell and hearing out further.

A soft noise caught my attention, and my eyes flew open, searching for the source. There were very few aetheric street lamps in this area, but the blaze provided some light. Behind a stack of crates, a small Strix child with the visage of a snowy owlet huddled crying. They held a hand to their chest. I rushed to them, crouching down.

"What happened, hatchling?" I asked, keeping my voice as calm as possible. My size was often intimidating for adults. Children had mixed reactions, either delight at how tall I was, or terror. The owlet was happily the former.

"Oh, you're a big'un," they said, their words slurring through their tears.

"Yes," I agreed, smiling as best I could, given the circumstances.

"But you've a kind smile," the owlet reasoned. Something had scared them, that much was obvious. "My mama's over there. She won't talk to me. I tried t'help her, but she didn't even look my way. I tripped and fell, see." They held their little hand out to show me. There was a piece of broken glass stuck in their palm, their taloned fingers quivering.

"That must hurt," I said, after identifying the Strix in the line of silent firefighters that was likely the little tyke's mama. Her eyes were black as the others, though the eyes of the Strix and Corvidae were always dark. But no Strix mama I knew would ignore their hatchling. No wonder the child was afraid.

"Can I help you?" I asked.

"Which House are you from?" the little one asked, suspicious of me. "Not one of those cratties, are you?"

The way the owlet said "crattie" was an obvious accusation, but I could only agree. The aristocrats of Pravhna were a terrible lot. I laughed softly. "No, hatchling. I'm no crattie. Just a common Vilhar, like you."

Many of the fey saw themselves as separate from their brethren, using the word Vilhari to distinguish between the fey that were not indigenous to Sirin. If history were to be believed, we all crashed here on a starcraft thousands of years ago and the elementals and Oscarovi were forced to let us stay. As I could not remember an upbringing where I'd learned that history, or the subtleties of our society, it was all the same to me. Strix, Corvidae, sirens, howlers, and my kind. We were all fey. All Vilhari.

"Will you let me help you, then?" I asked. "Now that you know I haven't a House to answer to?"

The owlet nodded, holding their hand out a bit more. I was no surgeon, but I could tell the glass was wedged in such a place that it might keep the littling from being able to use the hand again. I couldn't help with the fire, nor could I solve the problem of the adults' current bespelled state, but I could solve this.

"Close your eyes," I begged the owlet. It would be better if they didn't watch.

It was a risk to use my power this way. While many could wield celestial power, control over empyrae, its purest form, was rare. It might draw unwanted attention, and I'd worked so hard to keep my abilities a secret, but the child's hand was worth it to me. They squeezed their eyes shut tight, burying their face in their uninjured arm.

"This will hurt for a moment," I warned before pulling the glass out. The littling was brave though, and did no more than wince. I couldn't help but smile as I covered their hand with my own. I used a bit of my celestial power to knit the wound back together, my magic doing the internal work a skilled surgeon might. It was a dangerous thing to do this in public, especially so close to a blaze started with empyrae. I had no doubt that I'd risked making myself a target. If anyone saw what I did, they might think I'd set the fire.

"How did you and your mama end up here?" I asked, wanting to distract the owlet from the extra pain the healing would cause.

"Mama's a night guard for the rubber factory, 'nd I have a cold. So I had to come to work with her tonight."

The little one sniffed a little, their tears obviously compounding the severity of their congestion. My healing work was almost finished, but I would have to cauterize the wound. The owlet winced, but did not so much as cry out.

"Did you see who did this?" I asked as I sent a tendril of cool aether into the closed wound to soothe the cauterization.

The littling nodded, eyes open now and wide, staring behind me. "T'was them," the owlet said through strangled sobs. "How'd they get back here so fast?"

I whirled round, standing quickly, keeping the child behind me. In the street stood four masked people. They wore dark, lightly armored clothes, and their entire faces were covered, but for slits in the masks for eyes. There was nothing showing in their appearance to distinguish whether they were fey or Oscarovi.

The two in front were obviously athletically built, but the pair that stood behind them were in shadow, their physiques difficult to make out in the moving shadows the dying flames from the fire cast—one or more of these people had to be the cause of all this, the owlet was right. The fire and the entranced people made more sense if it were a group controlling the working. I hadn't heard them approach, which was utterly impossible. Where had they come from?

"Run," I growled at the child. "Get to the Merc for help."

Hopefully, the Mercury Room would still be full of Halcyon Gate Syndicate folk at this hour. At the very least, Edith Braithwaite kept rooms in the pleasure house, and if the Syndicate leader was in residence, she'd be able to muster aid quickly. I tried to discern if any of the four figures were using aethereal power, but something dulled my second sight.

The owlet made haste behind me. One of the masked figures attempted to follow. I blocked them, delivering one swift punch to the head as they passed me. I was fast enough that they didn't even have the opportunity to duck. There was no way I'd get so lucky again.

No change in my second sight, nor in the entranced people. That one hadn't been involved in the working here. Another rushed towards me, obviously wise to my speed now.

This one was smaller than me, but more heavily muscled and moving at a preternaturally fast pace. One punch, quick as lightning, landed on my ribs, sending me backward as they pummeled me in the stomach. I leapt away, but I couldn't move fast enough to block as their hits flew at me, keeping me on the defense. Like the entranced, their movements were not quite natural.

Each hit came just a little faster than I could manage, as though my assailant adjusted each hit to meet my mounting defense. I blocked a punch meant for my face with ease, then another on its way to my gut. It was almost like dancing, with them in the lead.

I stepped forward at the same time they stepped back. I blocked as they hit. We were evenly matched, it seemed. I swept a foot out to kick their feet from under them. They slipped just out of reach in the nick of time, then pummeled me in the gut with those preternaturally fast hits again.

They leapt back, their feet dancing, every movement a frustrating taunt. The fight had no momentum. It was as though my assailant had no stake in the contest, no worry that I would harm them, and no intention of actually harming me. In fact, the more I blocked and averted, the more skilled their attack became. And yet, none of the hits were painful. They seemed to be purposely holding back.

Testing me.

The other two masked figures simply watched. Gut instinct told me something about this wasn't right. Had they expected me to be here? Of course, I had no way of knowing that for certain, but the thought persisted as I struggled to stay in the fight.

My opponent had moved faster than me the entire fight, never allowing me to land a hit. But now their movements lagged, as though whatever power allowed them to supercharge their speed was waning. If we fought much longer, I would overpower them. I slowed down, conserving energy, and my opponent matched my speed precisely.

Too precisely. This was wrong. If they wanted to kill me, they'd have done it already. I was a skilled fighter, more skilled than these two, but they had the advantage of speed and whatever force allowed my opponent to read me so easily. If I wanted to end this, I would have to use empyrae.

I ducked my opponent, now focused on staying out of their reach, rather than feeding whatever information they sought in engaging me in a fight. My second sight cleared, and I identified which observer was the source of all the magic being used in the street. I paused to consider the wisdom of lunging for them.

I took my eyes off my assailant for only a moment, but it was enough. All went dark.

When I opened my eyes, the sun had long since risen, and rain pelted my face. I glanced behind me. I was in a seated position, propped up against the door of The White Lady, across the street from the rubber factory. It was morning, but this far into the undercity, the clouds were low and the light was gray.

My entire body felt like a bruise, tender and inflamed.

The owlet sat next to me. "You all right, sir?" they asked.

I nodded, my face smarting from the places I'd been hit, but I was already healing. "I'm all right."

"What was wrong with those people?" the owlet asked. "They moved unnatural-like."

"Yes," I agreed, smiling at the littling's way of reasoning through a problem. I liked the way children thought about things. Straightforward, and so often right to the point. "What did you see after I went down?"

The littling shrugged. "I don't rightly know. T'was like I forgot to keep looking at you all. S'not possible that a person disappears, is it?"

It was an unlikely observation, but I believed the owlet. "Like a greymalkin? Or an elemental?"

The owlet shook their head. "Not at all. It's hard to remember, though."

That was a problem I understood all too well, having been hit too hard quite a few times. My amnesia complicated this situation. Something about the four masked figures felt familiar. But if they were—if I had some knowledge about who they were or why they could fight like that—it was not something I could access. Anything before Skye and Morpheus found me a year ago was simply missing.

Across the street, the fire had died down. The people who'd been fighting it were standing in a row facing the pub, eyes blank, though they'd resumed their normal appearance. Briefly, I wondered why no one else had shown up yet. Why was the undercity so quiet? First shift should have started, and this place should be crawling with people.

The air was heavy with power, as though a blanket had been tossed over this little part of the city. I wondered if that was what kept others from discovering what had happened here.

"Where'd you disappear to?" I asked the owlet. "Did you get to the Merc?"

The little one shook their head. "I was going to go to get help, but I got lost. Don't really know how. I've been coming here all my life, but I kept ending up right back here."

So I wasn't imagining the power that muffled the air. Something kept the littling in, and was probably keeping others out. I shifted position a little, thinking to get up, but the pain in my ribs was nearly unbearable. I would have to sit here for another few minutes and wait for them to heal.

The owlet looked as though they might cry at my wince of pain. "I'm so sorry you got hit so many times. They just kept hitting you after they knocked you out. One of them said it wouldn't slow you down for long. Is that true?"

I smiled, my split lip cracking open, spilling blood into my mouth. I was a fast healer, faster than most Vilhari, but this was more inconvenient than I'd prefer. I spat the blood out, away from the owlet, before answering. "It's true."

A fluffy brown raptor dove down from the low clouds that hung over the undercity. Rue, thank the Lady. Skye must have sent the vicious little howler off to find me when I didn't come back home. His arrival was fortuitous—the little messengers could make it through workings that kept other creatures out. The Syndicate needed to know what had happened here, and fast.

"Hello," I said, wincing at the effort to speak. I was already healing, but it would take time. "I need you to get a message to Skye."

CHAPTER 4

MINA

As the thunder of hooves came closer, I ducked behind the Broussard, a massive presence in the carriage house. I was still visible through the giant windows that let natural light in. We'd never converted the carriage house to aetheric power, so windows still did much of the heavy lifting in terms of lighting. Through the glass, bursts of crimson jackets flashed in the woods.

Hoofbeats were close enough now to make the floor vibrate faintly under my feet, and the sounds of the dogs grew louder. Viridian's family employed a kind of fey dog I very much did not want to encounter. There was only one choice right now, as my joints burned with pain. I wouldn't make it up the stairs to the apartment above the garage.

I would have to get under the Broussard if I didn't want to be seen. The shiny black autocar was high enough off the ground that I could roll under it rather easily. The stone floor was cold on my bare skin and my back ached uncomfortably while I waited. I tried my hardest to lengthen my breath; even a heartbeat might catch the attention of House Montclair's fey hounds.

After my ostentatious rise out of the oubliette, my magic was weak, and I was even more exhausted than I would have been after simply climbing the sea stairs. I didn't have much energy left, but I drew a muffling spell around me with the last bit of magic I had. My fingers moved quickly to weave the working that brought a net of aether over me. It was one of my favorite spells. I'd been a child who benefitted from being as difficult to find as possible.

I tried to get comfortable now, but the floor made that impossible. It was foolish to not at least consider they might be looking for me. I hadn't much in the way of memories about the day I went into the oubliette, but there were two things I knew. Maman had sentenced me to isolation, and Helene and her fiancé Viridian were the last faces I saw before the sea covered the opening to the oubliette. If House Montclair was on the hunt, I had to assume Viridian knew I had escaped.

It took some time, but as the hares had promised, they drew the hunt off—shouts rang out among the riders as they spotted their quarry. The sounds of the hunt faded, but did not completely disappear. My eyes drooped, then fell closed. I neared exhaustion, which was strange to think about. The fetch did everything a body should do. It sent all the usual signals that I needed to do vital things like sleep and rest, but I did not actually need to do any of those things to survive.

The muffled sound of a dog sniffing the carriage house door stole my breath. My body tensed in preparation to fight, but the hellish creature did not so much as bark. The sniffing stopped, and the sound of the creature's footsteps fell away. Perhaps the hunt was for a mundane quarry, after all. Still, I needed to keep my wits about me until I was sure they were gone. I closed my eyes, not to sleep, but to pull up memories of Maman's books on forbidden magics.

Inside my memory, pages spun by until I found the ones I

wanted, the words I wanted to remember. *Fetch, doppelganger, automaton*: consciousness attached to a clever bit of technology and magic. Magic that the high echelons outlawed long ago, and for good reason. Whatever I had been *before*, I was not now. Remembering that was at least part of what had gotten me thrown into the oubliette. The rest was just beyond this memory, and I struggled against the slippery block that kept me from knowing more.

Frustrated, my eyes flew open. I turned my attention back to the hunt, listening hard, but there were only the sounds of birds singing in the forest to greet me. A sigh of relief brought fresh air into my lungs—I had been holding my breath.

I rolled out from under the Broussard, staring at it for a few long moments, thinking things through. There had to be clothes somewhere in the carriage house, but if there weren't, I was going to have to get to the village and steal some. A loose plan took shape in my head. If I could not make Maman and Helene pay for their transgressions, I could find out who deprived me of that pleasure and make *them* pay.

But first, I needed clothes, and to get to Pravhna. The season had undoubtedly begun, and I had the best chance of finding out what truly happened here in the city. Somershire was too small to even have an investigative unit. If a case had been opened regarding the fire, the records would be in Pravhna. I opened the driver's side door of the autocar, feeling around for the key Maman usually tucked into the crack of the front seat. I hated the idea of driving, but I did know how.

We hadn't been able to afford a driver in years, so Maman had taught Helene and me both to drive, casting it as another of her eccentricities. People thought Helene and I were practically wild things. The difference was that Helene was so beautiful and charming that they overlooked it. My beauty didn't get me very far, as I lacked Helene's social graces.

The key wasn't in the front seat, and though I doubted I'd find it in the back, I looked anyway. When I came up with nothing, I searched under the seats. The glimmer of a small beaded evening bag underneath the passenger side front seat caught my attention. I stretched to reach it, my exposed skin scraping against the metal underside of the seat, but I managed to fish it out. It was one of Helene's favorites. One from her second season out—the season Viridian proposed.

How did it get here? Helene was meticulously careful about her possessions. A vague memory of Brigitte, who'd played the role of nanny, governess, and lady's maid to Helene, crossed my mind. When Maman had been obsessed with selling off our precious possessions to fund her secret projects, Helene and Brigitte had hidden things from her. Perhaps they'd hidden the purse here.

Not what I'd been hoping for, but helpful all the same. I scrambled into the cold leather backseat, curling into myself as I stared at the purse. My fingers traced the floral pattern of the golden beads, emotion clouding my next move. What had become of my sister? It seemed unthinkable that she could die.

Maman had been so miserable as to have become dull over the years. But Helene was different, as cruel as Maman, but cunning. Vivacious. Alive. But the hares said they saw the body, and it was impossible for them to lie. Deceive, yes, but they had *seen* the bodies. My fingers drifted over the beads of Helene's purse, the smooth texture of them pleasing—soothing, somehow. Without my sister, would Viridian even care what became of me?

That was the real problem. I didn't know why the oubliette had been necessary to begin with, so it was impossible to determine what kind of threat Viridian was. I still needed the answers I'd planned to extract from Maman and Helene. The faster the better. I opened Helene's purse.

A silk scarf, a ring of brass keys, and a small bit of paper money were the only things in the purse, save for a few spare hairpins. The silk scarf was plain, the color of a stormy sea. Helene had used it on long drives to protect her hair when Maman insisted on having the windows of the autocar open to "get the air on us."

I examined the keys carefully. None were for the car. Three were for Somerhaven's many locks, and were now useless. One was for Orchid House in Pravhna, and one was a mystery to me. No matter, the key to Orchid House was all I needed.

Getting to Pravhna was a problem. The Broussard was easily recognizable as Maman's—it would draw too much attention. I would have to take the train. I needed as much time as possible to get to Orchid House with no one knowing I'd returned, so that Viridian couldn't make moves to stop me. Once in Pravhna, society would take notice quickly enough, and that was exactly what I wanted. I wanted them to see me, to be curious, to ask questions. It was the only way to draw out whoever might know more about what Maman and Helene had really been doing.

For a few moments, I debated between driving the Broussard to the station in Somershire and hiking down. Both were risky, but it would be better to make it to the station without Viridian stopping me than to be caught in the woods. Of course, that required finding the car key, and I needed to find clothes.

My chemise was tattered and soot-stained. There was no way I could march into the train station and buy a ticket wearing only this. Now that my body had calmed, my senses returned. The vague sound I'd been trying to block out was my teeth chattering. I needed to find something warmer to wear, now.

Even a coat and a pair of shoes would help. As the house was no longer an option, the apartment upstairs was my only hope for both clothes and the key to the Broussard. Before Maman fired the driver, he'd lived upstairs. It was possible he'd left something behind that I could put on until I got to Orchid House, and I was certain he'd had at least two keys to the autocar. I crept through the garage, carefully watching the windows for signs of stray hunters, or their terrible dogs. The narrow door to the stairs stuck when I pulled it, but wasn't locked.

After a bit more effort, it came open, nearly hitting me in the face. The sight of the dust-covered staircase to the apartment elicited a quiet groan. I took the first step gingerly, my entire body recoiling from the feeling of placing my tender, cut-up feet on the dusty stairs. Despite this, or perhaps because of it, I was more determined than ever to find shoes.

As I dragged my body upwards, I cursed. Part of me missed the oubliette. The only good that had come from being trapped in the hole was that for a time, I'd forgotten about my pain. It hadn't disappeared, but I'd forgotten it, along with everything else. Now that I was lucid, the agony of movement was unrelenting.

It will get better, I promised myself. *I just have to get used to it again.*

Luckily, this was nothing like the sea stairs. Just one short flight and I'd entered the apartment. Every surface was covered in the same thick layer of dust the stairs had been. I gritted my teeth. Touching it would be awful, but it was necessary. It was possible, of course, to weave a spell to clean the dust from this place. However, using magic of any kind might draw attention if Viridian had access to Maman's surveillance nets.

That had been one of her many secret projects, developing spells that monitored magical use and other disturbances. Any information left on that would be in Maman's workroom in Orchid House. Getting into her inner sanctum was another knot in this tangled mess, but that was a problem for another hour. I ripped the hem from my chemise in the cleanest part of the garment, tied it around my face to protect my airways from the dust, and began my search. There was precious little to go through, so it went quickly.

The tall dresser and trunk at the end of the single bed yielded nothing, but in the tiny closet by the stairs, I found a coat. It was long, made from thick brown tweed, and blessedly clean. On the hook beneath it hung a small bag of forgotten laundry, and from the faint smell of lavender that still clung to it, it must have been clean as well. Inside, I found a set of the driver's clean long johns, and several pairs of heavy socks. I took them all, and revealed one last happy surprise, a pair of boots.

They were the wrong size for the big Strix driver, but I hadn't time to wonder who they might have belonged to. I slid one foot in and found they fit me well enough, just a bit tight in the toe box. If this was the best I could do, it would be enough.

I took my armful of treasures downstairs to the tub that had been used for washing hounds, back when the manor was lively enough for such things, long before Maman's time. It had no hot water. I dreaded making myself colder, but my trip into the house had left me sooty and bedraggled, which would catch the attention of curious villagers. It was better that I be as inconspicuous as possible. First, I rinsed the tub, then shed my dirty chemise, rinsing off as quickly as I could.

I used the laundry bag to dry myself, then scrambled into the long johns, socks, and boots. When I finally wrapped the overcoat around me, I'd stopped shivering. As I buttoned the coat, something in the left pocket banged against my thigh. I reached in to find the Broussard's spare key.

A thrill rushed through me as I opened the garage doors. Something had worked out. I climbed into the driver's seat. It only took a moment to put Helene's stray hairpins to use, pulling my hair into a simple chignon; then I tied her scarf around my head, affixing it under my chin. It was a universal style this time of year for women in this area, tweed overcoat and a scarf to keep the wind off the ears. I glanced at my reflection for a moment in the rearview mirror. The face staring back at me was presentable but exhausted, my gray eyes puffy and inflamed, my pale skin dry and dull.

This wouldn't do in Pravhna society, but it was perfect for the Somershire train station. I would be utterly forgettable as I made my way to the station. No one was likely to recognize me if I kept my head down and didn't speak much. Not that any of that would be a problem. I hadn't a single friend in the village. Now that Helene was dead, I supposed I hadn't a friend in the world.

"How sad," I murmured as I started the Broussard. "The only person I truly loved died before I could kill her myself."

Was it true? Would I have killed Helene? As I pulled out of the carriage house, I pushed the thought aside. There was relief in not ever having to find out, and that was a gift.

CHAPTER 5

MINA

The drive down the mountain was harrowing. Even though Maman had taught me to drive, I wasn't any good at it. Still, I made it down in one piece, and unseen as far as I could tell. A thicket of blackberry a few miles outside the village was the perfect hiding spot for the Broussard, key still in the ignition. If some villager wanted the thing, they could have it—it was too distinctive to drive into town without being recognized. Besides, I would never drive again if I could help it.

I trudged into the forest, listening hard for any signs of the hunt. They were unlikely to come this close to the village, but it was best to make certain all the same. The woods were close, overgrown with moss covered brambles, the pervasive mist that covered all of Sirin crawling along the forest floor. Elementals often hid within its depths.

The walk into the station was just long enough to make my joints scream with pain. My mind drifted to strategy, a surefire way to dull the agony of a long walk. There was the obvious: get to Orchid House, and into Maman's workshop, but I had to plan for some unfortunate realities. Getting in would be difficult.

Her inner sanctum at Orchid House was undoubtedly guarded by dangerous spells, and she and Demophon would have planned for them to last long after her death. Most Oscarovi used magic sparingly, unless they were inspirited, as maintaining any working drained their lifeforce. Even the inspirited largely could not maintain spellwork after their deaths, but I knew Maman had found ways around the usual rules.

It was Maman's greatest shame that I had not proven a good enough witch to attract an elemental familiar. Not every Oscarovi was inspirited, but to maintain any kind of power in Pravhna, it was practically a requirement. She had berated me about it every chance she got, perhaps to make up for the unsatisfying fact that to maintain her own power, she had to hide my lack. Though power itself was not my problem. It was only doing as others did, making a show of things.

Maman's perspective was incomprehensible to me. She was a paradox—one of the most naturally talented witches of her generation, creative beyond comprehension. I doubt even Helene comprehended the ingenious aspects of her power. I certainly didn't, and it had caught me by surprise. It had always struck me as odd that she was so concerned with what others thought of us.

There had to be something in that particular inconsistency. It itched in the back of my mind, restless to be understood. If only I could remember what it was I knew. The only way to find out might be to ferret out the people who'd helped her. That much I did remember. There were others, though Helene and I never knew exactly who they were— shadows that lurked behind closed doors all my life.

A bubbling creek startled me out of the daze I'd been

walking through the forest in. My heart beat hard in my chest, panic rising in me. I should have been paying more attention, for the hunt, for stray villagers—what had I been thinking, letting my guard down that way? I had only meant to dull the pain a little, not lose track of time and space altogether. I needed to be more aware of my surroundings.

The oubliette had dulled my senses; sharpening things should be a priority for me.

I was just outside the village now, approaching a well-worn path that ran along the bubbling stream. Ahead, I recognized the footbridge, its railings built from bent willow branches. As I approached, water elementals took the form of various flying fish, jumping out of the water in prismatic glory.

Had Helene known who Maman's conspirators were, and what they were up to? Was that why she'd been killed? I paused on the footbridge, mesmerized by the crystalline elementals. I wondered how I might get hold of records regarding the fire once I got to Pravhna, and if it was even worth it.

All citizens were allowed to examine public records regarding events, which was what made it so unlikely that whatever had been written down about the fire was the truth. A twig snapped nearby, and my eyes darted towards the noise. It was only a cat, a sweet-faced little calico, running back towards the village with a small rodent in her mouth as a prize. A swarm of thoughts rushed back at me as my heartbeat slowed. After so long in the oubliette forgetting, it was overwhelming to think so much.

The best thing to do, unfortunately, was to move. My feet were already aching, sharp, biting pain shooting through the tendons in my legs with every step. Long breath after long breath did nothing for the pain itself, but with every step towards the train station, I grew reacquainted with it. Soon, I was able to think again.

The cityguard was corrupt, bought off by the highest echelons. If the fire at Somerhaven had been the result of foul play, which it most certainly had been, nothing of any use would be in those records. A stray thought reminded me that anyone with the ability to use empyrae would be nigh impossible to imprison, or to confront.

That was a problem for later, though. Now, my only avenue for finding out what truly happened, and what was at the heart of all this, was to re-enter Pravhna society. Secrets were currency amongst the upper echelons. I would have to find ways to gather enough to make clever exchanges.

That was going to take careful plotting. Without Helene, I would likely be lost in my overwhelming thoughts. Weak sunlight hit my face as I exited the thick forest. I'd walked slowly through the woods to conserve energy, but I sped up as soon as my feet hit cobblestone. I skirted through back alleys, avoiding the main thoroughfares and quaint shoppes of the village. Unlikely as it might be for someone to recognize me, it was better to be careful now.

Somershire Station was much as it had always been when I arrived. My heart thumped, creating a rhythm in my body that thrummed with anxiety. By contrast, the station was slow and sleepy, which wasn't to my advantage. It would have been easier if it had been a busy morning—I would have been just another face in the crowd. As I stood in front of the ticket window, reading the placard that named all the stops on the line out of this station, I noticed prices had gone up.

Before I could think too hard, it was my turn. The clerk was a kind-eyed Corvidae, with their beak stuck in a book. They asked me for my destination without looking up from their reading. I counted the little wad of money from Helene's purse carefully. There was just enough for a third-class ticket to Orobov. My heart sank. I couldn't get all the way to Pravhna.

"Next train to Orobov," I said quickly, not wanting the attention that waiting much longer to answer might draw from the line forming behind me.

The clerk didn't so much as look up at me, but printed the ticket and handed it over. I moved quickly out of line, doing some quick calculations in my head. Orobov was an outer ring suburb of Pravhna, and at the rate I walked, it would be mid-morning by the time I got to Orchid House, if not later. This was worrisome, and frankly dangerous.

I sat down on one of the hard benches in the station, keeping my head down while I tried to sort everything out. Exhaustion clouded my thinking, as I went round and round with myself. I'd used too much magic trying to free Demophon from Maman's ring. Sadness hit me. Cruel as Maman could be, Demophon had always calmed her. I would have liked to have seen the wolverine elemental one last time.

A little family of Oscarovi I didn't recognize entered the station, catching my attention, though I didn't know why. They were nobody remarkable, just parents, a baby, and a toddler. Their clothes were well made, but they'd been mended many times. They bought tickets to one of the northern aeries, and one of the adults spoke to the toddler about seeing the sirens as they sat down. The little girl, who had lush dark curls and glowing umber skin, tapped her cheeks. "They've got people-faces?"

"Yes, darling," one of the mothers answered, distracted by the cries of the colicky infant in her partner's arms. "Though we're *all* people. You know that."

The little one pulled on her other mother's pant leg, ignoring the correction in a babyish way that held no malice. "And birb bodies?"

Neither answered the child, who frowned. She turned to me. "Birb bodies?" she asked, toddling forward a few steps.

I nodded once, as it seemed no one else would answer her. She smiled at me. I did not smile back, wanting the child to look elsewhere. I was upset by the thought of walking from Oborov to Pravhna, worried that I might push myself too hard, when the toddler spoke again.

She was right in front of me now, her chubby little hands reaching for my knees. "Shiny eyes," she cooed. I recoiled from her touch, squeezing my eyes shut.

"Yes, Zell, the lady has shiny eyes," said one of the mothers. My eyes flew open, but neither of the parents was looking my way.

The little one stumbled into me, and the mother who was not holding onto the infant jumped forward, scooping the toddler into her arms. "Apologies," she said to me, while soothing the little girl, who looked as though she might cry.

I nodded once and looked down. The woman stared at me for a long moment. "Have we met? You look so familiar to me."

"No," I replied, shaking my head. "I don't think so."

"Mel, doesn't she look like someone we know?" the mother replied, bouncing the toddler on her knee.

Mel looked up at me, frowned a bit, then shook her head. Her curls were the same as the toddler's. "A bit familiar, I'd say."

My heart beat wildly. They weren't people I'd met before. My memory for faces was excellent. Names, not so much, but faces I always remembered. How was it possible they recognized me? Then it struck me. I hadn't even considered how Maman might have explained my disappearance. If they'd pretended I'd gone missing, had my picture been in the papers?

I almost spoke again, but they'd gone back to their children, fussing over them with the kind of loving frustration that parents with small children are easily forgiven for. Something deep inside me stirred with longing for something I would never have. The fetch was sterile. I'd read it in every one of Maman's forbidden texts about the topic. I'd never even gotten my moon.

Maman took all that from me. The thought was so clear, so poignant I knew it was memory, not suspicion. Everything wrong with me was Maman's fault, or at least I'd believed that the day I'd confronted her. Rage rose in me, and I knew that if I spent another moment here, my eyes would glow in a way the women across from me wouldn't be able to ignore.

I got up. "Have a lovely trip to the aerie," I said softly, the sound of my voice speaking to others strange, after so long with only myself to talk to. "Please excuse me." There was no chance that they'd even remember me in a few moments, so engrossed by their little family as they were.

As I moved away from them, out of the station proper, my anger with Maman expanded. I shut my eyes tight, leaning against the whitewashed brick wall of the station. The mere buzz of the aetheric lights was overwhelming, my shoes suddenly too tight, the collar of the coat itchy on my skin. My jaw clenched, as I attempted to force some of the stimuli to retreat, but it didn't work.

It was as though I could hear everything, and then for a moment I *did*. I could hear the mothers inside the station talking to their children, the clerk turning the pages of her book, and from around the corner, an argument.

I've told you time and time again to leave me be, Hippolyta.

That's fine. Then I guess I'll go to the rags about your little affairs when I get back to the city.

Have you any idea how easy it would be to rid myself of you?

I do. That's why I made certain to let Karnon know where I was off to.

You wouldn't dare put that brute Archambeau on my tail.

I'd like to keep him out of this, if you'd just give me the information I asked for. Where—

My feet moved, as though drawn to the voices. Quickly, I opened my eyes, stopping myself from going forward another step. The overwhelming rush of noise retreated. I could no longer hear everything happening around me. I was out on the platform now. It was empty, but the sound of low voices came from around the corner of the station. I couldn't make them out so clearly now, but one of the voices was familiar.

Viridian Montclair. What was he doing here? Hadn't he been with the hunting party? I froze as the sound of his voice drew closer. "Stop showing up at these events, *Hippolyta*," he warned. The emphasis he put on the other person's name was pregnant with disdain. Whoever she was, Viridian hated her. "You may think you have the upper hand, but I am very willing to prove you wrong."

A part of me wanted to round the corner and confront Viridian, but my fear of the oubliette was too great. It would be wise to run, but I couldn't do that either. I was as stuck as I'd been at the bottom of the oubliette, and if he came round the corner, I'd be caught. The woman was speaking again, but I could no longer make out the words. My fear had manifested into a roaring flood that suffused every particle of my being.

I stood stock-still, not hearing, seeing, or tracking time until a woman a head shorter than me bumped directly into me. She was dressed beautifully, and her face—well, her face put Helene's to shame, and that was saying something.

"Get into the station. *Now*," the woman hissed, pushing me forward. Somewhere in the distance, wings flapped. I had forgotten Viridian had the ability to transform into an eagle. In a daze, my body moved without much of my help. The tiny, stunningly beautiful brunette pushed me, maneuvering me around the corner and into the lavatory, which was a single, private toilet at this station.

She locked the door behind us, then turned to face me, whispering, "Wilhelmina Wildfang?"

I hadn't the wherewithal to lie. It felt as though I was back underwater, moving in slow motion. "Yes."

The brunette, who Viridian had called Hippolyta, glared hard at me, her hazel eyes narrowing. She was a vision, like a vengeful goddess out of an ancient tale. "You foolish girl. What are you *doing* here? Do you *know* who I was just speaking to?"

I came back around a bit more, a glare of my own forming. "Viridian Montclair. What of it?"

Hippolyta sighed. "I know you probably think he is wonderful, since he was engaged to your sister, but that man is dangerous."

My eyebrow arched with interest. I dismissed the condescension in the other woman's voice. Maman had frequently made light of my tendency to forget social niceties as a kind of quirk. People often thought me rather naive, and the way this woman was dressed told me she was likely familiar with my reputation in society. "Why do you think that?"

Hippolyta leaned against the heavy wooden door of the lavatory. "If you knew what I do about Viridian Montclair, you'd suspect him, too."

I laughed, the sound dry and unfamiliar to my ears. So, this woman knew the *real* Viridian Montclair. Unfortunate for her, but fortunate for me.

Hippolyta misunderstood my laughter as dismissal. "Fine," she said as she unlocked the lavatory door. "Take your chances then, if you don't believe me."

I slammed the door shut, reaching over Hippolyta to lock it again, murmuring, "I didn't laugh because I don't believe you, but because I *do*."

The small brunette turned, her eyes flaring with curiosity. "You know something about him."

I nodded once, then pointed silently to the train station around us, then cupped my ears to suggest that anyone could be listening. Hippolyta nodded, her eyes widening. I shrugged, pointing to the door. I could only hope she understood I meant that we should try to leave together. It would be easier to talk openly on the train. I showed Hippolyta my ticket to make my point.

The brunette rolled her eyes as she read my ticket, snatching the ticket away from me before unlocking the lavatory door. "I can do better than that, Wilhelmina Wildfang."

CHAPTER 6

ASHBOURNE

Wicked storms stole into the city on the heels of the usual morning fog, and now rain pelted the cobbled street outside the office. A cello suite played softly in the background as I flipped another page in my book without reading it. I glanced at the clock, my mouth twisting as I calculated how long Skye had been gone.

"*Shit.*" I swore in pain. My lip was still healing, even a few hours after my return home from the fire.

Morpheus growled from the office window, but stretched out, his great paws flexing, silver spotted fur shining in the firelight. The feline was only dreaming, not responding to my foul language. Not that the greymalkin would care much about my swearing, curmudgeonly as he was. Still, Skye rarely swore, so I tried to watch my language.

I glanced at the clock again, refocusing my attention. My partner had been gone for over an hour. As far as trips to the Merc went, that wasn't long, and it was better that she reported the devilry at the rubber factory than me. The Aestra in the *Aestra & Claymore* sign on the front window came first for a reason. Skye's name had weight in Pravhna, even in the undercity, where cratties like her old world family's House were despised. Unlike the rest of them, the name Aestra was respected, in no small part because of Skye herself.

Skye's clever tongue would weave a better tale for the Syndicate leaders than I could hope to. She'd been saving me in one way or another for nearly a year, and this morning was no different. I'd been lucky that she and Morpheus found me out cold by the river last winter, with no coat, no money, only an enormous claymore strapped to my back. When I woke, I had no memory of my past, or what I was doing in Pravhna, only my given name.

I turned the pages of the book back to the beginning of the chapter I hadn't been reading. The book was a new gothic romance, bought from my favorite bookstore down the lane. It was full of haunted manor houses and a sinister love interest, typically my favorite genre, but I was distracted. Likely, I'd stay so until Skye returned with news on what was to be done about the fires. Halcyon Gate got lucky last night; no one had died. Other districts hadn't been as lucky.

Perhaps another cup of tea would help. As I got up from my desk, stretching my long legs, movement outside the door kept me from heading back to the little kitchen behind the front office. My shoulders tensed, the bulk of my muscles still sore from the fight. A delicately boned Strix woman stood outside, reading the sign on the window before pushing the door open.

The woman had a scarred screech owl visage, and was dressed smartly in a vibrant ochre tweed suit, covered with a lush fur overcoat, a bowler hat pulled low over her brow. The gloves that covered the taloned fingers of her hands had a rich sheen to them. Everything about the Strix woman was an ostentatious show of wealth. I paused, feeling wary as she shook her umbrella out the door, depositing it in the stand. I hoped this wasn't about last night, or the child I'd helped.

The Strix tended to stick together and if the littling had told about my power… Well, I didn't want to think about that. I hadn't asked the tyke to keep it a secret. They hadn't even seen exactly what I'd done. They'd been so upset I'd chosen not to draw attention to it, figuring they'd likely forget most of what had happened. But if this woman was here to interrogate me, I might be in trouble. It wouldn't do to let the truth of my abilities out.

"You're the private investigators, yes?" she asked, skipping niceties altogether.

I straightened up, breathing an inward sigh of relief. She was a potential client, not the child's relative. In that case, I needed to think quickly. Skye typically handled new clients.

"I'm the Claymore," I said, stumbling over my words a bit, then realizing I'd been unclear. "I'm Ashbourne Claymore," I clarified. "Typically, Skye does the intake, but she's out right now. Apologies."

This wasn't starting off well. The Strix narrowed her eyes. "Because she is the female?"

I frowned, not understanding. My amnesia worked strangely, according to Skye, whose mother was a renowned physician in the upper city. According to my partner, amnesiacs usually remembered most things about society and the greater world, but forgot their personal details. I was different. It seemed I'd forgotten many things about our world and society at large, as well as my personal history.

"Does Mlle Aestra do the intake because she is the female? Do you view your partner as your secretary?"

I frowned deeply. "We can't afford a secretary, I'm afraid. I do most of the clerical work though. I hope that won't keep you from contracting with us."

The Strix sighed, already exasperated with me. "That's not what I meant."

I saw my mistake instantly. In some aeries, there were strict divisions of labor, based solely on sex, rather than gender. When I'd learned that fact, it had surprised me, and confused Skye and Morpheus.

They were unsure how I could have gone without such basic knowledge for all my life. Skye had wanted to take me to see her mother, but when I'd seen how uncomfortable the idea made her, I'd refused. Relearning stray facts about the world and how society worked had been part of my recovery.

It was as though I was learning most things anew. Memories of my past were elusive, and I did not chase them. My life here was good, and a feeling in my gut told me that whatever lay in the past should stay there. Still, moments like these were always awkward, and I needed to do better. Business had been a bit sparse lately.

My eyes glanced off the stack of bills on Skye's desk, as I gestured to the seating area up front. "Typically, I'm just the muscle. Skye's really best with people. That's why she does the intake." I put another log on the hearth as I spoke. "Please, sit," I urged the Strix woman. "Can I get you some tea?"

"No," she said, sitting gingerly, as though she thought the leather sofa might be dirty.

It was not, of course. We're meticulously clean, and I think the office is rather cozy. It was obvious in the way the Strix woman turned her beak up at the office that she did not agree. I took a seat across from her, a wingback covered in dark green velvet.

"How can I be of service, Madame…" I waited for her to fill in her name.

The Strix woman sat on the very edge of the couch, perched as though she would fly away if she could. "My name is of no importance. I was told you take cases no one else will… Ones of a more unsavory nature."

The woman's clothes had obviously been made at one of the haughty ateliers up top. She likely saw our usual clientele as unsavory, but the reality was that most of our cases were rather mundane. We specialized in finding lost people, and most of our business was reconnecting families. The fact that this woman found our rather wholesome clientele unsavory elicited revulsion in me, souring my stomach enough that I hoped it didn't show on my face.

Pull it together, man. I wracked my brain for what to do next. Skye's method for handling situations like these was to feign confusion. She claimed it often urged the subject to reveal more than they otherwise would. "I'm afraid I don't know what you mean."

"Apologies, Mr. Claymore," the Strix said, her tone gentling into pure condescension. "I meant no offense. I come as a go-between for my long-time employer. Someone of good standing, who has an enemy trying to destroy everything we've worked for."

There was genuine emotion in the woman's voice now. I believed that she believed what she said to be true. "All right. What would you like us to do to help? Gather information? Assess the threat?" All were our first steps in building up to more actionable commissions.

"No," the Strix replied, her dark eyes shining. "We'd like you to eliminate her."

What had this woman heard about me? Was it possible that word had gotten around about this morning already? I didn't see how, but I had no idea how the trance those people had been in worked. Maybe they remembered how easily I'd fought off the unnaturally skilled opponents. They'd gotten the better of me in the end, but everyone in the undercity was a fairly good judge of a fighter's prowess. I had no need to be the best, but there was no doubt in my mind that anyone who'd seen that fight would know that I was more than I appeared to be.

Morpheus stretched in the window, growling in his sleep. The Strix startled at the noise coming from behind her, and turned to look at the greymalkin. "I don't believe your cat likes me," she murmured, her eyes widening at Morpheus' considerable bulk.

"That's no cat, Mistress," I replied, my outward expression grim, though inside I had a laugh at the Strix's expense. Morpheus was deep into his midday nap; there was no waking him. Still, if the Strix was unnerved by him, that was fine. "Have you ever met one of the greymalkin before?"

"Oh," the Strix woman said, thoughtful now. "My apologies."

She didn't answer my question. I shrugged, as it didn't matter to me if she couldn't identify a fey cat. It was time for this woman to go. I hated to lose business, but I knew Skye would have done the same if she were here. "We don't do that kind of work, I'm afraid. You'll have to go elsewhere."

"That's not exactly true though, is it?" Her words sent a chill through me. *Did* she know about this morning? But how could she? Her head tilted to one side, a shrewd expression on her avian face. "You have certain unusual talents, do you not?"

My skin prickled in warning at her words. This woman knew more about me than she was letting on, and with how little I remembered about my own past, that was dangerous. She had to go, and now.

I crossed my arms over my chest, puffing it out a bit, hoping that my sheer size might be enough to convince the Strix that I meant what I said. "We're not the right agency for the job. You might try Wingate and Stravinski down the road a bit. They won't do merc work either, but they'll serve you well for an investigation, which I'm afraid we cannot provide."

The Strix tilted her head in the other direction, her intense expression unnerving. "We want you."

I said nothing, keeping my expression blank, but stony. Morpheus breathed deeply in his sleep, and I matched the rhythm of my breath with his—calm and even. Inside I roiled with alarm, but outwardly, I was cold serenity defined. I hoped she understood the chill in my stare to mean, *if you put the little world I've built for myself in any kind of danger, I will end you.*

"Fine then." The Strix sighed, apparently accepting, for the time being anyway, that I would not budge. "But keep an eye out for a woman named Wilhelmina Wildfang. She's trouble, and we'll pay for whatever you can dig up on her."

The Strix's eyes went to the stack of bills on Skye's desk, lingering on the telltale blue envelope from the Bureau of Taxation for a long moment. She appeared to think hard about something, then rose and moved towards the door. "We can have your tax fee cleared in an instant, and so much more. Consider our offer, Msr Claymore. Wildfang is a menace to all we hold dear."

Her gloved hand was on the door, but she paused, waiting, I imagine, for what she implied to sink in. That this Wilhelmina Wildfang was a threat to the very thing I protected by rejecting her employer as a client. She thought she was good at the game, leading me to believe she had information on my past, and that the woman she wanted murdered could hurt my future. I wonder what made her think I was such an easy mark, but it wasn't worth following up on.

Whoever Wildfang was, I'd bet good coin the Strix woman was the real danger. I narrowed my eyes, but slightly. "Good day to you, Mistress."

Her little hoot of laughter as she stormed out of the office was derisive, and though the sound did no such thing, it *felt* as though it echoed. Long after she'd left, I stood with my arms tightly crossed, fuming. The Strix had stirred up worries I didn't know I had and still couldn't name. Not that I wanted to.

I was so fixated on calming myself that I missed Morpheus waking. *Is Skye still at the Merc?* he asked as he jumped down from his cushion in the window. *I'd like lunch at a reasonable hour.*

The beast rubbed against my legs affectionately, purring. "Still gone," I replied.

Morpheus glanced at the clock that sat on the mantel. *She should have returned by now.*

He was right. Skye had been gone too long. "Let me get my coat and we'll go."

Morpheus dissolved slowly into nothing, his voice the last to leave. *I shall not walk in the rain.*

Of course he wouldn't, damn feline. I, however, would have to go on foot. Nothing about this day felt right, and if Skye was in trouble, she could handle herself. I knew that well enough, but a dark mood took me, and part of me relished a bit of a tussle. As I pulled my overcoat from the rack at the back door, a crooked smile curved my lips.

All this energy had to go somewhere, didn't it?

CHAPTER 7

ASHBOURNE

A few blocks away from the office, the rain cleared off, though the air was damp from the storm. The undercity bled into a dense forest at the base of the mountain Pravhna was built upon, and mist from below curled around my feet as I walked. It hung in the air, clinging to pant legs and clay flower pots bursting with chrysanthemums.

Lower down, deep in what was known as the dark districts, a canopy of trees blocked even the dim sunlight we sometimes got here. That was where the mist came from. The mist and the elementals. A gust of wind caused the clouds around my feet to billow up towards me off the cobbled walkway. I shoved my hands in the pockets of my overcoat as the mist reached waist level, not wanting it to touch me. It was irrational—the midnight blue stuff was harmless, but it gave me an unsettled feeling. There were echoes, deep in the recesses of my mind, of billowing mist that I daren't examine too hard.

I cleared my throat, as though doing so would banish thoughts of life existing before all this—before Pravhna and the undercity. My stomach growled as the scent of street food drifted past me. A street vendor, just a block away from the Merc, sold roasted chestnuts and candied apples at the center of a roundabout. They'd set up their stand at the foot of an enormous marble statue depicting a wide variety of Vilhari and Oscarovi. I'd been told it was a tribute to the brave soldiers of the undercity who'd fought in some long ago war against an extraterrestrial threat.

Vaguely, I understood the war had been the reason that the Vilhari and the Oscarovi had finally come together as a blended society—that the foe they fought against had alchemized the two groups. I struggled to recall the name of the invaders, but could not. It was all basic stuff, things school children knew by heart, and yet it was all still a mystery to me, as were the intricacies of Pravhna society.

It was easier here in the undercity, where people didn't pry about a person's past. But it was more than that. People in the undercity were nothing like the fussy upper crust cratties, whose neighborhoods of ornately carved limestone buildings were decorated with sedate gardens, put to bed the moment they dried up in the autumn. I passed a cluster of Oscarovi flower vendors, all calling out prices for their bright wares as I went. A few of them were familiar to me, and I waved as I crossed the street.

Here in the undercity, the avian fey gathered festive flora in their travels into the dark districts below. The Oscarovi used their elemental magic to spell them to last longer than they naturally would and sold them in beautifully arranged bundles. This time of year, our district had the feeling of a perpetual carnival.

The Mercury Room, or the Merc as most of Halcyon Gate called it, was up ahead. I slowed as I approached, honing my focus. Doing business at the Merc meant having my wits sharpened to a knife's edge. I always took a moment to clear my mind before entering the Syndicate's inner sanctum.

The pleasure house was a tall, four story building, whose imposing limestone exterior bore carvings of Strix knights and siren queens and oracles over the enormous arched doors. Flowers spilled out of boxes affixed to the sills of leaded glass windows. Huge aetheric lamps were lit even in daytime, their green glow and the curls of wrought iron flowers and bats luring customers in.

After one last steadying breath, infusing my still-aching muscles with a bit of cool relief, I entered the pleasure house through a side door. The back hallways were crowded. I nodded at various people from the neighborhood as I made my way to the atrium at the center of the building. There was a bar set up there, and at night musicians played and the tables were cleared off the floor for dancing. A paper bag labeled "S. Aestra" sat on the bar, near the till. Skye had ordered lunch.

The Strix bartender nodded at the bag as I read the label. "She paid, but she's talking to the boss."

I followed the golden-eyed Strix's gaze up to the mezzanine. Skye was easy to spot. Her shining white hair was cropped short, from where she'd cut off her Chevalier's braid when she left the upper city for good, a tradition among the Syndicate organizations, apparently. Today, she was dressed in her usual attire of slim-fitting trousers, tall leather boots and close fitting shirtsleeves that clung to the athletic muscles of her arms and shoulders. She'd tossed her gray wool overcoat over the back of her chair.

Her expression was serious as Karnon Archambeau leaned towards her, talking animatedly in a low tone. Archambeau was the Halcyon Gate Syndicate's unofficial leader, mostly because of his infectious charisma. He was a short man, but sturdily built, with tawny skin and a sharply intelligent face. The Oscarovi's dark eyes were serious as he fiddled with the pendant that channeled his elemental familiar. There was no hint of amusement in the motion of his hands—he was troubled by whatever he was telling Skye.

So, what I'd encountered this morning wasn't a fluke. We were right to report in. The undercity thrived, in many ways, because of organized crime, but Skye could never shake the feeling that the consequences of their rule were too steep. Privately, I disagreed. The cratties' hold on the upper city was just as cruel. It just looked nicer on the outside, while the Syndicate was open in their brutality. I didn't need to explain that to Skye. She understood it perfectly and wanted better from everyone. That was where we differed. I expected the worst from people and was glad when they surprised me with better.

On the mezzanine, Skye nodded while Archambeau spoke, her face grave. There was nothing of her usual serenity in her posture. Her shoulders hunched around her ears, and every so often she covered her mouth in what I knew was deep horror. Inwardly, I swore.

Signs had been cropping up for months that something rotten was happening in the undercity. First, there'd been more missing people than ever, more odd murders and unexplained crime. And now, these strange, unquenchable fires that did not spread. Our closest guess was that a new player might be attempting to take control of the Syndicate as a whole.

The Syndicate was a loose organization that operated throughout the undercity. Each of the large lower districts had multiple Syndicate leaders that ran things, taking bribes, offering protection, and keeping our communities prosperous. In the Halcyon Gate, we had four: Karnon Archambeau led the Oscarovi, Vionette Celestine the Vilhari, and Edith Braithwaite the Strix and Corvidae.

THE HOLLOW PLANE

The fourth leader, who went by the pseudonym Chopard, operated in secret, ostensibly acting as liaison with the dark districts. It was brutal work, but it kept the more dangerous Syndicate elements out of everyday life. No one had ever seen him. In my mind, he was a likely candidate to be the cause of all this trouble. Perhaps he'd been bought out by one of the darker elements in the Syndicate. This morning had proven that if that were true, all of Pravhna needed to be concerned, not just the undercity.

Anyone who could wield that kind of power was beyond dangerous. From the looks of things, Archambeau already knew what was going on, and the news was bad. Karnon Archambeau wasn't a selfish man; in fact, quite the opposite. He cared deeply about the undercity being run in the ways he saw fit. Though Archambeau and Skye disagreed on many of those points, they shared a belief that the only way denizens here would be taken care of was by their own.

I could take the bag of food and go, now that I'd confirmed nothing had gone wrong with the Syndicate, but something in my gut told me to stay. I slid onto a stool, glancing at the bartender. "Ale, please."

The Strix nodded. He was new, and I didn't know his name. They always had the new ones work the day shift for a few months before taking on the riotous nighttime crowd. "Dark or pale?"

"Pale," I said, keeping my eyes on Skye. The Vilhar could hold her own, but I'd never assume we were safe at the Merc just because we had good standing in the neighborhood.

While I didn't *think* we were in trouble from the way Archambeau was talking, there was no predicting the Syndicate. The bartender slid a glass of pale ale across the luxurious wood bar. I waited to take a drink. Something about the way Skye sat back on the ornately carved settee worried me.

Skye glanced down from the mezzanine at just that moment, her silver eyes locking onto mine. The same chill that went through me on the walk over seeped deep into my bones. Skye held my gaze for a long moment, then turned back to Archambeau. I settled into my stool. There was no way I was leaving now. I turned my attention to the bag of food, opening it to peek inside. It was cold.

"Want me to send it back to the kitchen for a warmup?" the bartender asked, a knowing look in his eyes. "The new sous chef is Oscarovi. They don't mind a bit."

I nodded. "That would be great. Could you have them add an extra helping of the plain poulet as well?" That would appease Morpheus' temper for having been made to wait. There was no telling where the greymalkin had got off to, but as he wasn't here, it was my duty to make sure there was enough lunch to keep him happy. Or at least *less* grumpy than usual.

The Strix took the bag away. "Of course." As he walked away, it looked like he let out a sigh of relief. I couldn't say as I blamed him. There was an atmosphere of tension in the pleasure house that was odd for a weekday afternoon. The usual games of cards were nowhere to be found, and there wasn't a courtesan in sight. The chill spread through me, aching as it went.

Archambeau's voice raised a measure, making him just loud enough to be heard down in the atrium. "...one remembers anything afterward. How is he *doing* it?"

Magic that alters memory is old and complex. The Oscarovi usually can't manage it, even those inspirited with the most powerful elementals. As far as I knew, the most powerful among the Vilhari couldn't do spells like that either, not without a fair amount of inconvenience, anyway. Minds are complicated things, hard to manipulate for even short amounts of time. It's why love and memory spells are unreliable and short-lived, if they ever work at all.

I scanned the atrium bar to see who else was interested in what was going on here today. The pink velvet chairs were empty but for a large man, with long dark brown locs pulled into a neat ponytail, wearing a wine-colored suit. His thick legs were crossed in a casual way that suggested he was at ease—well at ease, as anyone who saw the future might be.

I raised a hand slowly in greeting when Muse felt me watching. My emotional range was frustratingly limited, at times. I felt things outside my fairly even keel, but I didn't stray very often from a rather defined set of emotional parameters. Today, things were different. A feeling of an aperture widening came over me as Muse's dark eyes turned my way.

"Ashbourne." Muse's sonorous voice boomed across the atrium, a bright smile flashing white. As always, his umber skin was the epitome of vibrant health. The man always looked infuriatingly well-rested. "Good to see you."

Muse didn't get up though, or motion for me to join him, which was typical of the seer. Muse and Skye were acquaintances on good terms, and little else. The seer had made it clear he wasn't interested in being friends with "anyone who gets themselves into as much trouble as the two of you regularly do." Muse's table had a full glass of *le fey vert* resting on it, and he appeared to be reading a book. From the state of his full glass, I doubted he'd come to the Merc for a hallucinogenic drink and a relaxing afternoon.

Motion in my peripheral vision caught my attention. I looked up to find Skye, with the bag of food in hand. Her face was smooth and serene, but there was a steeliness in her eyes that concerned me. Skye nodded to me. "Let's get lunch to Morpheus, before he destroys something in retribution."

I started to slide off my stool, making ready to follow Skye home. Time seemed to slow, as instincts I didn't quite understand came awake within me. From secret corners, eyes were upon us. Muse looked up from his book at the same time I reacted to the odd feeling. Deep sadness lingered in the seer's eyes, clarifying further when his gaze rested on me. I wondered what he saw, but also—I had the strong sense I didn't want to know.

Skye paused. She looked around, but then seemed to sense the truth of the matter: by day's end everyone would know what she was about to tell me. "We've been hired to investigate Chopard. We're to uncover his real identity."

I had been right. This would mean war in Halcyon Gate. The peace of our district was dependent on the Syndicate leaders getting along. This was unheard of. I glanced back at the mezzanine. Karnon was gone. "What about Edith and Vionette?" The other two Syndicate leaders had to agree to something of this magnitude.

Skye's countenance was outwardly cool, but I saw the worry in her eyes. "They are in consensus. Chopard is the source of the arsons. His people have been spotted at two different scenes, as well as the masked combatants you fought this morning. He brought the fight to us, Ash. There's no other way."

She was right, of course. There were strict rules around how the Syndicate operated, and Chopard had been flouting them for too long—he'd gone too far this time. I thought of the little owlet, and the blank look in those people's eyes. The way that after the working that had turned them into mindless automatons fell away, they'd still be hollowed out, empty shells. I hadn't even asked if they were all right.

"The people from this morning…" I said, trailing off.

"Two are dead," Skye said, her eyes gentling. "The littling you helped and the mother."

"What?" the room spun out beneath me. The owlet was only a little sick, just a cold, and I'd fixed their hand. How could this be possible? "But the child wasn't even affected by the spell."

Skye shook her head. "We don't know how it happened, Ash. But when Vionette's doctor arrived an hour ago, they were both gone."

A stab of fear ran through me, laced with righteous fury at the hatchling's death. The feeling was old, familiar to me, though I refused to examine it further. I drew myself up, my spine lengthening as my feet hit the rough wooden floors. Skye looked back at me over her shoulder, her expression shifting as mine did. The mixture of fear and anger were a warrior's constant companions, and my partner wore them as comfortably as I did when the need arose. Skye's face was a mirror of mine, her eyes hardening into those of the Chevalier she'd once been.

Each step we took towards the Merc's back doors was a transformation. The mild-mannered private investigators we'd been two days ago melted away, and warriors of a different grade altogether walked out into the bustling streets of the undercity.

"I'm so sorry, Ash," Skye murmured as her pace picked up. "This isn't what I wanted for us."

I paused for a moment, knowing she wouldn't say more out here in the open. That apology was the end of the peaceful life we'd built together over the past year. I could run from this, build the feeling of safety I so cherished again —albeit somewhere else, without her or Morpheus, neither of whom would ever leave Pravhna.

The thought was fleeting. Skye looked back, sorrow and resolution embattled in her silver eyes. My feet moved forward until I was at her back—where I belonged—the menacing shadow to her beacon of light.

CHAPTER 8

MINA

A bit reluctantly, I followed Hippolyta back into the lobby of the train station. It was nearing the time for the next trains to arrive. The station was filling up with people. A few villagers I recognized appeared to be dropping visiting friends or relatives off, but none stayed. Anyone going into Pravhna for work would have left early this morning.

No one gave me a first, let alone a second, glance. My makeshift disguise had not worked on Hippolyta because she was uncommonly perceptive. Everyone else here went about their own business, with no mind for others. What had been such a hardship in my lonely childhood was now a boon. No one knew me, or cared to know me. All was the same as it had ever been. There was a cold comfort in that.

One of the mothers from before was talking with a clerk, a worried look on her face. "But we were told the baby would ride free."

"So sorry, ma'am," the clerk said. "They do ride free, 'til the northern stations, but…"

Hippolyta shooed me away. "Go find us a seat. The station's filling up and we've a bit to wait."

She was right, of course, but worry set into my stomach as I sat. She'd been talking with Viridian. Arguing, yes, but still in his company. Was it possible he knew I was out, and they'd plotted this together? Some part of me rejected that notion immediately. Their argument had been quite genuine, as was her hatred for him and his for her. Still, he might be blackmailing her into helping him.

But again, that didn't fit well with the conversation I had overheard. I watched Hippolyta buy two tickets to Pravhna. As the clerk gathered them for her, she glanced at the woman I'd talked to before. I searched the station for her wife, and the two children, but the station was crowded now. Winged Vilhari and Oscarovi in giant hats mingled together with Strix and Corvidae alike, the soft roar of a bustling day filling my ears. The station was a colorful riot of feathers and fabrics.

It took me a moment to find the little family amongst the crowd. I had to crane my neck a little, over the newspaper of the Oscarovi sitting next to me, to find them. They had changed seats and were crowded between a Vilhar with the brown wings of a sparrow and a Strix couple who were fighting over who had eaten the last cheese streusel from the bakery in town. The baby was crying, and the toddler clung to her mother. All their eyes were wide with distress.

It had sounded like they might not have accounted for the cost of taking a fourth member of their family north to the aeries. Not a crisis, certainly, but a disappointment. When I looked back up at Hippolyta, her eyes had found the wife and children. There was a mixture of sadness and desperation in her eyes I recognized acutely: loneliness. The kind of loneliness that ached in your gut, making your bones brittle and cold. The kind that gnawed on you at the edges, unrelenting and cruel in its persistence.

The clerk talking to the other mother said something to

Hippolyta, who nodded. I'd missed some exchange between them. The woman looked confused for a moment, then smiled gratefully, clasping Hippolyta's hand in hers. I watched as the clerk came back at the same time, handing four tickets to the woman, and two to Hippolyta. They spoke for a moment before parting ways. Hippolyta paused, watching as the little family reunited, their trip to the northern aeries back on schedule as planned.

The loneliness in her eyes lessened a measure, though the sadness behind it stayed. I had no idea if I could trust Hippolyta, but there was no doubt in my mind that we could help one another.

Hippolyta purchased us two first-class tickets to Pravhna. We would have to share a sleeping car, but that was not a problem. First-class cars contained two small beds, piled high with jewel-hued silk linens, in the bedroom, in addition to a beautifully appointed sitting room and lavatory. Neither of us spoke further about Viridian until the train was well underway to Pravhna.

Hippolyta had been "freshening up" in the lavatory for long enough that my thoughts had wandered. It was as though a ticker tape ran rampant in my mind, a carousel of fragments driving me into what felt like a trance. Pieces of the day Viridian and Helene put me in the oubliette accosted me, unbidden and out of order. The mechanics of what had happened were there, but the specifics eluded me. I'd woken that day plagued with troubling dreams.

And something else, though at first it stayed just out of sight. That morning, I *remembered* Papa. As the memory emerged, I nearly laughed at the impossibility of it. Alastair Wildfang died before Maman gave birth to me. And yet, I remembered his face, handsome, if rather plain—and the sound of his voice, gravelly and time-ravaged, much like my own. I could have dismissed remembering his face as mere fancy. There were portraits of him at Orchid House. But I had remembered the sound of his voice. I'd remembered it and told Maman.

That morning, I'd struggled to grasp onto the memory, but it disappeared before I could catch it. Whatever came next was a blur, an opaque film drawn over the memory. I saw myself, as though I floated above my body, talking to Maman, pleading with her for the truth. Feeling returned to my body, I was coming out of the trance, but I latched onto one last image. I'd woken at the bottom of the oubliette, Viridian and Helene completing the spell that locked me in, their faces disappearing as the sea rushed in to cover the hole.

"Wilhelmina!" Hippolyta's voice cut through the sound of my screams, echoing in my mind.

My vision cleared as I looked up at the woman's beautiful face, confused as to where I was. Her mahogany hair was tucked behind a pointed ear. *I was on a train, with a perfect stranger, hurtling toward Pravhna. Right.*

My eyes narrowed. "You're Vilhari?"

Hippolyta brushed the hair forward again, her cheeks flushing. "Yes, Wilhelmina, I am."

"Mina."

"What?"

Mother and Helene had always called me Wilhelmina. It had never seemed to fit me correctly, but it was an old family name, one I didn't particularly like or want. "Please call me Mina."

Hippolyta blinked once, frowned deeply as she searched my face. For what, I wasn't certain. Understanding people had never been my strong suit. The woman's large hazel eyes softened ever-so-slightly, her heartbeat slowing to a strong, regular beat.

A smile spread across her face, lighting it with overwhelming beauty. "Call me Poe." She lowered her voice to a whisper. "Not Hippolyta. *Ever.*"

"Why?" I asked, forgetting to soften my words into the more palatable tone Helene had begged me to use, claiming that my bluntness offended others.

Poe seemed to like it, though. The name fit her better than Hippolyta, which matched her regal beauty, but not the wickedly sharp intellect the woman obviously possessed. "Poe" fit the danger I sensed the woman before me might pose to any who got in her way. There was a kind of ruthless determination in Poe that was like a mirror of what lived inside my heart.

"The surname Endymion is common enough, but Hippolyta isn't," she said.

That was true. It *was* a unique name. "Viridian knows it, though."

Poe gritted her teeth. "Unfortunately, yes." She sank into the plush, seafoam green chair next to mine before going to work pouring herself some tea. The train's first-class china was exquisite, painted with snakes and a dark floral motif. For a brief moment, I considered stealing it. It would fetch a good sum on the black market—having been made especially for the railroad. It's what Maman would have done—it's the kind of thing she *had* done, or forced Helene and I to do, dozens of times.

Poe interrupted my thoughts. "In attempting to get what I need from him, he got something from me first. I'm certain he doesn't know what it means, though."

"Why?" I asked, hoping she would reveal more.

The smile on Poe's face was a sharp, cruel thing. "Because if he did, one of us would already be dead."

How interesting. Their conversation at the train station had sounded dangerous, a push and pull of secrets and threats. That clarified the state of things between them, if not the exact nature of their conflict. Neither seemed to have the advantage over the other, but as Poe hated Viridian, it warmed me to her, though perhaps irrationally so.

A cool calm settled over me. "You'll have to make him pay for whatever he's done to you."

Poe set the teapot down so gently it didn't make a sound, her eyes raising to mine. "I intend to."

We stared at one another for a long moment, neither of us offering more. The calm stillness within my chest spread throughout my body. A desperate, lonely feeling chased the stillness, one I was all too familiar with—one that had gotten me into trouble when I was younger. Giving into it always broke my heart, but something deep within me reasoned that all people couldn't be bad. That somewhere, there must be someone I could trust.

Trust was dangerous, too fickle a beast for my taste. "How did you get into a House Montclair country party if Viridian didn't want you there?"

Poe smiled, her grin a wicked thing. "I had three invites to the party. Not even Viridian could keep me away. It was just the opportunity I needed to put pressure on him." Her face fell. "I worked hard to make those contacts. Viridian kicking me out doesn't serve my purposes."

"What do your companions think happened to you?" I asked, wondering if her social standing had been harmed at all.

Poe sighed. "When Viridian had enough of me, I claimed I'd come down with the vapors and needed to go home and rest. But we were seen having words."

"I see," I said, thinking over what that might mean for her social status.

Now Poe's eyes narrowed sharply. "What do you see?"

I shrugged, trying to appear casual, though I don't think I fooled Poe. "I've never heard of you, and yet…"

"And yet I'm invited to weekends in the country with some of the highest echelons," Poe finished for me. Her tone was void of inflection, her face and body still, but not rigid. There was no way for me to read her, to tell what she might be thinking.

"Yes," I agreed, making sure to sound as neutral as she had. I was trying harder with Poe than I had in a long time. I didn't want her to immediately dislike me. But the fact remained that I had no time for friends. What I needed was an *ally*.

I stared at the teapot for a long time, not certain what to say next. In times like these, I worried my emotions were broadcast outside my body, that everyone could tell how I felt, even when I was uncertain. The train's low rumble as it hurtled towards the city soothed me somewhat, making it easier to think.

Reasoning through a problem always helped at a time like this. I took a sip of my tea—which was utter perfection —mulling over my next move. It was obvious Poe knew at least the basics of what had happened at Somerhaven. Her explanation would tell me more about her as well.

I took a cleansing breath, smoothed my face, and asked, "What can you tell me about the fire that killed my mother?"

For a long moment, confusion clouded Poe's eyes, then that deep sadness from before welled in them. It was as though whatever she felt was less about what she was about to say, and more about something deep within herself. "Your mother and Helene."

The elementals had said it, but with no evidence, I hadn't really believed it was possible. "So it was confirmed? Helene really is dead?"

Again, Poe looked confused, but she nodded. "Yes, Viridian identified the body. He was quite shaken."

That struck me as an odd thing to say. "Were you with him when he found out?"

Poe's cheeks flushed. "Not like that!"

Now it was my turn for confusion, but I caught on quickly. "I didn't mean to imply that you were…"

A shaky laugh spilled from Poe's pretty lips. "Of course you didn't. I'm sorry to have implied that you *would*. Sometimes our peers can be unkind."

I nodded once, though not sure if I understood completely. There was no question that our class could be cruel. I knew that to be true from painful experience. But it was difficult to understand why or how anyone could dislike Poe. I observed her for a long moment—her sharply defined features, her perfectly styled clothing. Everything about her was subtly better than what most of our peers could manage, even with the help of the modiste and a lady's maid.

"They are unkind to you because you are so beautiful."

Poe let out a little laugh, the sound less of delight than relief. "I suppose they might be. How I look has opened doors, but…" Poe's hands fluttered in a way that seemed uncharacteristic for her, given what I'd seen so far.

"But it makes things very hard, doesn't it?"

Poe nodded. "It does. People underestimate me."

"My sister experienced something similar when she was very young." Memory slipped down my throat, cold and slick. I swallowed hard. "My mother taught her to use it as a weapon."

Poe's eyes narrowed. "A lesson I've learned as well, though I had no mother to teach it to me."

The way Poe's voice cracked, ever so slightly, around the information moved me. Determined as I was not to make friends, every moment in her presence made me question my resolve. *Remember what happened with Rebecca and Caralee,* I reminded myself. *Remember how badly this can all turn out.* Childhood wounds did not heal easily, and I did myself no favors by forgetting.

The tension in the train car had thickened to a nearly gelatinous state. "So, my sister and mother are both dead," I said. "What does everyone think happened to me?"

Poe's eyebrows raised. "You don't know?" She shook her head. "Of course you don't...Your family said you were kidnapped—about six months before the fire—there was an investigation, but no leads were ever found."

"Who led the investigation? Which investigative unit, I mean?"

Poe shook her head. "The IU was dismissed. The Baldwin Agency was brought in—*oh.*" I sipped my tea, regulating the rapid increase in my heartbeat as Poe put the pieces together. She was *very* smart, which was incredibly satisfying. "They're on House Montclair's payroll."

Yes, they certainly were. The knowledge was disappointing, but I couldn't afford to let my emotions get the better of me. My eyes deadened, emotionlessness spreading over my features. "You don't need to convince me that Viridian Montclair is up to something bad. I know quite well what the man is capable of."

"So you weren't kidnapped then?" Poe asked.

I stood, suddenly feeling very tired, though of course the fetch did not actually need sleep. "It all depends on how you look at it. I was imprisoned against my will, by the very people who claimed to be looking for me."

I'm not sure why I told her—it was an instinct more than anything. A test, yes, but one part of me was sure she would pass.

Poe's long lashes brushed against her cheeks as she stared down at her hands. "I'm so sorry, Mina. I don't know what that would feel like... but I imagine it's terrible." The kind of sincerity that cannot be faked laced her words, drawing me in, tightening around me like a snare.

If this was a ruse, part of her incredible social skills, I needed her with me. If she could deploy sincerity this way, whether real or a performance, she was an asset I couldn't afford to lose. There was, of course, the possibility that her actions and emotions all stemmed from genuine interest in my wellbeing. I stared at her for what felt like a very long time. So long, in fact, that she looked up at me.

I found the answer I was looking for in her eyes. There was real concern and sadness there, paired with shrewd calculation. She'd hurt her reputation by getting kicked out of the Montclair party. Poe needed me as much as I needed her.

Whatever this woman was looking for, she wondered if I could help. The idea was staggering. No one had ever so much as wondered if I were an asset to their success before. I had only ever been a burden.

The idea of someone needing me terrified me, more than I could accurately understand. I backed away from Poe. "I think it best if I get some sleep now."

"Of course," Poe said softly. "I noticed that you might need something to wear to sleep in. I put something of mine out in the lavatory. It will be too short for you, of course—"

"Thank you," I said, cutting Poe short. "That is very kind of you."

Inside the lavatory, the aetheric light's greenish glow was tempered by a glass sconce, casting a pool of light into the little room. A beautiful loose dressing gown, made of the finest silk, lay over the warming towel rack. I was tempted to wash, but the shower in the lavatory was like a coffin, small and enclosed. Too much like the oubliette. I settled for keeping the door open, and washing quickly. Not much water got onto the floor, but I soothed myself with thoughts of the giant bathtub at Orchid House.

When I'd dried, I slipped into the dressing gown, which probably dragged the floor on Poe, but only skimmed my calves. Still, it was lovely to wear something so fine—and clean. I stared at my face in the lavatory mirror for a long time. My face didn't appear to have aged a day since I reached maturity. This was typical for Oscarovi, who were not technically immortal, but were so long lived that they might as well be, especially with the use of their jewels. But I wore no jewel, partnered with no elemental familiar for use of magic.

It was my greatest shame. An Oscarovi of my status without an elemental pair was considered incomplete, a failure. There were ways to hide my incompetence, but Viridian likely knew the truth about me and could use it to his advantage. That was something I'd have to be careful about. Yet another thing to be wary of.

In the mirror, as my emotions rose to the surface, my eyes glowed golden as the empyraen magic I wielded as easily as aether. Shadows flickered around my fingers, little clouds of aether, friendly as spirits for me. Yet another of my shameful eccentricities. This was not natural.

I was not natural.

I met my eyes in the mirror, as though looking at a stranger. Maman told people I took after Papa, an explanation for my dark hair, umber in color. But Papa's hair hadn't been this color. Brown, yes, unlike Maman and Helene's nearly platinum hair. But Papa had much fairer hair than mine, barely brown, and his features were nothing like mine, upon closer examination of my face.

The most common use for a fetch, before the Oscarovi High Council had outlawed them, was bringing back a lost child. It was nearly impossible to knit an adult's consciousness to a new body, but children were easier. Though the practice did work sometimes, it had also resulted in terrible monstrosities. Some people's essences never attached properly to the fetch, and they grew to be tortured individuals.

It had been considered unethical, and the practice was outlawed. As early as my twelfth year, I had suspected that Maman might have broken the rules, wanting to bring something of Papa back into her life. That perhaps she'd lost the baby she was pregnant with when Papa died and built herself a fetch to carry the child's soul. *My soul*. That maybe that was why I was so strange, never being able to fulfill Maman's desires for my potential, why I was always in so much pain.

But as I aged, I'd dismissed that as the fancy of an unhappy child. Unhappy families were not so uncommon, after all. In the oubliette, the memory of my childhood fear returned, confirmed by my lack of actual need for sleep or sustenance. Still, the entire time I was in the hole, I'd never once considered there might be another reason for Maman to put whoever I *actually* was in the fetch. I forced myself to do so now. I still could not remember why she'd done it or who I was, but staring at myself in the mirror, I understood.

The fetch looked nothing like my family because they were not *my* family. They never had been.

CHAPTER 9

MINA

The train entered Pravhna well past midnight. Though there was a station closer to Orchid House in the upper city, Poe needed to get off at Halcyon Gate Station and thought it better to hire a cab to take me to Orchid House. She explained that some of the tittle-tattle rags had been sending novice reporters to haunt upper city stations at night, catching sight of anyone sneaking into or out of the city in clandestine hours and printing the information the next day in features some of the rags called "comings and goings."

I'd never been of much interest to the rags. My time in society had always been brief. Maman allowed me to come only to events that would be odd if I'd not been present. She portrayed me as a naive, quirky child—a disappointing late bloomer and an introvert. After a few social blunders in my teenage years, it was an easy thing for most to believe. She'd never spent money on outfitting me properly for society, preferring to dress me in unflattering garments that disguised anything attractive about me.

As I followed Poe off the train, admiring the beautiful job

her modiste had done to tailor her overcoat to every curve of her petite form, I wondered what might have been different if I'd been allowed to dress as I pleased. I had an eye for beautiful things, but no clue how to go about picking them out for myself. I envied Poe that ability as we prepared to part ways.

Halcyon Gate Station was run down, its grandeur faded, all peeling acid green paint and dusty chandeliers. Only the cracked painted floor tiles remained vibrant, depicting a forest scene, rife with elemental spirits in flat line drawings. I stared at the drove of indigo hares, peeking out from behind the trees and in the mist. Odd that they were depicted here.

Poe took a long breath in, holding it as she frowned, then handed me some money. "This should be enough to get you to the upper city safely." Her words came out in a tumble and the frown deepened into her pretty face. "I hope everything works out for you, Mina."

The way she looked at me was hesitant, as though she did not want to leave me any more than I wanted her to go. But I couldn't find the words to say that. We'd only just met. I wasn't sure how to tell Poe Endymion that while I most definitely needed her help to navigate the upper echelons, I probably needed her friendship more.

Instead of finding those words, I took the money, returning the sentiment, as was polite. "I hope things work out for you too."

We stared at one another, a kind of longing I wasn't used to building between us. I'd experienced romantic crushes before, the desperate rushes of yearning building to a fever-pitch, lust mixed with infatuation. This was nothing like that. Instead, Poe felt like a missing piece of me. Something about her was kindred—her keen intelligence, her sadness, the sense I had that like me, somewhere in the thick of things, Poe had been deeply betrayed.

Poe's long brown fingers stretched towards mine. I looked down at our hands as Poe placed her card in my palm. "Call on me if you need anything."

I nodded, not knowing what to make of the offer, or the desire I had to offer something in return. Poe smiled at me, then finally nodded. "All right then."

She turned to go, picking her bag up. Without thinking, I caught the sleeve of her coat. It was as if my hands had acted on their own. "Wait."

Poe turned, her brows knitting together as she looked up at me. I wasn't sure what I was about to say, but I didn't want Poe to go. Our stories intertwined, creating a connection that had not yet clarified, but the part of my mind that always worked ahead, that always puzzled together the unseen pieces—it *knew*. Poe was important.

Before I could try to explain any of that, my skin prickled with the feeling of being watched. Covertly, I glanced around. The station was empty, but for the clouds of mist that crept in, curling this way and that across the mosaic tiled floor.

"Someone's here," Poe said, keeping her voice barely above a whisper.

"Yes," I agreed.

Poe and I stood completely still, though both of us clearly braced ourselves for whatever might come next. The feeling of eyes on us receded slightly, as though whoever observed us knew we knew. When it disappeared completely, she let out a tensely held breath. My shoulders sagged a bit.

"The rags?" I asked, thinking of what she'd told me about the tittle-tattles.

Poe shrugged, her dark brows furrowing. "Maybe."

We stared at one another for a long moment while I gathered my courage. "Do you think there's a way we might help one another?" I prepared myself for her to question my statement in a dozen different ways, rapidly calculating as many good answers as I could come up with. "I'm sure you have a life to get back to here, but—"

"Yes," Poe agreed. "I've been trying to sort out how I could broach the subject all night, but I didn't want to scare you off."

Now it was my turn to breathe a sigh of relief. "So, will you come stay at Orchid House?"

Poe grinned. "And play out the season together?"

I nodded. She understood my line of thinking then. We seemed to complement one another well. If we worked together, perhaps we would both find what we sought.

"Then let's get a cab and get out of here," Poe said, picking up her bag and marching towards the street.

I followed her into the night. On the misty sidewalk, several children, none older than twelve, stood smoking something that smelled of clove and vanilla. They were a mix of Vilhari, Oscarovi, and Strix. Poe hailed them, handing the little Strix girl that approached her a copper. "Grab us a cab going uptown, yeah?"

"Yeah," the little one with the visage of a tawny owl responded.

Poe tugged on the littling's sleeve. "Someone with a clean conscience, or Herself shall hear about it."

Poe said "Herself" like it was a name, and not just any name, a significant one. The little Strix' eyes widened. "Yes'm. I understand."

She ran off into the night. Interesting. It was as though Poe was speaking another language, though I understood her words perfectly. I cast a long gaze back at the undercity. In the distance, intense string music played, accompanied by the sounds of reveling in the streets. One of the undercity's infamous street balls was taking place, just a few blocks away. My body reacted nearly immediately to the music. A forbidden part of me longed to disappear into that music, to turn my back on whatever waited for me at Orchid House and never look back.

"So then," Poe said, stepping between me and the tantalizing din of the undercity.

It was all she needed to say to bring me back to myself—and my need for the truth. There was no room for such fancies as disappearing into the night. I was not built to let things go. "We'll help each other. You need access to society—and I need help navigating it."

Poe moved closer to me, our shoulders touching, her voice low. "Aren't you going to ask me what I'm looking for?"

I looked down at the beautiful woman. "I suppose we'll have plenty of time when we're alone to spin our sad tales, won't we?"

Poe's eyes narrowed slightly. "You don't seem like the type to trust so easily."

I smiled then, a rare thing for me, given how wicked Maman had always said it made me appear. In the undercity, the buskers' music swelled into an appropriately tense tango. "I said nothing of *trust*, Hippolyta."

Poe's smile matched mine. "Won't we make an interesting pair?"

"I doubt that's the word our enemies will use," I mused, keeping my eyes moving for any other unexpected appearances.

A child ran by us, leaving the station, headed towards the street ball. Poe reached out, snatching the littling by the back of their collar. Their visage was that of a snowy owl, and Poe's eyes narrowed shrewdly. "What color is the peony in winter?"

A secret code. Poe was becoming more interesting by the moment. She was obviously well connected, which could only serve both our purposes.

THE HOLLOW PLANE

"Black as the day is long, Miss," the little one answered.

"You know who I am?" Poe asked, keeping her voice soft as a cab rounded the corner, the first Strix child riding in the front passenger seat.

The second hatchling nodded.

"Tell her I'm back from the country."

The hatchling nodded again, and Poe let them go. They disappeared into the night. Her eyes narrowed slightly. "Something's afoot," Poe murmured. "The children are afraid tonight."

I hadn't noticed that, but now my mind raced, trying to pick up the pattern in what was happening around us. A picture formed in my mind, but was too vague to make out. It was frustrating to have to wait, but just a little more time and it would clear. It was unfortunate that I was particularly bad at waiting.

The cab pulled up to the curb, the first Strix child jumping out to join her companions. As they rushed off into the night, the driver got out of the car. Like the hatchling, he was Strix, with a barn owl visage. He wore a bowler hat and a tidy suit.

"Fulston, Mlle," he said with a tip of his hat. "Fulston Braithwaite."

Braithwaite? Not one of the famed Syndicate leader's family?

Poe nodded back, smiling. "One of Herself's, then."

This got more interesting by the moment. "Herself" must be none other than the famous Edith Braithwaite, Strix leader of the Halcyon Gate Syndicate.

"Indeed, Mlle Endymion." The cabbie nodded at me, but did not ask for my name. It was discretion, I realized, not rudeness. "Where can I take you this evening?"

"Uptown," Poe said. "And make it quick."

Fulston nodded, taking Poe's bag from her. "Indeed. Best not linger here for long."

THE STREETS WERE dark in the upper city, the gas running low in the wee hours for conservation. When the denizens of our neighborhood had voted down aetheric lighting, they'd been told this was a risk, as had the higher echelons who'd done the same. No one had even a shred of fear that poorer lighting might make our streets more dangerous.

We had the cityguard for that, and not one person voting had cared for their safety or convenience in patrolling the streets at night. No matter, I didn't need to see to know what Orchid Boulevard looked like as we rounded the corner onto the two hundred block. My mind's eye envisioned the tall limestone townhomes lining the street, neatly kept and statuesque.

Looming. Intimidating with their elaborate stone ornamentation, various faces and looping, curved lines making each house unique, even as they were made from the same pale stone. I kept my breath even, forcing it in and out of my lungs.

"Are you getting out?" Poe asked.

I hadn't noticed the car had stopped. I *had* to start paying better attention to what was going on around me, but everything was moving so quickly. Too quickly, perhaps.

"Yes," I answered, following Poe out of the car, while Fulston gathered Poe's bag.

"Shall I carry this inside for you?" the young Strix asked.

"Just up the steps please," Poe replied.

He did so with alacrity and was back in his car and down the street before they could even say goodbye. "Edith will pay him," Poe explained in a soft voice, but I hadn't been worried about that. Perhaps I should have been.

Still, it confirmed that the name Braithwaite wasn't a coincidence. Fulston was a Syndicate man, and somehow Poe was connected to the Halcyon Gate organization. For now, I pushed that aside, starting up the steps, toward the front door. Not a curtain on the street had shifted. It was the dead of night, but I had no doubt that by morning the entire street would know someone had returned to Orchid House. My mind raced, reevaluating the situation as I retrieved my key from my pocket. Poe stood behind me as I unlocked the door.

"Welcome to Orchid House," I said as I pushed the heavy door open. "Lux."

Lights flickered on in the front hallway at my words, sparkling crystal chandeliers reflecting on the marble floors and the grand staircase. There was not a speck of dust, and a hint of Maman's jasmine perfume still lingered, as though she had just stepped out.

"Oh my," Poe said, mouth agape as she entered. "I knew your family was wealthy, but…"

"We are not," I corrected her. "*Were* not."

Poe raised her eyebrows, dragging her suitcase and carpet bag inside. She gestured at the space. "I beg to differ."

I understood how she might make this mistake. It was one Maman had anticipated. She knew people saw Orchid House, well kept and looking like *this*, and then didn't question why they were never invited to Somerhaven for long weekends, or why the Wildfangs rarely spent an entire season in Pravhna. Our peers chalked it up to Maman's reputation for "academic" sensibilities, meaning that she was strange, and not much else.

"It's the last of it. There's nothing else. No money, and of course the country house is gone."

Poe nodded as she closed the front door, wandered through the two story entry hall, and grimaced at the staircase, carved from a creamy marble in a shape meant to resemble an artistically rendered spine. It was beautiful, but absolutely grotesque. "But this house. It's worth a lot."

I scowled, only seeing the monstrosity of the place. Elegant yet disturbing art dotted the long hall that ran through the center of the house. "The entire house is like this —from the fireplace with a gaping maw, to the spinal atrocity that is that staircase. It's gorgeous and horrible. My father had a macabre sense of design."

Poe gazed up at the oblong spiral of six flights of stairs. "We can work with this, though. Is there a telephone?"

I nodded. "In the study. Come."

Poe followed me through the house. It was a rather simple layout on this floor. The formal parlor, with its horrific fireplace, to the left of the entryway, the private sitting room to the right. We passed Maman's study and the dining room, as I made my way back to the housekeeper's office.

Poe's mouth hung open, as she examined every impressive but gruesome piece of art. Some paintings depicted horrific scenes of violence, others creatures not of this world. There were a few family portraits scattered in amongst the gallery of macabre images, but not many. I avoided looking at the statues at all. Since I was a child, they'd scared me.

My heart beat faster the further into the house we went. I wished Orchid House had been the one to burn down. Somerhaven had been oddly constructed and ancient, freezing in both the summer and winter, but it hadn't been *this*. All my worst memories lived here, where there had been no escape from how deeply I disappointed Maman.

The sound of footsteps behind me stopped as I entered the housekeeper's office. Poe wasn't following me anymore. I turned, backtracking through the hall until I found the

THE HOLLOW PLANE

Vilhar in the library. She smiled prettily at me, clearly meaning to comfort me. "*This* place isn't so bad."

I coaxed a few more lamps into lighting. Poe had obviously used the command, but the house responded most reliably to one of its own—and apparently it still recognized me as such. I wondered why it recognized the fetch as a genuine Wildfang, when I was certain I was not one. That wasn't how domicile magic worked.

Spaces were like people in some ways; they had remnants of magical history that made them nearly independent entities, and as such, there were only two ways they recognized someone as part of a family—blood or marriage. The fetch literally could not be either, so Maman must have found some way around the rules. Which, come to think of it, was just like Maman. Describing her as academic was more accurate than the social slight was meant to indicate.

"It's one of the nicer rooms in the house," I said, feeling almost wistful for the afternoons I'd spent hiding here. This had been my refuge as a girl, the only place in the house besides my attic bedroom that did not feel menacing.

There wasn't room for art here, just books, and most of them were novels. Papa had loved to read, or so I was told. Helene and Maman rarely spent time in pleasurable pursuits, so whenever they read, their taste tended towards spellcrafting and treatises on working with elemental spirits.

Maman's study was just next door, where all of her books were located, as well as the locked door to her workshop. But this had been Papa's domain. As a child, I'd imagined we would have been the best of friends. That my life would have been different, if only he'd lived, because he loved these magnificent books. Now, I wasn't so sure.

Poe walked around the room. "Would it be all right if I took some reading material?"

"Of course," I replied. Poe suddenly looked very young,

her eyes wide and hungry. It reminded me that though Poe Endymion had access to what seemed like quite a large sum of money, she might not have grown up with the same resources I had.

"What do you intend to do while you're in Pravhna?" I asked. We were safe here, in the strictest sense of the word. The house's wards would recognize Poe as a guest, since she was invited in along with me. None could enter without my permission. It was time to discuss some of what we'd avoided, thus far.

Poe set down a small mountain of books on one of the heavy library tables at the center of the room. She leaned against the table, her beautiful face glowing in the lamplight. "I am looking for my family—and I have reason to believe the Montclairs know where they are."

She stopped there, but her expression was so serious, so dark, I wondered if the family Poe searched for was alive, or if she simply wanted to know what had become of them. The anguish written on her face—in the wet luminosity of her eyes, the drag of grief on her mouth—evoked a kind of envy I'd never known. I could not remember caring for *anyone* that way.

And no one has ever cared for me that way either, a voice in my head snapped back. The envy gave way to an ache in my chest so profound I was rendered speechless.

When I finally found my voice, venomous irritation came spilling out. "And why do you believe *I* can help you get access to that information?"

Poe's smile was shaky, as though she'd instantly forgiven me for being so rude. "I know you didn't have the best luck in society. I do actually know a bit about you, though not much." She came around the library table and reached for one of my hands.

I stepped back, drawing my hands quickly behind my

back. I blinked several times, as though it might slow the panic racing through me. "Don't touch me." My tone was too sharp, my ears ringing with the sound of my blood rushing through my veins. The dull whine of the aetheric lights.

Poe's voice broke through. "I'm sorry. I should have asked."

My entire body froze. Forming words was a struggle, but I pushed some out, trying to remedy the damage I was sure I'd done. "You meant to be kind."

Poe nodded. "I did. But if you don't like to be touched, it wouldn't be a kindness to touch you."

Her words shocked me. So few people thought that way. "It's not that… Not exactly." I dragged my eyes back towards Poe's face. I expected to find pity in Poe's eyes, but instead found something else. *Understanding.* "It takes me some time to get used to people. To want them to touch me."

Poe stepped back, and again, her eyes were full of the kind of understanding that came from experience, not pity. That only deepened the ache in my chest. I looked out the window, watching moonlight hit the golden leaves of the black oak in the neighbors' garden. Knowing what to tell Poe and what not to was tricky.

No one needed to know about my body, about the fact that I might not be *real*. But Poe should know about the oubliette, about Viridian's role in putting me there. "Have you ever heard of an oubliette?"

Slowly, Poe shook her head.

I walked towards the library window, painfully conscious of the fact that the locked workroom was just on the other side of the wall. It called to me, begging me to unlock its secrets. Now was not the time. I focused on the scene outside. Looking at the moonlight on the oak tree soothed me. "It's a kind of hole—a deep, magical hole, used to induce a confusing mental state that causes its victim to forget."

"Like amnesia?" Poe asked, drifting towards the window herself.

"Something like that," I replied. "It's a kind of torture."

"Ah, I see why you are so angry with Viridian and your family then," Poe replied, after I had not spoken for a while.

I gazed into Poe's face. It was clear she had seen some of the worst of the world, but still, she was a person searching for her family—because she loved them. I presumed they loved her in return. "Yes. I only just made my way out this morning. I was headed back to Somerhaven to question them—to find out why they did it. But of course…"

Poe's mouth fell open, then abruptly closed. She was catching on to the fact that I didn't much like pity, or being comforted. That would make things easier.

I needed to redirect the conversation to something more useful for us both. "I don't know what the papers said about the fire…"

Poe looked as though she were trying to remember the specifics. "The investigators said it was a kitchen fire. They found your sister's lady's maid's body near the oven, where they said the fire originated. An accident."

I shook my head. That wasn't possible, given the traces of empyrae I'd detected. A lie then. But who'd concocted it? Viridian was the most likely culprit, but *why* had he lied? He had to have known someone used empyrae to start the fire, and how rare the talent was. But I couldn't explain that to Poe without opening up a line of questioning about myself that I wasn't ready to explain. We were revealing ourselves, but only bit by bit. Poe had certainly not told me as much as I was telling now.

Still, I added the necessary information: "The fire was not an accident."

Poe didn't ask me how I knew, as I had not asked Poe why she believed the Montclairs knew what had happened to her family. Secrets were power, and neither of us wanted to give over all of what we knew to the other. But Poe had spent time with Viridian—it was possible she could tell me more about what had happened to me than she even knew. I needed to take risks if I were to get to the truth.

I took a sharp breath in, considering my next words carefully. "I was placed in the oubliette for remembering some secret my family kept, though the oubliette did its work. Now I can't remember what I knew."

To my surprise, Poe's reaction was completely absent of pity. In fact, her eyes hardened. "So you aren't *just* looking for the truth about the fire."

"No," I replied, relieved that Poe reacted as I would have preferred. She hadn't revealed if she knew more than what she'd already said. That was fine. I wouldn't press her. This was only the first night, I reminded myself, and this was a long game. Much as I wanted to solve this quickly, I was going to have to settle in.

Poe leaned against the deep windowsill, looking up at me. "What would you have done to them, if you'd found them this morning?"

I focused on the tree for a long moment, thinking of how to answer. "Gotten to the truth." I looked down at Poe. "By any means necessary."

Poe was not disturbed in the least by my admission. "And when you had it?"

"I suppose I would have gotten revenge."

Poe nodded. "I like that."

"What about you? When you find out what's happened to your family, what will you do?"

Poe smiled. "The same, I suppose. Someone has to pay for what's been done."

That was most satisfactory to hear. I took a deep breath. "Viridian Montclair helped Helene seal me into the oubliette. It would seem we have a common enemy."

Poe's shoulders shook with laughter. "I thought as much—not about the oubliette, of course—but I *knew* he was involved with you going missing."

I didn't have to ask *how* Poe knew that. It was obvious we'd both been piecing things together since the moment we met. Poe plopped onto the window seat. I sat next to her, each of us leaning against the opposite edge of the windowsill, staring at each other.

"We're going to need a very good plan," Poe reasoned. "And probably some extra help."

I nodded. "You should know, I don't have any money. And I haven't a single friend in the world."

The smile on Poe's face didn't falter. "But you have all this." She gestured at the house. "It's the perfect backdrop for a ruse. Your grand reentry into society as Lady Somerhaven."

I frowned. "That will be a costly venture to do correctly and I am terrible with society functions."

"But I am not," Poe said, one delicate foot kicking out from under her skirts. "And I happen to have nearly unlimited funds."

"How?" I asked.

Poe leaned forward. "You keep your secrets, love, and I'll keep mine."

It had to be Syndicate money, but I wasn't going to press the issue further. Poe would tell me when she saw fit. "That will be just fine."

"Now, I must get a call in to Jeanne Laquoix, if we'd like to be outfitted for the season," Poe said, trailing a finger along the hem of the dressing gown that peeked out from my coat. "You're going to need something better to wear."

CHAPTER 10

ASHBOURNE

My tea had gone cold for the third time. I was rather annoyed, but I wasn't going to make another pot or reheat the old one. It would only go cold again. Skye and I had been up all night discussing our next move, and though she'd made several excellent arguments, I wasn't convinced we needed Syndicate backing to do what was being asked of us. I added another log to the fire in the office hearth, hoping that if the room warmed up a bit more, the cold tea wouldn't bother me as much.

"Explain this to me one more time, Aestra." We only called one another by our surnames in a disagreement. "Why is it worth getting in bed with the Syndicate? We can investigate this on our own."

Skye rolled her eyes. "We've talked this over a dozen times now, Ash." She wasn't angry with me, which was good, but it didn't stop me from being mad at her. "We need the money."

"We can find another way." I was wrong, and I knew it, but I was worried. Spun out of control by the thought of the owlet I'd helped and their mother dying. Worried sick that we were getting ourselves into something we'd never dig our way out of. People who helped the Syndicate this way were in for life. It was one thing to be on good terms with them, and another to work a complex job like this.

I needed Skye to understand what she was asking of us both—what we were tying ourselves to. I wasn't actually arguing against what she wanted us to do at this point; we both knew she'd already won on that count. I'd follow Skye into a burning building, knowing I wouldn't walk out.

But she needed to see what we'd give up by taking on Syndicate backing. Our freedom, our reputation for impartiality in the district, would all be in jeopardy once people knew we were working under Syndicate pay.

"Chopard is buying up abandoned warehouses, near the Achera," Skye said, repeating the information that Vionette Celestine's spies had picked up. She was the richest of the Syndicate leaders, and had a whisper network that extended across oceans.

"Who cares?" I growled. "Why should anyone care that some rogue Syndicate leader buys up some empty buildings?"

Skye didn't answer because I knew the answers all too well. *Everyone* should care. Chopard was buying up buildings openly, and was suspected of burning others down. There were more murders and unexplained disappearances in the undercity and medial districts in the upper city than there had ever been. Something was brewing and Chopard was at the center of it.

Some in the undercity defended the mysterious Syndicate leader. The businesses he protected brought in more revenue than any others, and from the outside, no one could tell exactly *why* that was. Many of the business leaders in the Halcyon Gate were now more likely to work with Chopard than any of the other leaders. Going against Chopard was dangerous, and we were a miniscule operation. Even with Syndicate backing, it was functionally just me and Skye. Morpheus helped with cases, of course, but the cat was only so much help in a real fight.

We had to take the job—Skye's sense of honor demanded it—but this was the end of life as we'd known it for the past year. A desperate part of me screamed for me to keep fighting, to preserve what we had. But Skye wouldn't be the friend I loved so dearly if she didn't want to do this. I moved to sit at my desk. Morpheus was nowhere to be found this morning, tired of our arguing, I assumed.

Skye's countenance was steady; she was committed to this, committed to helping the undercity she loved, and she wanted my help. Needed it—needed the skill we both knew I could provide if things went sideways. *And they* would *go sideways; shit like this always did*. The thought appeared out of nowhere, haunting me, sure as any ghost.

I growled, flinging my head onto my arms. I wanted a different scenario to argue against. One where the Syndicate was blackmailing Skye, or manipulating her into helping with this horrid plan. What I absolutely did not want was for Skye to be doing this because she was a good person. Because she cared about the people of the undercity, and her honor was worth more than their safety. I couldn't argue with that kind of logic. And I certainly couldn't say no to her.

You're throwing a fit, Morpheus reasoned from the corner of his desk, materializing out of nowhere.

I raised my head to look at both the cat and Skye, in turn. "Fine."

Skye raised a snow-white eyebrow.

"Fine," I repeated. There really was no use in arguing any further. I would follow them anywhere and they knew it.

All I was doing now was wasting our precious time. "We'll help the Syndicate figure out who Chopard is."

As I said the words, the eerie widening feeling came upon me again, just as it had in the Merc. Instead of an aperture opening, this felt like oblivion gaping at the edges of the life I'd carefully built with Skye and Morpheus. And we were all about to slip right over the edge into it, though neither Skye nor the cat seemed to care.

If only I could be more like them…but I was selfish, wanting only the peace we'd cultivated here. Undercity be damned, for all I cared; but I'd already agreed, and Skye was moving forward. "Braithwaite has an informant, someone who thinks she knows Chopard's identity," Skye said, turning her attention back to her journal. "She'll give us a name and location later today, but we're to liaise between her and the Syndicate."

"Why?" I asked, curious despite my reluctance to do the job at hand.

"We're a legitimate operation," Skye explained. "We've never been in trouble with the upper city authorities."

That was true enough. We'd even worked with them a few times, when our clients needed the help. Skye had severed her social connections when she gave up her life as a Chevalier for House Aestra, but most people in the upper city still liked her, and were willing to talk to her if need be. Her name was still good wherever she went.

She was lucky her mother hadn't put up a fuss. Privately, I thought Elspeth Aestra was still hoping Skye would come home. That whatever row they'd had could be mended and that all this business in the undercity was nothing more than a phase. If that's what she thought, then she didn't know her daughter very well. Skye might someday find peace with her crattie family, but she was never going back to the life she'd lived before. If there was anything I knew, it was what turning your back on the past looked like, and Skye was a classic case.

"So the Syndicate is willing to use your affiliation with House Aestra as an asset," I remarked, needing to be sure Skye saw the full picture. Sometimes she could be a bit of an idealist. "When this is over, your name might not have the same cache up top that it does now."

Every line of Skye's angular face seemed to liquify with emotion. She stood, clapping a hand to my shoulder. I nearly groaned. My argument had the exact opposite effect I'd hoped for. "I know, Ash. It's worth it. We can't let Chopard get away with this. We have to know what he's up to before more people get seriously hurt."

Again, I couldn't argue with her honor, and she knew what she was getting into. There wasn't anything else for us to discuss. Much as I feared I would come to regret this, it was time for me to stop protesting.

"I'm in. Let's liaise for the Syndicate."

Skye patted my shoulder, then glanced at Morpheus. "Do you want to go tell her we agree?"

The greymalkin blinked once and then disappeared into thin air. Off to tell Herself then. Edith Braithwaite would be pleased. She'd been dying to get Skye on her payroll for years, from what I gathered.

"Disconcerting as fuck, every single time," I complained as the last of the greymalkin's tail dissolved.

Skye snorted as she settled back into her chair and opened her journal. She was in good humor now that I agreed, but I felt I needed to offer some kind of apology, or explanation. "You know why I hesitated…"

She looked up from her journal, leaning back in her desk chair, running fingers through her cropped white hair. "I know. And I promised you back then that I'll never tell a soul what you can do. You've got things under control now, right?"

I nodded, but it was time to tell her. "Someone already knows, though."

Skye, always sharp, put down her pen. "What do you mean, someone knows?"

"Yesterday, while you were at the Merc, a Strix woman came in, asking for us to do a mercenary job. I think she knew about me."

Skye didn't ask how I knew that she'd known, or try to poke holes in my statement. She never questioned my instincts. She stood up from her desk, her mind already working on the problem. "Did she give her name?"

I shook my head, watching Skye pace the floor between our facing desks. She did this when she needed to think. "Did she work for someone, or was she doing the hiring?"

"Said she worked for a crattie who'd been wronged somehow. By someone named Wilhelmina Wildfang."

Skye frowned, then went to the wooden file cabinets that made up the wall behind her desk. She walked past our case files, into the territory where we kept track of bigger issues throughout the city. Murders, organized crime stings, Syndicate operations, and settled in missing persons. Why hadn't I thought to look the name up? I was tempted to smack myself in the face, but instead I got up. Skye would likely be a few, tracking the woman's name through the files. Now that we were done with the hardest part of things, there was no use in drinking cold tea.

I busied myself with the kettle and teapot while Skye flipped through file after file. She'd seemed to find something, setting a file aside, but then kept searching. Finally, as the timer for the tea was about to go off, she raised a newspaper clipping in the air. "Found it."

I poured us both huge mugs of a grassy green concoction, stirring in a lump of honey for her, and taking mine plain. Skye drifted over, taking the mug I'd prepared for her, reading the clipping quickly. "Wildfang's an Oscarovi socialite, though it sounds like she wasn't all that popular. Her sister though, Helene, she was a real beauty, extremely popular with the upper set. I remember her."

"Was?" I asked, sipping my tea. It tasted of spring fields, and just a hint of citrus.

Skye held up the first file she found. "She died in a terrible fire at their country home in Somershire a while back. Remember that?"

I made a noncommittal noise. I didn't keep up with the news the same way Skye did.

"Anyway, the mother, sister and lady's maid all died in the fire, but the younger sister, Wilhelmina, she'd been kidnapped shortly before that." Her voice rose just slightly in volume, off its even keel. "Viridian Montclair was engaged to her sister, the one who died. He offered a reward for anyone who knew anything about where Wilhelmina had been taken after the rest of the family died, but the case went cold."

"He's one of your set?" I asked, keeping my voice as uninterested as possible. Skye didn't like to talk about her family.

Skye nodded. "He's a real piece of work. If he hadn't had a rock solid alibi for the fire, I'd honestly think he had something to do with the whole thing."

I took another sip of tea. "He's that bad?"

Skye nodded, her jaw clenching tight at some memory of the Vilhar, perhaps, but she didn't say anything else.

"So, if the Wildfangs were associated so closely with Montclair, do you think Wilhelmina is trouble? One of the upper crust might have an axe to grind with her family?"

Skye shrugged. "Hard to say."

"Didn't the article say she wasn't liked very well?"

My partner glanced back down at it. "Not exactly. It's there between the lines, though." She looked up at me over her mug. "You know, nobody liked me much up there either."

She was wrong about that, applying how her family felt about her to them all. I'd seen it time and again. People loved Skye Aestra, in both the upper crust and the undercity. She was nothing short of a legend. But I never argued with her when I knew she was worried about her family. That wasn't my place.

I set my mug down and crossed my arms, giving Skye a rare grin. "Maybe this Wilhelmina's our kind of girl."

Skye grinned back. "Let's not rush to murder her then."

Her timing was so snappy, and her smile so unexpected, that I threw my head back and laughed. "Fine by me."

Skye looked back at the newspaper clipping. "She was probably just awkward. I wish I remembered her. She's about my age, a little younger maybe. Twenty eight, I think." She handed me the clipping. "She's pretty."

I took it from her, gazing at the grainy photo. It showed a pale young woman with large, serious eyes framed by neat but heavy brows and long lashes. Her nose was small and sculpted, cheekbones high and sharp, her mouth a generous downturned curve. She wasn't pretty—she was beautiful. I stared at the photo for a long time.

"Oh," Skye said, stretching the short word into many syllables. "You think Murder Girl is *gorgeous*."

My cheeks burned as I handed the clipping back. "She's fine enough, I suppose." I wanted to change the subject, and quickly. "The mother and sister died in a fire? Think it has anything to do with this Chopard stuff?"

Skye frowned, scanning the article again. "Nothing here would indicate that it does, but it *is* an odd coincidence."

Silence spread between us, chilling the air in the room

despite the roaring fire in the hearth. "You don't believe in coincidences," I mused, swirling the liquid in my cup a little.

"No," Skye replied, obviously lost in thought. "But now that I think about it, it's a little odd, isn't it, that on the day someone comes to ask us to *kill* Wilhelmina Wildfang, that the Syndicate hires us to help them identify Chopard?"

There was that aperture-widening feeling again. "Do you think *she's* Chopard?"

Skye grimaced. "That doesn't really make sense. From the little I remember about her, she's rather talentless."

I stared at the ceiling for a moment, noting a place that needed to be repainted. "She could be hiding her true power."

"I suppose," Skye mused. "But I think someone who has the kind of power to do what you witnessed the other night would be hard to disguise, don't you?"

She had a point. The kind of power that both Oscarovi and Vilhari wielded had a signature to it, an aura that was obvious. There wasn't a way Wilhelmina Wildfang could be as dangerous as Chopard and no one had noticed. Before I could give it another thought, Morpheus reappeared. The greymalkin immediately began licking his back foot. We knew better than to rush the cat in the middle of an emergency bath, so we stayed silent.

We're to go to 213 Orchid Boulevard in the upper city today at three to talk to the informant. The two of you should clean up if we're headed out of the undercity.

"Did Edith give you her name?" Skye asked. "The informant?"

No, the cat replied. *We were interrupted. Chopard burned another abandoned building last night, this one in Kyovka.*

Skye shook her head. "That's not good."

It is not. There is one more thing—the Strix child Ashbourne helped—

"The one that was killed?" Skye interrupted.

Yes. Their body went missing from the morgue this morning.

I swallowed the lump growing in my throat. It had the same bitter taste the visit from the Strix woman had left in my mouth. I glanced at Skye, who avoided my eyes. So she felt it too. This was going to get ugly.

CHAPTER 11

MINA

Jeanne Laquoix and her small army of Oscarovi sewists waltzed in at seven o'clock on the hour and did not take so much as a break until they were done at lunchtime. I had no idea it could be so grueling to have a visit from the city's most important modiste. When they left, I collapsed into a chair in the front sitting room we'd used for a makeshift studio.

Two racks of finished garments stood in the entryway, ready to be taken upstairs, which was a marvel in itself. "Oscarovi sewists are..." I trailed off, unable to accurately describe what I'd seen.

The talent and skill involved with using aether to complete an artisanal task, especially with the aid of a spirit, had been dizzying to witness. Demophon and Maman had a tenuous relationship, having made a tense alliance when Maman was young, but the spirits that worked with the sewists had been *happy*.

That was how it was supposed to work—the joining between elemental and Oscarovi was meant to be joyful.

Helene's had been with Ariston, an elemental that took the form of a tiny firedrake when it manifested, channeled through her ruby. The spirit would curl around Helene's shoulder, purring like a cat when she was a child, hissing at anyone who bothered her. I'd always been jealous. My sister had attracted Ariston long before she came of age, and they'd grown together.

Today I felt that same envy, watching the jewel-like spider and bird elementals that aided the sewists. The silent, serene communication between Oscarovi and familiar. The seamless coordination of movement—it was beautiful, and yet utterly devastating to watch.

Poe, who was changing back into the dressing gown she'd worn between fittings, nodded. "It's amazing, isn't it? There are Vilhari sewists of course, but the elementals add a certain something to the process." Poe fastened the dressing gown and sat across from me. "I notice you don't wear a jewel."

"No," I replied, wishing she would not have noticed so easily. I was going to have to do something about this, and quickly. I wondered if the sewists had noticed.

Poe seemed to sense my reluctance to say more. She leaned towards me, under the guise of making herself more comfortable in her chair. I wanted to tell her that it was a sheer impossibility—comfort had been the least of Maman's priorities when selecting furniture for Orchid House.

We were still seated in the parlor, where the walnut armchairs were carved in an ornate floral depiction of oleander and foxglove, and the upholstered backs and seats covered in a rich silk fabric that depicted a garden of poisonous plants in a pale aqua shade that somehow made the subject material more ominous, rather than less. The entire room was decorated in what Maman had termed "a poison motif." Frescoes painted on the walls depicted Oscarovi dancing in a poison garden, expired Vilhari victims at their feet, looking as though they were simply sleeping, but for their bruised lips and stained fingers.

When Poe resigned herself to the fact that the chair itself was the problem, not the way she was seated in it, she spoke. "It's fine that you haven't managed to inspirit yet."

I tilted my head to the side, curious to know what Poe was getting at. Surely she knew I should have done so already, but she was being rather delicate about the whole thing, which I could appreciate. "However, I think it would be better if people thought you had."

I gestured pointedly around the room. "There were almost a dozen people here today. They have seen me without a jewel. I don't think an obvious lie is the way to start things off."

A slow smile spread over Poe's face. "But *have* they seen you without a jewel?" She stared at my chest, where a long pendant Poe had casually draped over my head right before the modiste had arrived was tucked between my breasts, resting against my skin, blocked from view by my corset. I'd thought nothing of it, as Poe had also slipped a large ring onto one of my fingers and dressed my hair in the low profile chignon popularized by the Ballets Vermeil.

"I thought you were just making me presentable for the Maison Laquoix," I murmured, drawing the necklace out of my gown to look at it. It was nothing remarkable, but I was impressed by Poe's ability to anticipate the kinds of details that would help us later on. "Why didn't you tell me?"

Poe smiled. "I didn't want you to be nervous about it. And it was necessary that you be totally natural about the jewel, or it would appear as an object of interest."

"Ah," I breathed. "But if I'd fidgeted with it, I might have given myself away."

Poe nodded. "And you kept it tucked in the entire time, so no one has seen what it looks like. You can choose anything you'd like now. Oscarovi move their jewels into new pieces frequently, do they not?"

I wanted to laugh. "The rich ones do."

"Besides," Poe said. "It isn't as though you don't have power. You radiate with it."

I glanced at her, worried about what she might have surmised, but Poe's face was neutral, as though it were perfectly normal that I "radiated with power" while not actually possessing a jewel.

Poe stood as a soft chime sounded in the front hall. We'd received a calling card. "You can tell me all about it when you're ready, Mina. I won't ever pressure you to explain things to me. We all have secrets."

Poe left the room, presumably to fetch the correspondence, and something tight in my chest released as I got up to follow her into the hall. The way she said "we all have secrets" struck a chord in me. Whatever Poe was hiding had depth. This wasn't only a case of a missing mother; there was more to it than that.

As we walked together to Maman's private sitting room, Poe's fingers flew through a small pile of calling cards. She sorted through them with speed. Though I couldn't see them from my vantage point, she appeared to have a very definite criteria. "It would seem that Pravhna society knows you've returned."

She handed a select few to me. They were from people I would rather not see, friends of Maman's who'd always given me a distinctly bad feeling. It was overwhelming to read the invitations and requests to call. I wasn't sure how to sort them out. At the secretary desk, Poe separated the remainder of the cards into different piles.

"Those are the ones we both need to see first," she said,

as I added a log to the dying embers of the fire. "The ones we need to accept right away."

She was right, of course; the people who I liked least amongst Maman's acquaintances were the most likely to know what she'd been up to. I wondered how Poe had known. "How do you know which to choose?" I kept my voice soft, in case Poe needed to concentrate, curling into the velvet covered sofa. This room was only marginally more comfortable than the parlor, but even a little more comfort was welcome.

Poe looked up, her brown skin glowing with the pleasure of having been successful in our first morning back in Pravhna. "I follow society very carefully… I see… patterns in how it moves."

I smiled at the way she phrased her ability. It was so similar to how I thought about things, but about a subject I knew so little about.

My expression caught Poe's attention. "What did I say?"

I blushed, feeling embarrassed. "Patterns—I like them."

"Mmm," Poe hummed. "But you see them differently than me, don't you?"

No one had ever asked me a question like that before. I was stunned. "Yes, I suppose I do. Not with people, exactly. People and why they do things… That's hard for me to read, in the moment anyway. It's hard to describe."

Poe nodded, looking as though she were putting something fascinating together. "Maybe it's more like you see the patterns in what people do, events and results, while I see patterns in the *why*."

My eyes widened as I considered the implications of what Poe had said. "We could be unstoppable."

Poe grinned, her smile making her even more dazzlingly beautiful than she already was. "I'm afraid you're right." She looked down at the last card she held, and the smile faded.

"Edith Braithwaite is sending a liaison for us. The Syndicate wants to use our eyes and ears."

Now Poe's Syndicate connections emerged. I was pleased, feeling the blurred edges of the greater picture that formed in my mind clarify slightly. "Why would *we* agree to something like that?"

Poe gestured to the racks of clothing still sitting in front of us. "Because they paid for all of that."

This was excellent. "Oh," I said softly, allowing it to appear that I'd just now understood the depth of Poe's connection to the Halcyon Syndicate. It was always better if I didn't seem too far ahead, especially with new people. "They are interested in finding out what happened to your family?"

Poe shook her head. "No, they're trying to find out more about a person they call Chopard."

"The fourth Syndicate leader of the Halcyon Gate?" I said, wanting to show Poe that I knew something about how the undercity operated. I had a strange desire for her to think I was better informed than I probably was. It was something I'd have to be careful about. I changed tactics slightly. "Is it true that no one knows their identity?"

Poe nodded. "Yes, but Edith's had suspicions for a long while that it might be someone from the upper city."

"And you think it's Viridian," I said, my mind racing ahead of me. That would explain what she might be holding over him. The upper echelons would reject him entirely if they knew he was involved in organized crime. Not that many of their businesses were any better, but it would be the principle of the thing.

Poe shrugged. "It might be. At the very least, he's dealing in something he shouldn't in the undercity. I've caught him there far too many times. He's visiting pleasure houses, and I've confirmed the types of places he's visiting are not," she paused, swallowing a look of pure disgust. "To his taste... the places he visits in the upper city are *vile*."

I did not want to know more, but a chill slipped down my spine. The upper city made quite a show of being set against flesh work, all while having some of the most terribly regulated brothels in the city. If *that* was Viridian's taste, then it was no wonder he couldn't find what he was looking for in the undercity. The pleasure houses there were places to find actual pleasure, where both sides of the coin had a good time.

My eyes fell shut; it was the only way to stop the onslaught of sensory input rushing toward me. Often, the frustration of sorting out the irrationality of cruelty and injustice brought me to tears, but nothing like this. Perhaps the morning's flurry of activity had taken a greater toll on me than I'd assumed. I'd been so interested in the sewists' work that I'd failed to account for the fact that it had been a very long time since I was around so many people.

"Mina, I'm sorry. Have I upset you?"

My face twisted. "People think I am insensitive." It was hard to get the words out. My very short time in society had exposed me to cruel truths about how I was perceived. "But I feel *everything*. I'm afraid this morning may have worn me out a bit."

Poe was quiet for a long time. She didn't speak until I opened my eyes. "That must be very difficult."

I nodded once, unable to form words.

Poe set her pen down. "What we're going to do may be hard for you at times. I want you to promise me that if it's too much that you'll tell me, that you'll let me help take care of you."

No one had ever understood me so easily, quickly, or fully. It almost felt like a trick. Something to manipulate me into trusting Poe. I let my mind free, let it examine the issue from all sides. Poe wasn't rushing me to speak; in fact, she seemed extremely patient. I considered what Poe had said before about patterns and people. "You're like me, aren't you? You see it all, and feel even more."

Poe's smile was sad. "Yes, I suppose that's true."

"How do you keep it from overwhelming you?" I asked, desperate to know what Poe did to remain so obviously at ease.

"I don't," Poe answered. "It just *looks* like it doesn't."

My heart thumped in my chest, as I let that idea sink in. I looked Poe over. Her casual, elegant posture, the way her face was schooled into a perfectly pleasant expression. If this was an act, no, not an act… A mask. Beautifully crafted, elaborate in construction, and practically flawless, but a mask all the same. *How could anyone who felt what we did keep that up?* "That must be exhausting."

"Yes," Poe said, adjusting the piles of cards into neat piles, her voice perfectly collected and almost cheerful. "It is."

I looked for the tell that this was not Poe's real countenance, and found nothing at first… except… Around her eyes, there was the slightest tightness. Something most would read as "smiling eyes," but I read the exhaustion in that tiny bit of tension. Emotion broke apart inside me, my breath quickening at the idea that Poe was bearing all this alone. "Who takes care of *you*, then? When it's all too much?"

Poe's silence was all the answer I needed. We were a pair, and if I believed in Fate, I might have believed the Lady brought us together for a reason. As it was, I was simply grateful to know someone like myself, someone who would not find me embarrassing, or awkward.

"Well," I said, breaking the silence. "Perhaps I can try."

When Poe looked up, there was no trace of her smile.

Her hazel eyes were wide with surprise. "That would mean so much to me. Thank you."

Neither of us seemed able to find more words on the matter, so I asked the next logical question. "When do the liaisons arrive?"

CHAPTER 12

MINA

We only had an hour to get ready. I changed quickly into one of the dresses the sewists left. I would have preferred pants, but apparently the high-waisted style I preferred took longer to make than the dresses that had been constructed so quickly. Poe buttoned the back of the creamy lace dress up for me.

I had taken back my old room, at the top of the house. Though it was in the attic, it was quite nice. I'd always loved it here, far away from the rest of the house. It was quiet. My walls and ceiling were painted indigo, dotted with six and eight pointed golden stars that made strange constellations, like none in Sirin's sky. I'd painted them one winter, after being left here alone night after night while Maman and Helene enjoyed the season's many parties. I could have had a room downstairs; it wasn't as though Maman had exiled me here. This was just more my taste.

The view from the round window under the slanted ceiling looked both down the steep mountainside, into the misty forest below, and upwards to the upper echelons of Pravhna, rising above the clouds, where the richest in

Pravhna lived. There were Oscarovi up there, as well as Strix and Corvidae who'd made good. But mostly the highest echelons were occupied by the high Houses of the humanoid fey. They wielded the generative power of aether so easily that most had made their fortunes long ago—their families so obscenely rich that many needn't ever work again.

High above Orchid Boulevard, an airship drifted out of the cloud cover. Air elementals took the form of serpentine dracons and rode the warm wake of the ship before fading back into the clouds. In the distance, a group of Vilhari, taking brunch on a high terrace, stopped to watch the elementals before returning to the lavish party they were having. When power was all that mattered, the Vilhari would always rise to the top.

I turned away from the window to look at Poe, who wore a beautiful lavender directoire gown. The dress draped around her curvaceous figure, setting her rich brown skin aglow, and bringing out the amethyst sheen in her dark hair. I sighed, almost wistful.

"What?" Poe asked, glancing in the mirror. "Is something wrong with my hair? Sometimes I don't get the back right."

I shook my head, sitting down on the bed to watch her put the finishing touches on herself. "No, you're literally perfect."

Poe nodded once, the corner of her mouth tugging downward, her mask falling only momentarily, but enough that I caught my mistake. Inwardly, I chided myself, remembering this was a point of sensitivity for Poe. I needed to try to fix things. "Helene struggled with something similar. People expected less of her intelligence, because of how she looked."

The other woman said nothing, but seemed to wait for me to say more. "Like you, my sister was far more than her looks." I stepped closer to Poe, but did not attempt to touch her. "*And* like you, my sister was all the more dangerous because people underestimated her."

Now Poe smiled, a genuine thing, the miniscule tell of tension around her eyes disappearing into an abundant crinkle that set her entire expression sparkling. "Thank you, Mina," she said, her voice rough with an emotion I couldn't identify. Poe clarified almost immediately. "It feels good to be seen."

My head bobbed once. I was pleased to have said the right thing. There was a clenching in my chest that was not altogether unpleasant, a delicious ache I almost didn't recognize.

Friendship.

Downstairs, the bell at the front door rang. The liaison was here, and I still had to finish lacing the tall boots I wore under my dress. The floor-length directoire style wasn't one I favored, and I was relieved that shorter dresses were as popular for daywear as longer gowns now. However, they were a bit chilly in the colder weather. Tall boots were *en vogue* this season for both fashion and practicality, as they kept the wearer a more comfortable temperature.

"Don't forget your pendant," Poe called as she hurried downstairs.

I laced the dove gray boots as quickly as I could, slipping the pendant Poe had given me over my head and under the high collar of my dress, so that only glints of the gold chain showed through the lace. The creamy shade of the dress was nearly the same color as my skin. Because the dress was sheer lace, it made me appear practically nude. As I hurried past the tall mirror in the attic hallway, I thought Maman would have found the garment scandalous. She would have made me change immediately. Helene would have liked it.

I paused to look at myself, turning a bit to look at the way the dress flowed perfectly over my curves, drifting to and fro

THE HOLLOW PLANE

as though it had a magic of its own. It was remarkable how the right clothes made me feel like myself, though I wasn't certain what that meant yet.

From my vantage point on the stairs, I heard Poe talking to the liaison, who she had not yet let into the house. "Skye Aestra, what are you doing *here*?"

As soon as I heard the name, I hurried downstairs faster, then crept silently toward the front hall, wanting to eavesdrop. A familiar voice was speaking. "Edith sent us to talk— are *you* her informant?"

"Come inside, both of you," Poe hissed.

"You mean the three of us," a deep voice replied. The voice was so resonant it had to belong to someone quite large. My skin prickled with goosebumps, as though the sound of that voice had crept under my skin.

As though compelled by the sound of the stranger's voice, I entered the receiving hall to see Poe glance down at something. "Fate spare us, is that a greymalkin?"

An enormous cat strode into the house. I'd never seen anything like it; its silver ticked fur gleamed, covering its considerable bulk. Instead of the tall pointed ears that many common felines possessed, it had short, rounded ears, placed further down on its head. When it turned to face me, it wore a look of incredible displeasure.

I am Morpheus, the cat said.

Of course, I knew what a greymalkin was, but they were rare enough to be considered extinct in some circles. I wasn't sure I had ever seen anything that was simultaneously so distinguished, adorable, and absolutely grumpy at the same time. The howlers, Pravhna's vicious messenger birds, were a close second, but the feline could top any ranking, should someone make one.

"I'm Mina," I replied to the fey cat, making a little bow to it, as I'd been taught. Growing up in Somershire had meant a certain amount of education about customs regarding the wild fey, who were to be treated with the same amount of respect as the elementals.

You know the old ways, the cat said, obviously pleased.

"I grew up in the north," I answered, as though that explained it all. And for the greymalkin, it seemed to. I turned to face the two people that now stood inside the entry hall to Orchid House.

They were similar and the inverse of one another at the same time. Both were Vilhari, with pointed ears, sharply planed features, and the bulky muscular bodies of trained fighters. The woman had short snow white hair and silver eyes, while the man was dark-haired, with the golden eyes of a hawk. Instantly, I wondered if he turned into one. He was head and shoulders taller than the woman.

Both were dressed impeccably in tailored frock coats, waistcoats, slim pants, and tall boots. Their clothes looked freshly purchased, rather than handmade. This did not matter to me in the slightest, but I filed the information away nonetheless.

Of course, I recognized Skye Aestra. I was sure I'd never seen the man before, though something about him was familiar. Perhaps, on second thought, it wasn't familiarity, but that he was so outrageously beautiful that it was difficult to tear my gaze from his golden eyes.

As when he'd spoken, it felt as though invisible fingers trailed over my flesh, leaving a wake of shivering goosebumps. A flame that regularly burned low in me flared to life, a coiled beast at the core of me, suddenly ravenous for something to eat after too long asleep. My cheeks heated.

Don't embarrass yourself, said that pesky voice inside my head. Quickly, I bowed my head first toward the woman, eyeing her rapier. "Chevalier, it is my pleasure to meet you again."

THE HOLLOW PLANE

The man snorted, as though he might laugh, but his serious face didn't change. A stab of shame fluttered through me for a mere moment, as though I might have said something wrong. However, Skye rolled her eyes to the ceiling, as though her companion was perpetually frustrating her this way. She held a hand out to me in greeting, clasping my forearm when I offered mine in return, and kneeling before me.

"Thank you, mistress, for the honor you bestow me in recognizing my station. But I am Chevalier no longer. House Aestra no more."

She spoke in the cadence of the high fey houses. I sensed that while Skye was no longer a Chevalier for her House, that she was still bound by her honor. It was clear she didn't remember that we'd met before.

My attention slid back to the man, drawn back to him as though by some wicked force, heat pooling in my belly as I looked him over. He was almost too tall, both long-limbed and heavily-muscled at the same time. And he stared right back, his beautiful features sharpening by the moment in observation of *me*.

His expression confused me, something between a glare and interest radiating off of him. It was difficult to tell if he was simply an intense person, or if he immediately disliked me. My cheeks flushed deeper in response to the perplexing attention, while my spine straightened. Whether he hated me or admired me was none of my concern.

Skye glanced from the man, then back to me several times, then down to the greymalkin, who seemed to speak only to her. I noticed how carefully she avoided looking at Poe as she spoke. "This is my business partner, Ashbourne Claymore. We're here on behalf of Edith Braithwaite to talk to Mistress Endymion."

Poe rolled her eyes. "Stop it with the Chevalier routine,

Skye. Mina knows I've been working with the Halcyon Gate." Poe was obviously flustered. "This is Wilhelmina Wildfang, but the way. The new Lady Somerhaven."

Both Skye and Ashbourne paled slightly, glancing at one another as though sharing some private thought. It passed quickly enough, but it was another thing to file away for later. They'd both reacted specifically to my full name.

Did they know something about me? Something about Maman and Helene, or the fire? Immediately, my nerves set on edge, but I shoved down the hypotheses, which felt as though they reproduced in triplicate. Still, I was left with the question: why were the Syndicate's people so interested in me when they were here to see Poe?

This morning Poe had explained that her association with the Syndicate leaders began with a simple friendship and had grown into something more mutually beneficial. She and Vionette Celestine had met in a popular atelier several years ago, and formed a slow but close friendship over their love for couture.

It developed further when Poe revealed that she was looking for her family, and her belief that House Montclair held the key to finding them. She'd begun helping Vionette by posing as a socialite, a wealthy country heiress from Brektos, across the Pontus Axeinos. Vionette paid her handsomely, funded her wardrobe each season, and Poe passed along any information she gathered that was useful to the Syndicate. In doing so, she'd become quite popular with the three known Halcyon Gate Syndicate leaders.

Something in me tingled, a familiar feeling, as though a piece of the blurry picture in my mind had shifted, though I couldn't yet say how. It seemed we'd arrived back in Pravhna just in time for something, and while others might chalk this up to Lady Fate or coincidence, I preferred another explanation.

One or more of these people, whether they knew it or not, drew us together. That was the way of things. Our desires and fears moved us, not something as amorphous as Fate. I motioned towards the dining room. "Would you care to join us for lunch?"

The greymalkin was the first to go, leading the way as if he owned the house. Skye shrugged, then nodded, and the rest followed. Ashbourne Claymore's eyes followed me the entire way into the dining room, practically branding me with his narrow focus. I glanced behind me, keeping my eyes cast down, my lashes brushing my cheeks. Through them, I caught the heat of his stare. Desire and fear both mixed plainly on his face. If Ashbourne Claymore hated me, and he very well might, his craving for me was just as strong.

CHAPTER 13

ASHBOURNE

In person, Wilhelmina Wildfang was even more infuriatingly beautiful than in the photograph of her in the newspaper. As we followed her through the long hallway, to the dining room at the back of the house, I understood why I hadn't recognized her at first. In the newspaper she'd been dressed plainly, her hair hanging around her face in an unfashionable way. Here in her home, in real life, she was nothing short of breathtaking.

The lace gown she wore revealed pale skin that was nearly lucent, and her cloud of dark hair had been curled and twisted into a knot of waves that defied gravity in its simplicity, framing her lovely face to such perfection I felt as though I might write poetry about it. When Poe Endymion said her name, the weight of the Strix woman's visit slammed into me. Someone wanted this beautiful creature, luminous as the moon, snuffed out.

That could not stand. It wasn't just that she was beautiful—beyond compare, really. But her eyes held a keen intelligence that made me suspect there was more to her than doll-like perfection. Then came the guilt of having even been in a room with someone who wanted her dead, and letting them escape with their life.

If someone had expressed a desire to have Skye or Morpheus killed, I would have ended them, without guilt, sorrow, or second thought. But I let a woman who wanted Wilhelmina Wildfang dead walk free, and now a war waged inside me. Stay on this job and protect her by staying at her side, or abandon Skye and the Syndicate to hunt down the Strix woman and end her?

You are spiraling, Morpheus chided, without so much as looking back at me, as I found my seat. *Get a hold of your good sense, man.*

The greymalkin's words snapped me back into focus. The cat was right. I *was* spiraling. I only just met this woman, and no matter how deeply my instincts told me to protect her, she had not asked for that. She had not welcomed that kind of attention. And I had my friends to think about. My *family*.

Wilhelmina Wildfang was part of the job. That was the way it must stay, unless she asked me for more. Still, as I watched her move about the dining room, setting plates of food out, heat flushed through me. Skye shot a pointed look at me, as though to say, "What *is wrong* with you?"

I had no answer for that. Temporary loss of perspective? Attraction so intense I nearly went feral over a woman I just met? I almost chuckled at the thought of myself racing through the city, rage-fueled and blazing with celestial fire for this woman. I pinched the bridge of my nose. What *had* come over me?

As we took seats around the table, Poe and Skye began talking, though my focus had splintered apart. I could do little more than watch Wilhelmina move about the room, which was beautiful, in a macabre kind of way. As dining rooms went, it was quite small, just big enough for a heavy round table with a marble top, surrounded by six upholstered chairs. The only other piece of furniture in the room was a buffet, but it really didn't need other decor. The walls were plaster reliefs depicting intricate scenes of various violent acts. I couldn't help staring at them. They were beautifully rendered, but horrific.

Wilhelmina must have noticed my attention. "Awful, isn't it? Not my taste." Her words carried the cadence of sarcasm, but none of the tone. Instead, there wasn't a hint of inflection in her raspy voice, and her face was a smooth mask of serenity. Her utter lack of reaction to my rudeness stirred something primal within me.

She left the room before I could answer her, presumably to get more food from somewhere in the back of the house, Morpheus at her heels. Apparently the greymalkin was going to micromanage the serving of lunch—so very like him. With her gone, I could think a bit more clearly, and a wave of relief rushed over me.

While it was obvious I was attracted to her, what I felt for Wilhelmina Wildfang was different, instinctual. Base in a way that both relieved me and made me uncomfortable. Something in the back of my mind stirred, a remnant of life before the coma: a memory that I'd felt this way before for someone. I pushed that thought away, hard and fast. That was all well and good, but I would not open any door that obviously led to my past.

I turned my attention back to the conversation between Poe and Skye. "…on the beach. She doesn't remember anything about being kidnapped—but it's all been a lot for her." Poe dropped her voice. "She doesn't have many friends, and I can't leave her—so I'm staying here for a while to help her get settled."

Poe leaned towards Skye as she spoke. Skye cleared her throat, canting her body away from the other woman. Poe caught the movement and drew back, her movements sharp, hurt flashing across her face. She opened her mouth to say something, but Skye spoke, also keeping her voice low. "You're staying here because her sister was engaged to Viridian Montclair. Does she know you're using her?"

Poe's expression shifted quickly from hurt to cold fury. "Mina and I are honest with one another. A privilege I don't actually owe *you*, Skye Aestra. How did you get the job as my liaison?"

They exchanged barbs, verbally dancing in a fashion I found dizzying. *Mina*. Poe had called her that several times. *Perhaps she preferred not to be called Wilhelmina*. But why should I care about that? This was just a job, one I wanted done quickly so we could return to our former uneventful lives. I hardly convinced myself. Since the moment the Strix woman asked me to kill Wilhelmina Wildfang, I was invested, though I hadn't known it at the time.

The woman in question returned, carrying a plate of unseasoned canard, chatting amiably to the greymalkin. I watched the way Wilhelmina pulled a chair out for Morpheus, offering him the entire plate of meat. The cat began to eat, his purrs eclipsing the sound of Poe and Skye arguing.

Mina's eyes were serious as she watched the Vilhari volley polite insults back and forth. One lush eyebrow quirked slightly, as though she found what went on between them mildly interesting, but not at all disruptive or disturbing, despite the fact that their volume increased by the moment. My focus had narrowed to the point that I could only see and hear Mina, who fetched a plate of escargot from the buffet for Morpheus.

The dress she wore looked to have been made especially for her, its high collar accentuating the length of her neck. And that face. I had to work not to stare at her face, but also to keep my eyes from sliding down every delicious curve of her body. Yes, a war waged in me. Rationality versus the roar of carnal desire that mounted with each passing moment. I didn't even know this woman and yet I wanted to pull that soft body close to mine, protect her with every instinct I had.

What foolishness.

Poe and Skye were practically yelling at one another now, but it was as though I was trapped underwater, my gaze fixed firmly to Wilhelmina Wildfang, as my body came embarrassingly alive for the first time in what felt like eons. My eyes dropped to the ground, desperately trying to avoid lingering on her full breasts, or the perfect swell of her hips, but her boots, tall and closely fitted, didn't inspire any less lust.

The way they clung to her ankles, caressing the curve of her calves—I could not recall another time that leather had me quite so bothered. Her dress was a popular length that fell halfway between her knee and ankle, and each swish of the creamy fabric entranced me further.

"It's not as though you called on me," Poe spat at Skye, breaking my fevered reverie. "You knew where I was."

"You made it clear I couldn't *do* anything for you. But you've got *her* now, I suppose." I'd never seen Skye jealous before, and now she oozed with the emotion. Across the table, Mina's eyebrow quirked up again.

"It is not like *that* between us," Mina said, her voice low and calm as she glanced at Poe. "I need help, and Poe can help me."

Morpheus looked up from his meal, his paws sweeping elegantly over his whiskers a few times as he swallowed. *We have gotten off track. Might we return to the reason we came?*

Both Poe and Skye immediately sat back in their chairs, staring at the table like guilty hatchlings. "My apologies," Poe said to Skye, after a long pause. "I wasn't expecting to see you today."

"Obviously," Skye snapped, but her expression softened

almost immediately when Poe flinched. "My apologies as well. We'll discuss our... personal situation... another time."

Poe's lips pressed together, as though she were suppressing another comment, but her cheeks flushed bright pink, and a little smile flickered at the corner of her mouth. She'd read Skye perfectly. I knew my partner was fired up because she liked Poe, probably more than she was comfortable with. I could relate. No one seemed poised to speak to get us back on track. Morpheus had gone back to his canard, whilst Skye was obviously putting her demeanor back together.

I would have to speak up then. "The Syndicate believes a series of fires in the undercity are Chopard's doing. We've been asked to liaise between you," I nodded at Poe, "and Edith—"

Mina interrupted me. "Does Edith Braithwaite believe the arson at Somerhaven has something to do with Chopard?"

Skye answered for me. "She didn't say so, but I'm inclined to believe she thinks there's a connection. I don't think we'd be here otherwise."

I nodded. It all made sense now, why we were asked to liaise. Herself always had the pulse of things, and she had eyes everywhere. She probably knew the moment these two got on the train together. What had felt like Fate or coincidence fifteen minutes ago now felt like Edith's machinations.

"So," Poe mused. "Whatever Chopard is up to, it started long before what's happening in the undercity."

"Which is what?" Mina asked.

"Someone's setting certain buildings on fire," I explained. "People have died."

Mina's brow wrinkled slightly. "I am sorry, that's tragic..."

Skye jumped in. "And at the scene, anyone who might

have witnessed the event is found in some kind of collective trance. They remember nothing when they come out of it."

Poe and Mina glanced meaningfully at one another. They knew something. Skye and I both waited, but neither spoke up. Something to push on later, when they felt more comfortable with us. For now, there were other questions I could ask. "Mlle Endymion…"

"Poe, please," she interrupted.

"All right then, Poe. We were told you might have information for us after your trip to the country."

Poe frowned. "I'm sure I do, but I'll need you to be a bit more specific if you don't want to hear every detail of the last week of my life. What's she looking for?"

Chopard has burned several abandoned buildings on the Achera. His activities are ramping up, becoming more frequent, Morpheus explained. *One in Kyovka last night, in fact.*

"Kyovka?" Wilhelmina asked. "Please, eat, all of you. I'll be right back."

She left the dining room, walking at a brisk pace, her heels clicking against the marble floors. One of Poe's eyebrows arched. "And Edith thinks I have information about this?"

Skye shrugged. "You must, or she wouldn't have sent us."

Wilhelmina returned with a map as Skye spoke. "This may be why." She pushed a few of the plates aside, spreading the map on the table. "This is Kyovka here," she said, pointing to a tiny village, high in the mountains.

Poe's eyes widened. "Oh—oh. I mean, I suspected him of it last summer, but it came to nothing… In fact…" She glanced at Skye. "The night we met…"

Skye's eyes narrowed, then she shook her head. "I can't believe it. He's just not…that smart." My partner leaned back in her chair, crossing her arms tightly across her chest.

"Though I'm afraid it *is* possible that he has the power to be Chopard, and he certainly has the resources."

I sighed. All eyes turned towards me. "Apologies," I said. "Might someone explain?"

"This is Kyovka," Wilhelmina repeated, a long finger tapping the map, "And this is Viridian Montclair's country estate—where Poe just spent the week."

Her finger traced a huge plot of land, and right on the border of that land, far to the west, was Kyovka. "So you believe that Viridian Montclair *is* Chopard?"

Skye covered her mouth with a hand. "It would explain a lot." She touched Poe's hand lightly to get her attention, then snatched her own back, as though she'd made a terrible mistake. "The night we met—he had you cornered in that alley. Had you accused him of being Chopard? Is that why he was so angry with you?"

Poe stared at her hand for a long moment, as though Skye had burned it. "Not in so many words, but I hinted that I knew something. I wanted information in return for keeping what I believed was his secret."

Her last words were accompanied by a deep blush and a pleading look at Skye that my partner ignored. "It wasn't enough? What you had on him—it wasn't enough to get the information you were looking for?"

Poe shook her head, still blushing. I got the feeling Poe's emotions were rarely so on display. She appeared to be struggling to compose herself, shifting uncomfortably in her chair.

Skye threw up her hands. "Maybe because it isn't him. I've known Viridian Montclair my entire life. He's unpleasant, but he's just not *capable* of the things Chopard has done."

I felt the moment Wilhelmina's mind changed on the situation. Her chest expanded as she drew a long breath in. My body betrayed me, my pants uncomfortably tight as I watched her breasts push against the fabric of her dress. This was not the time for such observations, but again I was made all too aware of my embattled interior state.

When she spoke, I fell headfirst into the rich tenor of her voice, the low, breathy unevenness of it, as though her vocal cords had been damaged in some way. "If there is *any* possibility that Viridian Montclair is Chopard, then we will need to work together."

Her words surprised me out of my body's hunger for her. Skye also returned to herself, her attention turning to Wilhelmina, as she formed coherent thoughts more quickly than I could. "Why is that?"

My heart beat faster by the moment, as Wilhelmina considered her words. Morpheus was busy cleaning his face, but it was obvious he paid close attention to the woman who'd fed him. His feline eyes raised to mine, as though he cared to emphasize Wilhelmina's words.

"Montclair imprisoned me."

CHAPTER 14

MINA

Poe was angry with *me* now, but not by much, if I read her correctly. It was getting easier to do, and for some reason she was more open around Skye Aestra. Still, Poe was obviously annoyed with me. "You can't just *tell* people that, Mina. It's not strategic."

On some level, I knew that. But we'd already talked this over. To get to whatever Montclair knew about both our families, we were going to need help. And there was no one in the upper city to trust. But these two—I had known who Skye Aestra was my whole life. She was Helene's age, and my sister had *hated* the Chevalier. She'd made fun of her adherence to old Vilhari codes of honor, and sneered at her kindness, calling it "misplaced idealism."

The fey cat, Morpheus, told me on our trip to the kitchen that all these qualities had earned Skye Aestra an irreversible trip to the undercity. Apparently, the Vilhar didn't talk about it much, but she'd parted ways with her House. Her title was void, she was expelled from the Chevaliers, and ever since she'd been making her living in the undercity, solving mysteries, righting small wrongs. Helping others in ways no one would dream of in the upper city.

One of those people was the enigma of a man she'd brought with her. Ashbourne Claymore was in a strangely similar situation to my own. She and Morpheus had found him a year ago, beaten and unconscious. He'd been in a coma for three days, and when he woke, he'd simply integrated into their lives, having no memory of who he'd been before. Now they were a little family. According to the cat, both would rather not be working with the Syndicate, but whatever Chopard was up to, it was heinous.

They were the kind of people who wanted the world to be a better place. I had no such illusions. The world was exactly as terrible as it was because people were terrible. But it would make them easier to mold to my purposes. If Poe was invested in hero types, that was her prerogative, but I saw only opportunity.

So I held up a hand to stave off any further chiding. "We need *help*, Poe. We can't go up against Montclair on our own." Poe quieted, apparently willing to listen. "The two of you want to find this Chopard because he's doing terrible things, yes? You wish to stop him?"

Skye and Ashbourne both nodded.

"And you," I pointed to Skye, "believe Viridian Montclair isn't capable of doing these terrible things?"

Skye threw her hands in front of her, as though warding off an accusation. Perhaps I'd been too forceful with my words. Or perhaps it was the pointed finger. I forced my hand back to my side. I'd always used big hand movements when I talked. It had embarrassed Maman and Helene to no end.

I glanced at Poe, afraid to see the cringe of secondhand embarrassment that often accompanied my inappropriate social behavior. Poe looked like she might laugh, but not at me, at the look of deep worry on Skye Aestra's face. *Poe wanted to laugh at Skye, not me.* It was a distracting moment.

Skye sounded calm enough when she answered, but it was obvious she was attempting to regain her equilibrium. "If you say he kidnapped you, then I can admit I may have been wrong about what Viridian is capable of."

I had not said he'd kidnapped me. I said he imprisoned me, and I liked to be precise when I spoke. When others weren't it bothered me, and while I knew correcting others was considered rude, I couldn't seem to stop myself. "He didn't exactly *kidnap* me." Though I was not about to tell them all I knew, it was important they be fully aware of what Viridian could do. "He helped my family to imprison me in an oubliette."

Skye clapped a hand over her mouth, her silver eyes wide. Ashbourne went a slightly gray shade paler than he'd been moments before. So they were familiar with the mechanics of the oubliette and the way the spells to maintain it worked. I hadn't thought about it this way yet, but someone had to maintain spells on a long term basis. While Viridian might not have been old enough to have crafted the first spell for the oubliette, someone would have had to maintain or revive it, and that was no small feat.

There were too many similarities between the cases in the undercity and the fire at Somerhaven. The memory loss, the fires themselves. And still, I couldn't bring myself to say that Somerhaven had been burned with empyrae. I wanted to hold that information back until I was sure of something—I didn't know what right now, only that it wasn't time to reveal it.

"That is *torture*," Skye breathed, her brows knitting together. "Did you just escape… *yesterday?*" I nodded as Skye stood, wondering why she wasn't more concerned about the similarities between the cases. "Then we will go. You should be resting."

Ashbourne shook his head, reaching for Skye's arm to stop her from leaving. "If Montclair is capable of such magic, he'll come for her. We can't leave them to fend for themselves."

Skye's jaw twitched. "This isn't the job, Ash. *They're* not the job."

"But maybe they should be." The look that passed between the two of them was rich with some personal meaning.

Skye took her seat again, shaking Ashbourne's long arm off her. "How would we manage something like that? We'd have to—"

"Move in," I interrupted. "Yes. I think that may be necessary. Though the house is safe enough—Maman was an expert with wards—I think we need the extra eyes and ears. I'm not opposed to helping the Syndicate take Chopard down, as long as Poe and I get what we're after."

"Which is what, exactly?" Skye asked, her gaze pure steel.

I glanced at Poe, looking for her consent. She nodded once, resigned apparently to the fact that we could, in fact, use the private investigators. "Information about what's happened to both our families. We have very different motives, but Poe and I both believe House Montclair is at the center of our troubles. If Viridian Montclair is your problem as well, working together benefits us all."

"We can't just—move in here," Skye said, obviously flustered. "We have other work."

It was Ashbourne's turn to roll his eyes. "Not that you could tell from our ledger."

Next to me, Morpheus grumbled. *Here, lunch might be on time.*

Skye's mouth dropped open. "I am late *one* time—"

Ashbourne rose. He hadn't even touched his food. "We will discuss this in private and return to you with an answer this evening."

Poe nodded, standing up as Skye did. "I'll walk them to the door."

I was tempted to reach out to touch the greymalkin's head to say goodbye, but decided against it. The cat jumped down from his chair, and seemed as though he would stalk away without farewells, but instead, he bumped his head against my boot.

Skye looked back over her shoulder, shaking her head. I stepped forward, my hand reaching towards the Vilhar, then dropped. Poe and Ashbourne were already in the receiving hall, but Skye paused at my obvious attempt to stop her.

"Do you—" I hesitated. "Do you remember me at all?"

Skye frowned. "I'm afraid not. Have we met?"

That was truly embarrassing. I stared at the herringbone pattern in the wood floor of the dining room. "We danced at my debutante ball. It was a long time ago."

The tips of Skye's pointed ears flushed. "I'm so sorry, Wilhelmina. I don't remember that." She paused, then added, "I do remember your sister, though."

"Of course," I said, with a small bob of my head. Everyone always remembered Helene.

CHAPTER 15

MINA

When they'd gone, I stood for a long time at the arched windows in the drawing room, watching them disappear down the street. When an enormous maple finally obscured them from view, I let out a tensely held breath. I hadn't thought about the dance at my debutante ball in a long time. It had been the one nice moment in my entire season. Skye Aestra had seen that no one else asked me to dance, and plucked me from the sidelines—so debonair in her dress blues—a true Chevalier.

Of course, Skye didn't remember one dance; she'd had dozens that night. But it had been my only dance the entire season. Pravhna society ran on appearances, and Maman had allowed me only the basest of coming outs. But I was allowed no new clothes at the modiste, and hadn't even a ball gown. She then proceeded to tell people what a strange child I was, and that I had no interest in clothes.

It had made me an object of ridicule for a short time. Helene's friends Caralee Ellis-Whitely and Rebecca Smytheson pretended to befriend me, and then proceeded to tear me down in a way I didn't understand at the time. When

Helene revealed that the people I thought were my friends were actually poking fun at me, I was devastated. She, of course, was smug. After that, I was simply ignored. It was like I wasn't even there. But Skye Aestra was different. She had *seen* me, if only for a brief moment. I couldn't hold it against Skye for not remembering, but it stung all the same.

Poe came to stand next to me, leaning against the deep windowsill. "What was all that about?"

I glanced at her sidelong. "You heard?"

Poe made a grand flourish towards her ears. "They're rather good at picking things up."

The embarrassment of Poe having heard was almost too much to live through. "She didn't remember me."

"No," Poe said, sounding thoughtful.

"She'd have remembered *you*."

Poe turned, her arms crossing protectively over her body. "Is that what this is about? Do you like her?"

My eyebrows flew up in surprise. "*No!* I mean, I suppose I did when I was sixteen, but I'm not carrying a torch for Skye Aestra, if that's what you're worried about."

A little laugh escaped Poe, like a burst of wind. "Thank goodness. I thought our first fight was going to be over a girl, and I was so nervous."

"No need to be," I said, surprised to find myself as relieved as Poe was that there was no animosity between us. "I only meant that it is disappointing to always be so forgettable."

Poe didn't have an answer for that. She seemed to be the kind of person who thought before she spoke, if given the opportunity. I had no desire to rush her, nor to fill space with my own words. I walked over to the heavy brass racks of finished clothing in the hall. The racks were conveniently on wheels, and I pushed one down the hallway. Without asking what we were doing, Poe took the other and joined me. We made our way through the receiving hall and toward the back of the house, to the housekeeper's office.

The room was a cozy nook furnished with a sturdy wooden desk, pushed up against a bank of leaded glass windows that looked out onto the overgrown garden. The blackthorn and woody nightshade appeared to be in a battle for dominance, heavy mist creeping through their branches. Meanwhile foxglove, hellebore, and datura proliferated, still blooming long after their season. Maman's magic lingered in the garden, a haunting reminder that despite her irrationality and erratic behavior, her spells were strong. Stronger than her, apparently.

I turned away from the window to open what looked like an enormous closet door and pushed my rack inside. "To my room, please," I said, pressing my palm against the rectangular crystal plate just above the doorknob.

Poe stood behind me, quizzical, until I opened the door back up and the closet was empty. I pushed Poe's rack inside and shut the door, pointing to the plate. "Press your palm against that, and say 'to the Rose Room.'"

"Should I say please?" Poe asked. "You did."

I shrugged. "I like to be polite."

Poe tried it, then opened the door cautiously, as though she were afraid something might pop out at her. The closet was empty. "*How?*"

It was rather unique. All Oscarovi houses were somewhat magical, a byproduct of generations of magic running through them. But Orchid House had a few mysteries in its closets. "Maman's great-grandfather had an idea that they might eliminate servants entirely. The spell has never worked in another house, unfortunately, but it's become a part of the makeup of this one. Honestly, I think the house just doesn't like anyone unnecessary to be here, so it cooperated."

Poe shook her head. "The Oscarovi are rather ingenious, aren't they?"

I motioned for Poe to follow me. The grocery order I'd made before the Laquoix sewists descended upon us would arrive at any moment. We'd had breakfast and lunch brought in, but that wasn't economical in the slightest, and while Poe had access to quite a bit of money, I abhorred the idea of waste.

We walked down the stone steps behind the housekeeper's office to the ground level. The kitchen was a cozy haven, dark and perpetually spotless. The cabinets were painted a beautiful emerald shade, a sharp contrast to the rest of the house, where lighter colors ruled. When I entered, the kettle all but shivered in greeting.

Poe peeked out from behind me, wide-eyed. "Did the kettle just *move*?"

I nodded, then spoke to the kettle itself. "Water for tea would be lovely, thank you."

Flame flickered underneath the copper kettle. Poe took a few steps forward, leaning on the enormous wood worktable to watch as the water inside the kettle began to heat. "How is it doing that?"

I didn't have an answer for her. Orchid House had simply always *been* this way. Poe glanced up at me, through thick long lashes. "Really, Mina—I don't think this is normal—even for an Oscarovi house. Magic is science, not some nonsensical force."

So the Vilhari always insisted. Again, I shrugged. "I've never thought about it too much, to be honest. And I've been to very few other homes, so I wouldn't know."

Poe was silent after that remark, her mind obviously turning that information over carefully. It wasn't as though she didn't already know that I hadn't any friends. Anyone who'd followed the social seasons over the last decade with any vigilance would know that, and I knew Poe had. Perhaps she'd thought I'd accompanied Helene to her social engagements, and thus had friends by association. If she thought that, she hadn't known a thing about Helene—my skin flushed with anger at the thought.

Even now, the anger faded quickly, chased by my usual guilt for thinking bad things about Helene. It wasn't that I didn't know exactly who my sister was. It was just that she had been the closest thing I'd ever had to someone who loved me. Yes, she'd hurt me, more times and in more ways than I could count. But she was the only one who'd ever cared to see that I was all right after. To make sure I wasn't so damaged I couldn't recover. It was embarrassing to be so attached to someone who treated me so poorly, but I missed her all the same.

To avoid Poe's watchful gaze, I moved to the kitchen door, opening it to the autumnal air. I leaned against the doorframe, gazing upwards as a breeze floated down the alley, rustling some dry leaves that had gathered in a corner. The air was cool, but Orchid House was far enough up in the echelons to get a bit of sun every now and again. I closed my eyes, letting the the sun's rays warm my face.

A shadow falling over me broke my repose. Above me, enormous feathered wings blocked the sunlight. I stepped back inside the doorway as a siren landed with a small wooden crate in their talons. The fey creature set it down gently in front of the door. Her feathers were bronze, tipped with iridescent amethyst, and her face ethereal, that of a beautiful woman, with pale moonlight skin. "Order for Wildfang."

I made a little bow to the siren. They were revered beings after all—their terraced farms by the sea some of the only places food could grow in this region, high above Sirin's near-constant cloud cover. "Yes, thank you."

"Payment is due within the week. Will this be a regular delivery?"

I nodded in the affirmative as the siren held out a talon. A receipt and a contract for future deliveries were tied securely to her leg. Careful not to touch the siren too much, I removed the tightly scrolled bundle. "I'll have this filled out shortly."

"Sooner is preferable to later," the siren responded. They always sounded like that, speaking in the formal way of the old Vilhari.

As she prepared to launch, another avian fey dove into the alley—its trajectory shaky at best. The thing looked as though a cat and a raptor had collided rather hard, yielding a creature that was both adorable and incredibly vicious at the same time. Pravhna's little messengers, the howlers, were a distant relative of the gryphon.

"Oh dear," the siren crooned, her terrible voice full of concern. She stretched a wing out, rotating it slightly to catch the smaller fey. The little one bounced slightly, then perked up. Its eyes were large and dark as its head darted around.

Poe rushed past me into the alley, scooping the little howler into her arms. "Rue, you goose, what have I said about diving?"

The little fey chirruped loudly, in clear indignation. It trilled once at the siren though, blinking sweetly in clear gratitude.

The siren smiled, an uncharacteristic expression for one of her kind. "Be cautious, little one," she intoned as she took to the air. "The skies are not what they once were."

Something about the statement sent a shiver spider-walking down my spine. The sirens were known to traverse the spirit paths, to broker portents as mundanely as they did produce. I glanced at Poe, who cuddled the little howler to her breast, but watched the siren as she rose above the rooftops. When she met my gaze, the same fear that gripped me was reflected in the other woman's eyes. She felt it too, then.

"This is Rue," Poe said, by way of introduction.

I nodded to the little bird, bobbing my head in a little bow. They didn't speak the way the greymalkin or the elementals did, but it was known that they understood speech perfectly. "I am pleased to make your acquaintance."

The howler trilled at me, then hopped onto Poe's forearm, holding out his leg. A tiny piece of paper was attached, in much the same way the grocery receipt had been attached to the siren's leg. Poe removed it, slipped it into her pocket and kissed Rue's head, who made a series of pleased chirps, then took off again.

"No payment?" I asked, knowing messenger birds required something for their services, often shiny rocks or small snacks.

Poe blushed, making her look prettier than ever. "We are friends."

That was odd. The howlers were adorable, of course, almost to the point of being tempting to squeeze. But they were notoriously bad tempered, disliking humanoids, even their Vilhari kin. It was yet another piece of information to tuck away about Poe until a bigger picture formed.

I picked up one of the rope handles attached to the crate of groceries, and Poe the other. We dragged the crate into the kitchen and then went about the work of unloading it, Poe watching carefully where I put items away.

"You got them to bring more than just produce," she breathed.

A faint smile curled my lips. "The sirens may be the only people in Pravhna who like me."

Poe glared at me. "*I* like you."

I nodded once, but didn't prod further. That feeling could

always change. It did with others—Poe might not be any different. "What was the message that Rue brought you?"

"Oh, I'd forgotten it…" Poe fished the little piece of paper out of her pocket. There were actually two pieces of paper, rolled up together. Poe read the one on top first, then discarded it. "Rent's due at my flat in the undercity. Edith will take care of it. Someone's already billed her." Her voice trailed off, already reading the other message.

"They've agreed to be our liaisons—Skye and the others."

My eyebrows raised. "That was fast."

Poe shrugged, taking an apple from the ironstone bowl on the island and staring at it, as though it might hold the secrets of the cosmos. "Skye was always going to say yes. She's just angry with me."

As I finished loading the dairy and meat into the ice box, the kettle whistled. I took down a teapot from one of the shelves. "How did you meet?"

Poe drew a stool out of the pantry, and up against the worktable. "We met last summer at the Merc—well, outside it anyway. I was threatening Viridian, and she thought she'd rescue me." Her voice had slipped into a dreamy tone, as though whatever she was remembering was lovely.

I took a tin of Maman's favorite tea blend down from a shelf, scooping it into the teapot. It smelled of vanilla and bourbon, with just a hint of brown sugar. "But you didn't need rescuing, did you?" I asked as I poured steaming water over the leaves.

"No," Poe said softly. "I didn't need her to walk me home, or to kiss me either."

The pain in the other woman's voice struck a string in my heart that I wasn't aware actually *worked*. I identified the feeling quickly as envy, which was surprising in itself. I was envious of the other woman's ability to love so easily. Something inside me tightened. *Love? Surely that wasn't what Poe felt for Skye Aestra.*

Confusion gripped me, my muscles clenching to the point of pain. Releasing them with a deep breath did nothing for the pain, but just a little for my comfort. The feelings that had nearly overwhelmed me dissipated to a manageable level. Left behind was a wistfulness for someone lost that was both foreign to me, and all too familiar at once.

I blinked several times, as tears threatened to surface. "What nonsense," I muttered, not thinking.

Poe looked as though I struck her, but did not speak. I wasn't sure what to do, but realized my mistake almost immediately. "Not you. My mind drifted. I apologize. I'm not yet used to being in others' company."

The hurt drained from Poe's face. "What were you thinking of?"

Something about the question struck me as odd, but that was surely because no one had ever been interested enough to ask me such questions. "I was envious of your attraction to Skye—that you two might have a relationship—not because of *her*, but because…" I trailed off, not having words for the strange mix of nostalgia and longing I felt.

"Did you lose someone?" Poe asked, setting down a bag of flour, her dark head tilting to the side slightly.

I stared up at the uneven plaster of the ceiling. "I honestly don't know. There seems to be quite a lot I don't remember."

Poe stepped forward, her fingers stretching forward instinctively, as though she'd like to take my hands. She clasped them in front of her instead, to my relief. "You've only just returned. Give it time."

Footsteps in the alley kept me from answering. We both turned toward the kitchen door to find a tall Vilhari, dressed in the oxblood uniform of the cityguard, leaning against the doorway. The guard bore a strong resemblance to Skye Aestra, with her strong nose, and silver hair and eyes. Unlike Skye, his expression held no kindness, only cruel superiority.

"Well, Mlle Wildfang," the smug Vilhari drawled. "It appears you've returned."

CHAPTER 16

ASHBOURNE

As I expected, Skye's apparent hesitance to work with Mina and Poe was nothing more than a show. I got the feeling she did not want Poe Endymion thinking she was too eager—but I saw the signs of her interest in the pretty, tiny woman. Skye agreed to stay at Orchid House before we'd even gotten out of earshot of the house.

"Of course, we're going to stay with them," she said, her movements agitated, as she pushed a strand of fair hair back from her face. The wind raked cold fingers through it, tousling it again. Skye's mouth pressed into a grim line.

I could hardly keep pace with her as she wound down crowded streets in the upper echelon, and apparently neither could Morpheus, who disappeared to tell Edith that the deal was struck. The little bugger was likely napping in his favorite window at the office already, while I was stuck chasing after Skye.

She rounded corner after corner. I had to double my pace to keep up with her. It didn't help that our route home was a network of back alley staircases that lead back to the undercity and Skye was taking the steep stairs two at a time.

Even with my longer legs, the steps gave me vertigo, something about the descent putting me ill at ease.

"Skye," I pleaded, coming to a stop. The dark alley swam in my vision, and bile rose in the back of my throat. Skye had been rattling off our packing list, discussing what items we needed from our compact but well-curated armory. But she stopped, nearly half a flight of stairs below me, turning swiftly to gaze back up at me. There were four of her in my vision.

"Sit!" she exclaimed, rushing back up to me as I swayed. Her hands gripped my arms as she guided me into a seated position. *What was happening?* A spell like this had never come over me before. I took a few deep breaths at her guidance, swallowing the bile in my throat. It felt as though the alley was caving in on me, and I muttered as much under my breath.

Of course, Skye heard me. "You're panicking, friend. Just breathe."

Panicking? But why? I'd squeezed my eyes shut while I took deep breaths, but now I opened them a sliver, my vision bleary behind my long eyelashes. The depths of the stairs disturbed me on a level I couldn't quite understand. As far as I knew, I wasn't afraid of heights or enclosed spaces, having experienced plenty of both in the past year in my work with Skye. We'd taken these routes before. They were dangerous, of course, primarily used by the Syndicate and less savory characters. But they were quicker than the main roads and cheaper than public transport. Besides, we could handle ourselves.

So why was today like this?

The weight of my head grew heavier by the second. Sky guided it into my hands, her fingers cool on my face. "Keep breathing, Ash," she murmured. "Everything's all right."

The dizziness dissipated some, and then cleared. When I

raised his head again, the sight of the stairs no longer bothered me. Skye sat next to me on the stairs, her hand on my back.

"Are you all right?" she asked, her silver eyes narrowed.

I tried for a light tone as I stood. "That was odd, wasn't it?"

Skye nodded, but her face stayed serious. "I haven't seen you so unwell since right after the coma. Are you sure you're recovered?"

I nodded, taking a few experimental steps down. I was steady enough on my feet. "Yes, I think so." I reached a long arm back to pull Skye up.

She smiled up at me, but the concern in her eyes let me know she was still worried. "I wish I could take you to see my mother. She'd know what to make of this."

Skye rarely talked about her family, and typically I didn't want to pry. But if we were going to live in the upper city—possibly indefinitely—it seemed prudent to ask a question or two. Also, it would take the focus off me, at least for the time being. "Will you see her when we return to Orchid House?"

A long silence passed, the soft sound of our feet on stone the only noise as we descended the alley stairs. This time of day, when everyone was at work and the stairs were lit well enough with daylight, not many were about.

Finally, Skye let out a frustrated noise. "I don't want to, but it may come to that, eventually."

I hated to hear her distressed. I'd stayed away from the subject the entire time we'd known each other, but now I had to ask. "What happened with your family, Skye? Why did you leave your House and the Chevaliers?"

Her pale head shook a few times as we descended further. It smelled like the undercity now, like roasting chestnuts and woodsmoke. "My brother, Niall, and I could not get along any longer. One of us had to leave, and I knew he would not. So I left, and he stayed. My family disowned me for it."

She'd told me versions of this before, and I didn't like that she was still evading the question. I put an arm out in front of Skye, stopping her from moving forward. I kept my voice deliberately gentle, but firm. "That's not an answer. What was the problem between you?"

Skye threw up her hands. "What *wasn't* the problem between us?" She pushed past me. "But the end for us was when I made the Chevalier class, while he could barely rank in the cityguard."

I suppressed a groan. The cityguard were one of the most corrupt organizations in Pravhna. Outside the city, it was often better, but here they were some of the worst criminals of any echelon. They sought out bribes, dealt unreasonable amounts of violence, let cases in the undercity slip into oblivion… I paused.

"What we do, the investigative work—is it because of him?"

Skye nodded, her eyes filling with tears. "Because of *them*. I begged Niall not to join the cityguard, to take up *any* other profession. But my family didn't agree. I was asked time and again to let it go. When I caught wind that he'd been involved in a brutal raid on one of the medial district pubs, I asked one last time."

Each word she spoke was punctuated by a step downward and a tear sliding down her cheeks. "I love my family, Ashbourne. There was no one more loyal to House Aestra than myself. But the injustice of it, the hypocrisy. My parents especially… I couldn't take it."

"So you left?"

She nodded. "The night I met Poe. There was a terrible dinner, Niall and I screaming at one another. My mother said that if we could not find civil ground, one of us would need to leave. As though Strix being beaten for doing nothing more than operating a licensed pub in the upper city was excusable."

It was a story all too common in the medial districts—those that were just at the edge of the line between the upper city and the lower were often subjected to such unjust treatment. Money talked louder than anything else in Pravhna. The Strix that had owned the bar likely couldn't pay the exorbitant rents levied at businesses there.

I wanted to hug Skye, but she hated for anyone to acknowledge her sorrow. We'd come to the door that led into the undercity, anyway. Skye spoke a few arcane words—ones I had difficulty understanding or remembering, even after a year in the city—and the door opened. When we were on the other side, she shut it firmly behind us. We were in an alley in our own district.

The walk home was unusually quiet, as was our packing. I had been mistaken; Morpheus still had not returned from updating Edith on our progress with the Orchid House inhabitants. In the silent sorting of weapons and various clothes, I had too much time to think. My mind drifted to Mina.

The way her dark hair shone in the aetheric lights of Orchid House, the contrast of her long, bony fingers with her voluptuous body. The hint of skin under the creamy lace of her dress. My own skin heated at the thought, my trousers feeling tighter by the moment. It was as if something woke inside me, blooming even, and I couldn't stop myself from wondering what it would be like to—

"I've asked if you could pass me that dagger at least three times now." Skye smacked me with a tall leather boot.

Playfully, I snatched it from across the table at the center of our little armory. Some of the nicest memories of my life took place in this cozy little cellar, surrounded by weapons and gear. A lump formed at the back of my throat, just thinking about leaving.

"Apologies," I said, passing the dagger in question to her. "My mind was elsewhere."

Skye smirked slightly as I adjusted my pants. "Indeed."

Morpheus appeared on the table between us, stepping deftly around the array of blades Skye had discarded. *Your brother is at Orchid House, Skyeling. We must go.*

Firstly, I was shocked to hear the feline use a diminutive for Skye, but only for a moment. Our friend had gone utterly gray, as the fey cat must have known she would. He'd done his best to cushion the blow, but we were in the thick of it now.

Morpheus hopped down from the table, his usually dour face downright grave. *There is a cab waiting outside. I do not think we should leave them alone with Niall, do you?*

It only took a beat for the information to sink in, and then Skye was on the move. I wasn't entirely sure what the two of them worried Niall Aestra might do to Poe and Mina, but I didn't ask questions. I just moved, racing up the cellar stairs behind them.

CHAPTER 17

MINA

"Niall Aestra—what are you doing here? Missing persons isn't your beat." Poe's voice was calm, smooth as silk. Still, I saw the hint of tension in the set of her jaw, the skin around her eyes.

Niall Aestra—was this Skye's brother? Vaguely, I remembered that House Aestra had two primary progeny, but I'd never heard anything about Niall. Skye, when she was still living in the upper city, had been an object of attention. She was popular for her calm demeanor and unusual kindness, rather than the many other vile reasons that made people stand out in the upper echelons.

Niall moved to step inside the kitchen doorway, but Poe made a gentle tutting noise before he could hit the wards. "Now, now, Niall. You haven't been invited in. We haven't even seen official documentation regarding your visit. Besides, you are addressing *Lady Somerhaven*."

The Vilhar blinked once as his gaze slid to me—looking me over as if he couldn't believe such a thing were true. I took the opportunity to step forward. All day, I'd been watching Poe. Her manners were impeccable, and though I knew I wasn't capable of replicating her warmth, I had other material to draw on to find a public persona that suited me.

After all, I'd watched Helene—with her cold, imperious grace—navigate society my entire life. A mask of serenity gilded my face, as a sense of eerie calm came over me. I spoke slowly as I held out my hand. I was breaking through the ward, but I was certain that I could more than handle Niall Aestra, if needed. "I am pleased to make your acquaintance, Officer Aestra."

The command was implied, rather than openly given. I had effectively pulled rank on him. House Aestra was of higher standing than Somerhaven, but by the rules of echelon, I was titled and he was not. He had to submit to me.

As he took my hand, bowing uncomfortably, it became clear: he was here on his own agenda, not that of the cityguard. Corrupt as the entire organization was, they were beholden to the upper echelons in nearly every way. No district official would have sent Niall Aestra here without a partner, nor would they ever have sent an officer, rather than a detective. These thoughts spun in my head, piling atop one another.

Niall rose, letting my fingers go as though they'd burned him. He spun to face Morpheus, who materialized behind him. Wards meant nothing to the wild fey, but as Morpheus and the others were returning to stay with us, on my invitation, the house would now recognize them as it did Poe.

Niall openly sneered at the sight of the feline, who hissed right back at him. *Explain your presence.*

"I don't have to explain myself to the likes of *you*," the Vilhar growled.

The cat sat, casually bathing a paw, though his tail swished violently on the stone floor. *Speak quickly, before your sister arrives. These women are under her protection, and I doubt she will offer you grace for this unwarranted harassment.*

"I am here on cityguard business," Niall insisted, the timbre of his voice shifting erratically.

I glanced at Poe. A vein in her neck trembled slightly, though the rest of her countenance remained calm. "Of course, Officer Aestra. What can we do for you?"

She shot a lightning quick look at Morpheus, and I wondered if she was communicating silently with him. Morpheus nearly faded from sight, losing some of his corporeality. Immediately, I detected a shift in the atmosphere, as though the fey cat were no longer in the room, though I could still clearly see him.

Niall did not appear sensitive to this change. "I am here to inquire after Lady Somerhaven's wellbeing and to find out how she escaped her kidnappers."

Poe stayed quiet, but she nodded at me, almost imperceptibly. We'd discussed how I should answer this over our early morning tea. "I am unable to answer you, Officer Aestra, for I myself do not know."

His eyes narrowed in suspicion. "Are you claiming not to remember?"

I didn't react to his obvious disbelief. "I *claim* nothing, Officer. I am *telling* you, I do not remember." When he visibly winced at my haughty tone, I pushed harder, pleased this persona was working so well. "I hope you're not implying that I'm being deceptive."

"Of course not," he replied as a shadow swallowed him.

The kitchen doorway filled with Ashbourne Claymore, who was so large he eclipsed the light from the alley. "I should think not." The Vilhar's voice was low, carrying the icy chill of darkest winter in its undercurrent.

The ice in his voice had the opposite effect on me. Warmth spread through me at the sound of it. As Niall turned to identify the speaker, Ashbourne stepped into the kitchen. He was a head taller than Niall, dressed in only his shirtsleeves, which were rolled up, revealing his muscular forearms. His long hair was pulled into a messy knot at the nape of his neck. He wore no waistcoat or jacket, as though he'd stepped out of his closet, midway through undressing. I nearly blushed at the thought, but tamped the feeling down as hard as I could.

"Whose behalf are you here on?" Ashbourne asked, his head tilting to one side. He moved with the demeanor of the pantheroi of Brektos, all darkness and sleek cunning.

Niall took a step away from him, almost by instinct. "I'm here on behalf of the cityguard, of course. We had reports that there were lights on in Orchid House."

Some might call the expression that crept over Ashbourne's face a smile, but I saw it for what it was—a predator narrowing in on prey. "You took those reports, did you not?"

Niall swallowed. "I did."

Ashbourne leaned against the kitchen island, the picture of calm. "And does your superior officer know you're here?"

Skye's brother gritted his teeth, a noise so grating I had to suppress the urge to wince. "No."

The thing that was not a smile widened on Ashbourne's face. The man was pure apex predator. Something stirred in me, fluttering wildly in my belly. His gaze caught mine and my breath escaped me.

He didn't take his eyes from mine as he pushed off the worktable. "I think you should go, Niall. Scurry back to your superior officer. Let them know that Lady Somerhaven has returned, and is being kept *very* safe."

Niall's eyebrows raised. "I know who you are, Claymore."

Ashbourne didn't break my gaze, his tawny eyes smoldering. "Do you?" I heard the silent ending to his statement as though he'd spoken it aloud: *because I hardly know myself*. We were an odd pair, two people with broken memories.

No, I thought, in an almost breathless correction. *We are not a* pair.

"I will leave you to whatever this is." Niall backed out the kitchen door. "Tell my sister that I was here."

In my peripheral vision, I saw the way Poe's fists clenched at the vicious tone in Niall's voice. Any questions I had about how Poe felt about Skye were put to rest. Relief flooded me as Niall disappeared, the kitchen door blowing shut behind him.

CHAPTER 18

MINA

"Where is Skye?" Poe hissed as Morpheus materialized fully. Her eyes blazed with something I couldn't comprehend. She seemed almost desperate to know where the Vilhar was.

"Doing a perimeter sweep," Ashbourne replied. "She spotted someone else on your neighbor's roof when we arrived." He glanced at me, his heavy brow furrowing as the fingers on his right hand flexed and then clenched into a fist.

Poe's face changed. "I forgot to lock the front door this morning... There was a herd of elemental ponies in the street this morning... I went to watch them pass..."

"They're very rare," I murmured to Poe, whose smile was watery in return. "But the house won't let anyone we don't approve inside."

Poe frowned. "We?"

I nodded. "I reset the wards to allow you approval."

Ashbourne raised an eyebrow. "Didn't the two of you just meet?"

I glared at him, which elicited a crooked grin. My treacherous stomach flipped. "That's none of your concern."

Ashbourne laughed softly, shaking his head. It was obvious he liked something about my words, but I couldn't tell what. "How do the wards work?"

My stomach wasn't done with its unconscionable fluttering, but I ignored it. "When we are home, any resident of the house may allow someone inside by inviting them in. Otherwise, no one may enter, except creatures for whom wards do not apply."

"Like the wild fey," Poe murmured, glancing at Morpheus, who simply licked a paw in response.

Ashbourne stepped in front of me, pausing, his molten amber eyes boring into me. Once more, I had the impression that he was either extremely interested in me, or hated me outright—his intensity was difficult for me to read.

"Are you all right?" he asked, speaking to me as though I were a gentle lady, disturbed by Niall's obviously nefarious intentions. His expression softened some as he spoke. He really was uncommonly handsome.

"I am," I answered, suddenly wanting to laugh.

No one, in my memory, had ever looked at me like that. It was so wholesomely unwarranted, so deeply misguided. He thought me a delicate flower, when I was crafted from poison. Living in such close proximity to me, he would learn his mistake quickly. My eyes fell on Poe, who was already headed up the kitchen stairs, with the greymalkin in tow.

Ashbourne nodded once, and then turned to the kitchen stairs, taking them two at a time. I followed, though at a much slower pace. The pain was not so bad today, but there was no need to aggravate it into appearing and ruining my day.

No matter how much I liked any of them, they would learn the truth about me eventually. Whether it was the blunt honesty I often could not hold back, or the way my mind rotated every piece of information until it fell into place—

people always got to the core of who I was and recoiled. Every friend I'd tried to make in childhood. Helene, despite her own oddities. Maman, before I'd even had the chance to become a whole person.

At the top of the stairs, Ashbourne had waited for me. "It sounds like the perimeter is clear. Niall was alone."

"That is good," I murmured, almost lost in thought. "Did you bring your things?"

For a moment, Ashbourne looked confused. "No, we came as soon as we heard Niall was here."

I nodded, then frowned. "How did you know?"

Ashbourne sighed. "I haven't heard all the details yet, but the short answer is Edith Braithwaite."

I realized Ashbourne likely had no idea where to go next, so I motioned for him to follow me through the back hall, past the housekeeper's office. "The library is that way. Please feel free to take any reading material you like. My father was a great collector of fiction."

Ashbourne peeked in through the double doors that opened into the library. "Any romances?"

I stopped, raising my eyebrows as I turned back to the library. "Yes, there is an entire section, though I'm not sure anyone's ever read any of it. My understanding was that he appreciated the covers."

Ashbourne nodded, stepping into the library. "Romances often have lovely covers. I prefer a gothic romance, myself. Something about the windswept moors and ghost-filled houses satisfies me."

That made a certain kind of sense. He *looked* like the hero of a gothic romance, with his dark hair and impressive bulk. I wondered if he knew it—if that was why he enjoyed them, or if he was unaware of how closely he resembled the heroes he enjoyed.

Or maybe it was the heroines he liked to read about. My

mind swam with possibilities. *What were heroines like in gothic romances?* For the life of me, I could not remember, but suddenly had the burning urge to find out.

"What about you?" he asked.

I frowned, my stream of thoughts regarding gothic heroines disturbed. "What about me?"

His brows knitted together, as though he wasn't sure what I didn't understand. "What kinds of books do you like?"

"Oh," I replied softly. No one had ever asked me before. *So many firsts, lately.* It was an odd feeling to be surrounded by people who seemed genuinely curious about me. "I enjoy adventure stories. Far-off lands and all that."

He looked fascinated, his stern expression opening further. "Not stories of dashing heroes and gallant grand gestures of love?"

Something in me quivered at the thought. "Love stories are not for me."

In one fluid step, he'd moved closer to me, his long legs taking him further than I imagined they might. It was a casual movement, but the heat of his body mingled with mine, in the chill library air. Rare golden afternoon light broke through the clouds, streaming in through the windows, hitting the sharp planes of his face. For the briefest moment, I was certain his amber eyes glowed. My breath caught in surprise, but as his head tipped downward to look at me, I saw it was only a trick of the light.

"And why are love stories not for you, Lady Somerhaven?"

The moment was far too intimate. We'd known one another for a matter of minutes, not even hours. *And still.* My chin raised, as though drawn upward by a force not its own. "Because love is a curse, Msr Claymore."

One dark eyebrow arched in response, one side of his

mouth quirking into a crooked smirk. He looked altogether too pleased with himself. "Is that so?"

Now he resembled the rogue princes in the adventure stories I enjoyed, wicked and sure of himself. He did not read gothics because he resembled their brooding heroes then.

How had our heads gotten so close? For that matter, how had our bodies gotten so close? I'd only have to raise my palms to press them against the hard muscle of his chest. Something I was not about to do, but still... Flustered, I swallowed hard, embarrassed at how difficult it was to take a step backwards. Being in his orbit felt like grace.

In my second sight, a beautiful face flashed before me—not Ashbourne's. Pale, porcelain skin, hair like flame, eyes wild with fear. Fingers gripped my shoulders, shaking me as the face shouted, screaming words I could not hear, though I knew I wanted to. The face was so familiar, so precious to me. I reached out to touch it, but found myself falling through darkness instead.

I hit the ground hard, surprised to find the checkerboard pattern of the library's parquet floor underneath me. Hands still gripped my shoulders, but they were not the long fingers of the redhead from my vision. Or had it been a memory? I looked up into Ashbourne's dark, honeyed eyes. Like the memory, he was shouting at me, but I couldn't hear.

Not at first, anyway. When my hearing rushed back in, I realized he wasn't shouting, but *was* obviously quite upset. Poe and Skye rushed into the room.

"What happened?" Poe asked, skidding to her knees to snatch me from Ashbourne's grip. For such a tiny person, she was remarkably strong. She wrestled me into her arms, all fierce defense and blazing fury. "Did he hurt you, love?"

Ashbourne rose, his eyes alight with anger. "Of course I didn't hurt her. She collapsed." Skye clapped a hand to his shoulder, reassuring him, apparently.

I shook my head to corroborate. "No, he didn't hurt me. I remembered something."

Poe turned to Ashbourne quickly, the rage dying in her eyes. "I apologize."

He nodded once, then bent down, scooping me out of Poe's grip and into his arms with a degree of ease that surprised me. "Put me down. I can walk."

Ashbourne paused. "Can you?" His words were careful, and he looked as though he regretted touching me.

To my surprise, his touch was comforting. I was angry that he'd manhandled me, but I had no desire to pull away from him. There was something oddly right about his proximity, as though my body belonged in his arms.

Which was, of course, utterly ridiculous. A short huff of a sigh proved my frustration. "No."

"May I carry you then?"

It was as though the rest of the world melted away. There was nothing left but the two of us, staring into one another's eyes. The feeling that I had been in just such a place before echoed through me, a disconcerting sense of time looping to keep me both right here and somewhere else.

Ashbourne broke eye contact first, directing his attention to Poe. "Could you show me to the parlor? She should rest."

"I am right here," I insisted, my voice too loud and too sharp. "Speak to me."

He looked down at me as he followed Poe out of the library. His voice was a low rumble against me, sending waves of vibrations through my body. "I know exactly where you are, Wilhelmina."

This close to him, the desire in his eyes was plain. The pulse of resonance his voice sent through me was too thrilling, too stimulating—*it felt too good*. I was not allowed such pleasure, not in this body. Not that I could remember.

My breath caught at the same time his did, and once more, the world disappeared. I felt my grip on reality slipping.

And then he set me down on a settee in the parlor, his strong arms and sturdy chest receding from me at an unforgivable pace. It was as though I were one end of a magnet, and he the opposite. I had to stop myself from lurching forward, which was momentarily humiliating, until I saw the way every muscle in him tensed. Not in revulsion, but as though he too was holding himself back.

His breath came too quick for the little effort it had taken to carry me, the pace matching my own, as though each of us had traversed long distances to end up in such close proximity. Skye and Poe glanced between us, and then at one another. Skye shrugged and sat down on one of Maman's uncomfortable chairs, her face crinkling with displeasure as she did.

"Should I get us tea?" Poe asked.

I shook my head immediately. I didn't want Poe to go, but I did want tea. That might help steady me. Ashbourne stared at me, then moved. "I will get the tea."

"Thank you." My voice was soft as he strode out of the room.

I realized I'd needed him to leave; I wasn't sure I could concentrate with him there. It wasn't as though I'd never been attracted to someone before. I had. But I could not recall ever having such a strong reaction to someone else. I would need to develop a way to combat this, and to understand why feeling that way for him had triggered the memory; for now, I was sure that was what had occurred.

That wasn't something I was willing to discuss, but the memory itself was. I sat up, feeling focused now that Ashbourne was gone. My body ached more than ever after my vision into the past. My muscles had tensed too tightly during the episode, and now everything hurt.

Poe watched the effort it took for me to drag myself into a fully upright position. Though I'd done it as fluidly as possible, I was sure Poe had gauged my level of pain accurately. I was coming to learn that was typical of Hippolyta Endymion, who saw as much as I did, but interpreted it all differently.

"Can you tell us what you remembered?" Skye asked.

I swallowed hard, a lump forming in my throat at the thought of the woman. "I can tell you what I saw, but not what it meant."

Poe's expression fluttered between compassion and frustration as she squeezed her own hand in her lap. Gingerly, I reached out and took one of Poe's hands. Nothing about it was frightening; in fact, as Poe's fingers laced through mine, I found the touch comforting. I allowed my lips to raise slightly, the tiniest smile for Poe.

Poe grinned back, pure joy on her face. To my surprise, tears welled in her eyes. "Whatever you can tell us is fine, Mina."

A warm feeling oozed through my chest as her hands gripped mine. It was entirely different from what I felt pressed against Ashbourne, but it was a kind of attraction all the same. The feeling was pleasant, comforting even. No one had touched me much in my whole life. Not with tenderness anyway. It was a strange sensation to have so many people interested in me, affectionate with me.

Disconcerted by the flood of confusing feelings I had, I focused on the memory. "I saw a beautiful woman with flaming red hair. She was shaking me by the shoulders, shouting at me, but I couldn't hear her words. I don't know who she is, but I have the sense I *know* her."

Poe glanced at Skye, who shook her head. "There are almost no gingers here. Are you sure it was a woman? I know a few folk with red hair, but they're not women."

I frowned. "Why would you expect to know who it is?"

Again, Poe and Skye exchanged confused looks. Skye answered. "Because of the way we grew up, Mina. We know most of the same people, and there are very few people with red hair in the upper echelons."

I frowned again, wanting to argue her logic of assuming that the person I'd seen was someone of our social class. But Poe spoke. "The way your mother raised you was quite sheltered, wasn't it?"

I nodded. That much I couldn't argue with.

"All right," Poe reasoned. "Were there any redheads you can remember in Somerhaven? It tends to be a familial trait."

Slowly, I shook my head. It wasn't that I didn't follow Poe's logic. The most likely scenario was typically the right one. But neither of them knew what I did: that there had been a time *before* this life, a before that I could not yet conceive of fully. Perhaps I should tell them… But the thought of telling them what I really was, seeing their faces contort with revulsion after all this kindness—I *couldn't*.

CHAPTER 19

ASHBOURNE

I made tea in silence, even though Morpheus had reappeared next to me almost as soon as I'd made my way back to the kitchen. Emotions swirled through me, confusing my mind and body. I breathed deeply, narrating each familiar movement to keep my focus sharp.

Fill the kettle with water. Long inhale.
Light the stove and put the kettle on. Exhale.
Spoon tea into the teapot. Inhale.
Take the teacups down. Exhale.
Slice a lemon. Inhale.
Fill the sugar bowl. Exhale.

As I waited for the water to heat, I leaned over the long worktable at the center of the cozy kitchen, cradling my head in my hands. Morpheus sat next to me, diligently bathing, leaning his heavy body against my shoulder. If I didn't know better, I'd think the beast was trying to comfort me. I tried to let my mind go blank, rather than remembering what it felt like to hold Mina's body against mine.

It is strange, isn't it? the cat asked—finally done with his bath—*How both you and Wilhelmina have damaged memories.*

The feline's words were phrased as a question, but were spoken as a statement. Fact. It *was* strange. I stood, the knot in my brow deepening, as I considered what Morpheus had presented to me. It was an odd coincidence. Too odd to even be a coincidence, really. It smacked of omens, portents, and other uncomfortable topics. I hated all that nonsense with an intensity that suggested it was a long-held feeling. You couldn't do anything about a prophecy, and I preferred to do something about my problems.

The kettle whistled, and I turned to take it off the stove. I poured water into the teapot, then searched for a tray to carry everything upstairs. By the time I turned back to the worktable, I found Morpheus staring at me. His oblong head was tilted to the side, and his eyes had narrowed to an appraising glare.

Had I offended him somehow? The damn feline was too sensitive. "I'm sorry, old man," I apologized, hoping an advance on my remorse might help smooth things over between us. "What were we talking about?"

The cat's eyes narrowed further, and then he twitched, furiously licking his paw. The movement seemed a touch contrived, as though he would prefer not to return to whatever it was we'd been discussing.

Nothing of import, he finally replied, when the paw met some unknowable standard for cleanliness. He jumped down from the worktable, rubbing his head against the thick barley twist legs before trotting upstairs.

I found a tray and arranged the cups, sugar, lemon slices, and teapot, before following him, balancing the tray full of china easily. What *had* we been talking about? I shook my head. I was going to have to pay better attention—my burgeoning attraction for Wilhelmina Wildfang couldn't get in the way of doing my duty.

We were here for two reasons: to protect Edith's assets

and find out who Chopard was. Nothing more, nothing less. But my resolve broke almost as soon as I'd fixed it in place. As I approached the parlor, I smiled to see Morpheus already curled up on Mina's lap. It didn't help that she was so beautiful, but it wasn't just that. There was something so at odds about her, ruthless and soft at the same time. Her blunt utterances and obvious vulnerability mixed an irresistible cocktail of desire and protectiveness within me.

The women were already strategizing, so I laid the table with tea, pouring for each of them in turn as they continued without pause for my entrance.

"Mina's memory *could* be connected to Viridian somehow though, couldn't it?" Poe asked, her question directed towards Skye. My partner sat at a mahogany secretary desk situated near the front windows, a stack of paper in front of her.

Skye nodded as she scribbled notes, pausing to take her cup of tea with a grateful smile. "I suppose it could. Perhaps Mina met the woman from the memory at a country party?"

Mina shrugged lightly, her face a mask of impassive calm. But her fingers trembled slightly as she stroked Morpheus' back. He must have told her it was all right to pet him, because that was not something he typically allowed.

Poe, who sat on the same settee as Mina and Morpheus, took the cup I offered her. "House Montclair has connections to Brektos, so I don't think we can discount the idea that Mina might have met her in the country. That is, if your family attended Montclair parties."

Mina looked as though she were struggling to recall. "So much of the season before the oubliette is missing. But I was never asked to go to parties there before that. Maman and Helene always went without me."

I poured Mina's tea, dropping a slice of lemon and a

spoonful of sugar in without thinking. Her eyes narrowed when I handed it to her. "How do you know I take my tea that way?"

Morpheus stared at me, his silvery-green eyes wide, his gaze unsettling in its pointedness.

"I didn't," I admitted. "Just a good guess, I suppose."

The greymalkin sighed as he laid his head back on Mina's lap. Again, I wondered what I'd done to offend him so. All cats were like this, secretive about their many grievances, but Morpheus had to be the most curmudgeonly of them all. There was no telling what I'd done to displease him. He would either tell me or forget he was ever unhappy with me. There was no use in obsessing over it.

Mina's eyes relaxed as she took a sip of tea. She set the cup down on the table as I poured a cup for myself, sitting in the chair across from them. As I did, the bell rang at the front door. Everyone looked to me.

I chuckled; clearly I was to be the domestic help today. I stood, leaving my cup on the low marble table that sat in front of the settee. "Let me get that."

They returned to their conversation as I left the room. In truth, it felt nice to be needed for things so pleasant as making tea and getting the door. Too often, my primary usefulness with Skye was intimidation and fighting. Neither of which I minded much, but it didn't help to feel that was all I was good for.

I strode quickly through the entrance hall, trying not to let the impressively grotesque carved stone bother me. The house itself was a terror—beautiful, but horrific at the same time. I'd never seen another like it in Pravhna, but something about it was vaguely familiar. Likely, the artists the Wildfangs had hired had done other, similar work, only on smaller scales. Last winter, when business had slowed, I'd spent a dizzying month in the galleries of the upper echelons, drinking in all the art I could see, with Skye by my side talking over all the artists' influences.

I paused in front of a statue of a Vilhar soldier, my eyes catching on the odd wings the artist had chosen to give their subject. Utterly fantastical: six wings, more like dracons than birds. *Someone had a good imagination.* The bell rang again, more insistently this time, as though the visitor held the button down for longer than necessary. I swore under my breath.

"Coming," I called aloud.

I opened the door to find three Strix youths waiting for me, two of which were dragging huge trunks up the steps. The other had a trunk at his feet. "Herself sent us with your order from the Laquoix woman and the things from your office."

I'd never gotten used to people calling Edith Braithwaite "Herself," as though she were some kind of royalty. It was warranted, I suppose. To her people, she was better than any of the cratties. She cared about the people who were loyal to her, more than anyone in the upper echelons did. That much was certain.

I frowned at the luggage, not sure what could be inside, but the Strix just shook his head, handing me a clipboard. "Not for us to question the boss."

I stared at the clipboard until the Strix dragged a pencil from his pocket. "Sorry about the pencil. It's all I have. Sign for me, so Herself knows you received the packages."

I did as asked, then fumbled in my pocket for a few coins to tip the hatchlings. The one who'd had me sign shook his head. "None of that please, Msr Claymore. We've been handsomely paid." He lowered his voice, looking around. No one on the street was near enough to hear us, but several curtains shifted slightly. We were most definitely being watched. "The old girl says to report in a week's time."

I nodded, thinking Edith wouldn't appreciate these younglings calling her "the old girl," but that was an issue for another time. "Thank you for the delivery."

"Cityguard's been taken care of as well. The Aestra bastard won't come around again," the youth murmured. "Can't keep the press off you though—not for more than a few more days."

"Tell Herself we appreciate it," I murmured back, careful to look down as I spoke. Lip reading was more difficult than average people assumed, but it was still possible.

The three youths strutted off, chatting to one another in a lively, carefree way. They were headed back to the undercity, back to the Syndicate. I envied them deeply as I pulled the trunks inside. There was nothing about this house, or this part of the city, I wanted anything to do with.

Nothing except Mina. The thought ricocheted through me, wild as a stray bullet in a barrel, and just as dangerous.

I opened each of the trunks, trying to determine which should go where when we chose rooms. One was a combination of both my and Skye's things. None of the clothing we'd packed was there, only weapons and a box of files Skye had pulled from our collection. The other two trunks were full of finely made clothing, fit for dukes, not the likes of us.

"Did Edith send those things?" Skye asked, appearing out of nowhere. I'd heard her coming, of course, but was still impressed with her ability to sneak up on me.

"Yes—what do we need all this for? I thought we were meant to be their guards."

Mina and Poe both arrived in the entrance hall. Poe was immediately distracted by the host of calling cards in the bowl near the front door. She moved quick as a forest pyx as she sorted them.

Mina came to stand next to me, looking at the clothes in

the trunk I determined was for me. "It looks as though the two of you will be acting as our escorts."

I glanced at Skye. "Would that be… inappropriate? Escorting them and staying in the house together?"

Skye laughed, though she also had that worried look she got when I didn't remember something essential about how society worked. "No—no one cares about that kind of thing in the upper echelons. They bed whoever they want, whenever they want."

Poe looked up from her calling cards. When Skye's eyes met hers, they both flushed deeply.

Mina leaned over with intention, her eyes locked on the neat pile of shirts. I liked that she had noticed our friends' obvious attraction to one another, but was letting them have a private moment. She was uncommonly considerate for someone raised in the upper echelons. I'd never met a crattie I liked so well so quickly, other than Skye.

"These are lovely," she murmured. Her voice still sounded as though her vocal cords were damaged.

"Have you been screaming?" I asked, before I could think better of it.

She looked up at me, her eyes wide. "Yes. I believe I screamed for months on end in the oubliette."

Her voice did not so much as waver. She'd trembled in my arms, her heart fluttering like a panicked, wild thing after her vision, but had no reaction whatsoever to that. As she stood, she seemed unsteady on her feet. "I think I may have done too much today. I need to lie down for a bit." She began to walk away, headed towards the terrible staircase at the end of the hall. "Poe, can you show them how to send their things up the elevator? They can stay in the Oleander and Hellebore rooms."

Poe nodded. "Of course."

Mina turned, took a few steps, then paused. "Nothing in

the house is off limits to you, but a word of caution—my mother was very fond of poison and traps. Stay out of the rest of the bedrooms on the second and third floors."

There was a deadly chill in her voice. The fact that she didn't turn disturbed me more than I would have imagined it could. I wanted to see what her face looked like, if there was a mark of some horrific childhood lesson there, or pure fear. As it was, the ice in her voice was enough to send a lick of apprehension through me. What had we gotten ourselves into with this place, this family?

"Of course," Skye replied. "We wouldn't dream of prying."

Mina nodded, glancing sidelong behind her at Poe, her arm stretching out behind her ever so slightly, as though she reached for the other woman. "Would you come chat with me about those cards before you show our guests where to go? We need to decide which to accept."

Poe rushed forward, taking her arm as they walked towards the stairs. I noted the way Mina leaned against Poe, just a little, but enough for me to see things clearly. She was in more pain than she let on. Probably all the time from the practiced, careful way she moved. I watched as they made their way upstairs. Morpheus appeared behind them, following.

When the sound of their footsteps died, I turned to Skye. "She's in a great deal of pain."

Skye nodded, as though she'd noticed the signs I had. "I'm remembering a bit more about her now. I don't remember dancing with her during her season, but when she was a child there were rumors she'd been ill—and that's why she and Helene were kept from society."

Something about that struck me as a lie. The dead woman had obviously fixated on poisonous plants. Had Vaness Wildfang experimented on her youngest child? But why would she? I stared at a family portrait, tucked into a nook near a coat closet. It only portrayed Vaness, her husband, and a small tow-headed creature I assumed was Helene. The littling bore a strong resemblance to both her parents.

None of them looked a thing like Mina, and I wondered if perhaps she wasn't Vaness' child at all. If that was why she'd permanently damage a littling—revenge for an affair. It was the kind of thing we saw all the time in our line of work, sadly. I wasn't sure how that held relevance now, but I'd worked as a detective for nearly a year, and something about all this didn't make sense.

By contrast, the fires were too much of a coincidence to be ignored. What in the Wildfangs' past had drawn them into Chopard's web? I chewed it over in my mind, scowling at our weapons. I wasn't sure how to sort them just yet, so I worked to put the trunks back to rights and close them, while Skye watched. She was just as lost in thought as I was.

When I got the trunks closed, I asked, "What was the sister like?"

"Imperious. Beautiful beyond measure for an Oscarovi. Quite a prize for Viridian. He must be furious that he lost her."

"Why?" I sat down on the trunk that held my clothes. This was as good a place to talk as any. As far as I could tell, there were no comfortable seats in the parlor. I hoped the bedrooms were a different story.

Skye sat across from me, atop her own trunk, silently agreeing with me to not return to the parlor. "Viridian Montclair is rich, connected, and intelligent. But he grates on people's nerves. He struggled to maintain a match, though many were interested in the Montclair fortune. And in the past few years, there have been rumors about the kinds of pleasure houses he frequents."

I grimaced. "Not the ones in the undercity, I take it."

Skye shook her head. "No." She paused for a moment, listening hard for movement upstairs. I did the same, faintly sensing soft footsteps and voices, but not hearing anything distinctly. Poe and Mina were obviously talking still. Skye continued, "Muse could help her remember. She has to know something that would help us. The fire at Somerhaven, her imprisonment... I'm sure it's all connected to Chopard somehow. I can feel it."

I nodded, glad our guts still spoke the same language, that we still thought along the same lines. This mission was cloudy territory, and I had the feeling we were going to have to work on instinct more than either of us liked. Being aligned in our thinking would help ensure we didn't make mistakes.

I kept my voice low. "He could, but getting her to the undercity will be a problem. We're being watched, both openly, and I assume otherwise."

Skye nodded, looking up again, leaning forward. "Edith has eyes everywhere, but I'm fairly certain Montclair has people out as well."

"And your brother?" I asked. "Who's he working for?"

Skye shook her head. "I can't tell, but I doubt he'd have come on his own—someone tipped him off about Mina. I don't like that he's involved in this."

The sound of a door opening and closing upstairs urged me to lower my voice further. "The Strix woman that came to the shop—you think she's involved in this somehow?"

Skye stood, hearing Poe's footsteps as clearly as I did. "I think we should assume that this is *all* connected."

So she was sure then. It both comforted me and set my teeth on edge. Our instincts were built differently. It's what made us such a good team. Skye felt into the subtler side of things, people's feelings, patterns of behavior, when folk lied.

But I had a warrior's sense of a fight: when things shifted or turned. When my opponents were closing in on me—and I had that feeling now. Things were building in a way I didn't like one bit. The battle had shifted, but to whose advantage, I was unsure.

CHAPTER 20

MINA

For days after our arrival at Orchid House, we fended visitors off, claiming that I was still quite "done in" from my ordeal. In reality, we spent our time combing the garden for any kind of surveillance spells and reworking the house's wards to our specifications. Niall Aestra's unusual visit put us all on edge, and Skye and Ashbourne insisted we go slow. There was only so much I could do while Maman's workroom was still locked.

Poe and I also spent a good deal of time sorting the calling cards into strategic piles: ones we would never answer, ones we should answer for social reasons, and ones to answer to gather information on both Maman and Viridian's known associates. The trick was mixing the last two groups enough that it would be difficult for anyone observing us closely to determine what we were up to.

Every morning, I rose long before the sun to try the door on Maman's work room. I wasn't keeping it a secret from the others. It was just easier to think in the wee hours, partly because I was having no luck. My frustration was getting the better of me. One morning, on my third day of having no success, Ashbourne appeared beside me in the study, a tray of steaming tea in his hands.

He said nothing to me, just nodded, fixed my tea, and settled into a chair with his own cup, apparently engrossed in a book. He wasn't pretending to read while surreptitiously keeping an eye on me, either. I'd been suspicious when he sat down, but as I sipped my tea, the special calm that came over a room when someone was lost in a story seeped into me.

The man really had just come to keep me company. He seemed to intuit that I didn't want to talk, and just read while I tried every spell, sigil, and secret password I could think of. Nothing worked, but with Ash's calming presence, my frustration lessened. By the fourth day that he joined me, I noticed he had a little notebook he wrote in occasionally.

With sweat beading on my brow from my last attempt at the door, I slumped into the desk chair. The sound of Ashbourne's pen on paper caught my attention.

"What are you writing?" I asked, trying not to sound as grumpy as I felt. I wasn't annoyed with him. Quite the opposite, in fact.

He looked up from his notebook. "I'm keeping a list of all you've tried so far."

"Oh." That was rather thoughtful of him. "There's no need. I'll remember."

His expression was one of thoughtful repose as he continued writing. "The list is not for you, it's for me. I think things through by writing them down."

I wiped the lingering sweat from my forehead with a handkerchief. "Does that work?"

Ashbourne nodded once, then looked up. "It does. For me, anyway."

His golden eyes met mine and a feeling of ease crept through the atmosphere in the room, smoothing all the rough edges that threatened our peace. We didn't talk more.

He went back to reading as I pulled down some books from Maman's shelves to read about astral travel, if only to clear my head.

Companionable silence filled the room like a balloon gently inflating. It hugged me, my heartbeat even and my breaths deep and cleansing. It was true that Ashbourne's mere presence had the ability to send me into paroxysms of lust, but there was also this—whatever *this* was. He, Poe, Skye, and Morpheus all drove the loneliness of the oubliette away.

Morpheus. "Could Morpheus get in? To the workroom, I mean."

Ashbourne looked up. "Call to him."

I'd learned the cat could hear a summons from great distance, so I said his name under my breath, adding, "Could you please come to Maman's study?"

The greymalkin appeared at my feet. *Yes?*

"Can you get into locked spaces?"

Most, he answered, staring at the door. *But not that one. That one only opens with a key.*

"A real key?" Ashbourne asked. "Or a magical one?"

The greymalkin seemed to shrug, then rapidly licked some patch of offensive fur on his back leg. *It is difficult to say. The spell is quite complex. A ward around the inner room connects to the lock itself.*

Ashbourne set his book aside to come stand next to me. We both stared at the door. There was no lock. Morpheus curled up by the fire and closed his eyes, having nothing else useful to say, I assumed.

"Have you come across any evidence there's a lock?" Ashbourne asked. "You did several spells to reveal what's hidden."

I shook my head. "No, nothing."

"You don't use a jewel," he said simply. There was not a

hint of judgment in his voice. "And yet you are adept with magic."

I nodded, sighing. He was more observant than I'd thought. I might fool people I was around for short periods of time, but I couldn't fool anyone I lived with—a fault Maman had reminded me of constantly. "Correct."

He stepped backwards, sinking back into his chair. "Was your mother resentful of that ability?"

I leaned against the bookshelves, not knowing how to answer that. It was all so complex. "Perhaps. It's not unheard of among us—the Oscarovi have always had access to magic. Some simply have more natural talent than others. But it's rare to have power as strong as mine without the help of a familiar." There was more I could say, but delving too deep would dredge up things I wasn't sure how to explain. Things I wasn't ready for him to know about, first among them that this was not even my real body. That *I* was not real.

He nodded, but said nothing in response. I could not tell him the rest, but I found myself giving voice to one of my most vulnerable realizations—offering it to him like a pearl. "If it had been Helene, I think she'd have been proud. Since it was me—she was ashamed."

I don't know if he understood that I'd pulled something from the horrible dark place at the core of me, that this was a gift. His face was calm, but anger flashed in his eyes, fierce and protective. *Of me.*

"Why?" he asked. "What reason could she have had to be ashamed of *you*?"

The way he said "you" sent shivers through me—as though he could not imagine finding fault with me. The shivers expanded into vibrating waves of heady pleasure. Something was changing inside me, shifting to make room for these people and their apparent care for me. The path I walked now was dangerous for someone like me. I had too many secrets, and it took me far too long to sort out what people's intentions were.

I shrugged, shaking my head. It was time to put my emotions back on more solid ground. "If I knew that, I'd probably remember why I'd been put in the oubliette. I have a strong suspicion the two issues relate to one another."

"So do I," he said, his expression dark. He didn't elaborate, and I didn't push the conversation further.

BY THE END of our first week together, we'd come up with a solid plan for how to deal with the inevitable questions about where I'd been and what Ashbourne and Poe were doing with us. Since many of the upper echelons had seen Poe at Viridian's country party, we agreed it would be better to hinge my "rescue" on Poe and Ashbourne. As Ashbourne had made a trip out of town the month prior, we concocted a story that he'd found me wandering the beach, soaked to the bone, with no memory. He'd been to one of the aeries just north of Somershire around that time, so it wasn't out of the realm of possibility.

Skye had an isolated little cabin near the Achera River and he'd stayed there for a few days, before traveling north, right past Somershire. In our story, he'd taken me there to recover, until I remembered things like my name and where I was from. We rehearsed telling the story exactly the same repeatedly, then Poe made us tell it more "colorfully," including shared details, from our own perspectives. She even gave us points to argue over, such as whether or not he'd given me his coat right away.

And then we began taking turns about the neighborhood, both in pairs and as a foursome. We let the story slip out, bit by bit, as we naturally ran into many of the people we planned to call on, on the promenade. By our second week together in Pravhna, we began taking callers. There were nearly a dozen each day, Oscarovi and Vilhari alike. None were any of Maman's closest confidants or Helene's friends. Poe wanted to wait for us to meet some of them in public.

She also surmised that this would put anyone who might be anxious about what I might know about Maman's plans on edge. As a result, I was exhausted by endless small talk and the sheer pressure of being around other people. Even alone in my room at night, I felt Poe, Skye, and Ashbourne acutely. It was as though I could hear their very breath and heartbeats, setting me to tossing and turning. Only Morpheus, who melted silently between the limen and the waking world, was gentle on my sensitive perception. Sometimes I didn't know he'd been sitting next to me until he purred, soothing my frayed nerves.

The days inched by slowly, as I did little more than sit quietly and speak in measured tones. But Poe insisted this was the way to meet all our aims. According to her, trying to eke information out of the highest echelons of society was something of a long game. Maman had often expressed similar opinions, though of course, her goals were different from ours.

Calling cards came in daily, the bowl in the hallway filled with more requests to meet with Maman's closest known associates, as well as a few names I did not recognize, but who Poe assured me were people we wanted to be interested in my return. I grew more restless with each passing day.

There was no word from Viridian, nor from any of Helene's set, and instead of relieving me, this made me even more anxious. Poe assured me that we were right on track—that all was unfolding exactly as we'd planned. Though, of course, this part was *her* plan. Even Skye had to admit that

Poe's insight into the upper echelons was far more nuanced than her own.

Ashbourne had little to say about it all, though we'd begun an ongoing game of Squires Spades, leaving our spread out on the table in Maman's study to return to in quiet moments. He told me about the books he read, even trying some of my recommendations and giving me his thoughts.

"Needs more romance," was his usual comment.

I found one of his favorites, *The Gentleman Rogue,* tucked in the basket I used to carry things with me between downstairs and the attic. Though I hadn't started it yet, a brief perusal proved that some passages were quite explicit. I wondered if this was an attempt at seduction, then dismissed the thought. We were simply sharing books with one another, and he enjoyed romances.

One morning at the beginning of the third week I'd been home, we took the morning off from callers at my request. We had been invited to one of the Institute for Research on Interstellar Life's exclusive luncheons—my first public event—and I needed peace to gather myself.

I was headed downstairs after dressing for the lecture when Ashbourne strode in the front door. He'd taken up the habit of a morning constitutional and had been gone an unusually long while. From what I could observe from the front windows, it had made him quite popular in a short time.

I couldn't blame the neighborhood for their interest. Dressed in Mme Laquoix's best, he was a sight to behold: every bit the polished gentleman, though nothing could alter the rugged beauty of his face or the sheer size of him. He was at least a head taller than most Vilhari, who were frequently taller than Oscarovi to begin with.

I couldn't help but think of the description of *The*

Gentleman Rogue's hero ravishing the heroine as I stared at him. I only realized I'd stopped on the stairs when he spoke. "The neighbors say Viridian has arrived at his town residence."

My chest tightened. So the game had changed. "We knew he'd return eventually."

Ashbourne nodded tersely. "And so he has."

He seemed to avoid my eyes entirely. *The Gentleman Rogue* was most definitely not a method of seduction then. Disappointment seeped around the edges of the thought, frustrating me. I took the last few steps of the staircase, moving through the entry hall into Maman's private sitting room, just off her study.

It was the coziest room in the house, decorated in plush cream velvet brocade curtains, with four matching chairs that sat in a circle in the middle of the room. I sank into a chair, waiting for Ashbourne to follow me, which he did. With a few whispered words, the hearth sprang to life. Ashbourne gave it a withering look, and likely for good reason. It was ostentatious, the marble carved with poisonous flora.

"What was your mother's obsession with poison?" Ashbourne asked, breaking the silence between us. His voice was warmer than before, and he leaned towards me, interest in his eyes.

It was so difficult to read him. Was it possible that like me, he was fighting the feelings he had? While I had a few sexual encounters in my past, there had never been romance. I had no idea how to discern what someone felt for me in a romantic sense.

It seemed better to leave all that alone, for now. I wasn't sure how to answer his question. There was the truth, and there was the story I told myself. I never had to tell anyone else, for no one ever dared ask, but I had comforted myself with lies as a child. For some reason, I decided on the truth. "She enjoyed murdering her enemies."

His reaction was unexpected. Ashbourne merely nodded, one eyebrow quirking upward. "A woman with ambition."

"Indeed," I agreed, glad that he did not appear overly sanctimonious about the admission. It wasn't that I defended Maman's predilection for murderous behavior, but I also saw no need to become hysterical over it. There was nothing I could have done to stop Vaness when she lived, and now there was no need to. "The decor, I presume, was to remind people of the fact that not only could she kill them, she was proud of it."

"Excellent," Ashbourne replied, his voice too dry to be anything other than earnest.

What an odd reaction, I thought. *It is almost as if he admires her*. There were plenty of points on which Maman deserved admiration, but combining her ambition and tendency towards murder as positive attributes was somewhat unusual.

Something out the window caught Ashbourne's eye and he stood. "Whatever *is* your neighbor doing?"

I rose to join him at the window, sighing deeply. The door leading to the garden was locked. I fished the house keys out of my pocket, unlocked the door and stepped out onto the terrace. Ashbourne followed me, a warm presence at my back.

"*Miranda.*" I kept my voice low and calm. "What's all this?"

The question wasn't necessary; it was quite obvious what Miranda Willsworth was doing. The pale Oscarovi was yanking on vines of the bittersweet that crept up the wall toward her own garden.

She startled when I spoke, then paled to a grayer shade of white. "*Wilhelmina*. I didn't think it was true."

Everything about Miranda was wan. Her face, her hair,

her expression—even her clothes. There was not a single interesting thing about her—unless you counted her sanctimonious attitude as interesting, which I did not.

"Didn't think what was true?"

I tried to keep my temper. One thing Maman and I had always agreed upon was that Miranda was a pain in the arse to live next door to. Honestly, I was surprised Maman hadn't poisoned *her* for all the times she'd meddled with her standing in the Royal Oscarovi Gardening Club over the years.

"Your bittersweet is out of control. It's getting into my garden," Miranda snapped, not answering me.

No matter; I knew what she meant. She didn't think I'd really returned, and she would have preferred it if I hadn't. This was her passive aggressive way of letting me know that she did not approve of me anymore than she had Maman.

Insufferable woman. I glared at her as she shoved her gardening shears into her apron and marched through the open gate between our gardens. "Get it taken care of, or I shall report you to the ROGC."

Before I could answer, she'd slammed the gate behind her.

"Did she just threaten to report you to a *gardening* club?" Ashbourne asked.

"Yes." I sighed again, turning to go back inside. It was the kind of thing Miranda was known for, and the ROGC did have an irritating amount of power amongst the Oscarovi high echelons, so it was something to be conscientious of. Before I knew what was happening, Ashbourne had me in his arms, flat against the deep doorframe.

"Stay quiet," he warned, turning my body so I faced the same direction he did, though his grip on my waist did not loosen. "Do you see them?"

Our view was of the street, as we were on the northside terrace of the house. A block down the street, two cityguard detectives made their way toward Orchid House. Though they were dressed in civilian clothing, as all detectives were, they wore brass eagles pinned to their lapels.

"They're coming here," he warned. "Go inside and warn Poe."

I nodded as he pushed me into the house and disappeared around the terrace, towards the back of the house. "Poe?" I called as quietly as I could.

Poe's dark head popped out from the parlor. "Are you nearly ready to go? The cab will be here shortly."

"Detectives," I breathed, my heart pounding too fast. "A block away."

Poe moved quickly, back into the parlor. I followed, feeling queasy. Something soft brushed the exposed ankles of my boots.

I looked down to find Morpheus at my feet, rubbing his face against my leg. *Fear not, Mina, we will not allow them to harm you.*

Poe looked up from the secretary desk, where she was gathering up her papers, and locked them inside the part of the desk that folded down. "Of course we won't let them harm her, why would you say something like that? Mina knows that."

The cat simply blinked at her, expression solemn as usual.

"Oh," Poe breathed. "*Oh.*"

I wasn't sure what Poe was realizing, but we didn't have time to discuss it. There were footsteps on the front steps. "What do I do?"

"Stay calm," Poe said. "Like you did with Niall. We knew they'd come—you're ready." She guided me towards a chair by the fire, placing one of Ashbourne's romances—not *The Gentleman Rogue*—in my lap, open to a page in the middle. "Read," she commanded. "Do not look up until after I announce them."

I did as I was asked, as well as I could anyway. My mind swirled with worry; knowing Viridian had paid off the detectives in Somershire, what might he do here? My eyes glided over the words on the page of Ash's book. It helped to think of him as Ash, like Skye and Morpheus did. Even Poe called him by the diminutive of his name now. My breath evened out, giving me the appearance of serenity. Morpheus flopped down at my feet, reclining on one massive side, so that his enormous bulk was on display.

He was bigger than most domestic canines, though he would not consent to being weighed, no matter how many times I'd pleaded. He appeared to be sleeping until Poe led the detective into the room.

"She's just in here, Detective Brenton."

Outside in the entry hall, I heard the sound of Skye chatting amiably with the other detective. They'd split them up somehow.

The detective made a small bow in my peripheral vision, but I still did not look up. Poe had not announced them yet. "Mina, this is Detective Brenton. She'd like to ask you a few questions."

Now I looked up, placing my right index finger inside the book as I closed it. I was grateful for it, as my hands had begun to shake, and clasping the book kept that from being visible. Poe really was three steps ahead in situations like these.

I inclined my head slightly towards the chair across from me. "Please, sit, Detective."

The Oscarovi woman sat, looking incredibly uncomfortable. She was a wiry thing, with dull blonde hair pulled into a severe bun at the top of her head, and a sour expression. "We've come to close your case, Mlle Wildfang."

"*Lady* Somerhaven," Poe corrected, her tone somehow sweet and sharp at the same time.

"Of course," Detective Brenton replied. "My apologies, Lady Somerhaven."

"It's quite all right," I said, keeping my voice low and soft, as Poe had instructed. "It is a change for me as well."

The detective, who had been staring nervously at her hands, looked up, a slight expression of surprise crossing her face. *Perhaps no one in the upper echelons has ever spoken to her with kindness*, I reasoned.

"Can we get you some tea?" I offered.

This too seemed to surprise the detective, flustering her a bit. "No, thank you. That is not necessary. I have a few questions for you before we can close your case."

Poe sat on the settee, pretending to take up a book of her own. Anyone who looked at her would think she was relaxed, and perhaps she was. After all, the Syndicate had said they'd taken care of the cityguard. But there was no telling who was working with whom in the corrupt organization, so being too sure of anything would be a mistake.

I made every effort not to look at Poe, but I couldn't help but see Morpheus, who opened his eyes now, stretching his paws out in front of him. His razor sharp claws shone in the firelight, and then he yawned, showing all of his teeth. The fey cat stretched as the detective watched him, horror growing on her face as she realized he was no mere housecat.

When he rubbed his face against my legs before turning twice to curl up at my feet, Detective Brenton's mouth fell open. The greymalkin were legendary for their vicious tricks, bargains that often ended in gruesome violence. Not many people had met one, but everyone had heard terrifying tales of deals gone wrong with the fey felines.

"Perhaps I can make things a little easier for you," I said when Morpheus had settled, glaring at the detective, even as he fell asleep. "As I'm sure you've heard, I remember very little about my time away. In fact, from what I understand, I don't remember the months leading up to my disappearance either."

Detective Brenton nodded, taking a notebook out of her jacket pocket. She jotted down a quick sentence or two, then looked up. "An oubliette could do something of the sort."

I had answered questions about where I'd been in myriad ways over the past few days, but no one had asked follow-up questions when I said I couldn't remember anything. In fact, most had reacted with nothing more than sympathy, seeming to like me more for what I'd been through. People often liked those they perceived as outsiders better when they thought they suffered.

I didn't allow my surprise to show. "I suppose you're right." My head tilted to the side, as I rested my chin on my hand, staring into the fire. "But so could any number of memory-altering rituals and spells, if someone were talented enough to complete them. We've spent the time since I was found searching my mother's library." I paused to turn my head slowly toward the Detective, making firm eye contact. "I am sure you already know about my mother's library."

Vaness' famed library contained records of some of the worst spells and rituals that the Oscarovi had ever successfully performed, many of which were now outlawed. Detective Brenton swallowed hard.

I raised my eyebrows, attempting an innocent expression. "I have none of my mother's interest in such things, of course. But you must understand that I've tried quite hard to find out what happened to me, and come to no conclusions."

The detective looked as though she wanted to ask a follow up question. She had the look of someone who needed the last word. I spoke before she did. "A good conk on the head might have done me in as well. I was covered in small wounds when I regained my senses, but of course, they all healed so quickly it is difficult to know what lasting damage there might be. I am afraid I have no answers for you."

The detective nodded once, looking disappointed. "We understand you have not yet met with Viridian Montclair."

This was not an unusual line of questioning, but it was beginning to seem a bit vigorous for detectives in Herself's pay. The truth was, we had no idea if the detectives were loyal to the Syndicate. Many took bribes with no loyalty in return. It was a dangerous game, but plenty played.

Best to be on guard. I let a small smile creep onto my face. Skye had noticed how unsettling it was the previous evening at dinner, and I was interested to try it out. Detective Brenton was clearly unnerved. Behind her, Poe hid a smile of her own.

"No," I answered. "I have not yet had the pleasure of seeing my brother-in-law." My hand flew to my mouth, my eyes gone wide. "I—I mean… He would have been, you know… If Helene had not…" I let myself trail off. I couldn't quite bring tears to my eyes through false emotion, but I hadn't had a second cup of tea yet. I suppressed the incoming yawn, the necessary tears welling in my eyes creating the convincing effect that this whole line of questioning upset me.

It had the desired effect. Detective Brenton appeared more uncomfortable than ever, and I got the distinct impression she wished she were anywhere but here. It was time for this conversation to end. Any member of the upper echelons would consider this all the information the cityguard would need.

I rose to indicate that I was finished with the encounter. "Is that all? We really must make ready to go. Our autocar will be here any moment, and I do hate to keep the driver waiting. You know they are on such tight schedules."

Detective Brenton nodded. "Of course, my lady. Thank you for your candor."

"Shall you close the case then? Since I have arrived home without harm, and am now in such good care?"

The detective hesitated. "Would you like us to close the case? If you feel yourself in danger…"

Was the detective actually concerned for me? I hesitated for the briefest of moments, but saw a hint of alarm in the way Poe's finger tapped against her thigh. Not concerned then, something else. Best to send her on her way then.

I smiled again, hoping it would have the same unnerving effect it had before. "I am in no danger now that I am back at Orchid House, and amongst those who care for me."

The detective glanced at Poe. "Have the two of you known each other long?"

This was most definitely a more aggressive line of questioning than most of the upper echelons would consider appropriate. Poe looked as though she would answer, but I wondered if it might be better if I did instead.

I kept smiling, my face aching with the effort, as I lightly touched the detective's elbow to guide her to the door. "No, though I wish we had. She is so good to me."

The detective looked a bit flummoxed, as though she wasn't sure how the tables had turned on her. The sickly sweet tone in my voice was nausea-inducing. But the character I had developed, the one I was forced to play to get the information we needed, would say such things. Over the past few days I'd seen the benefit of being perceived as wide-eyed and innocent. Tongues loosened, the usual wariness I was used to dissipating with every effortless-seeming kind word.

Though the detective seemed less dramatically affected by my feigned innocence, her shoulders relaxed a measure, as though something was confirmed for her that she'd suspected all along.

"Of course," Detective Brenton replied. "Unfortunately, because of Msr Montclair's claim that you'd been kidnapped, we are unable to close the case officially. But we will do our utmost to ensure that your privacy is respected."

I paused, widening my eyes a bit further. "Whatever do you mean?"

We stood in the doorway of the parlor now, and I saw that Skye had already ushered Detective Brenton's partner back out the front door. Though Poe stood behind me, my muscles tensed at the detective's statement.

"A member of the upper echelons was kidnapped, Lady Somerhaven. We can hardly appear not to take that seriously, glad as we all are that you have returned safely."

There wasn't time to think of how best to react. I let my face relax, hoping that dropping the smile would help me appear to take the cityguard's efforts at face value. "I appreciate that. Please keep us abreast of whatever you uncover."

The detective's pale eyebrows raised slightly as she stepped towards the door, which Skye held open for her now. "Of course, my lady. We would be happy to. Good day."

I inclined my head, but only slightly. "Good day, and thank you for coming." I turned before the detective could say another word. "Poe," I called out, injecting as much frivolous cheer into my voice as possible. "Is this what I'm wearing to the lecture?"

Poe matched my tone perfectly, warmth suffusing her answer. "I should think you'll need a coat, love."

I disappeared into the parlor as Poe shut the door behind her, my heart beating wildly. When the detectives had cleared off the front steps and retreated down the street, I spoke. "They weren't Edith's people, then?"

Poe shook her head, her mouth twisting thoughtfully as she made her way out of the parlor and down the back hallway towards the housekeeper's office, where we'd been keeping our coats. "Apparently not."

Skye met us there. "They weren't Edith's and they're not Viridian's either, though they're almost certainly on *someone's* payroll. We have another player in the game."

CHAPTER 21

MINA

The car pulled up, its driver a Strix woman dressed in the Braithwaite crew's signature tweeds. I'd begun to recognize the subtle patterns and textures of tweed that only Herself's people wore. Though I wasn't sure what they signified, it was a useful way to tell them apart from civilians.

Ashbourne was nowhere to be found. I hesitated as Skye handed Poe into the car, then held out her hand for me.

"He'll meet us there," Skye murmured to me when I took her gloved hand. As she said nothing else, I thought it better not to ask further questions.

The sunny autumn morning had clouded over, mist billowing up through the streets, out of the undercity, or rather the forest below the undercity. I glanced up at the skyway, watching the airships peek out of the clouds as they passed by. Seeing the sky at all still felt a bit overwhelming after the oubliette.

As Skye helped me into the car, my joints protested. The stress of the detectives' visit had aggravated me, apparently, and the rest of the day would be difficult as a result. I'd have to be careful not to speak too much at the lecture. The pain always brought my defenses up, and I would be liable to say something unpleasant if provoked.

Skye sat in front with the Strix driver, chatting amiably as they pulled away from the curb. Poe joined in from time to time, saving me from having to speak. The autocar wound up the narrow Pravhna streets, passing into posher neighborhoods than my own, where residences took up whole blocks, garden walls spilling over with explosions of autumn flowers.

When we passed into the university district, the buildings grew larger and more impressive. The mist had not yet reached this echelon, and up so far, the near-perpetual cloud cover was less intense. Up here, everything was brighter, but I was not so foolish as to let the atmosphere take me off guard.

Here, where the most powerful ruled, was where I must be the most careful. Everyone was a suspect now, and it would be foolish to assume anything but that the myriad ulterior motives of Pravhna's ruling classes would be on display. I barely registered the conversation happening around me, wondering instead where Ashbourne had gotten off to.

He was still a mystery to me, his mere presence a distraction. I had never been prone to flights of fancy when it came to romance, though I felt attraction for many. Early years of crushing social rejection had stopped me from believing I had a romantic future. Maman certainly had not made plans for me, focusing all her attention on Helene.

My sister hadn't cared for Viridian Montclair even one tiny whit. She'd been betrothed to him as nothing more than a power move, as most people of our class were. That was something Maman had no experience with. To have heard her tell it, Papa had been the love of her life, his death at sea a tragedy she never fully got over.

Maman and Helene still felt real. Present. Every day at Orchid House, I expected one of them to stalk through the front door or around a familiar corner and scold me. It was difficult to believe either were truly gone—that I'd never see them again. Hard as I'd tried to keep track in the oubliette, time had blurred, even when I'd had an accurate count of days. Being trapped in an unchanging hole, affected by the memory-altering magic, made it feel like I'd seen my family only days ago.

Next to me, Poe laughed at whatever the Strix driver had just said. I shifted uncomfortably as the autocar bounced over an uneven section of cobblestones. The streets were narrower here in the university district, making it harder to avoid rough spots in the road.

"Ack," the driver muttered. "Looks like there's a fair bit of congestion ahead. You'll be late for the lecture, I'm afraid."

Poe craned her neck to see, then pulled her watch from the pocket of her emerald gown. She'd unbuttoned her close-fitting frock coat. "We have a half hour until we need to take our seats."

"We're just two blocks away," I said.

Skye looked over her shoulder, into the back seat. "We ought to be dropped off at the front door, though, for propriety's sake."

I stifled a sigh. Propriety was a damn pain most of the time. Poe grinned though, pointing to the little shop out the window. "Problem solved. We'll get out here."

I leaned forward, trying to see what Poe pointed at. I wasn't familiar with this area of town, but the shop was new. Its sign was freshly painted and read "Armande's" in gold lettering. The driver pulled out of traffic and parked. Skye got out first, then helped Poe and me out. As I stepped out of the car, I saw what had attracted Poe's attention.

The most fashionable set of Oscarovi and Vilhari were crowded inside the shop, all of them sipping frothy concoctions. Behind a massive marble bar, a dozen attendants scooped ice cream into fluted pink glasses, topping it with various sodas, syrups, and whipped creams. Some of the liquid sparkled in glittering swirls, while others changed colors as the glasses were passed to patrons. Stands of oversized cupcakes towered on shelves behind the bar, and chandeliers dripping with jewels hung from the ceilings. It was no wonder so many were crowded inside. The place was a sugary fantasy come to life.

I scanned the crowd for familiar faces, only to find that I knew most of the people inside.

Many of Viridian and Helene's friends were among the crowd. My heart's pace picked up as we moved towards the door.

"Brace yourself," Poe warned as she took Skye's outstretched arm. "It'll be a viper's nest in there."

That was precisely what I was hoping for. Finally, it was time to confront them. As I trailed behind Skye and Poe, I composed myself. The ice cream parlor was packed tightly with Oscarovi in ostentatious hats and Vilhari who smelled of hothouses and imported perfume. I bumped into a winged Vilhar, dropping my bag. When I retrieved it, I was separated from Skye and Poe. I took a few steps forward as the crowd shifted. My entire body was abuzz with anticipation as the people who'd made me miserable my entire childhood came into view.

Caralee Ellis-Whitely and Rebecca Smytheson sat around a tall marble-topped wrought iron table, surrounded by sycophants. While this was not the group I suspected of knowing why I ended up in the oubliette, there was no love lost between any of us. I was about to walk over to them, several cutting remarks already playing in my head, when Viridian Montclair appeared in the crowd.

He wore an expertly tailored cerulean jacket, the color of a clear morning in the upper echelons. It stood out amongst the darker jewel tones of the season, a discordant note clanging against a symphony of well-practiced melody. The crowd seemed to contract with my severed breath, my lungs straining to take air in. My joints burned with pain, but I did not close my eyes against my mounting terror. There was nowhere to run, even if I wanted to, which decidedly, I did not.

He saw me at the same moment I saw him, and as we made eye contact a smirk haunted the corners of his lips. His arm slipped around Caralee's slender waist. Her dark brown hair was curled into ringlets, tied back with a saccharine looking pink bow. She gazed up at him adoringly, then followed his line of sight straight to me. Something darkened in Caralee's pale green eyes—an intelligence I would not have expected before the oubliette.

I had underestimated my sister's sometimes-friend, perhaps gravely. The two of them had vacillated between rivals and friends for years, the line between the two almost indistinguishable. Though I felt no protective loyalty towards Helene, something about Viridian's arm snaking around Caralee's waist troubled me.

The move was so obviously calculated. Viridian Montclair did nothing by happenstance, but what did this mean? I was nearly immobilized by the swarm of theories crowding my mind. It was as though my body refused to move until it had a plausible explanation for all of this. I was panicking.

Viridian whispered something to Caralee, then began to move through the crowded ice cream parlor. I took the opportunity to search out Skye and Poe, but they'd disappeared in the crowd. My heart thumped hard, but I steeled myself, refusing to move for Viridian Montclair.

It wasn't as though he could drag me out of here by force. Not even the high Vilhari houses had that kind of power, and House Montclair was a middling echelon at best.

Higher than the Wildfangs, but not above reproach, certainly. I spotted a sliver of his ostentatious cerulean coat the moment before he emerged from the crowd in front of me.

"A bit close in here, isn't it?" Viridian said with apparent ease. There wasn't a hint of worry in him. He knew that I knew what he'd done. There was no mistaking it in the smug smile that crept from his mouth alone, straight into his eyes. He leaned into me, his mouth grazing my ear as he kissed both my cheeks, and took my hands in his. "I'm sorry I wasn't able to get to you sooner."

It was an obvious threat, but a cleverly disguised one. I refused to allow myself to give into the fever pitch of fear that blossomed in me like Maman's deadliest flowerbed.

Viridian squeezed my hands so tightly I nearly gasped, caught completely off guard. Why hadn't I expected him to behave exactly this way? Perhaps it was that he'd always seemed a bit off-kilter, like he could never quite find his footing in social situations. As difficult as he was, I'd always felt empathy for his situation.

I had been wrong. Wrong about Caralee. Wrong about Viridian. Wrong about so many things. My hands were clammy in his, but I couldn't yank them away. People were watching. My voice abandoned me, along with all the things I'd planned to say to him. I'd rehearsed dozens of biting remarks, clever things I yearned to say to put him in his place, to force him to understand that I would have vengeance for what he'd done.

And now, the moment had come, and he had the upper hand. His grip on me tightened as he straightened up, looking down on me, his cold eyes imperious. "You should have waited for me in the country, Wilhelmina. There was no need for you to travel alone."

A warm hand spread across the small of my back, and a familiar voice rumbled through me. "There you are, love."

Someone pressed a kiss to the top of my head. I tensed for a brief moment, and then my body came unfrozen. Viridian let go of my hands as Ashbourne pulled me into his side. The feeling of his body against mine was comforting and distressing all at once. "So sorry I'm late. Who's this?"

"Viridian Montclair," I replied, using every effort to keep my voice steady as I leaned into Ashbourne. "Helene's betrothed."

Viridian flushed, and behind him, in the distance, Caralee fumed. So they *were* together now. "We have much to discuss, Wilhelmina. We should go somewhere private."

It was a slight not to introduce himself to Ashbourne, but Viridian wasn't known for his manners. Ashbourne's fingers pressed into my flesh, soothing in their unexpected familiarity. The touch radiated through the base of my spine and deep within the recesses of my body. My confidence returned.

"Do we?" I asked, keeping my voice light and sweet. "I understand you handled things with Somerhaven after the fire. I haven't seen Maman's lawyer yet. Do we have affairs of some sort to settle?"

It was a polite way of implying that I suspected him of asking for money. Around us, the crowd tensed. Among this set, there was nothing more vulgar than to discuss finances.

Viridian flushed again. "Of course not."

My eyes landed on Caralee's right hand ring finger. The smile everyone found so unsettling found its way to my lips without effort. I lowered my voice, but not by much as I locked onto the enormous sapphire ring Caralee wore. The entire crowd followed my gaze. Caralee's face flushed beet red, and her hand disappeared under the table.

"What an interesting choice of engagement rings," I

murmured softly, putting the subtlest bit of quivering sadness into my voice. There were a few sympathetic murmurs. Ashbourne's hands pressed gently into my back, encouraging me.

"It is a family ring, Wilhelmina. You know that," Viridian spat. I had him off-kilter now.

"Was she wearing it? When you—when she—" I made a show of burying my face in Ashbourne's chest, his arms going around me immediately.

"Oh, Mina," he murmured, as though he spoke just to me. As though the entire shop wasn't hanging on our every word. "Love, don't cry."

I pressed my face against the hard muscles of his chest, my shoulders shaking with hidden laughter. Around us, people whispered, clearly swallowing my supposed grief whole.

I caught only one comment, but it soared through my thoughts. "Do you think he washed it before he gave it to Caralee?"

That brought another round of laughter on, so much that tears streamed down my face. I composed myself and drew my head away from Ashbourne, looking up into his golden eyes.

There was a glimmer of amusement behind his stony mask. The corner of his mouth twitched slightly. He was enjoying this as much as I was. He drew a handkerchief from his jacket pocket and dabbed at my face.

"Beautiful as ever," he whispered.

There were nearly audible swoons, and one "Who is *he?*" in the crowd. We had to stop. It was tempting to twist the knife further, do more damage to both Caralee and Viridian, but Poe had cautioned me against too many public theatrics. The upper echelons had no trouble turning shows of emotion against the unwitting.

I took a big deep breath, making it obvious I was calming myself before turning to Viridian, though I made eye contact with Caralee. "My apologies. I only miss Helene. All my warmest congratulations to you both."

It was the right thing to do, and I hoped wherever she was in the crowd, Poe was proud. I daren't look for her, though. The rage in Viridian's eyes was like nothing I'd ever seen. Ashbourne's every muscle sprang to life, tensed with readiness. I half expected him to throw me behind him. Viridian's fury was obvious.

"You will regret this," he hissed in a voice so low no one could hear him but Ash and me.

Now, suddenly, he was Ash, not Ashbourne. Something had shifted between us, the alteration both imperceptible and monumental at the same time. As if he read my mind, Ash pulled me tighter into his body, his arm snaking around my waist in such an intimate way the world nearly fell away. My breath stopped in my lungs, fluttering like a wet, newborn thing.

"Use caution, friend," Ashbourne warned, using the same low tone. "People are watching."

The ice cream parlor was silent now, everyone openly hanging on the drama of every breath that passed between us.

"Just who do you think you are?" Viridian sneered. "Have you even a House, Vilhar?"

It was an insult amongst the Vilhari to suggest they had no lineage, but Ash did not so much as react. He only smiled. I enjoyed the way my diabolical smile made others uncomfortable, but this—this was something else. The finely planed angles of Ash's rugged face smoothed into something stately, cold, and deadly all at once.

A marble hallway lined with statues, the smell of cypress trees and bergamot carried on a hot breeze, flashed in my mind. It was only a moment, but I was transported to somewhere else. I tried to grasp onto the memory, emblazon it onto my conscious mind so I wouldn't forget—and then I was thrown back into the present moment, as though I never left.

Movement in the crowd stopped Ash from answering as Elspeth Aestra strode forward. Viridian's face smoothed into something more pleasant almost instantly as Skye's mother, revered surgeon and pillar of Vilhari society, placed a hand on Ashbourne's arm.

"Darling," she crooned, in a vibrant, musical voice. "Wherever is my daughter?"

Near the till, the sound of someone clearing their throat caused everyone to turn their heads. "Right here, Mother."

"Perfection," Elspeth remarked as she took my arm. "We must be on our way, I'm afraid, Viridian. Tell your mother I said hello when next you write to her."

Viridian bowed, retreating in a huff. Conversations started again. Elspeth's grip on my arm was too tight as she guided me towards the door. In the crowd, I saw Skye and Poe making their way in the same direction.

"It is good to see you, Wilhelmina," Elspeth said as she dragged me through the crowd. "We will be late for luncheon if you do not hurry, though."

I opened my mouth to explain that we were going to the lecture, but Elspeth Aestra's face was so stern I dared not speak. Outside the ice cream parlor, a grand white Studevale stood idling. It was the most beautiful autocar I had ever seen. A tall Vilhari with the wings of a red-tailed hawk stood waiting next to it.

Skye and Poe hurried out of Armande's after us. "What are you doing here?" Skye whispered.

"Get in the car, dearest," Elspeth said again, speaking at a normal volume. She laughed as though wrangling an unruly child, as she kissed her daughter's cheeks. "It seems you've forgotten our luncheon engagement today."

Skye raised an eyebrow. "My apologies, Mother."

Elspeth's eyes slid to Poe. "Mlle Endymion, how lovely to see you. Please, do join us."

Poe made the tiniest little bow, a show of reverence for Mme Aestra's high rank. "Thank you, your grace."

There was a twinkle in the surgeon's eye that I liked, but Skye practically glowered as we got into the back of the autocar. It was a crowded fit, with me squeezed between Ashbourne and Poe, Skye and her mother sitting opposite us.

When the driver pulled away from the curb, Elspeth's smile faded. "Niall is missing."

CHAPTER 22

ASHBOURNE

Skye flounced back on the bright white leather upholstery of the Studevale, rolling her eyes. She was the picture of teenage angst, and it struck a protective note in me. My partner so rarely appeared young or vulnerable, but she had reverted to some childlike state in her parent's presence, and it brought worry upon me. There was much left unresolved between them, and being drawn suddenly back into family business would not help the situation. Skye was bound to be upset, even if her mother's arrival had rescued us from what was about to be an uncomfortable standoff in the ice cream parlor.

"Mother, *please*," Skye whined. "Niall's off somewhere with his cronies, like always."

"He is not," Elspeth said with crisp surety. "He went missing shortly after he visited Orchid House. I've had him tailed for some time, but my man lost him." She glared at the driver, who glanced apologetically in the rearview mirror.

Skye sat back, her expression melting from incredulous to professional. I'd seen that look hundreds of times—it always meant there was a development in a case, that the knots Skye was unraveling were making sense to her at long last. "Why did you have Niall followed?"

Elspeth Aestra's silvery-blue eyes filled with tears. Tears that, I was certain, were at least partially manufactured. From everything Skye had ever told me, Elspeth was too controlled to cry in front of strangers unless she wanted to—and she thought it was to her advantage. "I made a mistake, my darling. You were right, I should have stopped Niall from joining the cityguard."

Apparently, Skye agreed with me about Elspeth's demeanor. "Oh, cut the tears, Mother. It's not necessary. I agree that Niall being missing is important." She locked eyes with me, a question there.

I knew instantly what she needed. We'd developed an unspoken shorthand in the past year. "We'll look into your son's disappearance, Madame."

Next to me, Mina shifted a tiny bit to look at Poe, who cleverly had no reaction at all. Even the slightest movement of Mina's body set mine alight. I was far too attuned to her, but Viridian's confrontation had awakened something within me I couldn't deny much longer. The closer we got, the more danger she was in.

To stay clear, I'd need to untangle what made her so alluring, but Mina was difficult for me to understand. It was a mistake to think she was innocent. Mina was as mercurial as Poe, changing as needed to fit the scene she was cast in. However, unlike Poe, whose resilience appeared to spring from an endless well, Mina tired of any ruse quickly, her base nature overriding whatever part she was playing.

I had to wonder if that was part of the attraction. Where I'd tamped every bit of me I didn't want to confront down, she was still free, still wild in a way I couldn't quite identify. Privately, I thought our strategy should be to play into that. Whatever lay beneath the veneer of sweet society ingénue ought to be let out. Every time her lips curled into that terrifying little smile, heat lashed through me. I wanted to see more of that, more of her strength—whether for my own selfish reasons, or that of the mission, I couldn't yet say.

I was so lost in thinking about Mina, I'd failed to track the conversation Skye and her mother were having. Things had grown heated in my inattentive moments. "I don't know what you want me to do, Mother," Skye sighed. "I'm working on an important case, and I can't just drop everything to look for Niall."

"I know what you're working on," Elspeth said, her voice barely louder than a whisper.

Next to me, Mina shivered slightly, her eyes drifting to mine sidelong. *Do not become so distracted you fail to protect her*, a voice inside me cautioned.

"A small group of us has been tracking the movements of this 'Chopard' for some time," Elspeth said, smoothing an invisible wrinkle from the skirt of her directoire-style gown.

Skye sat forward as the car slowed to a halt. We'd stopped in front of a rather nice hotel, The Palais. Nice for people like me and Skye, but for people like Elspeth, practically invisible in the scheme of things. It was neither fashionable, nor run down. It was indistinct, the perfect place for a clandestine meeting. Despite how people often behaved in the mysteries I'd read, places like this were far better for secret goings-on than seedy back alleyways and places of ill repute.

"We've connected Chopard's movements to Wilhelmina's return," Elspeth said. Mina sat forward, Poe went on high alert, and Skye gritted her teeth with obvious frustration.

"How?" Skye demanded.

"Yes," Mina added, her voice deadly soft as Elspeth's. "I'd like to know the same thing."

Elspeth shook her head. "We do not have time for this now. The four of you have an appointment with Muse."

That explained how they'd connected Chopard to Mina. Whoever Elspeth was working with, they must be doing something the seer agreed with. Muse didn't work with cratties, unless he had a very good reason. Skye had always trusted Muse, which was good enough for me.

Fury brought color to Skye's cheeks, though I saw a flicker of relief in her eyes at the mention of Muse's name. Like me, she'd already reasoned that if Muse was willing to help then her mother likely wasn't up to something evil. Though perhaps Skye already assumed that. I hadn't even the barest hint of memory or feelings about my own parents and thus had trouble empathizing. I tensed in her defense, but she didn't need my aid. "If you think I'm going to simply go along with whatever you say without question—"

Elspeth leaned toward her daughter, taking her hands. "Skyeling, I would never assume something so foolish. You've had a mind of your own since the moment you drew breath. Don't you see, my darling? You can move in places I cannot. House Aestra needs you more than ever." It surprised me to hear the sincerity in Elspeth's voice, and I was not so jaded as to immediately suspect her of manipulation.

Perhaps that would be a mistake in any other circumstance, but I knew the kind of loyalty Skye inspired. That had to come from somewhere, and I suspected it came from the kernel of decency I detected in Elspeth Aestra. "I know you think I've been irresponsible with your brother, my politics, and probably hundreds of other things. But if you've ever trusted my heart, please know I want the things you want. I want to see things get better, rather than worse."

Everyone in the car hung on Elspeth's words, waiting to hear how Skye would react, myself included. I would go any direction she chose, follow her down any path she picked out.

After what felt like millennia, she nodded once. "Our methods will never be the same, but I believe that much. Shall I ask for Grandmother at the front desk then?"

"No need," Elspeth said with an expression that bore lines of relief. "We chose The Palais because it has private tea rooms."

That phrase seemed to mean something to Skye, who nodded, resigned somehow. What was that about?

Poe too seemed to pick up on what I had, though I couldn't discern from her vague expression what reaction she was having, and then her face changed. The nick of understanding morphed into an earnest smile. "I see where you get your confidence from," she said, looking first at Elspeth, then to my partner. Pleasure shone in Poe's eyes as she gazed at Skye. For a short moment, I wondered if the world would stop turning, just for them.

A little smile crept onto Elspeth Aestra's face as she looked between her daughter and the tiny fey woman opposite her. She suspected what the rest of us did then: the two of them were in love. My chest tightened with emotion at the prospect of Skye's happiness. There was nothing I wanted more than for her to be loved and cared for in every way she could have it.

"Muse and your grandmother both are in the Opal Tearoom. Tell the concierge," Elspeth commanded.

"You're not coming?" Mina asked.

Elspeth shook her head. "No, I have another engagement I must get to. I will call on you, though, later this week. As my daughter is residing with you, it would be strange if I did not."

Rubbish, I thought to myself. She's been shunning Skye for months. This was apparently our signal to leave the autocar though. Skye nodded and got out, helping Poe as she went. I followed suit and helped Mina onto the brick sidewalk in front of the Palais' front gates.

"She's giving us a gift," Poe murmured to Mina as they linked arms. "Her calling on you will open the upper echelons to us."

Mina nodded, obviously understanding what this would mean. Her family name certainly had status, but not like that of House Aestra, which rubbed elbows with the old aristocracy, the last of the Vilhari high courts. Rumor had it in the undercity that House Aestra had been consul to the Court of Aether's queen. Elspeth Aestra was granddaughter to the second-in-command on the Avalonne, the ship that brought the Vilhari to Sirin. Turning the information over in my mind brought up the uncomfortable feeling that always arose when I had cause to think of the Vilhari's history. It should feel like *my* history, the proud history of my people, but more than ever, it did not.

As I followed the women into The Palais, my gut twisted into knots. I had never allowed Muse to read me. I didn't want to know who I was before, or what I was looking for. My steps faltered, my body hesitating. Skye cast a look over her shoulder, immediately knowing I'd fallen behind. Her mouth opened to speak, but soft fur brushed my pant leg.

Morpheus materialized fully, finally deciding to join us. He said nothing, as was his way, but his bulk against my leg was a comfort. There was a plea in Skye's eyes I could not ignore. She needed me, not just to come with her now, but to stay the course and keep my promises to both her and Morpheus. Those promises spoken and unspoken were a comforting weight on my heart, the core of what kept me grounded. My feet moved quickly once more, as long strides caught me up to my friends.

I will not turn away now, I promised myself. *This is my family.*

CHAPTER 23

MINA

Behind us, I felt it deep in my sense of spatial awareness when Ashbourne paused. I nearly turned, but Poe's pace did not slow. She didn't have the same sense for her surroundings that I did, nor the odd connection I'd formed with Ashbourne. *Why was he hesitating? What worried him?*

I longed to turn and ask him, but I kept stride with Poe. Skye fell a half step behind us as Poe greeted the Oscarovi who manned the doors. When Ashbourne's footsteps renewed, relief fluttered in my chest. I shook my head to clear it, focusing instead on the lobby of the hotel. It was modestly but tastefully decorated. Dark wood paneling on the walls echoed the coffered ceilings, which dripped with crystal chandeliers.

An enormous marble podium served as a front desk, and the concierge looked up as we approached. The chestnut-haired Vilhari was dressed in a serviceable gray wool pantsuit, tailored to the generous curves of her body. Her brown skin shone with either well-applied cosmetics or good humor. Perhaps she was simply talented with glamour. Whatever it was, it had a nice effect that I wouldn't mind learning.

"Mlle Aestra," she said in greeting. "Your grandmother awaits you in the Opal Room. Do you know the way?"

Skye nodded. "I do, thank you."

This was a place of discretion then, no unnecessary pomp and circumstance. Of course, I knew there were a handful of places like this all over the city, bland enough to never catch anyone's attention, but clean and discreet. Maman had used such establishments frequently in the last years of her life, but I never knew what she was up to.

Poe squeezed my arm, as though to confirm my previous thoughts. Elspeth Aestra was intimidating, but very good at whatever she was playing at. *No, not playing*, I thought. Whatever the head of House Aestra was up to, it was nothing so inexpert as playing.

Skye led us down a narrow hallway behind the front desk. Tall, heavy doors were staggered on both sides of the hall, each with a gold placard next to the door naming the room. No sound emanated from any of the doors, but vaguely, I sensed occupants in many of the rooms we passed. There was a heaviness in the air I could not identify, as though gravity were different here. I had the heady sense for a moment that I could feel the earth beneath the hotel, pregnant with some massive power, vibrating beneath the surface.

Tempted as I was to dismiss this as foolishness, I was learning to trust my gut more. These impressions rarely led me astray, so long as I kept an open mind about what they might mean. I glanced back at Ashbourne, who appeared to note something in the atmosphere, as I did. His eyes lingered at the door of a room labeled, "The Emerald Room."

"The sound-proofing spells are excellent," he murmured as I fell back to walk alongside him. It was almost a reflex now, and not just because it was obvious that Poe and Skye wanted a moment alone.

Our performance in the ice cream parlor had shifted

things between us. While I knew he was playing a part we'd agreed to, there was no ruse to it. We hadn't agreed to act as though there were a romantic relationship between us. The way he'd acted, not to mention the way I'd responded—the way my body had responded—there was no doubt in my mind that was real. I wanted him, and there seemed very few reasons not to indulge if he wanted me as well.

Would it be a distraction? Possibly, but also, I was wise enough to know that if I did not inject a bit of pleasure into my life, my senses might deaden from stress. Yes, to keep sharp, it might be just the thing to let Ashbourne in a bit more. It was more than that, and I knew it, but it helped to tell myself that a bit of physical release was all I sought.

Poe and Skye murmured to one another as they fell in step. The hallway felt endless, and my legs ached with the effort of walking, even on a flat surface. I'd slowed down considerably, but Ashbourne matched my pace. The way he moved when I did, as though in perfect choreography, brought heat to my belly, gathering in my core. What would it be like to be alone together? To move this way, in perfect call and response to one another, in bed? The possibilities were tantalizing, cutting through the pain I was in.

The toe of my boot caught on the carpeted floor. I barely stumbled, righting myself easily, but the jolt sent pain lashing through my joints. He didn't offer his arm, or even look askance at me, but his body oriented towards mine, ready to catch me.

"I will not fall," I said, my tone curt. It felt as though he'd read my mind, the images of all the ways we might please one another dancing in my head as I considered allowing myself respite from all this pain. "There is no need to prepare yourself for a swoon."

A smirk lifted a corner of his lips. "I shouldn't think so. *You* would never swoon."

The tone of his remark was familiar, as though he knew me well. *Had our short time together been enough for such familiarity?* To my surprise, my lips quirked in reflection. "I would not."

"But you are in pain," he added, his voice even and deep, without a hint of condescension.

"Yes," I admitted. There was no use in denying it.

Ahead of us, Skye and Poe rounded a corner at a divide in the hallway. Try as I might, I could not hurry my steps. I'd done too much the past few days, and the increased activity was catching up with me.

"They will wait for us," Ashbourne reassured me.

There was a glimmer in his eyes, an expression that seemed reserved for me. His eyes didn't light in the same way for Skye or Poe. His actions and countenance let me know he cared for Skye and Morpheus, rather deeply, in fact. But between us there was something else—something deeper than the heat that gathered between my legs—something that keened and growled just beyond the surface of my conscious mind.

Ash has a talent for making people feel safe, Morpheus said as he materialized near my feet. *But he rarely uses it.*

I couldn't respond, the greymalkin's observation nearly stopping me in place. *Was that what this was?* We rounded the corner to find Skye and Poe waiting for us, just like Ashbourne had said they would. They stood in front of a plaque that read "The Opal Room." Skye nodded as we caught up to them and then knocked.

The door swung open under her touch, revealing a staircase cut from opal, its pale fire revealed by the aetheric glow from ornate gold wall sconces. The walls were gilded as well, a sharp contrast to the more sedate appearance of the hotel.

Ashbourne shared a meaningful glance with Skye who nodded once. "This is part of things here. Each 'tea room' is set up this way. You'll see why."

Not even a hint of surprise crossed Poe's face. She was cool as ever. Had she been here before? I wouldn't put that past her. There was so much about her I still didn't know, and she held information close. At the very least, if she knew what to expect, then we were unlikely to be walking into an ambush or other trouble.

There is nothing to worry about, I told myself. Until I looked down at the staircase. My jaw clenched, frustration mounting. *Why must things always be so difficult?*

The stairs were polished to a high sheen. They would be slippery. The soles of my pretty boots were not built for my stability, and sharp pain already shot through my feet. I had no doubt that someone would catch me, should I fall, but the embarrassment of such an occurrence was more than I could comprehend at the moment.

Poe had already followed Skye downward, their soft conversation drifting up to me, though it was muffled as they descended the staircase. Morpheus, as usual, had already disappeared. Ashbourne waited for me though, watching me hesitate with brows furrowed. He glanced down at the slick staircase, then at my shoes. His arms stretched out towards me, an offer of help.

I opened my mouth to protest, but he shook his head, his eyes soft as his fingers stretched towards mine. I took one step down and my knees wobbled. The steps were too much for my terrible balance. Ash took another step back up the stairs. He was as steady as could be. There wasn't a hint of pity in him, only the silent promise that I would get down the stairs without injury or embarrassment.

He lifted me, turning without even so much as a quiver in his muscles. I expected another of those wicked smirks of his, as though he'd won something. But I was surprised. Ash's face was calm, concentrated even. This was not a seduction, or a game to determine which of us had the most power. It was a simple offer of help. He was strong and steady enough to carry me, and I was unable to descend the slick stairs without trouble.

This was kindness, I realized. A kind of protectiveness I wasn't used to. The kind that sought to shield from harm, rather than control. I was glad then that I did not have to walk on my own because the thought of such generosity of spirit was dizzying.

He'd carried me before. This time, I was fully present, and able to feel the increased pace of his heart, thumping against my hand, which was pressed to his chest. My cheeks burned with the sensation of being so closely perceived. In response, I tucked my chin to my chest and closed my eyes, grateful for the assistance, but fighting shame for needing it.

Near the bottom of the stairs, Ashbourne turned, setting me down slowly so that I wouldn't slip. Immediately, I was sure I would have fallen had I attempted to go it alone. My feet ached too much as I stepped down, taking his outstretched hand for stability, the joints in my knees and hips burning.

When my boots touched the rough stone at the bottom of the staircase, my knees buckled, catapulting me into Ashbourne's hard chest. He righted me without so much as a word, his breath hitching as his fingers closed around my waist. So he wasn't so unaffected by my presence. I looked up as he pulled me against him, heat pooling first in my chest, then sinking lower and lower still as his eyes dilated.

"Are you steady?" he asked.

"No," I answered honestly, but it had nothing to do with the pain rushing through me, swirling amongst the blaze of desire lit within my core.

Ashbourne swallowed hard. "Nor am I."

His head dipped slightly, and my lips parted as though by instinct, my back arching into him as one of his arms snaked around my waist, pinning me to him. My breath came in sharp gasps as his hand rose toward my cheek, his thumb grazing my jawline. His face was so ruggedly handsome it was almost painful to look at, as though carved from the finest marble. Even now, he didn't smile, though his lips curved, sensuous in a way that did nothing to cool the flames of desire licking at every sensitive nerve in my body.

Steps brought us both back to the moment, and Ash's grip on me slowly loosened. "You are a beautiful distraction," he murmured as Skye came into view behind him.

"Everything all right?" she asked, her voice a little too bright, eyes sparkling with the light of someone who knows a delicious secret.

"Quite," I answered, my voice high and shrill.

Skye hid a smile as she turned. "This way."

As we followed, my eyes adjusted to the dim light. The sound of water falling filled my ears. It was not a trickle, nor a burbling stream, but the sound of a rushing waterfall. The stone beneath my feet was rough, and though the walls surrounding us were smooth, I could see they'd been carved into rock.

"Are we underground?" I murmured, half to myself. The path was lit by lavender bioluminescent lichen and fungi from below, and some kind of glowworm from above.

"Yes," Skye whispered back, her voice reverent in the dark. "This place is special."

It was indeed. The path widened into a garden that opened up onto a terrace made from a pale white stone. On each side of the terrace, intricately carved arched doorways flanked the common space. Beyond the terrace, graceful skyways crossed the cavern, carved in similar patterns. Lush plant life sprung from window boxes and common spaces alike, scenting the humid cavern with petrichor and perfume.

From somewhere deep inside the cavern came a dim

glow of some artificial light, though aetheric power did not fuel it. There was no telltale hum of the aether, only the quiet sounds of water and faraway music. On some terrace I couldn't make out, someone played a harp quite expertly.

We were not alone.

There was an entire city here, underneath the hotel. The architecture was familiar to me, similar to what the high echelons of Vilhari society preferred, but much more intricate. Witchlight lanterns glowed with soft golden light from within the buildings—and in the distance, I could make out a few dark figures, here and there. This place was far from abandoned.

"What is this?" Ashbourne breathed.

Skye smiled. "The wreck of the Avalonne."

I frowned. "How is that possible? This is a city."

"*Part* of a city. The rest of the ship was destroyed in the crash." Skye's eyes widened with sadness as she gestured towards what was left. "This is how my people traveled the stars."

I had seen models of the Avalonne, renderings of what the great ship the Vilhari arrived in four thousand years ago might have looked like. They were nothing like this. Nothing even close to this scale, magnitude, or beauty.

A sliver of unnerving realization skittered up my spine. If this city was only part of the ship the Vilhari had traveled in, the Oscarovi were lucky that they had not wanted to crush us, but only live together in relative peace. When the Ventyr came to conquer Sirin, all that changed. We saw the power the Vilhari had, and we had to adapt.

A shadow of memory danced at the edges of my mind, teasing me. I walked to the edge of the terrace, resting against a stone balustrade so I could crane my neck downward. Waterfalls spilled through arched stone ducts that looked to be made specifically for such use. The memory eluded me, refusing to emerge, but something about this place made whatever came before the fetch feel closer—more tangible.

I chased my thoughts backward, as Ashbourne spoke about the ship with Poe and Skye—back to the Ventyr—another race of winged people, though very different from the Vilhari in many ways. Papa had been a scholar of their ways, studying the stories they left behind after their invasion, until his death. I'd learned much about them as a child, from his books in Orchid House, and now my mind wandered, wondering what that had to do with me.

But it was no use—the memory slipped out of my grip, leaving only the spectacular view of the Avalonne. The impression that I'd almost touched an answer to all that was missing lingered, bitter in my mouth.

"Come," Skye said, touching my arm lightly. "My family's quarters are this way."

CHAPTER 24

MINA

House Aestra's "quarters" were nothing short of a small mansion. Inside, the structure was made of the same white stone as the rest of the city. Furnishings were sparse, but spare in nature, a contrast to the intricately carved stone.

Skye led us to a curved room that looked to be positioned directly under the spillway of an enormous waterfall. The water roared softly behind an invisible barrier. No stray droplets marred the floors under the arched windows that looked out onto the waterfall and the Avalonne. The walls on the opposite end of the room were covered in various mosses and lichens, some glowing softly in the dim light of the room.

Golden orbs danced just below the domed ceiling, which was painted to look like the night sky. The constellations surprised me—they were none I was familiar with. An enormous round table, cut from the same stone as the city itself, sat centered beneath the dome. Two tall figures sat across from one another amongst the many chairs. Skye pulled out a chair for Poe and she sat. Ashbourne held another out for me, and I sunk into it, grateful to finally be off my feet.

On one side of the table sat Mirabelle Aestra, the head

of House Aestra and Skye's grandmother. Though we'd never been formally introduced, she was familiar to me. As the head of one of the high houses of Pravhna's elite Vilhari, everyone knew her. Mirabelle's shining white hair hung long down the back of her midnight blue gown. Her skin was the same moonstone-pale as Skye and Elspeth's, and she was rail-thin, like Elspeth.

There were fine lines around her eyes, the only sign that she was aging. And yet, I knew she was nearly four thousand years old. She was born here on Sirin, shortly after the Avalonne's demise. The sheer length of her life was astounding. Oscarovi could live to be a thousand, but it was rare, and we were mere husks of people by that age. I swallowed hard, wondering what the longevity of the fetch would be like.

"Welcome to Avalonne," Mirabelle said as we settled into our seats. "Are you all acquainted with Muse?"

The others nodded, but I had never met the man sitting across from Mirabelle Aestra. He was tall, dressed in crisp white shirtsleeves and a dove gray waistcoat that matched his well-tailored pants and the frock coat that hung on the back of his chair. A sparkle of cosmetics on his rich brown skin caught the witchlight, his tawny eyes shining mischievously at the sight of us. He was a head taller than me, even seated. His arms and shoulders were heavily muscled, and his waistcoat fit his soft middle perfectly. Muse's ebony locs were braided in a thick multi-strand plait that hung down his back, showing his arched ears.

"Hello," he greeted us, then nodded once to Mirabelle as he rose from his chair, walking towards the arched end of the room, near the windows that looked out on the waterfall. As he went, his footsteps grew softer; the closer he went to the waterfall, the less I heard.

"Skye, would you go first?" Mirabelle asked. "While I explain things to your friends."

THE HOLLOW PLANE

Skye bowed her head, then got up from her chair and joined Muse by the windows. When she joined him, I could see their mouths moving, but no sound reached me. Something at that end of the room silenced all conversation.

Mirabelle smiled, a serene expression, but severe as well. When she spoke, her words seemed directed at Poe. "What do you know of the Court of Winds?"

Poe's face did not move a muscle. "Only that the Courts were a part of the old world, but not this one."

Mirabelle's smile was practically feral now. *What was this about?* "Come now, Hippolyta."

A snarl so vicious it startled me came out of Poe. She stood, tiny and imperious. "What is the meaning of this?"

At the other end of the room, Muse held Skye's hands in his, their faces calm, eyes closed in concentration. The contrast between the two scenes at play simultaneously was jarring. Something about this was wrong—my heart beat faster, empyrae flaring to life within me, in defense of my friend. Under the table, a hand curled around my knee, warm and firm. I glanced at Ashbourne, whose face was stone, but his eyes burned. The message was clear: *stay put*.

"Don't worry, little Strider," Mirabelle said. "Your secret is safe with me. Not even my daughter knows."

I didn't have to know what Mirabelle was talking about to know she was threatening Poe. Fury rose in my heart, gripping me like a vise. My fists clenched as Ashbourne's grip on my knee tightened, sending a pulse of warmth straight into the apex of my thighs.

This was no time to imagine that hand creeping higher—and yet... *What would it be like to have Ashbourne's fingers on my bare skin?* My mind wandered, merciless in its imagination. In the very real present, his palm moved, inching upwards by only a fraction of an inch, but my breath hitched slightly.

Heat pulsed in my core, all my focus on where I

wanted his hand. My eyes slid to his face, where the faintest curve of a smirk played on his wicked lips. It did me no good to see it, for then my imagination went wild with what it might feel like to have his mouth on me. He was distracting me—he'd felt my power flare to life —*but how?*

In my second sight, a vision flashed—*a dark head, buried between my thighs. Cries of pure ecstasy tumbling from my lips as my fingers gripped the hair of that head, pressing fangs deeper into my flesh.* The vision broke, my eyes swiveling to Ashbourne's face. Though his expression had not changed, something in his eyes shifted, desire replaced with fear.

I flinched away from his touch, his hand retreating. His fear at whatever had passed between us infected me. So much so that I didn't notice when he left, and that Skye was back in her seat. Time moved strangely, and the vision played over in my head, getting blurrier each time I tried to remember it, as though a barrier had been erected in my mind. It was as though I'd gotten too close to something, and now it retreated from me with unsettling speed.

Muse approached the table, leaving Ashbourne by the windows. "Poe," he said, nodding. "Has anything changed since last we met?"

Poe shook her head. "It has not." She offered her hand to him, and he took it, closing his eyes for a moment. When he opened them, his mouth turned down slightly. "I am sorry, love."

Her chin wavered only slightly, then clenched. "I expected as much." She turned to Mirabelle. "What do you hope to accomplish with all of this?"

Ashbourne stepped towards the table, but did not sit down again, avoiding my eyes, locking his gaze firmly upon Mirabelle. This told me that while he trusted Muse, he did *not* trust Mirabelle Aestra. Skye's ears pinked at the tips, as though she were embarrassed not to have been the one to ask such an important question.

Mirabelle sat straight in her seat, her serenity unwavering. "We merely want more information about the connection between Wilhelmina's sudden reappearance, Chopard's actions, and Niall's disappearance."

"For what purpose?" I asked.

Mirabelle's silver gaze turned on me. "That is not your purview."

Poe stood. "But it is *mine*, Mirabelle Aestra. You have no right to deny my claim to the information Mina asked for."

The sharp breath from Skye's direction had both my and Ash's attention. The former Chevalier stared at Poe in awe, though I could not immediately discern what had elicited such a reaction. It was clear that she'd violated some kind of hierarchical nonsense the Vilhari cared about, but I couldn't immediately determine what it had been.

Mirabelle scowled in response, at first. The sour expression turned, though, shifting into a smile that sent chills through me. "You only have to command me."

Poe stretched to her full height, which was not tall in inches, but imposing in other ways. Her eyes fell half-shut in a regal glare, the set of her shoulders squaring as her spine lengthened. Aether swirled around her fingers, staining them a dark, midnight blue, her nails curving into wicked talons. "House Aestra, you are held to account by your superior. The Court of Winds shall report now to the Court of Aether."

"The lost court?" Skye whispered, her eyes widening further.

Though the Oscarovi didn't care much about the Vilhari's unnecessarily detailed ancient lore, the lost court was the stuff of legends. We grew up with "lost heir" imposters running rampant in Pravhna—Vilhari claiming to be the long lost ancestor of the missing Aethereal princess were a constant source of news. They were all charlatans, of course, trying to seize power in the highest echelons. Their downfall was as much a source of interest as their arrival.

Mirabelle's voice lowered with obvious pleasure at the hush that had fallen over the room. "Name your rank, child, and I shall comply."

Skye's eyes had gone so wide and her skin so gray that Ashbourne came to stand behind her. Morpheus appeared, lounging at the center of the table. While I did not quite follow what was happening, it was obvious this was an important moment. Poe was utterly magnificent, raptorial and fierce.

"You know that as heir to the Court of Aether, which no longer has a representative on Sirin, that my rank is meaningless, Mirabelle," Poe pleaded, glancing at Skye, then myself.

"Say it," Mirabelle hissed. "If you want the information, declare yourself."

The command ignited the indignance I'd seen in Poe before. "It is not yours to command me, Mirabelle Aestra. Henceforth, you shall refer to me only as YRH, Lady Endymion, or simply by Poe." Poe paused for effect, before unleashing one last command. "Call me *child* again, and you'll find out why my rank surpasses your own."

YRH? I asked Morpheus. The greymalkin obviously understood what was happening.

The cat's long fluffy tail swished twice in agitation, but he answered me. *Your Royal Highness. Hippolyta is the lost heir to the Court of Aether, the Strider Princess. Her great, great grandmother was on the Avalonne as an ambassador when it crashed.*

Poe was the *real* lost heir. Immediately, my mind began to twist and turn, pulling various threads, connecting and reconnecting them as the new information changed the pattern. I spun through the little I knew of the old fey courts of Vilhar, what had been on the worlds they left behind when exploring the cosmos in their great ships. I only knew the basics: Vilhar had six elemental courts, four terrestrial, and two celestial. Aether was one of the ruling courts, the Court of Starfire its only equal. The Avalonne had been populated mostly with representatives of the Court of Winds, but an Aethereal princess had been aboard as well, with a portion of her retinue. If Poe was the lost heir, that changed so much.

A pit formed in my stomach. *What was she doing helping me?* Poe didn't need access to society at all. If she'd wanted it, she could be a member of the highest echelons. She would *be* the highest echelon. The look she bestowed on me was one of remorse, and a promise to tell me everything later. I tried to take it at face value, but a seed of doubt once sown cannot be easily dislodged.

Mirabelle had laughter in her voice when she answered. "Certainly, YRH." Poe glared at her, and the laughter died, but slowly. "We believe there to be a connection between these events. They all bear a similar weight, according to the sybil at Orrery."

Some thread in the pattern I was trying to form thrummed as Mirabelle spoke, its vibration discordant. Quickly, I tried to locate it inside my mind, but it quieted, fading from notice almost as soon as my attention turned to it.

"And my people?" Poe asked. "Does their location bear weight as well?"

"We don't know yet," Muse said, placing a hand on Poe's arm. "Though there was no change when I read you, that means nothing until I read Wilhelmina."

Unlike when Mirabelle had spoken, the pattern was silent as Muse spoke. That much made sense, at least. I had wondered if he was one of the sirens' children, and now I was sure. Sirens existed almost completely in harmony with Fate and rarely disturbed events—unless they were meant to—and they could not lie or deceive. Something in the nature of that thought pulled at my memory, but like the discordant thread of a few moments ago, it disappeared.

It was obvious now that Muse was one of the siren's children, though he was a rare genetic anomaly that appeared as a bipedal humanoid. They often acted as inconspicuous ambassadors for the High Aerie, and if the sybil at Orrery was involved, then Muse was likely one of her progeny. The threads connecting everything tightened further. Soon, a bigger picture would form.

"How do you know that?" Ash asked.

Muse stared at him for a long moment, his eyebrows raising slightly. "Because I've read the rest of you, and I *know*."

Ash looked away quickly, his eyes falling to the floor. "I see."

I pushed my chair back, standing. "You may read me next."

Poe was looking for her people, her family, folk she obviously loved, and who loved her back. If *that* was what she was seeking, I understood her secrecy. Though our motivations for learning more about our families were very different, if I could change the course of things for her, it would be worth the risk.

Muse nodded, and beckoned me towards the windows. I followed him, the feeling that someone had wrapped a blanket around my head increasing as we neared the windows. I still could not hear the waterfall outside, but neither could I hear the conversation going on at the table.

"You see things as well, don't you?" Muse asked as he

stared out the windows at the falling water. He did not move to take my hands, as he had the others.

"I have been having visions," I explained. "But only for a little while."

"Even so," he said softly, "I cannot read another seer."

"I'm no seer," I scoffed, moving to stand next to him, our shoulders nearly touching.

"Anyone with visions is a seer."

I sighed. There was no need to hide the truth from Muse. He would be able to tell what I was as soon as I took his hands. "They're less visions, and more memories. Suppressed memories. I was in an oubliette for nearly a year, and this body is not my own. I remember nothing about my life before."

Muse turned to face me. "A fetch? That makes more sense. I will not be able to read you at all then. But I *can* help." He opened his hands in offering.

I moved slowly, placing my hands in his. "What do I have to do?"

"Just close your eyes," Muse said. "If there is anything on the surface of your mind that might help you understand what's happened to you, I should be able to retrieve it."

I stared at him for a long moment.

"I will not be able to see what you do. Whatever your secrets are, they will be safe from the others, and I will not tell them about the fetch, so you need not worry about that."

My eyes fell closed as Muse's fingers closed around my hands. Warmth flowed through me, comforting and calm. Time slipped out of forward motion, loosening its grip on me as I shifted between, into the limen's dark heart, and through to elsewhere. Out of time, out of this reality, I found myself at the edge of a rocky cliff, a slate blue sea stretching out before me.

The redhead from my previous vision walked ahead of me, obvi-

ously older now, and dressed strangely. She spoke to a similarly dressed, tall woman with short dark hair and golden brown skin. I looked down at my hands, which were incorporeal. Their conversation was faraway, but I could just make out the sound of their voices.

"...after Okairos, you must find my sister. She will need your help as well."

I couldn't hear the other woman's answer, but the red-haired woman locked eyes with me, as though she could see me.

"Open the door, Lumina. Free Sirin and I will come to your aid."

The voice echoed in my mind as the vision blurred. Now, I was immobile on a table, trapped in my body, my corporeal eyes frozen open as two dark, winged figures I could not make out moved above me.

"Work quickly, Penthe—we haven't much time."

"The curse is complete, but the loophole… It won't work. She doesn't love him."

"It will work precisely because she does not. It is what makes it the right loophole.*"*

"That makes no sense."

"She is still young, Penthe, and under her father's influence. Away from it, her capacity will be greater than you know. She's the one we've waited for."

"The first of Alcyone's three?"

"Yes. Tighten the loophole, and she will open it with time."

My eyes opened. I was back in my body, back in the fetch. The space between my shoulders ached, a phantom pain that would not relent. I was tempted to try to reach the spot with one of my hands, to try and touch the space that hurt, but did not. None of my pain manifested quite this way.

Muse smiled at me. "Did you find out what you wanted to know?"

None of what I'd seen made any sense to me whatsoever,

but a hunch struck me. "I don't know yet. Have you ever heard the name Alcyone?"

Muse's eyes widened. "Yes. She's quite famous amongst my people. On the old world, eons ago, she delivered a prophecy. One that spoke of a great disturbance in the cosmos, an imbalance of power, and the three who would make it right."

My heart beat faster. The three who would make it right. What did that mean? "Can you tell me the prophecy? Or is it written down somewhere?"

Solemnly, Muse shook his head. "I don't believe it is, and I am sorry, I don't know more than what I've told you. My mother would be the one to ask."

"The sybil at Orrery?" I asked, heart sinking. The Orrery Aerie was across the Pontus Axeinos in Brektos. Traveling there was an impossibility right now.

Muse's expression was open and gentle. Under other circumstances, he might be someone I could like. "I am sorry I cannot tell you more. For what it's worth, something is blocking you. I can't read you, but I sense whatever it is."

"Could it be the after-effects of the oubliette?" I asked.

"No." Muse's head shook thoughtfully. "The magic of the oubliette would have worn off moments after you escaped. You did escape it on your own, didn't you?"

"You saw that?" I breathed, wondering how that was possible, given what Muse had said.

He laughed, loud and hearty. "No, I assumed it. There's bits and pieces of you in all the others' surface memories, and from what they think of you, it seems like something you'd be capable of." His eyes sparked with interest. "That's a story I'd like to hear someday."

"But not now?"

"No, now I'm going to tell Mirabelle that my reading was

inconclusive. That you haven't been out long enough to tell how you connect."

"Can you do that?" I asked. "I thought you had to tell the truth."

Muse chuckled. "It *is* the truth. *You've* been telling everyone the truth."

I frowned. "About what?"

Muse took my hand again, squeezing hard. "That you don't remember what happened before the oubliette."

"Oh yes," I murmured. "That is true."

I felt no need to pull my hand out of his grip. There was something about Muse that was inherently right, inherently safe for me to be close to. "Will you tell them about the fetch?" I asked, turning my head toward the windows. He'd already promised, but I had to be sure.

"No," he replied. "That is your business, just as Poe's secret was hers. Despite what Mirabelle Aestra thinks, I don't serve her. That's not how the Courts worked, not originally. Her kind has forgotten, but they will be brought to account."

His words had the tenor of portent, and I had no desire to press further. Somewhere in the recesses of my mind, a part of me that existed long before this body whispered that no good had ever come from prophecy. It might be a blessing that I could not reach the sybil easily. Whatever was at work here might be bigger than my concerns, but I was happy to help these people as long as my needs were being met. Right now, however, they were not.

"Do you know anything about my mother and sister that might help me remember the things I've forgotten?" I asked.

Muse shook his head. "I've never had occasion to learn anything about them. I am sorry, Mina. You're the one person here I'd really like to help, and I cannot."

"You don't like Poe?" I asked, feeling shocked.

"I like her just fine," Muse replied. "But her path was set

long ago. There's nothing I've ever been able to do to help her. You, I'd like to help. I have a feeling you're the kind of person it pays to be owed a favor from."

At that, I had to smile. "Then you would be a rare one. I don't allow myself to be in positions like that."

Another of Muse's hearty laughs filled me to the brim with comfort. He drew a card from the inner pocket of his waistcoat. "Come visit sometime. For drinks, for fun, for whatever."

I took his calling card, with the distinct feeling that Muse didn't give it out to just anyone. "Thank you."

He bowed slightly to me, then walked back towards the table. I stayed in the quiet for a moment, watching Muse tell them I was no help. I exited the muffled solace of the windowed nook to hear him saying, "It is my conclusion that the four of you are connected. Both to one another, to Chopard, and likely to Niall's disappearance, but not enough has transpired to find out why that is."

Mirabelle Aestra sighed sharply, shoving her chair back from the table. "Then this was a waste of time." She flung a hand at Skye as she stalked out of the room. "Show yourselves out."

Skye nodded, stoic and unreactive. Muse followed Mirabelle, mouthing a silent apology as he went. When Mirabelle and Muse's footsteps disappeared into the upper regions of the Aestra's quarters, Skye spoke. "Shall we find someplace to talk?"

Morpheus was nowhere to be seen, and I envied his ability to blink in and out. Teleportation was a rare and desirable gift that I very much wished I possessed. I considered asking to stay right here—my body ached and fatigue wasn't far behind—but I saw clearly that Poe and Skye wanted to be away. They were both out of their seats and inching towards the door. An old fear of inconveniencing others with my pain fluttered through me.

Slowly, I sucked air in through my nostrils and brought the mask of calm down over the screaming agony that rose in me like an unholy chorus as I stood. Something about unleashing the vision had aggravated my corporeal form. But this was nothing I couldn't manage. I stood without so much as a grimace, proud of myself for hiding the intensity of my body's protest.

My legs crumpled underneath me, and all went dark.

CHAPTER 25

ASHBOURNE

M use's words echoed in my head, spinning around like a top, torturing me. *Whatever you do, you cannot tell Mina about the offer from the Strix woman. If you do, things go wrong for her. Very wrong,* he'd said, right after he read me. It was a warning, one I took seriously, but it pained me to keep it from her. Especially after the way she'd reacted to my touch, the heat her arousal ignited in me.

Before I could do *anything* about that, I needed to tell Mina everything about the Strix woman and her claims, especially if it was connected to all of this. But neither could I risk her safety, and telling her would do just that. Muse was trustworthy, not just because sirens cannot lie, but because he was a good man, one who stood behind his word no matter what. His reputation in the undercity was unassailable.

Lost in my thoughts, I didn't notice the shake in Mina's muscles as she stood. When she fell, the part of me that was attuned to her recognized something was amiss and I moved without thinking. I only caught her in time to keep her head from hitting the stone table. Poe clapped a hand over her mouth, presumably to keep herself from screaming.

"We need somewhere to go," I whispered. "No one can see her like this."

Poe nodded. "Come with me."

Surprise lit Skye's eyes as Poe moved with purpose, out the front door of House Aestra's massive quarters, into the wreck of the Avalonne. As wrecks went, this one was in fairly good shape. I tried to focus on our surroundings, rather than Mina's scent of iris and white musk. Had my sense of propriety not been firmly in place, I might have nuzzled the space between her shoulder and neck as I adjusted her body to be carried a longer distance.

No one would have seen me do it, but I couldn't trust myself not to linger there, breathing her in. Already, my head spun with her nearness, desire for her racing through my veins. Now that I understood the depth of my need for her, I wouldn't touch her again 'til she begged for it. Something sweet and thick filled my mouth, the taste familiar and strange at the same time. I swallowed the liquid seeping from the roots of my elongated canines.

Faint memory tickled at the back of my mind. This had happened before, with another I'd wanted… I shook my head. There was nothing there for me. Here and now, I wanted her, and only her. She was the only one I'd desired with this kind of intensity since I awoke from the coma. I wanted to keep that for myself, so I diverted my thoughts with purpose.

The Avalonne was a feat of engineering I could not comprehend. The ship itself must have been beyond my puny imagination, for this was a true city, as large as Pravhna, if not larger. We followed Poe through the narrow stone walkways and steep stairs. In the dim light of the phosphorescent plants, the stone sparkled a bit with a faint luminosity of its own.

We took a spiral staircase that looked over a waterfall that fell hundreds of feet, into the misty darkness below. The view stirred something within me, memories of a labyrinth in the mist conjured in my mind. So long as they were not memories of another lover, I let them drift in and out. The less I paid attention to them, the more likely they were to disappear, without effect.

Poe had stopped in front of an enormous arched doorway, drawing a ring of keys from an interior pocket of her heavy coat. Next to her, Skye's mouth fell open. "I've walked past this door so many times, wondering what House it belonged to."

Poe glanced sidelong at Skye. "I don't come here often."

Something about the statement elicited a smile from Skye, a private joke between them, perhaps. The thought of them having jokes to share pleased me as Poe pushed the door open.

"Welcome to House Feriant," Poe said, her voice quiet. "Please never mention this place to anyone."

I pushed past Skye, who'd stopped dead in her tracks. "Hippolyta Feriant. You *are* Hippolyta Feriant."

The name meant nothing to me, but clearly it did to Skye. This seemed like a private conversation though, and Mina stirred in my arms. "Where should I take her?"

Poe's brows immediately furrowed. "Upstairs, second floor, to your left. Any room will do."

Another spiral staircase sat at the end of the entryway, and as I carried Mina up, Skye and Poe's voices carried— they were arguing again. Mina woke to the sound, her face thoughtful against my chest.

"Do you know why they're fighting?" she asked.

"No," I murmured as I stopped at the top of the stairs. The hall stretched out in two different directions. I went left, choosing the first door I came to.

Mina's hand dropped to open the door for me when she

saw I'd paused, worrying I'd have to put her down to open the tall, heavy thing. She turned the doorknob, and I pushed the door with my shoulder. The room was pristine, lit by soft witchlights that glowed brighter as we entered. A scent of jasmine and rose hung in the air, as though the room had just been cleaned. There was a canopied bed on one wall, made from heavy, spare wood, hung with diaphanous white curtains. It looked a little like a giant cube. There was no other furniture in the room, save a simple wood bench at the end of the bed.

"Where would you like to be?" I asked.

She looked around. "In a bathtub."

I set her down, watching her sink onto the bench at the end of the bed before I strode across the room. Tall, arched doors took up nearly the entire wall opposite the bed. When opened, they revealed another, bigger room. It was the biggest bathing chamber I'd ever seen. In a nook at the front of the room sat an oversized bathtub.

"There's one in here," I called to her. From downstairs came the sounds of a muffled fight.

"Please run the water as hot as possible," Mina said from the other room. "If there is salt, I'd take some."

There was a shelf carved into the stone wall next to the tub that held various bath accoutrements. I could identify the salt easily enough, but the rest was a mystery to me. Once I had the tub plugged and hot water flowing, I dumped a generous heap of salt in, and went to fetch Mina.

She sat where I left her, obviously listening to the fight downstairs with interest. "So, she's a princess."

I nodded. "It would seem so. Would you like some help getting into the bathroom?"

Mina looked as though she might say no, but when she tried to get up on her own, she winced. I rushed in to help, gripping her forearms before I could think twice. She flinched, grimacing as she recoiled from me.

"I apologize," I murmured. "I should have asked."

She nodded, but said, "Please don't let go. I do need the help."

Together we moved towards the bathtub, her body leaning heavily on me as we went, but she was tense, pulling herself upward with each painful step. Her hands shook in mine.

"Please let me carry you," I pleaded. "There's no need for this. I can see how much pain you're in."

She glanced up at me, her mouth set in a determined, grim line. "You cannot possibly know how much pain I am in."

I stopped, refusing to move another inch. If this was her successfully hiding the true measure of her discomfort, that concerned me. "Show me then."

She stared at me for a long moment, and I thought she'd brush my pleas off, but she closed her eyes. The shift was subtle as she loosened her grip on the mask she wore to keep herself secret. Her shoulders drooped, her spine sagging, her head heavy on what now seemed like a too-weak stalk of a neck. When her eyes opened, I could all but hear the screaming inside her. There was no haggardness in it, only pure suffering, endured over a lifetime. Silent tears slipped down her cheeks, her breath ragged in her chest.

"Let me carry you," I repeated.

"Fine." Her whisper of a voice was barely audible.

Picking her up in this state was different from before. She was both heavier and lighter at the same time. The weight of her pain was unimaginable, but besides that, she felt empty in a way I could not understand. She lay her head on my shoulder, her tears staining my jacket.

In the bathing chamber, I found a bench, a smaller

version of the one in the bedroom, and sat Mina down. The room had warmed with the hot water and she was steady enough for the moment, so I returned to the bedroom. I stripped out of my overcoat, frock coat and waistcoat, and rolled my shirtsleeves past my elbows. When I returned to the bathing chamber, she was pouring more salt into the tub, along with various oils and dropperfuls of liquid from different bottles.

Her own coat lay in a heap on the floor, and her hands shook as she found and replaced bottle after bottle. When she could not open the last stopper, I stepped in to help.

"Just one drop of that one," she said. "It has an analgesic effect, but is very potent."

I did as she asked. The tub was full now, and the water shut off automatically. Both of us startled at the realization that it had done so of its own accord. A tiny smile of wonder played at her lips.

She practically vibrated with exhaustion, and though I wanted to give her privacy, it was clear she could not do this alone. "I can help you. I can even close my eyes, if you like. But you need help."

When her eyes met mine, they burned with life. "I don't want you to close your eyes."

My breath caught. Even in this state, with her pain so evident, she was more alluring than any lover I could remember. She turned toward me, her arms hanging at her sides as she leaned against the marble wall. Her eyes did not leave mine as I stepped towards her, my hands going to the buttons on her blouse first. Every button brought her creamy skin further into view, my breath catching at the beauty my fingers revealed.

She leaned forward when I finished, so I could slip it off her shoulders. Her face burrowed into my chest. "There's buttons on the back of the trousers."

I found them, undid them, then pushed them away as she stepped out of them. Under her clothes, she wore a silky ivory camisole and a pair of matching bottoms. My hands hesitated slightly as she pushed away from my chest and turned from me.

"It will be easier for me if I can face away from you," she explained. For a moment, I thought she spoke of modesty, but she braced herself against the wall, allowing me to push the silk bottoms down over the generous curve of her hips. When they lay on the floor, she leaned back against me, her knees buckling.

My arm went around her in an instant, pinning her to my chest, my hand splayed across the bare skin of her abdomen, pushing her camisole aside. Her breath came quicker now as she pulled it off, over her head. I closed my eyes for a moment, trying to still my blood, but she turned in my arms, every delicious curve of her pressing into me as she did so. When I opened my eyes her face was lifted, watching me.

"What is this between us?" she breathed. "Or am I mistaken?"

It was as though she spoke to herself, but I could not help answering. "You are not mistaken."

Her arms went around my neck, and my heart nearly thumped out of my chest. She waited, watching me carefully. "You cannot hurt me more than I'm already hurt."

It was as though she'd read my mind. "What would help you, Mina?" I whispered.

"To feel pleasure amidst all this pain," she answered.

CHAPTER 26

MINA

The words came out of me unbidden and without thought for consequence. It was wholly unlike me, but the pain had caught me, its claws gouging holes in my good sense. Ash's reaction was unexpected. Many men, given the right opportunity, would have ravaged me then and there.

And if he'd have done so, I would have welcomed it. What came next was worse. His mouth met mine, in an infuriating combination of restraint and strength, as he lifted me aloft. His lips were firm and slow, but his tongue tangled in mine with wild abandon.

Hot bath water hit my skin and he paused. "Is it too much? The water, I mean."

"No," I murmured against his mouth. He lowered me into the water, looking only at my face. It wasn't the gaze of false modesty, but one bordering on obsession. As though he wanted to memorize every line of my expression as his fingers grazed the sensitive skin of my jaw then ran down the line of my neck to trace my collarbone.

I'd always hated the way my collarbones disappeared beneath my flesh, when Helene's protruded in such a delicate way. But Ashbourne's reverence made me rethink my stance, the touch reverberating through my entire body as his lips met mine again.

Now that I was settled safely in the tub, the tenor and rhythm of his kisses changed. I was too exhausted to touch him more than to cling to the collar of his shirt, but his hands moved enough for the two of us, pulling out the dozens of pins that held my hair in place.

One grazed my scalp as he did so and I cried out. He broke the kiss, but I pulled him to me, crushing my lips against his. He seemed to understand. There was no way to be gentle with me. Everything caused me some measure of pain now. The only thing to do was to mix pleasure with it so fully that I might find relief.

My hair undone, his fingers moved through it as he kissed me, massaging my scalp to a degree of sheer bliss. Every strand of my hair felt too heavy for my head to carry, and his touch sent shivers of pleasure through me. The heat of the water and the combination of his touch made my eyes heavy.

"You're exhausted," he murmured as he left a trail of kisses from my jaw to my earlobe.

I nodded once, unable to speak now. Ash drew away from me, watching me for a long moment, as though making some determination about what would happen next. His fingers continued to stroke my scalp, pulling gently through my hair to keep it out of the water as I sunk deeper into the hot suds.

"Close your eyes, love," he said.

I shook my head. "Can't fall asleep in the tub." The words came out awkwardly, slowly, and I couldn't be sure they'd exited me in the same order I'd thought them in, but he understood me.

"You're safe," he whispered, sending a shudder of pleasure through me. "I won't let you drown."

There was no way to be sure of that, but the littlest bit of relief had brought all my defenses down and I lost all sense.

I woke in my attic room at Orchid House, my dressing gown tied securely around me. Pillows supported every aching part of my body in an expert placement that surprised me. I raised my head slightly to find Ashbourne sleeping in the chair by the window. The curtains hung barely askance, letting in a sliver of the night. Outside, rain fell in steady sheets.

Slowly, I sat up, listening to the sounds of the house. Rain on the roof, Ashbourne's soft breathing. My pain had receded while I slept, the medicinal bath in the Avalonne helping immeasurably. Careful not to push myself too hard, I swung my legs over the edge of the bed. My muscles were stiff, but nothing was so painful that I couldn't go downstairs for a cup of tea.

I pulled the knitted throw from the end of my bed and covered Ashbourne with it. He hardly stirred at my touch. It was hard not to stay and ponder the sharp lines of his face, the curve of his lip. However, I needed to brew a cup of herbal tisane if I was to feel at all myself when the sun rose. I stole out of the room, closing the door softly behind me as I went.

The back stairs in the attic went straight to the kitchen, but I stopped on the first floor to check the lock on the front door. Viridian knew I was back, and a part of me feared he might come here. I couldn't be sure that my adjustments to the wards would keep him out. When I was satisfied the front door was locked, I checked the terrace doors. Skye had fallen asleep on the divan in Maman's study, a book open on her chest, Morpheus stretched out next to her on his back, snoring lightly. There was no blanket to tuck them in with, so I made my way downstairs to the kitchen.

Though it was dark, I saw Poe without trouble. She stood in the kitchen doorway, a crystal rocks glass hanging from her fingertips as she watched the rain. I know she heard me enter, but she didn't turn to face me. "Are you feeling better?"

Her voice carried a chill I hadn't heard before. "Yes," I answered, turning the dial on the aetheric lamps over the oven so they provided just enough light to make tea by. The green glow was eerie in the midnight hour.

The silence between us was uncomfortable, but I decided to let Poe direct the conversation. When the kettle was on to boil, I turned, and she sat on a stool at the worktable across from me.

"Ashbourne said you prepared your own bath." Poe's words were obviously an accusation, though I could not make out exactly what wrong I'd done.

"I did," I said slowly, spooning tea into a brass basket.

"How did you know what to put in it?"

Another accusation. Still, I didn't understand. I sighed, resenting the fact that she did not simply say what she meant to and tell me whatever I'd done wrong. "I read the labels."

She frowned, as though confused by my reaction. "But *how*?"

"With my eyes, how else?" I hissed, beyond frustrated with her ridiculous line of questioning.

Poe shook her head, her molars grinding audibly. "How did you read the Old Vilhar, Wilhelmina? Who taught you?"

The question was simple. *Who taught you?* Three simple words unmoored me. Three simple words cut the strings that bound me to this plane. Memories slammed into me, out of order and nonsensical, faces and bodies blurry, but emotions all too clear. As I rose out of the emptiest place of my very long existence, the day I'd remembered it all to begin with became all too clear.

The day I'd caught Maman and Helene, playing with forces neither of them should have trifled with. *Maman.* No. Vaness Wildfang was no more my mother than the teapot I held in my hands, but somehow—somehow, Helene still felt like my sister. That horrifying sentiment shook me out of the stream of memory.

Poe watched me carefully, her hazel eyes sharp. "You've remembered something."

A slow, wicked smile draped over my face as I poured my tea, more relaxed than I'd been since I rose out of the oubliette. "Enough to destroy those that harmed us."

Poe's laugh was soft and dangerous. She pushed her teacup towards me. "Tell me everything."

CHAPTER 27

MINA

We talked long into the night, taking our tea to the study. While the majority of my memories were like watercolor paintings, I understood them well enough to glean that I'd lived a long life before the fetch. I worried at first about telling Poe, given the stigma against unnaturally created life.

Her response surprised me. "After all that happened, perhaps it was a boon."

That was certainly true. Though many things still escaped me, I knew now that the redhead from my visions was my true sister. A half-sister, anyway. When my own mother had died, my father was forever resentful that I resembled her so closely, but could not be *her*. For as a youngling, I showed no sign of having her immense powers, only the most mundane spark of what she'd been, and my father was nothing if not ambitious.

But my father remarried, a woman I loved, and who became like a second mother to me, even after she had children of her own. Twins, a boy and a girl, both far more talented magically than I had any hope of becoming. I could not remember any of their names, and only impressions of their faces. I remembered the wars that lasted lifetimes, the pain of being loved by my stepmother and half-siblings, but never pleasing my father. And then all went dark for a time, though my impression of pain, fear, and an intense longing hunted me still. It had always been there, deep in the pit of my stomach.

"And this was all somewhere else?" Poe asked, setting aside her tea, now gone cold. "Another world?"

I nodded, glancing at the clock. The sun wouldn't be up for another few hours, but night had turned to the wee hours of morning. "Yes, but there was time between when I arrived here and when the fetch was made that I still don't remember. Only that I grew up as Wilhelmina Wildfang."

"So the fetch has grown, just as a real child would?" I nodded as Poe bit her bottom lip. "I don't know much about how a fetch is supposed to work, but…"

Again, I nodded. "That's not how it's usually done. The Oscarovi's fetches were static, everlasting and strong, but they did not age."

"So Vaness had access to some technology or magical knowledge the other Oscarovi didn't."

"Yes," I answered. "I believe that's the only conclusion we can come to. She captured me, and what's more, I think Papa—her husband was involved. I remember him, from before the fetch. Whatever they were doing, he was helping her."

"Why though?"

I had no answer for her. Memories still floated through me, quietly organizing themselves in my mind, but none made much sense yet.

Poe drew a sharp breath in. "But how did you get here? Was it a ship?"

My answer had been theorized about thousands of times

over Sirin's long academic history, but never proven. "I believe I came through a portal. Through the limen."

"Like the Ventyr?" Poe asked, naming the only extraterrestrial force to have come to Sirin since the Vilhari.

I paused then. She'd taken the news about the fetch so well, but this was different. From the time we were small children, we learned about the Elemental War. We had named it so because it was the first time the elementals of Sirin agreed to pair as familiars with the Oscarovi, making our kind as nearly as powerful as the Vilhari. We had needed that power when the Ventyr came to conquer us.

They were much like the Vilhari in some ways. Stronger than the Oscarovi, with more technical prowess. They had come with the intention of conquering Sirin, and by the elementals' grace and the strength of our alliance with the Vilhari, we had beaten them back. We had become unconquerable.

I still thought of the Oscarovi as my people. It was easier than the truth. The Ventyr were despised on Sirin. It was one of the few things we could all agree on. Telling Poe wouldn't be like it was with the fetch. She might hate me.

I took a deep breath before answering her, knowing I had to be honest. "Not *like* them."

Poe leaned back in her chair, her eyes wide. "*With* them? You're one of them."

I stared at the ceiling for a long moment, tracing the clouds painted there with my eyes. "Yes, and no. I believe I am a high ranking Ventyr, though I cannot remember my name, or the names of my family. I have the strong sense I was left here to be punished. Isolated."

The silence between us made me anxious. I longed to fill it with words, but I stayed silent. There was nothing I could do now. If she hated me, if she feared me, I would have to endure it.

"What was the reason for the punishment you endured?" Poe asked. "Why were you left here?"

I sighed. "That I still don't know. I first remembered all of this—it's why I was imprisoned in the oubliette—on my twenty-eighth birthday."

"Your celestial anniversary," Poe added. "That is a special birthday for the Oscarovi, is it not?"

I nodded, wistful sadness gripping my chest. "But not for me. Maman and Helene had nothing planned for me, other than the barest acknowledgment." It wasn't that I wanted the kind of lavish party that people like Caralee Ellis-Whitely had. We didn't have money for such things.

"Maman refused me the ritual. She told me no elementals were interested in pairing with me, that the forest had denied my soul a pair."

This elicited another sharp breath from Poe, her eyes widening. "Your family's familiars were mountain elementals?"

Rain struck the study windows in violent torrents, obscuring my view of the garden. "Yes, that is the Wildfang tradition."

"That is rather cruel," Poe said, sadness caressing the hard edges of her response. "Mountain elementals are the most powerful, but pairing with them is a vicious process from all I've heard."

I stood, pulling my arms around me for warmth. What she said was true. Mountain elementals required a trial before agreeing to pair as an Oscarovi's familiar. The ritual could be brutal, but I had longed for it just the same. All I had wanted in my childhood was a familiar, but I had been denied over and over. My celestial anniversary had been my last chance; after that, I would have been too old. I had been desperate that night. There was one log left in the basket by the hearth, and I bent to put it on the dying fire. "I went into the forest at Somerhaven to plead with the old ones."

Behind me, Poe was silent. I didn't have to turn to know she wore a shocked expression. No one in their right mind would do such a thing. The Oscarovi were indigenous to Sirin, but the elemental spirits, they *were* Sirin. The old ones were their eldritch gods, the nameless elders that spawned the spirits. They were elementals, and *more*. Creatures best left to forgotten places and legend.

One did not treat with them and live to tell the tale. I had been foolish to do what I did, going to the standing stones to demand reconsideration—or at the very least—an explanation for why I'd been rejected. I got my answer, the forbidden knowledge I'd sought. I was given the reason for my pain, my neglect, my isolation. In the standing stones, the old ones showed me the truth of my body, the carved out reality of my existence.

But all I said to Poe was, "They showed me what I was, and I confronted Maman."

Poe made a little noise. I turned and saw tears streaming down her face. "I am so sorry you were treated that way, Mina."

There was no doubt in my mind that Poe understood more than I'd said, that she had some ability to see beyond a person's words and into their souls. I'd suspected she might have auric abilities for some time—that she could read emotions and possibly even surface memories. It was a rare gift among the Vilhari, one that presented only sporadically. It was treasured, though without proper cultivation, it could be maddening for some. Clearly, she'd mastered her ability to read others. There was no other way she could read between the lines of what I'd told her and the swirl of emotions and memories that flooded me now.

"There's no reason for you to be sorry, but I appreciate the sentiment."

Poe wiped her eyes with the back of her robe's sleeve. "When I met you in the train station, I knew there was something special about you, about us."

I turned my back to the fire, letting my backside warm for a bit. The feeling was delicious on my still-sore muscles. "Oh?" I wasn't following her train of thought.

Poe nodded. "Yes, I read auric energy."

Well, there it was. I'd known, but there was something gratifying about hearing her tell the truth.

"And there was something familiar about yours." She flexed her hands out in front of her, staring at them for a long moment. "I can't see my own aura, but I feel it. And there was something familiar in yours. Something that made me think immediately that we might be connected."

The excitement in her voice was contagious. "And what do you think now that we've spent time together?"

She stood, coming to stand next to me, her backside to the fire as well. "Oh," she said, with a tiny smile. "That does feel lovely. This place is freezing."

A little chuckle bubbled up from my chest, breaking up the tension that had gathered there since she confronted me in the kitchen. It was going to be all right with us.

"What do you know about House Feriant, about the Court of Aether?" she asked.

I shrugged. "That the Court of Aether ruled Vilhar alongside the Court of Starfire, and the heir was on the Avalonne, as some sort of ambassador. And of course, that the representatives of the Court of Aether disappeared after the Ventyr were beat back, leaving the Vilhari without a ruler."

Poe nodded. "That's the basics. But like the vast variation in the Court of Winds, there are also variations in the ways the Court of Aether presents."

My rear began to feel as though it might catch fire, and I moved to sit on the plush rug in front of the fire. It was the softest textile in the room. Why Maman could not have invested in more comfortable furniture was beyond my comprehension.

It would be painful to get up from the floor, but at least I'd stay warm. "Like the differences between the Strix and Corvidae?"

Poe sat next to me, crossing her legs under her billowing robe. "Yes. The Courts of Aether and Starfire have fewer variations in that way, though there are many fey creatures that made their homes with us. The draconae, for one..." Poe trailed off, deep sadness in her eyes. "I'm sorry. I don't know how I can miss a place I've never seen, a life I've never had."

Gingerly, I took her hand. It felt good to do so as her fingers closed around mine. "Thank you," she whispered. "It's kind of you to comfort me, considering that you actually remember the home you left behind. I only have stories."

The memories I had were sparse, but she was right. I did have them, and more would return. What she felt was a different kind of pain, missing a life she never had a chance to live. "We don't have to have the same experience for me to feel empathy for what's happened to you," I explained.

She smiled. "The point I was trying to make was that a good portion of the Court of Aether were winged, much like the Court of Winds… But different."

"Different how?" A yawning hole opened in my gut.

Poe pulled her hand from mine, but gently, then pushed herself into a standing position. She closed her eyes, and the atoms in the room shifted. The change was nearly imperceptible, but for the six feathered wings that flexed behind Poe. They were midnight blue, the color of aether, glimmering in the firelight with a faint iridescence that shifted green and purple.

Their formation was as familiar to me as my own face. Now I remembered what else I had lost, long before anyone put me in the fetch. A great howl of grief welled within me, but I only said, "Your wings are like the Ventyr's. Avian, rather than draconic, but the same otherwise."

Poe nodded. "This is not common knowledge amongst the Vilhari on Sirin, Mina. But I think it explains something… On the Court of Aether's home world, on Neamor, House Feriant had feathered wings. House Larae, draconic."

My heart beat faster at the name. "House Larae?" The way she pronounced it, laa-ray, was not the word I was familiar with. "Not, Larai?"

"Lah-rhye, laa-ray," she sounded the words out as one of her wings stroked my back. "Do you miss the sky, my sister?"

Tears fell unbidden, streaming hot down my cheeks. While I could not make the faces of my family clear in my mind, I saw their wings. I *felt* my own. Three sets of draconic wings, just like what Poe had described. The ache between my shoulders was nearly unbearable now that she'd said it. It did not matter how many baths I took, nor how many massages. That particular pain never went away. Even in the fetch, *I missed my wings*.

Loose memories gathered, spinning through me, clustering into stories that made sense. The first time I'd flown, my mother tossing me to the wind, off the top of a tower with a joyful whoop, diving after me as my wings found purchase in the air. My father's angry scowl as he watched my mother sicken and die. The day he married my true mother's second-in-command, and the way Orynthia treated me as her own. The day the twins were born. And the war, the never-ending war.

My mother was Larai. It was why my father wanted her so badly. Her people were unconquerable, and his only choice had been to ally with them, taking their queen for his wife. Was it possible that the Larai were somehow related to House Larae? I swallowed hard, understanding what must be an ancient truth. "The Ventyr are Vilhari. We're all the same people."

"Yes, they are ancient relations. Lost but never forgotten," Poe breathed. "I don't know much, but from the records I found in the Avalonne it is why the ambassador traveled with the Court of Winds. She hoped to find some hint that the Ventyr, our lost people, still lived."

Had the Ventyr known all this when they came to conquer Sirin? Had my parents known we were one people? If they had known, would it have mattered? I wished I remembered more. In time, perhaps I would, and I could give Poe some of the answers her ancestors had sought. It wasn't enough to make up for what the Ventyr had tried to do here, but if my mother's people had been loyal to House Feriant, perhaps that would be enough for her.

Poe let her glamour cover her wings, and sank back down on the rug next to me. Her frown deepened as she chewed something over in her head. "I would like to find my mother, and the last of House Feriant."

"The lost court," I murmured, thinking of the truth about Poe's heritage. We hadn't had a chance to talk about her revelation in the Avalonne yet. "How were you separated from them?"

Poe shook her head. "Much of what I remember is a blur. I was only five when it happened. All I remember is that there was a disturbance in the middle of the night. Fighting. My mother's lover, Euryale, was the one to bring me to the Avalonne. She was injured though, and died before she could do more than tell me how to access our family's quarters, and the wreck itself. I wasn't left with much."

It was all too much sorrow. We had not deserved such terrible childhoods. I had not deserved two terrible childhoods, but I would not say that. I didn't want Poe to think I was trying to compare.

Instead, I asked, "Why were you in hiding to begin with? Why did they disappear?"

Poe's sorrow was palpable now. "I'm not certain. From the little I remember being taught, they were afraid of something. I was never to talk about House Feriant, never supposed to say my full name."

"But you think they're alive somewhere?" I asked.

Poe's smile was watery. "No," she replied, her voice breaking over the word. "All I want now is to know who killed them, and to find their bodies. I want to do the rituals, to grieve for them."

"And after that?" I asked.

Her eyes hardened. "I want what you want."

"Revenge." I offered Poe my arm. My memory might be fractured, but I remembered what it was to make an oath amongst my mother's people. The Larai were kin to House Feriant, and that was enough for me.

Poe clasped my forearm, her fingers curling around my skin as mine gripped hers. When she called me sister, she meant it. We were more than friends. We were family, and I would not let her down.

CHAPTER 28

ASHBOURNE

I woke to the walls shaking, a lightning strike hitting someplace too close for comfort. Mina was gone from her bed, but I sensed her and the others downstairs. My heart slowed as I assessed the situation. Everyone was safe. Morpheus and Skye slept, while Poe and Mina talked in her mother's study. I couldn't make their words out, but they were calm enough in tenor.

All was well. There was nothing to worry over. I pinched the bridge of my nose, a soft blanket falling off me. Mina had covered me before getting up. Memories of her touch, of her mouth, of her naked skin, came flooding back. I took cool air into my lungs, hoping for relief.

None came. I wanted her too badly. There was only one way to resolve these feelings: I needed to move. Technically, there were two ways, but the one I'd prefer wasn't an option right now. Someone needed to do a perimeter check anyway. I adjusted the massive erection in my pants, then slipped my frock coat back over my shoulders as I stood. I'd been sitting on it, and it retained the heat of my body.

I took the stairs two at a time, not bothering to be quiet.

Mina stepped out of the study, her robe dragging on the floor behind her, dark hair spilling around her face and shoulders. "You're awake."

The rasp of her voice was too much. The thin fabric of her robe clung to her, revealing the way the chill in the air had peaked her nipples. My head swam with ideas—so many ideas about the ways I'd like to touch her. I could not stay and listen to her without dropping to my knees and begging her for release. I swallowed my baser urges, clearing my throat in an attempt to gather my wits. "Someone needs to do a perimeter check."

"Is something wrong?" Poe asked, poking her head out the door.

"No," Skye said from the doorway of the drawing room, Morpheus just behind her. Wonderful, everyone was awake. "But with Viridian back, and our trip to the Avalonne, it's probably best that we set up a watch." She stepped forward. "I am sorry, Ash. I should have thought of it myself."

I nodded, feeling bad about her obvious guilt. I only wanted to get out of the house, to find something useful to do with myself. There was never a moment I wanted Skye to feel as though she'd made a misstep, especially not when she had been resting.

"Go back to sleep," I pleaded. "I'm sure all is well."

Skye yawned. The enormous grandfather clock in the back hallway made a soft noise, its cogs and gears turning as the stars on its face shifted slightly. It was a quarter past five. Technically a decent hour to rise, but we'd had an extraordinary day.

"Please," I said as Poe and Mina both yawned in chorus with Morpheus and Skye. "All of you to bed. I will do a perimeter check and then make mushroom tarts for breakfast."

"With cheese?" Skye asked, heading for the stairs. "Something sharp?"

"Yes," I reassured her. "Plenty of sharp cheese. We have a lovely cheddar."

Mina looked back at Poe, reaching a hand toward the other woman. "We should sleep. There will be much to talk about later."

Poe nodded, taking Mina's hand. I noticed the way Skye purposely did not look back. She was still angry then. They'd done nothing but bicker since Mina lost consciousness. I'd hoped they'd have resolved things between them by now, but Skye felt betrayed by Poe's secrets, and I couldn't blame her for that.

Honesty, I'd found, was the most important thing in healthy relationships. It was the foundation of everything Skye and I had built together in our friendship, and it was the reason I needed to get out of the house. Muse had been clear that it was imperative that I keep the visit from the Strix woman a secret from Mina, but I still had doubts.

How could lying to Mina about someone who meant her harm be helpful? But Muse had made an important point. It wasn't that *not* knowing would cause her to be off her guard; it was the knowing that would prod her into making decisions that might ruin everything.

Something about that idea resonated deeply with me. While I could not be sure why that was, I knew the feeling of memory returning when it drew near. There was nothing I wanted less right now than to bring on visions of the past, especially when the people in the here and now meant so much to me. My coat hung in the front closet, in the vestibule. I brought it out, flipping the collar upwards against the storm as I opened the front door and made my way down the steps and onto the street.

The early morning was marked by the storm that raged

on outside. Rain fell in sheets, clouds rolling in the sky. Pravhna's storms were serious this time of year, and would remain so until the snow began. Water rushed down the steep streets, into the sewers that ran below the city. I had to wonder if the waterfalls in the Avalonne were overflowing right now, if the ship had ever been flooded out by storms.

I turned the corner on Orchid Street, and made my way up several blocks before doubling back when I was certain I hadn't been followed. It was hard to imagine who would be out in such weather, especially so early. But there was something about Viridian Montclair that reminded me not to get complacent.

He had a quality I recognized, though I could not pinpoint its origin. I knew in my bones' marrow I'd met others like him in the past, bullies who thrived on people believing their motivations were simple cruelty. Viridian Montclair was no fool, and I would not make the mistake of underestimating him.

As I slipped into the alley behind Orchid House, I was rewarded for my efforts. On the roof of the horrendous neighbor's house, the one who'd scolded Mina about the garden—what was her name? I could not remember, but there was an anomalous shadow on her roof.

Whatever my previous training was, I'd learned to pay attention to even the smallest details. The shadow was nothing short of suspicious. As I neared the neighbor's garden wall, my path to the roof became clear. The shadow moved, having spotted me as well.

"Shit," I swore, regretting that I'd told Skye I didn't need her.

There was no time to fetch her. If I wanted to know more, I'd have to follow alone. I raced back to the alley to follow the shadow. Nor was there time to scale the houses on Orchid Street. I would have to pursue them from below, hoping my efforts would fade from sight in the dark alleyways.

After two blocks, I nearly lost them, but gained a tail. So much for being lost in the darkness. There were two of them. But were they separate entities, or were they working together? I had to make a choice. Follow one or catch the other. Some trace of strategy or instinct told me it would be better to chase and let the tail follow.

I increased my speed and the length of my strides. No longer did I try to disappear. Speed was all that mattered at this point—if I could get ahead of my quarry, I could cut them off. As I pulled almost two city blocks ahead of the figure on the roof, I hit the high street. Rather than having back gardens, shop buildings extended all the way into the alley.

One had a ladder that went up the side of the building near the trash bins. I scaled the ladder as fast as I could. Near the roof, I looked back. My tail was on the same block, and had spotted me. *Good*.

The figure from the roof was catching up to me. I moved towards them, meaning to cut them off and confront them, but they paused, spotting me. They were a block away and hesitated for what felt like an age. And they then shifted shape, turning into a starling and flying away. As they rose higher, I noted that one wing appeared injured, though it did not seem to impede their progress any. Swearing softly, I stole to the edge of the roof to find my tail.

They hadn't followed me up the ladder, but had stopped in the alley, watching the starling disappear into the clouds. I caught sight of their scarred owl's visage as they slipped into the shadows, disappearing so quickly it was startling. What they'd done wasn't possible. They were simply *gone*. I scrambled back down the ladder, searching the alley for signs of them, but there were none.

It was as if they'd never been in the alley at all. I'd lost them both, but gained at least a little knowledge. My tail had been none other than the Strix woman, which was complicated, given Muse's pronouncement. At the very least, now I knew that she was far more talented at subterfuge than I might have expected. I wouldn't underestimate her again. The sinking understanding that she would return threatened to send me into a focused rage, but I hadn't time for that. Besides, if the Strix woman was headed anywhere immediately dangerous, it would be back towards Mina.

My best bet was to head back to Orchid House and keep watch. I made haste, pondering the starling, going over all I'd observed as I jogged. I had a feeling that both Skye and Poe would be good resources for which of the high families shifted into starlings. Sunrise threatened in the east. There wasn't anything else I could do now. I turned back towards Orchid House.

I'D JUST PUT the mushroom tarts into the oven and was filling the kettle with water when Skye appeared in the kitchen, along with Morpheus.

"Poe and Mina are still asleep."

I nodded, putting a bit more water into the kettle. Skye often needed an extra cup of tea on mornings when she hadn't slept well. From the shadows under her eyes, I had to assume she was still upset from the previous day's events.

She sank onto the stool across from me. I filled the kettle, then put it on the stove. The house would not fill it for me, the way it did for Mina or Poe, but as I set it down, the stove flared to life on its own, just as the oven had done when I began making the tarts. The house was getting used to me. I opened the kitchen door a crack. It was hot down here.

"We were being watched," I said, keeping my voice low.

Skye nodded, resting her elbows on the island and her head in her hands. "Did you catch up with them?"

I shook my head. "No, the first flew off before I could catch up. The other was the Strix woman from before." Muse had said nothing about keeping news of the Strix woman from Skye, and it was best that she knew what we were dealing with.

Skye raised her head from her hands, her silver eyes narrowing. "That isn't good."

"No," I said, taking a teapot down from the shelves. "It isn't. What's more, Muse warned me against telling Mina about her."

"What?" Skye gasped. "Why?"

I lifted my shoulders to indicate I wasn't sure. "He said knowing would set her on a disastrous path."

Skye leaned back slightly. I knew my friend well enough to see the wheels turning in her head. She was trying to put this all together, just as I was. "She's more than she seems, don't you think?"

My jaw clenched as my body reacted to the mere thought of her in the bathtub, her arms around my neck, her soft mouth on mine, pliable and warm.

"I meant from a tactical standpoint," Skye hissed, though there was laughter in her voice. "You've really got it bad for her."

Morpheus leapt onto the island, flopping down in front of Skye, the tip of his tail moving only slightly. *She is more than any of us bargained for, that is for certain.*

"Do you think she's a danger to us, or herself?" Skye asked, the question directed toward the cat. Her focus was sharp now, as though something about the feline's words or tone was concerning to her. She was better at reading him than I was. His moods seemed rather monotonous to me, but Skye sensed the subtleties in Morpheus.

I believe Wilhelmina is dangerous to the entire world, in the wrong situation. He stared at me as he spoke, as though waiting for me to react.

I had very little to argue with. Mina was most definitely dangerous, quite dangerous, in fact. I sensed a power in her she likely was not even aware of yet.

"Do you know something more specific?" Skye asked. "Or is this another of your vague premonitions?"

She said it with love, but apparently, Morpheus did not appreciate Skye's tone. He disappeared in parts, dematerializing from the tips of his ears down to the end of his tail in a slow, deliberate manner that expressed his displeasure.

She is dangerous and powerful, the cat said as he faded from sight. *We will need those qualities before this ends. It would be better that she were dangerous and powerful for us, rather than against us.*

When he was gone, Skye swore. "That's rather ominous."

I nodded, glancing at the clock above the stove. The scent of mushroom tart had increased a measure. Skye smiled contentedly as she breathed in the bouquet of rosemary, mushroom, and melted cheddar. "When will the tarts be finished?"

"Not for another half hour," I replied. "And then they must cool."

The kettle sang, and I moved quickly to bring it off the stove, then spooned tea into the pot to steep. Behind me, Skye spoke. "When I found you, you were such a fearsome sight, even passed out. Bloody and so damn *dirty*."

I chuckled as I brought the teapot and teacups to the island. "And now?"

Skye smiled at me. "Now you're my best friend." Her hand stretched towards mine, and I reached out to take it. Her fingers closed around mine, her large hand looking small and graceful against my rugged bulk. "Be careful, Ash. With Mina, I mean."

I nodded. "She's been through a lot."

Skye sighed. "That's not what I mean. Be careful with yourself. She's dangerous in more ways than what Morpheus meant." I frowned. "She's complicated, and she's not telling us a lot. You sense that, right? That she's holding a lot back?"

I nodded. "Everyone has their secrets, though."

Skye shrugged. "We don't."

I laughed, gesturing to myself. "We *do*."

"That's different," she said. "You don't have any memory of who you are, or what's happened to you."

"But I remember what happened at the rubber factory," I murmured. "And so do you."

Her expression went dark, thinking of the empyrean fire I'd used to heal the owlet the night this all began. We hadn't had time to discuss that further, with all that had happened since. Everything had moved too quickly. But in any other investigation, I'd be a suspect.

"Do we need to talk about it?" I asked. "It's an odd coincidence, given everything." Something about my words, and the kitchen itself, gave me the sense that I'd had this conversation before.

"There is no way that you're Chopard. I know where you were for every other fire," Skye murmured. "Besides, you used your empyrae to heal. We don't even know if you have the ability to use enough to burn buildings to the ground."

I nodded, appreciative of her trust, but she was hedging and we both knew it. There wasn't any need for more conversation. Skye was always straightforward with her words. I poured the tea, spooning honey into hers, with a little milk. Just a splash. She smiled up at me.

"The one that got away from me before," I said as I

poured tea for myself. "They turned into a starling and flew off."

Skye's cup nearly slipped from her fingers. "Was there anything wrong with one of its wings?"

I knew she would know who it was. "Yes, it appeared injured."

She shook her head. "Not injured. Well, not actively so, anyway. Niall broke his left arm rather badly as a child, on a voyage to Brektos with my father. It wasn't set properly, and it healed wrong. He's never been willing to have it broken again and reset."

"So, your brother isn't missing at all."

"It would appear not," Skye said. "But that still leaves us with questions."

"Yes," I mused. "Such as, who is he working for?"

CHAPTER 29

MINA

I picked at my mushroom tart while Poe combed through both the gossip rags and an enormous pile of calling cards. Ashbourne and Skye were off to the undercity to report to Edith Braithwaite's operation. Ash hadn't made eye contact with me all morning, nor spoken even a single word. One nod in greeting was all I got.

I wondered if I'd made that much of a fool of myself in the Avalonne, or if he was simply shy about physical encounters. It bothered me a little, but there would be time to address it later. Outside the front windows, a stream of umbrellas passed by on the street. The rain had continued into the morning. It was a typical Pravhna autumn, cold, rainy, and blustery.

Water elementals played in the rain, turning into beautiful goldfish with fancy tails and swimming through the air. They grew larger as droplets added to their mass, then splattered apart, only to reconstitute moments later. Watching them, it was difficult not to wonder what might have happened if the old ones had answered me in the way I'd hoped for—if I'd been given a partner in this life, rather than knowledge that had shattered any hope of happiness I might ever have.

Without speaking, Poe handed me the pile of tittle-tattles. *The Ladies of Chanticleer* publication was at the top of the pile, and the most popular of the rags. Poe tapped a long oval nail on its first piece, "Oscarovi Heiress Ostracized at Armande's."

"That's an abhorrent use of alliteration," I muttered. Poe made a non-committal sound, the nib of her pen scratching the paper she was making lists upon. A glance told me she was sorting invitations. It was time to move to the next phase of our plan, evening events in wider society.

It looked like we'd been invited *everywhere* from the piles Poe had sorted. I turned my attention back to the article in the Chanticleer rag. Through the author's lens, Ashbourne had valiantly come to my rescue, and I'd done little more than stand there looking pretty and "surprisingly vulnerable for the heir to the Somerhaven title."

I sat the rag down with an eye roll. "Surprisingly vulnerable."

Poe looked up from her list. "That's a good thing. They're underestimating you still."

I grimaced, but of course she was right. The longer society thought me a brainless socialite, guileless and without ambition, the better. People's lips loosened around those they underestimated. They forgot to be on guard, and that was exactly what we needed to untangle the knot of our multiple interests and how they wove together.

It was good that they didn't think I was like Helene or Maman. While Helene had been admired, she was feared. Apparently, no one remembered much about me other than my youthful awkwardness, which the Chanticleer author noted that I'd "blossomed out of." It was insulting to think people perceived me this way, but I reminded myself it was all for a purpose. A vain part of me was pleased that they noticed how beautifully I was dressed.

It didn't take long to scan through the other rags. Some mentioned the previous day's outing, but they were mere echoes of the Chanticleer's thoughts. Nothing original. That was the way it always was. The Chanticleer set the tone of things and most everyone else simply followed along.

"Where are we off to this evening?" I asked, setting the pile of gossips aside.

Poe pushed a hand-lettered invitation towards me. "This was delivered by one of the House's footmen this morning."

I opened the envelope, the heavy paper luxurious to the touch. Inside was an invitation to an intimate evening soiree at House Aestra. "This seems a bit last minute for Elspeth," I said as I scanned the invitation.

"It's a viewing for the Orilion Lights." Poe held up a handwritten note. "She says the sky will be unexpectedly clear this evening and the astronomers have deemed them likely to be visible."

I glanced outside, where rain still fell in heavy sheets. "Interesting."

"She also says that she's invited those she believes may have connections to Chopard, and some of your mother's possible connections."

Anticipation thrummed through me. We'd missed our opportunity to sleuth yesterday at the lecture, but gained valuable information from Muse. It was an acceptable trade-off, but it was time to begin our hunt for Chopard in earnest.

"If we are going, I need to respond," Poe said, staring at the front door.

"Have the two of you made up yet?"

Poe shook her head. "And I'd rather not respond without talking it over with her, but..."

I placed my hand on Poe's. "Respond. She'll understand."

Poe sighed. "All right. We'll need to begin getting ready, if we're to make it in time."

I glanced at the clock. It was a little before noon. The soiree did not begin until almost nine, which meant no one of consequence would arrive before ten. The lights wouldn't even be visible until midnight. How could it possibly take us that long to get ready?

∼

Six hours later, I understood. Poe had a rigorous routine to ready herself for a high echelon event like this one. This included several small, nutritious meals; treatments for the skin, hair, and nails; and one nap before the real work began. She'd left me to rest, but sleep would not come. Instead, I stared at the slanted ceiling in my bedroom, counting the slats of painted boards, as I'd done when I was little.

I was avoiding the onslaught of memories that flooded me every time I closed my eyes. Everything came back in the wrong order, and though I could discern the basics of my life before the Wildfangs found me, the nuance of it all escaped me. The memories of an extraordinarily long life rushed back, mixing with those of the past twenty-eight years. I was left muddled and confused, unable to find a comfortable position in bed, though my pain was not as intense as it had been the day before.

Downstairs, the front door opened. Skye and Ashbourne spoke to one another, then both came upstairs. I listened as they parted ways. Footsteps grew closer to the door of my room, followed by a soft knock.

"Mina, are you awake?" Ashbourne murmured on the other side of the door, so quiet I could hardly hear him.

So he did not want to incur Poe's wrath. I smiled at the ceiling. "Yes," I whispered, using the same caution. "Come in."

He opened the door, slipping inside on silent feet, then shutting the door behind him without a sound. I glanced at him. Propriety would have said I should rise from bed to greet him, but despite the fact that I resented being told to rest, I did actually need to do so.

"How was it with Edith's people?" I asked as he moved to the chair he'd slept in the night before.

"Fine," he said, removing his frock coat and rolling up his sleeves, as he sank into the chair.

The flex in his forearms was a little too arousing, if I was honest with myself. I'd just had a bath and had only put on my nightgown, since I was still too warm to get under the covers. Ashbourne seemed to notice this fact only after he'd sat down. A pink flush colored his moonstone cheeks.

He swallowed hard. "About yesterday, at the Avalonne..."

"I understand if you were just being kind," I interjected when he seemed lost for words. My voice went flat. "I apologize for my forward behavior. I hope I haven't made you uncomfortable."

"I am not uncomfortable," he said, defense edging his voice. "In fact, I worry I am altogether too comfortable with what happened between us."

Surely he wasn't one of those men that believed women needed to be protected from the wanton desires of men. There were a few of that kind in more conservative pockets of the upper echelons, but most folk didn't subscribe to that kind of nonsense. If he was one of those, I'd made a terrible mistake.

"I only meant that you are a client, Mina," he explained, obviously observing the way my eyes had rolled at my train of thought. "It isn't appropriate for me to bring clients to the heights of pleasure."

"Then you have nothing to worry over."

He scoffed slightly, then frowned.

Perhaps more clarification was necessary. "I only meant that not much happened between us. I hold every confidence that you might please a lover."

He stood slowly, his eyes falling half shut as he rose. "Oh?"

The depth of his voice sent shivers through me, my back arching slightly at the sound. "Yes," I said, planting my body firmly back on the bed. "I am certain you're quite capable."

He crossed his arms, looking down at me. "You don't sound convinced to me."

I raised my eyebrows, and my head, but only slightly from my pillow as I stretched my arms behind my head, arching my back again. "Perhaps I'm not."

The barest hint of a smirk played at his lips. He moved faster than I assumed someone of his size might be capable of. In a flash, he was bent over me, one hand pinning my hands above my head. "What," he growled, "do you anticipate it might take to convince you?"

"I'm not certain," I purred back. "I'd have to be presented with a sampling of your skills to really say."

His free hand gripped my jaw now, bringing my eyes to his. "Please, tell me you are not a virgin, Mina."

My eyes fluttered, rolling again. "Of course not."

He waited. We were still playing, but he was serious. "If you are a virgin, we cannot do this now."

I strained playfully against his hands. "I am not." He frowned, clearly worried I might be lying to him. It was good of him to be concerned, but he need not be. "There have been others. When I was younger—a teenager." I matched his seriousness now. "It has been a very long time, though."

Relief flooded his expression, replaced quickly with simmering desire. "Then we'll need to make this good, won't we?"

My mouth went dry at the promise in his words. I had no doubt that Ashbourne Claymore could make good on the fire burning in his golden eyes. One hand slid down my side, barely grazing the fabric of my thin nightgown, eliciting a shiver of pleasure that quaked through my whole body.

He held his weight above me, only applying enough pressure with his heavy body to give me the feeling of being comfortably caged. He shifted slightly, parting my thighs as he came to rest between them. His eyes didn't leave mine as his wandering hand moved lower, skimming the line of my hip now. The hand holding my wrists above my head flexed, and I opened my palms to allow him to lace his fingers through mine.

"Tell me where you want this hand," he murmured as he lowered his head to my ear. The sound of his low voice sent waves of anticipatory pleasure straight to my core as his fingers dragged lightly across the swell of my belly.

I was no blushing virgin, and I wouldn't pretend to be. "Inside me," I commanded.

His head pulled back from mine so our eyes met again, his fingers leaving my body, though I could not see where they'd gone. "Inside you?" he asked as his thumb grazed my bottom lip.

I glared at his purposeful misunderstanding of my words, but I dipped my chin, capturing his thumb lightly between my teeth. He let out a rumbling growl of pleasure as my tongue flicked over his skin. Two could play these games.

When I released his thumb, I asked, "Where do you want to put that hand, Ashbourne?"

His breath quickened at my words and a muscular thigh slid between my legs, an answer of its own. My arms broke free of his grip, flying around his neck. I pulled him down atop me, our mouths colliding in a fervent embrace. My hips lifted as I squeezed my thighs around him, desperately seeking friction. My joints ached, but his touch countered the pain in a bittersweet dance.

Some fluttering thing beat its wings inside my chest, my breath racing through me in feverish pants. His hard length pressed into my core, promising me sweet release with each thrust of our hips, then betrayed me as he pulled away. Again and again he moved against me, kissing me as hard as I kissed him.

My fingers coiled in his hair, drawing his head back so I could taste the skin at his neck. Something primal rose within me at the taste of his skin, and I had the insatiable urge to sink my teeth into him, to inhabit him so fully we could not be parted. I wanted him with a desperation I had never known with any other lover. There was no time—I wanted him inside me now.

A knock at the door caused us both to startle, our foreheads crashing into one another. "Mina," Poe chastised from the other side of the door. "That is *not* resting."

Ash buried his head in my neck, silent laughter shaking his shoulders.

"Let her rest, Ashbourne," Poe warned as her footsteps retreated. "Or I shall make you both sorry you defied me."

I stared at the ceiling for a long moment, cheeks flushed hot, Ash's body a comforting weight. My hands ran through his hair as I laughed along with him. He fell onto the bed next to me, pulling my back against his chest. "Poe may be a lost princess," he murmured in my ear. "But she certainly has the giving orders part mastered."

As his arms tightened around me, my backside pressed into him, seeking the proof that he wanted me still. His hand slid down to my belly, pressing firmly into my flesh, pinning me to him, a claim on my body. "Will you not sleep?"

I shook my head, my thighs pressing together. "How could I now?"

The arm that curved up from under me flexed. "I am not risking her royal highness' wrath," he murmured in my ear. "But we will finish this, Mina. You will scream my name before this night is over."

Desire snapped through me like a live aetheric wire, but Ash's arms only tightened around me. "Sleep, you beautiful menace."

Something about those words soothed my soul. Ash saw me for what I was, and he wanted me still. I sighed deeply, smoothing the ragged edges of my breath as my heart sought out the rhythm of his, thumping against my back. My eyes were heavier than I'd thought and before I was finished yawning, I had fallen asleep.

CHAPTER 30

MINA

When I woke, Ash was gone, but there was a note on my pillow that read, *I keep my promises. Dress accordingly, and do not take matters into your own hands.* I swore into my pillow, but couldn't help but laugh. It felt good to do so, and when the sound of my mirth died away, I rolled onto my back, breathing freely, a smile on my lips.

A voice inside me rose up, warning that I must not lose focus. That if I sought pleasure over purpose, I would lose. The voice sounded more like Maman or Helene than me, though, and I whispered aloud, "Lose *what*, exactly?"

There was no force requiring that I hunt down the arsonist who burned Somerhaven down. My survival did not depend on getting revenge against whomever killed my family. And why did I want to kill them, anyway? They'd done me a favor. My anger seemed silly. Childish even.

Nothing in the world could stop me from helping Poe, or Skye and Ash, for that matter. They had offered me aid without conditions, a kind of generosity I'd never known. But I could leave all this anger behind, if I so chose. I could help them find Chopard, and then leave with them. Wherever they went next, I could go too.

I could start over if I wanted. The promises Ashbourne's body made to mine could be fulfilled as many times as we wanted. My skin flushed at the thought, remembering his hands on me, his lips on mine. *Do not take matters into your own hands*, I reminded myself. My rebellious thighs squeezed together, my skin damp with the pleasure he'd wrought from me before my nap.

There didn't have to be more than this. I could have this winding affair, let my feelings get involved in ways that the voice that sounded like Helene railed against. It gave me pleasure to deny it.

I sat up in bed, my eyes meeting my reflection in the mirror on my vanity table. "I don't have to do as you did anymore," I said aloud. To Helene, to Maman. To all those who came before this body, before this life. The ones who'd wanted only to control me, to punish me.

And for what?

I could not remember now.

I only remembered the pain. The pain that had always been with me, in one form or another. Behind it, there was the promise that the well of agony would be endless if I stayed on this path. If I let all these memories in, if I unlocked Maman's workshop door, this would never end. But I had the power to stop. If I wanted to, I could.

I looked at the note again, my fingers moving over the words, thinking of the man who wrote them. Would it be so bad to fall in love with him? To give him my heart? Not tonight, or tomorrow, certainly, but someday.

My throat tightened with every passing thought, a sob clawing its way up my throat. On the sea stairs, I had promised myself that there would be no more tears. Not of this kind. If I let them out, could I let this go?

I nodded to myself, rocking my body back and forth as tears fell, sobs wracking through me as I relinquished all my anger to my tears. None of it mattered anymore. The memories that had crowded my thoughts before Ash knocked at my door receded to somewhere deeper in my mind. They were still there, and someday I could take them out, sort them, and understand why all this had happened.

But for now, I wanted this release. I looked around my room, knowing that when we were done here, I never wanted to see this house again. I would sell it all, and move to the undercity, or wherever my friends were.

My friends. My heart swelled with all the affection I hadn't yet let myself feel for them. For the first time in my life, I had real friends. People who saw me for what I was and did not care. Through the tears that still fell, I laughed. Maman and Helene had been wrong all along. I was worthy of love, and now they were dead. Gone forever.

I was finally free.

A FEW HOURS LATER, Poe put the finishing touches on my hair and declared me perfect. Diamond and sapphire encrusted pins shone in my masses of dark hair. I had no idea how she'd managed it, but the effect was one of undone beauty. The style was less severe than the sleek chignons that were popular now, but still unquestionably fashionable.

Poe was a genius, pure and simple. When she left me to put the final touches on her own ensemble, I turned in front of the mirror in the hallway. I marveled as the light caught the jewels in my hair, the subtle sheen of my dress. The gown was simple, made from a nearly sheer midnight blue fabric that billowed around my legs as I walked. The bodice was fitted, a corset built into it, the light boning covered in plush velvet that created an intricate pattern across my abdomen. It looked a little like I was wearing armor. But my favorite part of the dress was the high neck and billowing lantern sleeves.

The effect was heavy, elegant, and sensual. I was completely covered, but when I moved, hints of my pale skin showed through. I wore scant little under the dress, as that was how it was meant to be worn, but also, because of Ashbourne's note. My skin heated with the promise of his words.

He and Skye were out on some errand, though I had not caught what that was. I made my way down to the second floor, where I found Morpheus asleep at the top of the stairs. I sat next to him and he stretched out, his fluffy tail flicking my leg.

His eyes blinked open a few times before he sighed deeply, appearing to go back to sleep. *You are a good likeness for Akatei.*

"Who is that?" I asked, curiosity piqued.

Morpheus growled in irritation, but did not answer me directly. *Of course, you are not really a witch. Not truly.*

That stung a little, even if it was true. Though I thoroughly hated all Maman and Helene stood for, the Oscarovi were admirable. I wished I was one of them. I wore no false jewel this evening. Poe had promised me she was fetching me something from her own cache of treasures.

"I am no one," I mused. "Not really. Whatever I was before, I'm not now. And you're right, I'm not a witch."

That is not what I meant at all, the cat grumbled. *Have you considered you might be* more?

I was about to ask what he meant when the door to the Rose Room opened and Poe emerged. My mouth fell open. The dress she wore was seafoam green, which contrasted beautifully with her bronze skin, but the dress itself wasn't the marvel. The silver corset she wore atop the dress accentuated her every curve, a flexible cage that moved with her, giving her the appearance of a queen going into battle. She wore no other jewelry.

Poe needed no extra adornment; her face was so beautiful it was hard to look at her for very long. Joy crept through me, a grin stretching my cheeks so far it almost hurt.

"I don't think I've ever seen you look so happy," she said.

The tears I'd shed after my nap threatened to return, but I swallowed them. There weren't words for all the emotions I currently felt. Not yet. It was going to take me some time to find the words to tell Poe how much I appreciated her. I settled on, "You look like a queen."

Her smile was faint, as though her thoughts were far away. "Thank you. Tonight, I feel like one."

Downstairs, the front door opened and Skye and Ashbourne entered, both dressed in tuxedos and long, heavy overcoats. Skye stopped in her tracks when she spotted Poe. Ash shut the door behind her as the two of us watched them float toward one another.

Poe took Skye's outstretched hands. Skye fell to one knee, pressing her forehead into Poe's palms. "I'm sorry," she whispered, kissing each palm in turn, a gesture so intimate I blushed. "Forgive me, Your Royal Highness."

"Skye," Poe breathed. "Don't call me that."

Skye looked up, a devilish look in her eyes.

Poe bit her bottom lip, smiling. "Unless I ask you to."

From the top of the stairs, I struggled to stifle a delirious laugh. It was wholly inappropriate, but also, *I was happy*. The feeling left me giddy. Ash's eyes shot to mine, a slow smile spreading over his handsome face. He'd gotten a haircut, his long hair now shorn into a style that flopped into his eyes, but no longer needed to be tied back.

Morpheus, who still sat next to me, began to disappear.

"Where are you going?" I asked, looking down. He hadn't been around much lately.

I have an engagement of my own to get to this evening. He promptly disappeared, as though annoyed by my question.

Downstairs, Ash shook his head, then took the stairs three at a time to reach me. He sat a step below me, reaching for something in his pocket.

"I picked this up for you. Edith paid for it." He handed me a velvet box, his eyes dark with worry. "I wish it were actually *from* me."

I opened the box. Inside was a beautiful ring, an enormous black opal, set between the metal petals of two *orchis mascula*—a mildly poisonous orchid, whose roots were used in love spells, should one be foolish enough to craft one. It was a beautiful ring, stunning in fact. My heartbeat sped up as I ran a finger over the ring, testing it for traces of magic.

There wasn't even a hint. The ring had been made by mundane means, which was an enormous tell. My heart beat even faster now. A piece of paper was folded up inside the box. Ash shrugged when I pulled it out, showing it to him. I opened it. It was a note written in a neat hand that said,

Mina,

This was given to me to pass onto you when the time was right.

EB

I frowned. "Did Edith say where this came from?"

Ash shook his head, pulling the ring out of the box and looking at it closely. "No, and there's no artisan marks on it either." He closed his eyes, his fingers closing over the ring. "There's not a trace of magic on it. It's like it's empty."

I swallowed hard as he dropped it into my hands. It was as I'd suspected upon opening the box. The ring was a vessel —created with the sole purpose of being inspirited with a familiar. A black opal was a powerful stone, meant to channel an even more powerful elemental spirit. Goosebumps pricked my skin as I slid the ring onto my left index finger, the place anyone who knew what they were looking for would check. Inspirited rings were always worn as such.

Unless someone else held the ring itself, as we had just done, no one would know the ring was still empty. "Do you know what this signifies?" I whispered. "What people will think?"

Ash nodded, his mouth tightening. "It will make you an object of conversation… But also a target."

CHAPTER 31
ASHBOURNE

The rooftop terrace of House Aestra was beyond anything I could have anticipated. I thought I understood what the high echelons were like, how they lived, but this proved how wrong I was. The building itself was beyond comparison, a six story marvel of limestone and granite, twice as grand as Orchid House. The patterns in the leaded glass alone must have taken years to create, and an inordinate amount of money.

It shattered my understanding of Skye, in part, but mostly, it helped me understand her convictions better. That her honor was true, because she'd chosen the life we lived over this one, the undercity over this sparkling world. I loved her all the more for it.

The house was beautiful; tastefully decorated, art gilding every hallway. But Mina was the real jewel tonight. The dark fabric of her gown swirled in tantalizing fashion with even the slightest movement. As we made our way to the terrace, Skye, who had hold of Poe's arm, looked back at me, nodding once to confirm our plans. We'd agreed to go our separate ways for the evening. The four of us together was too much, too intimidating. But split up, we could cover more territory, talk to more of Elspeth's carefully curated guest list. Mina slipped her arm under mine, her fingers curling around my bicep as she leaned into me.

The feeling of her body so close to mine was distracting, but a pleasant buzz of pleasure, rather than the intense waves of desire I'd felt before. It was obvious from the way her pupils widened as she gazed up at me that she wanted all the same things I did. There was something comforting in that, a warmth emanating from her that hadn't before.

"Something is different about you," I murmured softly.

We stepped out the arched doors of House Aestra's impressive ballroom to the garden terrace. Mina nodded towards a bower near the balustrade. Further on, fire moths danced in the tall garden flowers, drawn by the ambrosia of night blooms. People gathered in groups, sparkling wine in hand, chatting under the unusually clear night sky.

"Could we take a moment?" she asked.

"Of course," I replied, following her lead.

The bower was covered in night-blooming honeysuckle, which was covered in fire moths sipping at the flowers. Mina's skin glowed like the moon under the dancing light of the flying insects. One lit on her shoulder as she sank onto the bench inside the bower. Its white furry body was larger than the others, and the glow it gave off was blue, rather than the pale silver light of the rest of the moths. She smiled as it rubbed its fuzzy face against her cheek. My breath caught in my throat, and my body froze.

The picture she made with the elemental creature so close to her beautiful face was like nothing I'd ever seen. Somehow, even with my missing memory, I was as sure of that as I was of the emotions brewing in me. This was more than lust, more than duty. I cared for her, wanted to see her satisfied in all things.

In that moment, I was sure of only one thing: I would do anything to give her what she wanted. Nothing would stop me from protecting her, from being at her side if she needed me, away if she asked it. I would journey miles to find anything she needed, extinguish any who harmed her, and someday, if she let me, I would love her.

The thought stunned me. I loved Skye and Morpheus deeply. They were my family, the deepest companions of my heart. We had forged trust between us with time and experience, in thousands of thoughtful actions and conversations. But this was an altogether different feeling. It was as though my heart already knew hers.

This woman *was* my fate. She was as inevitable as moonrise. Her eyes met mine as the moth whispered silently to her. She nodded once, acknowledging it, but her gaze did not waver. I wondered if she felt it too, the way Lady Fate had her talons wrapped around us. Would Mina buckle in submission, as I was about to?

I took one step towards her, my fingers grazing her chin, her soft jawline. I hesitated, not wanting to muss her hair. My thumb swept over her bottom lip, and she let out a gasp that wove between us, the threads of Fate's magic tightening. Mina's fingers closed around my free hand, tugging me towards her.

When my face was just inches from hers, our breath met in a moment so heavy with possibility I thought she might turn from me. But she did not. Instead, she whispered just one devastating sentence. "I want all of you."

I searched her eyes for telltale signs of lust, but found only raw vulnerability. Yes, there was desire there, as there was for me. It was not the base desire of bodies feverish to make quick contact. Instead, in her gaze, I found the longing that haunted me. Longing for some place to belong, just as I did. For some*one* who could love the monster I knew lurked inside me. I pulled her onto my lap in one fluid motion, wrapping my arms around her waist.

"Then I am yours," I replied. But it wasn't enough. I needed to know that she would promise the same. "Will you be mine as well?"

She nodded once, solemn as a priestess, and destiny ricocheted through me, wounding as it gave me hope. When my lips met Mina's, a drumbeat sounded in the recesses of my mind, menacing in its violent threat. Rather than warning me off the path I walked now, it drove me further, my grip tightening on the woman who kissed me with need that echoed my own. I deepened the kiss, my hands drifting now over the curves of her body, the silken fabric of her gown slick against my touch.

"Not here," I said, my mouth still on hers. The warning in my mind was clear. When I entered Mina, I could lose some measure of control of my magic. She would be safe, but no one else would be. I couldn't risk revealing myself. "I know what I said, but not here."

"What is happening to us?" she asked.

I shook my head, unsure, but glad it was not just me. "I don't know, Mina. Is this what falling in love feels like?"

A helpless little laugh let me know just how unmoored she felt. She was at as much of a loss as I was, then. "I don't know. I've never fallen in love before."

I hugged her to me. "This seems like something people are supposed to know, doesn't it?"

Her breath on my neck was distracting, but sweet in its comforting simplicity. "How do you know this isn't just lust?"

I sighed, knowing it was best to be frank. "I am not a monk, Mina."

She nodded. "Neither have I been chaste, as I said before."

"So how do *you* know?" I asked.

She shook her head, watching the fire moths floating around the bower. Music from further away on the terrace floated towards us. Someone was playing the harp. "For me, it is like I've always known you."

Her words pierced me. For the smallest moment, I thought I might panic, but I could not say why. "Yes," I said, the word slowly leaving my mouth. "Yes, that is exactly how I feel. How strange."

"What is strange about that?" she asked. "I've read some of your romances. Is this not how lovers often feel?"

At that, I laughed. "You are right. Perhaps that's what is strange. I don't have many... How to put it?" She waited for me to speak, her eyes infinitely patient, an expression I'd never seen on her face before. *I'd* elicited this from her. Patience from one of the most driven women I'd ever encountered. "Universal experiences," I finished when words found me again. "I don't often seem to feel or react the way most people do to things."

Mina slid off my lap, taking my hand in hers, pressing it to her lips. "Neither do I. Perhaps that is why we're so drawn to one another."

I nodded, feeling like someone had cut me loose. From what, I could not say, but the unmooring was not unwelcome. In fact, it felt as though an adventure lay before me, new and alluring. I stood. "So, we'll do this together?"

"Yes," she replied. "We'll do this together, and when it's done, when we find Chopard..." she trailed off, as though suddenly unsure.

I finished for her. "We will sail those waters together as well."

CHAPTER 32

MINA

His words sent a fissure through me, cracking into the wall that stood between me and the last of my memories. There was a thick mist between me and all I wanted to know, but one memory in particular floated back to me: the vision I'd had of the women standing over me, talking while they thought I was unconscious. *What had they said? Something about a loophole. Something about love.*

When the memory had first returned, it meant nothing to me. It was only evidence that there had been life before the fetch. But now I wondered—was love part of what I needed to end this? Were their words a benediction, rather than a threat?

If, as I was beginning to suspect, I had been cursed, then some essential part of my nature must have been taken into consideration. Vaness Wildfang was a terrible mother, but she had been a thorough teacher, and I knew that curses only worked if you truly understood someone.

If someone had cursed me before I'd ever encountered the Wildfangs, then it had been someone who knew me. Someone who knew that love did not come easily to me, and would not in any life, any iteration of my essence, as I was unlikely to ever trust another enough to love them. Someone who knew that every curse had to have a loophole to bind properly—and that truly loving another would be an appropriate one for me.

As I looked up into Ash's golden eyes, fixed on me like I was the moon he hung all his hopes upon, I knew. I could love him. And not just him, but Poe, Skye, and Morpheus as well. I'd been right this afternoon. This thing that had plagued me through lifetimes could be vanquished. Though I was not even sure yet what it was, what followed me, relentlessly haunting me, I knew I wanted it gone. And now I had hope. If there was a curse upon me, it could be broken, but there would be a price.

My pride, my fear—they would all have to go. Trust was not built on secrets. "This is not my true body," I said, without hesitation. "This is a fetch, a doppelganger. I am not real or natural." I paused, waiting for his face to twist with disgust. But like Poe, he merely appeared curious.

"You feel very real to me," Ashbourne responded, pulling me to him. The hard warmth of his body infused me with hope. I dared not breathe for fear he would change his mind. His head bent low. "And when I am buried deep inside you tonight, you will know just how real you are. Nature means nothing to me. I want all of you."

Tears welled in my eyes as a fresh wave of arousal flooded my core. This was what true desire felt like, emotion tangled with attraction so strong it could unthaw even the coldest of hearts. "Then, you don't care?"

He shook his head. "You could turn into a wraith, a White Lady, a ghoul, and I would still want all of you, Mina. I want *you*, not the vessel that carries you." The words were spoken with such depth of feeling, I wondered for the briefest moment if they were for me.

Wasn't this all too fast? Too soon? Shouldn't I be suspicious? Thoughts flooded me, trying to overwhelm me with doubt. I shoved them aside. For once, I wanted something good for me. Something that had nothing to do with survival or revenge. What I wanted now was a life, and I was willing to fight for it.

"Thank you," I said. Simple gratitude was all I could manage, the lump of emotion in my throat so potent I could not say more.

"Shall we get to work?" he asked.

I nodded. "And later?"

His grin was a promise, followed by a hard swallow, his throat bobbing with the same emotion I felt. "Later, I will show you what devotion means to me."

I'D VISITED some of the upper echelon's homes in my childhood, but House Aestra's terrace was like nothing I'd ever seen. The structure itself jutted out above the city, which peeked out from the mist and clouds below, where every so often, lights sparkled in the depth of the dark night. Up here, the air was crisp and dry, all the stars visible in the clear sky. There was no moon; Fate's lady hid her face from us in her monthly retreat inward.

The fire moths lit the fragrant flowers of the garden. Up here, where the sun could actually peek through the clouds, so many more varieties of flowers bloomed. Pravhna's climate was fairly temperate. Despite the fact that the autumn rain could be brutal, it was merely chilly, not truly cold, as it would have been in Somershire. Scattered amongst the overflowing flower beds were nooks meant for intimate encounters, marked by carved stone arches. Various delights graced tables and the trays that floated unaccompanied through the crowds.

Elspeth Aestra had pulled out all the stops for tonight's party, using so much magic I had to wonder who exactly was pulling the strings. Was she powerful enough to light the gardens and keep floating trays on their paths? Or had she a team of Oscarovi somewhere managing it all? That would be expensive, but she certainly had the capital to do something of the sort.

There weren't so many guests as to feel overwhelming, but neither were there so few that the party felt small. I couldn't help but be impressed. As Maman had not entertained much, I had very little idea how one pulled something like this off. From watching Poe, I knew the answer was "carefully." More than that, I might never know.

My fingers tightened around Ash's arm. If he meant what he'd said, and I believed that he did, my life would probably never look like this. There would be no posh parties, no giant townhouse in the upper echelons. No large events to plan or execute. Relief crashed over me. I wanted none of this. I wanted purpose, and most of all, peace.

Ash took a coupe glass from the tray that had paused before us. It was full of a sparkling rose liquid. I took a sip. Crisp apple burst on my tongue, followed by the sweet taste of burnt sugar and something vaguely floral. He sipped from his own glass and smiled. "Tastes like a day at the orchard."

A smile stole through me, reaching my eyes before it did my mouth. "It does, though I can't say I've ever been to an orchard. But this is exactly what I imagine it would taste like."

Happiness rolled off us as we stared at each other. That nasty voice inside me tried to make a remark, but I couldn't hear it. Over Ashbourne's shoulder, I caught sight of Caralee

Ellis-Whitley. "Will you hunt down one of those trays of cheese puffs?" I asked.

Ash followed my gaze, his brows knitting slightly, but he nodded. "I will." He brushed a kiss to my cheek, his breath lingering for a moment. Caralee looked up as his cool knuckles brushed over my jaw. "So beautiful," he murmured as he turned away. I watched him stride after one of the floating trays, stifling a laugh as it moved just fast enough that he'd have to jog to keep up.

When I turned back to the crowd, Caralee openly glared at me. I walked towards her, keeping my pace relaxed. There was no need to rush and risk tripping on the rough stone pavers that formed the terrace's many winding paths. Besides, it agitated Caralee, who so obviously waited to have a confrontation.

As I approached her, I noticed she no longer wore the ring Viridian had given my sister. I could practically feel my eyes glimmering with mirth. "Good evening, Caralee. You look beautiful tonight." It wasn't a lie; she was gorgeous in a ruby colored gown that draped alluringly over her tiny waist. Her mass of dark curls was pulled into a tight bun, and to my mind, the pale skin of her forehead appeared a bit strained. "I always appreciate someone who knows just exactly how much jewelry to wear to one of these events."

She fumed. My heart sang with the pleasure of it. The woman had tormented me for years when we were children, pretending to be friends for months on end, then embarrassing me at the most inopportune moments. All of it had been a game to her.

"Do you?" she asked as she regained her composure. "Have you been to many of these kinds of events, then? I don't recall seeing you."

Good. She was going to play rough. I wanted a fight. "Are you invited to many parties with the likes of House

Aestra?" I asked, taking a firm guess that she was here because House Montclair had been invited, and not on her own merit, which meant that Viridian was here somewhere.

Caralee's eyes blazed with fury. "At least I'm not here riding the coattails of some undercity hoodlum."

I felt Ash return before I saw him, felt him tense at Caralee's words, and my own fury rose to meet hers. "No, that's true, Caralee. You come riding the coattails of Helene's leftovers." I stepped closer to her, dropping my voice a measure. "How does it feel to know that you only have what you do because someone *murdered* my sister?"

Caralee gasped, sputtering. "How... *dare* you?"

It had been a calculated move, cruel, but it did as I hoped it would. Caralee searched the crowd for Viridian. She had never been the kind to stand up for herself. She moved in crowds of people who were just as small-minded and petty as she was. Helene had been just as vicious as she was, but never so small.

I'd hit her where it hurt the most, revealing an insecurity, and now she wanted Viridian to come put me in my place. I wondered if she knew that he'd put me in the oubliette. It wouldn't surprise me much if she had, nor would it surprise me to know that he'd kept her in the dark. Ash stepped up beside me, handing me a small plate of cheese puffs.

He followed my gaze, which tracked Caralee's. She had taken a few steps away from us, and was preparing to disappear into the crowd. Her eyes lit when she found Viridian. He was at the opposite end of the terrace, leaning against the balustrade. His coat was tailored close to his trim form, and was a deeper shade of crimson than Caralee's dress, but it was obvious he'd dressed to match her, which was unfortunate. The color did not complement his pale hair or skin one bit. Cooler colors suited Viridian better, I decided. He was deep in conversation with a shorter Oscarovi man, who faced away from us.

The man had pale skin and wan brown hair. There was nothing of interest about him whatsoever, except that he wasn't dressed for the party. His suit was nice enough, and had obviously been tailor-made, but the invitation had specified formal dress. When I turned back, Caralee had disappeared, melting into the crowd. No doubt she was off to tattle on me to Viridian.

"What a terrible woman," Ash said as we both watched the man speaking to Viridian. Ash was looking him over carefully as well. I wondered if he noticed the sartorial misstep. Likely he did. He had a careful eye for detail. "Someone should break all her fingers."

I made a non-committal sound as his words fully sunk in. My curiosity piqued. "Why her fingers?"

Ash swiped a cheese puff from my plate and popped it into my mouth. The melted sharp cheddar combined with a hint of tart cranberry jam and buttery pastry. It was divine. He smiled at my apparent reaction to the puff. "Because then she'd require help wiping her own ass."

My nose wrinkled at the picture forming in my head. It was an awful thing to say. Also, it pleased me so much I wished the crowd would simply disappear so I could tear his clothes from his body. "Wicked boy," I purred.

"Beautiful menace," he replied.

For a moment, it seemed we might forget ourselves and give into our passions without care for who watched. Across the terrace, the man talking to Viridian moved, his face briefly visible. It was a plain face, one most would forget the instant they saw it, but I'd seen it many times before.

"I know him," I said, careful to keep my voice low. "He is one of those who used to come to the house to meet with

Maman." I looked at the sky. "Often, on nights such as these."

"The dark moon." It was a statement, not a question. He'd scanned through as many of Maman's spell books as I had recently. The dark moon was ripe for many kinds of workings. Many of them neutral, but many dangerous as well. I had no idea if the timing was significant, but it would be lazy not to assume that it was.

The man shook hands with Viridian, and then turned. Ash took my plate from my hands, leaving it on a bench. "Come, we need to talk with him, then."

CHAPTER 33

MINA

Overhead, the Orilion phenomena appeared as Ash pulled me through the terrace garden. The lights must have been manifesting while I argued with Caralee. Now they danced in the sky, green and violet ribbons of light. Somewhere deep inside me, a resonance built in my chest, behind my lungs. It was as though some part of me vibrated in time with the celestial dance.

I took my eyes off the lights in time to see the faint blue glow of a loping gait, close to the ground. My breath stuck in my throat. It couldn't be. They didn't leave the mountain. The flash of a pale tail stopped my feet—I froze in place.

Ash looked back. "We'll lose him."

My heart beat faster. "Go. I'll catch up."

He shook his head, seeming to sense that I'd seen something important. "No, I won't leave you."

"Go," I insisted. Just beyond him, in a giant rosemary bush, a long ear poked out as a chill breeze kicked up. The hare was behind the bush, waiting for me.

"All right," Ash agreed, though he still held onto my

hand. "If I don't return, find Skye and Poe. I'll meet you at home."

I liked the way he said home. I nodded, pulling my hand from his grip. He'd lose the man if I stayed with him, and I would lose the hare. He flashed a quick, reassuring grin at me, then disappeared. A moment of envy caught me by surprise. It would be nice to be so mobile, so quick and free of pain. Even now, after a day of rest and preparation, my body ached. I flexed my shoulders slightly. The place between them hurt more tonight than usual.

Ash had the ability to free me from my pain, to make even the worst bouts of it pass, even if just for a short while. The little of his touch I'd already experienced was enough to know that the ways his body was attuned to mine would be more than a balm. In his embrace, I experienced ecstasy, however brief. That would have to be enough for me. As I made my way slowly toward the rosemary bush, I had the distinct feeling that it would be more than enough.

"Hello," I said as I approached the bush. "I see you."

The hare poked its head out. I couldn't be certain, but it looked like the one that had helped me escape the ruin's collapse at Somerhaven. *You have become distracted*, it said.

"I do not recall you giving me a mission," I replied, feeling tart. "You only told me you'd be watching and that all I do matters."

The hare glared at me, its vicious, cunning paws raising towards its chest. I'd seen common hares box one another before. Surely, this one did not intend to punch me. *You are impertinent.*

"Very likely so," I agreed. "But if you have something you need to tell me, I am happy to hear it."

The hare's head tilted slightly, its terrifying eyes reflecting the dying light of the Orilion. *My brethren dance to the songs of the stars. Can you hear the music?*

I glanced behind me. Sure enough, in the fading lights, air elementals, many in the shapes of serpentine dracon, undulated with the Orilion. Though the lights faded, the resonant music inside me had not. I felt the music, rather than hearing it, but I supposed that was good enough. I nodded. "Yes, I feel the music. What does it mean?"

It is Her song. She gathers us to Her. Which side will you choose?

I knew better, but the cryptic knots the hare spoke in were terribly frustrating. I sighed. "Whatever do you mean?"

Impertinent, the hare scolded. I didn't dare roll my eyes. Already, I'd pushed the rules of etiquette too far. *You must choose between this world and the past. She Who Waits does not mean you harm. But should you choose incorrectly, there will be consequences.*

"Is there some kind of rule that you cannot simply tell me what it is you mean?" Speaking so was a risk, but I was ever so tired, and the revelations of my day emboldened me.

I could have sworn the hare sighed. Its paws lowered, and it stared at the Orilion as it faded, the air elementals dispersing. In the crowd, near the balustrade, the hush that had fallen over the party broke. People began chatting again, and the Vilhari on the harp picked out a soothing melody.

We do not intend to cause you distress. But it is required that you choose without interference. This is our way.

A sharp gust of wind cut through the thin fabric of my dress. "And is this not interference?"

It is a reminder, the hare said before fading. *When you have decided, meet us at the standing stones.*

The mere mention of the standing stones struck fear into me. I'd trifled with the nameless elemental gods once and survived. My base instinct warned me not to think of doing so again, not without good cause. I fought against this new information. I had decided on another path. Anger and fear mixed within me, souring my stomach.

Fear won. I'd been too well educated on the lore of the

eldritch origins of the spirits, and the dangers they posed to the corporeal beings of Sirin. I could sell Orchid House, start a new life, whatever I wanted, but the elementals could find me anywhere. There was no running from this. Disappointment flooded me, adding urgency to fear's sharp bite.

A single tear leaked from the corner of my eye. "How will I know that I've decided?"

You will know, came the hare's voice, though it was gone.

I stood staring at the spot the hare had been for a long time, though if it were minutes or hours, I had no real idea. I had decided on another path—could I still have the life I'd imagined, if I was drawn deeper into this mess? A hand touched my arm. By instinct, I flinched, but relaxed as soon as I saw Poe. All made better sense with her by my side.

The hare was correct: I knew exactly which side I would choose. *Hers.* Poe was the kind of person who could change Sirin for the better. And I was exactly the kind of person who could support her from the shadows.

Oblivious to my monumental revelation, Poe smiled. "Skye went after Ashbourne. She said we should say our goodbyes and head home."

I stood staring at the spot where the hare had been for a long moment.

"Are you all right?" Poe asked.

"Yes," I said. I wasn't ready to tell her about the hare just yet. The encounter had unsettled me, and I needed to sort things out. "Should we find Elspeth, then?"

Poe nodded slowly, obvious concern written all over her face. "If something was wrong, you would tell me, wouldn't you?"

I took a deep breath. "This afternoon I decided that when we find Chopard, I want to sell Orchid House." I wasn't going to lie to Poe about the hare, but I needed time to think over what it had said.

"You want to sell Orchid House? But why?" Poe sounded genuinely shocked. "What about revenge and finding out what happened to your family?"

My chin quivered, but the warm, safe feeling I got when Poe asked me questions reassured me. Before the oubliette, I dismissed feelings like these, not knowing how to interpret them. Now, I learned to trust myself. And Poe.

"I don't want to know who killed them anymore. I want to be done with all of this." Gingerly, I took Poe's hands, waiting to feel the usual tightness in my chest at touching someone. I felt only comfort as her hands closed around mine, her expression open and earnest. "These past weeks have been the nicest of my life. If you'll have me, I'd like to help you find *your* family."

Poe nodded as I spoke. "Of course I'll have you. But..." she trailed off, her brows furrowing.

My voice dropped a level. "Whoever burned the house down did me a favor, Poe. I'm free. I don't need to know more."

"Muse said that all this is connected. You may find out more whether you like it or not."

She was right, of course, and I'd already considered that. "I know. And that's fine, but I only want to follow this as far as taking Chopard down. The only thing I want for myself now is a new life. One free from the upper echelons."

Poe nodded, then sighed. "You'll get quite a lot of money from the house. What will you do?"

Yes, that was exactly the point—we could stop depending on the Syndicate for money—but I didn't want to say that just yet. She needed time to adjust to the idea, and so did I. "I'd like to find out what I'm good at. I don't hardly even know myself. Vaness didn't raise me to have a purpose."

"I think that sounds wonderful, Mina." Poe took my arm, and we turned to find Elspeth in the crowd. "Will you come live with me? I have a little space you could use as a bedroom, and my neighborhood is darling. So many lovely cafes and galleries."

"Yes," I said, a picture of it forming in my head. Poe let out a shuddering breath, relief coloring her smile. She wanted this too. Hope fluttered in my chest, bright as a newborn chick. To keep myself from any earnest proclamations of undying friendship, I pointed across the terrace. "Look, there's Elspeth and Mirabelle."

Poe's smile was slightly smug; knowing, at any rate. She heard the unspoken proclamations, despite the fact that I'd clamped all earnestness down. I bumped her shoulder with mine, rolling my eyes a little. She laughed softly, nodding as though I'd spoken words she agreed with.

I'd watched Skye and Ash communicate wordlessly and wondered what it would be like to have someone like that in my life, and here she was. The oubliette had taken so much from me, but when I looked at Poe, I came to realize it had given me something precious as well. I said a silent prayer of thanks to Lady Fate, my first ever, promising to plant deadly nightshade to honor her name.

We made our way to the House Aestra matriarchs. Now that the light show was over, the party was breaking up. There were only a few guests left on the terrace. As we drew closer, Mirabelle spoke to Elspeth in fervent, hushed tones. When they spotted us approaching, Elspeth beckoned us to her.

She gripped Poe's arm as soon as she came within reach, alarm in her eyes. "Niall was here," she said, after looking around to make certain no one was within earshot.

"He stole something," Mirabelle added. "Though I can't say what yet. But he ransacked my study."

"Someone saw him?" Poe asked.

"Yes," Mirabelle answered, voice sharp. "Me. He nearly knocked me over, rushing out."

"He was hiding something in his coat," Elspeth explained. "Mother thinks he made a mess to hide what was taken. Where is Skye?"

"Following a lead," Poe replied. "We should get home. Will you send word when you know what Niall took?"

"Absolutely," Elspeth promised. A twitch near her jaw gave me pause. Was she nervous about something? "Go now before Msr VanGuerten makes his way over here. He says the longest goodbyes." She kissed Poe generously on each cheek, her hand lingering on the younger woman's face for a moment. "You are so lovely. I can see why my girl holds you in such high regard."

Mirabelle sniffed a little derisively but did not contradict the statement. Poe blushed. "I feel the same about her."

Elspeth beamed with pride, nodding vigorously. "How lovely," she said, emotion thick in her voice. She was impressed by Poe, happy that she was interested in her daughter. "How very lovely."

My gaze flitted between them, my heart swelling with happiness. When this mess was over, we had much to look forward to.

CHAPTER 34

ASHBOURNE

Skye and I nearly ran into one another. We'd been around the block twice, but the man Mina spotted had disappeared. My frustration mounted. Too many were getting away from us these days. It felt like I was always just a touch too slow for my opponents. I wasn't used to the feeling, and it unsettled me more than I cared for.

"Shit," I swore. "We lost him."

My partner paused before she answered me, her molars grinding together in vexation. She too was losing patience. Undoubtedly, this job was more complex than any we'd worked together, but the basics were the basics, and usually we made headway more easily than this. When she spoke, her voice was strained. "Let's widen the search a few blocks. What do you say?"

I narrowed my eyes, raising an eyebrow. It was unlike Skye to sound so unsure. But she was already walking, and I was right behind her. "What are you thinking?"

Skye picked up the pace. "A few blocks down from here, there's a little park with a smattering of crattie conveniences."

I snickered at the term. "Eateries with all the tiny food?"

She nodded, laughing along with me. It broke up some of the tension that frustration had built between us. "Indeed. What a foolish trend. You always go home hungry and it's twice as expensive as anywhere else."

The casual banter was the lifeblood of our relationship. It got us back on more solid ground. I saw her line of thinking, though. "It would be a good place to catch a cab. If he didn't have a driver of his own, perhaps he went there."

"It's a long shot," she replied, some of the agitation from before still lingering in her words. "But worth a look."

Of course, she was right. Skye was always thorough. We fell into companionable silence for a block. As we reached the square, Skye motioned to me that she would go left, and I'd go right. I'd given her a good description of what the man had been wearing and his build, though I hadn't gotten a look at his face. The goal now had to be to find out who he was. We could bring Mina to him, if necessary.

I began my walk around the square, still amazed by how clear the sky was this far up the mountain. The stars were beautiful, but it felt as though I might float away. Some part of me missed the cloud cover. As I walked, I watched the cab line gathering in front of the little cafes grouped together on the opposite side of the square. The man was nowhere to be seen, but I spotted Skye, whose eyes were fixed on a dark alley.

She glanced over one shoulder, found me, and made the smallest motion of one hand. I couldn't believe it—had she found him? Careful not to draw attention to myself, I strode across the little park at the center of the square. I reached Skye's side just in time to see what she was looking at. A car drove into the alley, one that had just been in the cab line. It had one passenger in the back: Niall Aestra.

The man from the party stepped out from behind some

trash bins and got into the car. Skye pushed me out of the mouth of the alley, behind an enormous pot of chrysanthemums. Someone had piled various sizes of pumpkins and gourds at the center of the arrangement. It was artistically done, and very convenient, as it hid us perfectly from sight. The cab pulled out of the alley and headed back in the direction of the undercity.

I shook my head. "He was talking to Viridian at the party."

Skye paused, grabbing my arm. "*Ashbourne*. They're headed toward Orchid House."

That was undeniable. Orchid Street was on the way to the undercity from here. Skye rushed towards the cab line, searching each big black autocar until she found a Strix driver wearing Braithwaite tweeds. She knocked on the window. The cabbie rolled it down. "What can I do for you?"

"We need transport back to Orchid Street, on the double. On business for Herself."

The Strix, who had the visage of a screech owl, raised her eyebrows. "Yeah?"

"Yes, yes. All the nonsense about velvet peonies riding at dawn."

The Strix clicked her beak. "Get in. I'll get you there."

THE RIDE WAS HARROWING, the Strix taking turns at a gut-wrenching pace. I was glad I'd only had one glass of sparkling wine, and no more than a dozen cheese puffs. But we got there in time to find Mina and Poe pulling up in a cab of their own, driven by Fulston Braithwaite, still half a block away. Skye patted the Strix's shoulder in relief, passing her the fare, as well as a generous tip. "What's your name?"

"Evelyn Masterson," she said, voice clipped as she glared

out the front window at Fulston Braithwaite. Perhaps they were in some kind of competition with one another. "But everyone calls me Evie."

"You're the fastest cabbie I've ever had," Skye said with a grin.

Evie passed her a card. "Faster than him," she said, nodding at Fulston. "You call me whenever you're on business for Herself. I'll get you where you need to go."

Skye glanced at the card, letting out a low whistle. "The boss doesn't give too many of these out."

The Strix nodded. "That's right. I'm the best. Or I will be when Fulston gives up."

So I'd been right. Skye flashed the card at me, showing me what had elicited the whistle. It was one of the most expensively made calling cards on the market, the kind that came in packs of a baker's dozen, rather than a box. It would let Evie know our exact location if we used it to call for her.

The usual calling cards simply appeared in hallways or mailboxes when you wanted to schedule a visit with someone and didn't take much magic at all. But something like this was expensive for a reason. Edith must really trust this slip of a girl. I was doubly impressed now.

"Thank you," I said as I got out. I glanced back at Skye. "Don't let the girls in the house."

Skye nodded, giving the autocar a pat as Evie drove off. I slipped inside. As soon as I entered, I knew we were clear. Morpheus lay reclining on the steps, cleaning his paws.

There is someone in the garden, he said as I was about to go back out front.

I wondered why he hadn't done something about it, but asking the feline to justify anything was a losing battle. I ran through the back of the house to the housekeeper's office, taking the stairs to the garden two at a time. Sure enough, a shadow lurked in the garden. The figure stepped out of the darkness, into the golden square of aetheric light on the stone patio.

She was tall, with rounded ears and golden brown skin. Her hair was short, like Skye's, but the style was different, strangely cut. And though she wore clothing that was regular enough, slim trousers and a long wool overcoat, her shoes were the oddest thing I'd ever seen: white, and made from a material I could not immediately identify.

"Ash," she said, breathing a sigh of relief. "I'm so glad to have found you."

I frowned. "Are we acquainted?"

The woman's brown eyes narrowed. "That's rather cold of you. A week in the limen together wasn't much for you, eh?" The woman laughed easily, as though she expected I would laugh along. She had a lovely smile, but it faded almost immediately. I sensed something about her, some power that did not make sense.

"Are you not Oscarovi?" I asked, more confused than ever. If what I sensed was right…it couldn't be. The stranger had empyrae in her.

"Of course not." She laughed again, but this time she backed away, obviously nervous. "I'm human. You know that."

"Human?" I asked. The word sounded familiar, but I couldn't place it. It was the root of humanoid, of course, but I knew of no people who claimed the name.

"Seventeen hells," she swore. "Do you not know me, Ashbourne?"

There was no threat in her voice, nor in her posture. It was obvious she knew me. A weight dropped into my stomach like dread. *She knew me*. Now I was the one to back away. "Whoever you are," I cautioned, "I don't want to know you."

Hurt flashed in her brown eyes, then determination. "Did you find her? Lumina?"

My mind caught on the name, a howl building from deep within my soul. "Get away from me," I growled. "Don't come back here again."

Her hands flew up in front of her, as though in defense, the sleeves of her overcoat falling down her arm. A tattoo of a compass glowed with celestial power. So that was how it got into her, this human. I shook my head. "Get. Out. Of. Here."

"I'm going," she agreed. "But I'll be back. Maybe Bayun can talk some sense into you."

My entire body vibrated with fear, empyrae mounting in my hands. I couldn't go in the house this way. When the woman disappeared, my entire body sagged with relief. Her footsteps traveled away from the house. I listened until they faded away, squeezing my eyes shut tight.

When I opened them, the yard was empty, and I felt a lingering sense of confusion. *What had happened? Why did I come out here?*

WHEN I GOT BACK in the house, Morpheus waited for me by the back door. *Did you find what you were looking for?*

I nodded. "All clear."

The cat turned his lamp-like eyes on me. *No one in the garden?*

"Not a soul," I said. He was in a mood then, because he stalked off, huffing in frustration. I went to the front to give the girls the all clear. The three of them sat on the front steps, Poe leaning against Skye's knees as Skye told them all we found out. Mina had made them a sound dampening bubble, but it encompassed the door to the house, so though

I could sense the spell working from the way the sound of traffic on Orchid was muffled, I could still hear them.

"The house is clear," I said, reaching out to help Mina up. I was tempted to scoop her into my arms and kiss her, right here on the front steps, but I wasn't sure how she would react to that.

She leaned on me as she stood. "These shoes are too much," she complained as she let her muffling spell go with a flick of her hand. Little tendrils of aether clung to her fingers. She tucked them into her pocket, sparing a moment for a tiny smile.

"Thank you for going on without me," she said as we walked into the house. Skye and Poe stayed out front, murmuring to one another about more mundane topics. We turned to look at them.

"Coming in?" Mina asked, though the quirk of her lips told me she already knew the answer.

Neither of them looked back at us, so engrossed in one another's eyes as they were. "Be in later," Skye said, her voice thick with concentration.

Mina let out an amused breath as I shut the door behind us. "You should have seen Elspeth Aestra saying goodbye to her. The woman has her sights set on Skye wedding the last princess of House Feriant."

I chuckled. "She's going to be rather disappointed then."

Mina looked back at me, her eyes sharp. "Why is that?"

I held up my hands in mock defense. Had I already done this—reacted just this way? *No, that wasn't right.* I grinned at Mina, banishing the odd feeling. "Stand down, little menace. I only meant that I doubt Elspeth will get a society wedding out of the pair of them."

"Oh," Mina said, a blush creeping onto her cheeks. "I apologize. I'm a bit protective of Poe."

I stepped towards her, our hands brushing. "I like it very

much. Your protective side, that is." Her eyelashes brushed her cheek, and I didn't think it was modesty, but she was battling some feeling. I bent toward her, bringing my mouth to her ear as my fingers wound through hers. "Did I detect a bit of that protectiveness when Caralee called me a hoodlum?"

"Perhaps," she said, her damaged voice low and sweet.

"Does that mean you care for me as well?" I asked.

"Perhaps," she replied, this time turning her eyes to mine. "You know I do."

"I do," I said, my voice dropping to its lowest register. Heat rushed through me. "And I believe I promised to show you the meaning of devotion tonight, did I not?"

"You did," she said, turning to the stairs. "The night grows short. You'd better get started, if you've any hope of making me understand."

I swept her into my arms, our mouths crashing together as she wound her arms around my neck. I pulled away just long enough to make a promise. "You will. And if you don't understand the first time I show you, then I'll simply have to demonstrate it again."

CHAPTER 35

MINA

I don't know how we made it to my bedroom. All I knew was the tangle of hands and the power of Ashbourne's body, moving mine at incredible speed. Everything slowed as he set me down in front of the bed. No fire was lit in my bedroom, the night air cold at the top of the house.

Slowly, I turned. "Unbutton me?"

The heat of his body warmed my backside, his breath caressing the shell of my ear as he trailed kisses down my newly exposed neck. "So many buttons," he purred.

The dress fell away from my body, leaving only the meager undergarments I'd adorned myself with. He turned me in his arms, his eyes hungry with desire. "What is this?"

"I believe they call it lingerie," I said, my words carrying a challenge and a bite.

He took them easily, swallowing them down as he dragged one finger over the laces of the close-fitting camisole I wore, sending shivers down my back. My fingers went to work as well, pushing his waistcoat off first, then moving on to the buttons of his shirt. He'd removed everything else before we came upstairs, so there was little else for me to do.

The laces loosened, and he pulled the camisole off me, exposing my bare skin to the chill of the room. My body sang as his hands cupped my breasts, warm as they stroked my pebbled skin. He looked me over, as though afraid he might hurt me.

"I am all right," I breathed as his fingers dragged down the curve of my hips, setting my skin afire.

"You are beautiful," he replied, his dark hair falling into his eyes.

In the dim light of the bedroom, the angles of his face were all in shadow. He might be threatening, his body made for winning battles, but I was more interested in the pleasure it would bring me. He turned my body in his arms, bringing the unclothed skin of my back against his bare chest.

"Lean into me," he murmured as one hand cupped my breast again, the other sliding down to the curve of my belly.

I moaned as his fingers pressed into my flesh. His hard length pressed into the silk of my undergarment, the only thing I was left wearing. "Will you let me show you what devotion means to me, Mina?" he whispered in my ear, his fingers sliding under the scrap of silk that covered me.

"Don't go slow," I begged. "I need you."

He let out a primal growl and turned me around, depositing me on the bed, his body covering mine. Our kisses came fast and hard, his body moving against mine in expert ways. Ways that cleared my mind of any thought but how I might get more of this feeling, more of this friction, this pleasure. My thighs squeezed around his, damp heat building between them.

"Please," I begged, knowing he would not relent until I asked him to. "I need you inside me."

His breath was as quick and labored as my own. My back arched with need as his fingers grazed over the curves of my body, then pulled the fabric of my undergarment aside, cool air meeting my hot, moist skin.

Ash's mouth met mine as his fingers found the places I needed him most. This was sheer torture and the height of gratification all at once. His touch was more than I'd hoped for and somehow not enough. My cries were desperate, pleading for him to go further, as I writhed against his touch.

Harder and harder he kissed me, his hand working in time with each thrust of his tongue, each nip of my bottom lip and then my neck, moving lower to my collarbone. Then his mouth covered one exposed breast, his kiss harder and more insistent now. Heat built in me, gathering into a tight knot at my core. My eyes fell shut as my hips moved with each circle he wove with his fingers.

Ash's breath was hot in my ear as his mouth left my breast, commanding me. "Open your eyes."

I did as he asked, finding his beautiful face hovering above mine as I whimpered with need. "More, I need more."

He nodded, his hands leaving me only for the time it took to remove his pants. And then he fitted his slim hips between my thighs, pushing me open for him. "Is this what you need?" he asked, his voice soft and husky.

"Yes," I murmured as his fingers closed around my chin.

"Don't look away," he pleaded. "I want your eyes right here."

I did as he asked, his body moving against mine. He entered me slowly, carefully, his face tender as I moaned his name. "Yes," he breathed as he filled me. I pulled him down atop me. I wanted him covering me.

"Don't stop," I said. "I want you hard and fast."

He had no verbal response, only the increase in speed I begged for. Our bodies moved in perfect concert, my pain fading as every delicious moment of friction and wet heat brought me closer to an edge I wanted more than anything.

When Ashbourne's mouth met mine again, drawn together as if by some cosmic force, white light flashed behind my eyes. My voice went ragged with my cries, my fingers wound tightly in his hair.

Every muscle in me clenched, my toes curling as his voice met mine. The power of his release took me over the edge and into another swell of ecstasy I hadn't known possible. Our bodies rocked against one another as we slowed, but could not quite stop.

He brushed a damp strand of hair from my face. "You are incredible," he murmured. "Better than I could have imagined."

I raised an eyebrow. "I did very little."

He laughed. "You did plenty. And you will do more before the sun rises."

"Will I?" I breathed, my breath quickening already, my body tightening around him once more.

"Yes," he promised, his words backed up by the reigniting passion that sparked between us and inside me. His hips pushed against mine—and I believed him. "You will take all I give you and more."

"I will," I moaned. "Give me all of you."

He did, over and over, until I knew Ashbourne Claymore's definition of devotion by heart.

CHAPTER 36

MINA

I woke up with a start, my legs tangled in Ash's, his fingers twisted in my hair. He mumbled something incoherent as I pulled out of his grip. What had woken me? I'd been dreaming, but could only remember snippets of the dream. Someone had been speaking to me, arguing with me. My thoughts raced as I tried to hold on to what was left. The argument felt important.

What are you doing here?
Saving you.
I sent word. I told you not to come.

Then hands gripped my arms, dragging me away. When the screaming began, I was shaken awake. I touched my face only to find that tears stained it. I'd been crying in my sleep. My heart pounded, its beat all I could hear—the memory of pain seared into me.

A hand pressed into my back, its warmth a reminder of the pain. I closed my eyes, fighting the tears that threatened to overtake me. "What's wrong?" Ash's voice was careful, as though he feared my reaction.

I shook my head. "It was just a dream."

"Was it?" he asked, sounding a bit relieved. "Or was it another memory?"

"I don't know." My words came out in a strangled sob.

Gently, his fingers closed around my arm, pulling me into his chest. "What do you remember?"

"An argument," I said, after a few deep breaths. "I was arguing with someone about saving me."

A thoughtful hum sent vibrations through me. "Would it help to tell me more?"

I shrugged. Truly, I didn't know anymore. The hare had said I would have to choose between the past and this world. Was there any use in thinking about what had already happened? "There was so much pain," I whispered. "And I told him not to come, but he came anyway."

Ash tensed beneath me. "What?"

I shook my head, sitting up. "It's what I said: *I sent word. I told you not to come.*"

All color had drained from his face, and there was a faraway look in his eyes. "Who were you speaking to?" he asked, his voice devoid of any emotion.

"I don't know," I replied, sitting up. "But I screamed it at him before they dragged me away. After that, it was all just pain." My hand crept over my chest and around the base of my neck, grasping for the spot between my shoulders.

Ash blinked a few times, color returning to his face as he focused on me. "That sounds terrible."

There was something oddly stilted about his words. "Is everything all right?" I asked, feeling suddenly tentative. Had I shared too much? Was this not what people did after intimate encounters? Though I'd had sexual liaisons before, I'd never spent the night with anyone.

A slow smile spread over his face, his fingers playing with my hair again. In the early hours of the morning, he'd washed it for me in the bathtub and it was still a little damp.

"Everything is perfect, except for your dream. I wish that hadn't happened."

He sat up, brushing kisses onto my face as he did so. In a movement so quick I could hardly track it, he'd pulled me between his legs, my back resting against his chest as his fingers traced lines over my skin. I pulled the blankets up, not wanting the chill in the air to get to us. Beneath the covers, he teased me, skimming all the parts of me he'd learned last night would make me moan.

My body was sore, in the best ways possible, but I did not think I could take much more pleasure without the consequence of real pain. I winced slightly as his fingers brushed my core. "I'm sorry," he murmured, his hands moving away, wrapping around me in a comforting embrace.

"Please don't be sorry," I said. "Last night was wonderful. I'll just need a little recovery time."

"Take all the time you need," he said, his words warming me. "We never have to rush."

Something about the way he said the word caught my attention. "Never?" I leaned my head back on his shoulder, looking up at him.

There was a glimmer of mischief in his amber eyes. "What are you asking me, love?"

I hesitated, not able to find the right words. He saved me from my struggle. "We have all the time in the world, Mina. This is not a bit of casual fun for me. Is it for you?"

I shook my head. "No. I'm selling the house when we've found Chopard." I paused, watching for his reaction. He only waited, steady, countenance open and curious. "I'm moving in with Poe."

"And what if she and Skye wish to live together?" he asked, a smile growing.

I twisted around, straddling him. I'd changed my mind about the pain. A little more wouldn't do me any real damage. His breath caught as our bodies met, and he pulled me to him.

"You beautiful menace," he growled, before kissing me hard.

Every nerve in my body sang for him, some with pleasure, others with pain. The mix was exquisite, dark and rich as he slid inside me, our movements slow and small.

"If they want to live together," I breathed as his fingers traced my spine, "then I will find a place for myself, and you will sleep in my bed."

"I doubt I will sleep much," he whispered, his hands covering my breasts. "If this is how it is to be between us."

My back arched, and he wrung a keening cry of agreement from me. My vision went dark at the edges, all the tension from the nightmare snapping out of me in one clean break. Another memory replaced it: the set of keys I'd found in Helene's purse. There had been one I hadn't been able to identify, hadn't there?

Under me, Ashbourne found release, his grip on me tightening as our mouths crashed into one another. When our bodies finally stilled, he shook his head. "You got the better of me, love. Are you hurt?"

"A little," I breathed as I climbed off him. "But it was well worth the trouble."

He caught my hand in his as I got out of bed. "I don't want you to push yourself too hard, Mina. I meant what I said. We have all the time in the world. Where you go, I go—until you tell me not to."

I had my robe half on, but I paused, listening to him. He sat up, pulling the robe closed, and tying the sash for me. "Perhaps it's too soon to say this..." For the first time since we met, he seemed unsure.

I touched his face, my fingers running over his cheekbones. "Whatever you want to tell me, it's right on time."

THE HOLLOW PLANE

"I want to be with you. Only you," he said. "And all else that comes after that."

His words dazzled me, simple as they were. Nervous energy flowed off him in waves as he waited for my response. "I feel the same," I said, after giving it a moment of thought. "There is no one else. I want to see where this goes."

Ash laughed, a sound so joyful it almost hurt to hear. What we were agreeing to was complex. Pain came with forging a connection like this with someone. But also love, and I was no longer afraid of love's weakening effect. Even the little taste of what was growing between us had me well fed. Love might make me weak in some ways, vulnerable, rather. But in so many others, it had the potential to strengthen me, lift me up.

Joy, I was discovering, was the antidote to pain. Living a life that meant something to me, with people I cared for, was far more important than anything else I'd ever wanted. This was no longer about letting Helene and Maman go, or forgetting them. Poe had been right the night before. I might have to confront all that at some point. Now, this was about finding the place I belonged, and I belonged wherever my friends were. Wherever Ash was.

I wrapped my arms around the man that had just offered me another avenue to that belonging. "Thank you," I whispered as he hugged me back.

"For what?" he asked as he stood, his arms scooping me up. He walked toward the door to my little bathing chamber.

"For setting me free."

Some point of confusion flickered in his eyes, as though his mind stumbled over my words. Then his eyes cleared, and he smiled at me. "If anyone is mistress of her own fate, it is you."

I wasn't so sure about that, but it meant something to me that he thought so. We dressed at a leisurely pace, taking time to help one another in entirely unnecessary ways. Every touch was bliss, every stray kiss a promise for the days to come.

As we walked downstairs together, arm in arm, I leaned on him. Stairs were hard for me, and I didn't care that he knew it. Letting even a little bit of my vulnerability be known felt like a victory.

Downstairs, Poe and Skye chatted amiably in the dining room. When we walked in, they held hands, and did not spring apart or show signs of embarrassment. Instead, they smiled at us, and Ash smiled back. I nodded once, happy that they too had found solace in one another.

Breakfast was quiet. Peaceful even. I could not remember another such time in Orchid House. Quiet was typically a sign that Maman was angry, and her silence had been deployed as a weapon. This silence was different, carrying with it the comfort of ease and a hint of joy that I had not ever felt in my family.

Morpheus consumed an entire plate of poulet, and then stretched out on the table, purring. Ash left for a bit, and returned with a pot of tea, pouring each of us our preferred serving. Once done, he sat, opening our morning's conversation with a return to the previous night's events. "I believe our first order of business must be determining who our mystery man is."

Skye nodded. "I can visit Mother today, see what she knows, and how he's connected to Viridian. If she doesn't know outright, perhaps someone in her circle might find out more."

Poe squeezed Skye's hand. "That is good thinking. As Mina is the only one who saw him, it might help to employ a sketch artist."

"Do any of you know one not employed by the cityguard?" I asked.

Skye smiled then. "Yes. I believe Muse's lover is an artist who does portraits, is he not?" Her question seemed directed at Poe, whose smile brightened as she answered. "Indeed, Arcturus has done work like that in the past. Mina, Muse gave you his card, didn't he?"

"Yes," I replied, getting up to fetch it. It took a short trip to Maman's sitting room to fetch the card from the secretary desk, where Poe had filed it away. When I returned, I cleared my mind, then pressed my finger to the card, making a request to see Muse and Arcturus at their soonest convenience.

The response was nearly immediate, and I imagined the two of them might still be in bed together. As I had just left such a happy state, it was easy to smile. "They will see us in an hour. We are to bring pastries from the Clotted Calf. What does that mean?"

Ash grinned. "It's the best bakery in Halcyon's Gate. Right around the corner from Muse's place. Tell him we'll be there."

I did as asked, then turned to Poe. "Are you coming with us?"

She shook her head, picking up a piece of correspondence sitting next to her plate. "Vionette Celestine wants to see me for lunch. I asked her to do a little digging for me on Viridian's past. He spent some time in Ismit last year right after Mina's disappearance, and Vionette has connections there."

"Good," Ash replied. "The more we know about his movements, the better."

Poe hummed a little in the affirmative. "Yes, I hesitated to ask before. Vionette can be prickly about her Ismiti connections. Her reasons for leaving were unpleasant, I believe. But I couldn't justify leaving potentially valuable information on the table any longer."

"Thank you," I said.

Poe smiled at me. "Of course, darling. We're narrowing in on something, I can feel it."

As we parted ways for the day, I had to agree. There was an air of possibility hanging around us, as though our story was turning, on its way to a new chapter.

CHAPTER 37

ASHBOURNE

Watching Mina pick out pastries and a variety of cheeses at the Clotted Calf was nearly as satisfying as having her to myself in bed. Nearly. But her excitement at deciding on various delicacies was unmatched, and so endearing I had to stop myself from hugging her. When she had nearly three large bags of treats, and the clerks were dizzy with her requests, I hazarded a touch.

As my hand pressed against the small of her back, she turned towards me, her arm slipping around my waist. In the most alarmingly domestic movement, she lifted her face to mine, her eyes closing. She expected to be kissed. The sweetness of the moment, and her trust that I would oblige, moved me.

I dipped my head to meet her mouth, keeping the kiss chaste as I could manage, but my blood sang at her nearness. It had taken all my effort the night before not to allow my magic to run loose. Even now, I felt the song of empyrae in my blood, and some primal instinct told me to take her behind the building and bury myself in her—in every way possible.

Her tongue slipped into my mouth, evidence that she too was thinking of more adventurous encounters. I pulled back, running my thumb over her delectable mouth. "You are a wicked girl," I murmured as the clerks finished bagging our goods. "*My* wicked girl."

She did not smile with her mouth, but the gleam in her eyes was enough for me. "If only I could show you what I'm thinking," she whispered.

"All's ready," the clerk behind the counter said, a brunette Oscarovi with a pleasant smile. She pushed the bags forward.

Mina took one, and I paid, then took the remaining bags. Outside the bakery, the streets of the undercity filled with people. There was a lively bustle and the smell of the bakery mixed with the distinctly green scent of the florist next door. Mina shivered.

"Are you cold?" I asked, concerned for her wellbeing.

"No," she replied. "Well, yes. But it's not unpleasant. This is my favorite time of year. For weather, anyway."

As we walked, she told me about autumn in Somershire, the fall festivals and the Hallowed Moon rituals. A note of sadness followed every word she spoke, chasing down what should be pleasant memories. From that alone, I understood that she had not been intimately involved in any of the happy events she recalled, but only watched them.

She had spent her life as an outsider. When this was over, when we found Chopard, I was determined to take her to every one of the undercity's ridiculous seasonal celebrations. For her, I would happily make friends, socialize, anything to wipe away the sorrow in her voice. Anything to show her how wanted she was now, and—I paused—now, and for a very long time to come.

It surprised me how much I wanted a future with this woman. How I wanted to watch her enjoy her life. I'd become so distracted by the thought, it took me a moment longer than it might have otherwise to notice we were being followed. I did not turn to look behind us. It would do me no good.

Whoever followed knew what they were doing. Whenever I slowed, even a little, they did as well. We were nearly at Muse's. Though I did not want to frighten Mina, I would have to do a perimeter check of the building as soon as I had her safely delivered to the seer and his lover.

"We're being followed," she said, her voice light as she broke through my thoughts.

She surprised a laugh out of me. "Yes." I bumped her shoulder with mine, careful not to unbalance her with my bulk. "How did you know?"

Mina shrugged. "Are we almost to Muse's?"

We were on his block, in fact. "Yes, it's just there."

Her pace picked up slightly, and though I knew it must cause her pain to do so, she climbed the front steps of Muse's building swiftly. A line of brass call buttons was embedded next to the door. Mina seemed to know which to choose already, and she pressed the third one from the bottom. The speaker placed above the buttons crackled to life.

A rough voice spoke. "Muse is in the bath. I'll be right down."

Moments later, a person as tall as myself, but twice as wide, opened the door. His chest was broad, covered in dark hair exposed by his unbuttoned shirt. He had a mass of dark curls haloing his bearded face and sparkling brown eyes. "Hello," he greeted us. "I'm Arcturus."

"Hello," Mina replied, her voice pleasant. "We are being followed."

"Ah," Arcturus said, eyeing the bags in my hands. "Let me take those then, and show Mlle Wildfang upstairs, yes?"

I nodded, handing off the bags. As Mina disappeared

inside the building, I narrowed my eyes at Arcturus, a warning.

"She is safe with us," he assured me. "Do what you need to make sure it stays so."

I nodded once, then turned, rushing down the steps. My gut told me to go back the way we'd come. I walked with purpose, knowing whoever followed wouldn't be out in plain sight, and would likely expect my pursuit, especially if they were after Mina, not me. I turned down several quiet streets, making a circle around Muse's building.

When I'd nearly come back to Muse's block, I caught the sound of a muffled struggle. I paused, locating the sound. It came from the garden level entrance to the townhome I'd just passed. I turned, racing back, before whoever followed me could escape. In the lower level entrance to the house, the Strix woman who'd asked me to murder Mina struggled with a tall, dark-haired young woman.

The Strix was overtaking the woman, or so I thought at first. But as I neared, I saw the truth of things: the dark-haired girl had a firm grip on the Strix's wrist, and the avian woman was punching her repeatedly, trying to get her to let go. I wasn't sure what to do, who to help, but before I could decide, a furry golden body rushed past me, streaking down the stairs.

"Don't let her get away," the dark-haired girl yelled to the cat, for that was what the little beast had been, I was sure of it. "She's one of *his*."

The Strix woman growled something I could not understand, some language I didn't know, and the girl snarled in response.

The cat arched his back, ready to fight, just as the dark-haired girl caught sight of me. She paused, distracted just long enough, and the Strix woman slipped her grip and ran, kicking the giant golden cat and shoving me aside as she went.

I made my way towards the stairs, thinking to see if the girl and the huge feline were all right. I lost sight of them for only a moment as I rounded the balustrade that kept folks on the street from inadvertently stepping into the staircase. When I reached the top of the steps, the girl and the cat were both gone. I ran to the bottom of the stairs, trying the door to the townhome.

To my surprise, it came open easily under my hand. The door swung open with an eerie groan. Inside, the garden level flat was empty. There was nothing inside, no furnishings, just layers of dust on the wide planks of the wood floor. And not a single footprint in the dust.

I stepped back outside, looking for another door, another obvious way the two of them could have disappeared. But there was nothing. Nothing at all. My breath shuddered through me. People did not just disappear into thin air. All the magic in the world did not allow for such a thing. I went back into the flat, sure I'd missed something.

I opened the few doors the little place had. There was only a tiny closet and a lavatory. No other door led to outside, and the walls were solid stone. I stood staring at the flat for long moments, wondering if I might be losing my good sense.

What other explanation could there possibly have been?

CHAPTER 38

MINA

Muse's flat was a wonderland. The walls were painted a rich peachy pink, and caught the light from the leaded glass floor-to-ceiling windows in a magnificent glow. Everywhere there were plants and comfortable places to sit. Plush velvet chairs in orchids and lavenders, sparkling chunks of raw crystals scattered about. Oversized pillows, covered in lush patterned fabrics, were strewn around a low stone table at the center of the room.

An entire wall was taken up by bookshelves, stuffed full of only fiction, most of it titles I'd never heard of. I was mesmerized by the books, wondering what it would be like to read as Muse obviously did, or Ash did. While I enjoyed the odd adventure story, I had rarely read for enjoyment. It wasn't that I didn't like to do so, but that Maman had not approved.

She'd called it a waste of time, and warned that too much fiction would rot my brain. Especially the kinds of books these were—mostly romances and fanciful stories about mythical creatures. Arcturus laid out tea just for the two of us on the stone table, as he asked me for my description of the man. Without thinking too hard, I told him, still staring at the books.

When he'd asked me a few questions, he got out a sketchbook. "Feel free to sit and have some tea. When I have a basic sketch done, we'll see if we're close."

I nodded, reading more of the book's titles. "Have you read any of these?" I asked.

Behind me, the sound of sketching stopped. "Oh, yes, most of them. Though only half are mine."

"Oh," I said, frowning. I'd seen no pattern in the way the books were organized. How odd. "Which half?" I asked, turning.

Arcturus looked up from his sketch, his eyes lit with merriment. "I have no idea, love. I hardly remember anymore."

"Oh," I said again. "I assumed you meant that either the top half was yours... or perhaps the left side. Are they organized in some way?"

The Oscarovi laughed now. "No, we just shove them in wherever."

I took my overcoat off, draping it over a lavender velvet chair. I arranged a few pillows, then sat down on the floor, across from Arcturus. A gold earring with a dangling pink opal hung from one ear.

I sat quietly as he sketched, not wanting to bother him. Behind the door to the bedroom, a radio drama played, and there were faint sounds of splashing. Arcturus winced, setting his pencil down.

"You are in pain," I said, my voice deep with empathy.

He nodded. "Yes, do you mind?"

I wasn't sure what he asked, but there was a large glass device for smoking poppy on the floor next to him. Did he use the stuff to help the pain? If so, I had no desire to stop him. "Of course not," I said.

He did not reach for the pipe, but instead whispered the words, "Venisci Acraea." *Come, Acraea*, he'd said in ancient Oscarovi.

The opal at his ear glowed with blue light for a few moments, before a large moth spirit appeared, an air elemental. "Acraea helps me when my hands hurt," Arcturus explained.

I watched as the moth fluttered around Arcturus' face. They communicated silently, before she landed on the bridge of his nose, flapping her wings several times. When she took to the air, his eyes glowed faintly blue. "She can see my vision for the image now," he explained.

The spirit hovered over the paper for a moment, then landed. At almost the exact same speed as Arcturus had drawn before, lines appeared on the page, while Arcturus massaged his hands.

"I thought you meant to smoke poppy," I breathed, amazed by the way they worked together.

Arcturus smiled. "I might later. It does help with the pain a bit, but I want to get this done for you first. Acraea was happy to help."

"How did you form such a relationship?" I asked, amazed. Maman and Helene had both acted as though their elementals were servants, meant to do their bidding. Even the Laquoix sewists, who worked in beautiful collaboration with their elementals, seemed to have a working relationship. This was something different, more intimate, deeper. It was what I'd always dreamed of. Someone who understood my pain and who *wanted* to help me.

"It has always been this way between us." Arcturus' eyes fell on my ring. He smiled at me, sympathy in his eyes. "You are not inspirited, then?"

I realized my mistake instantly. My eyes widened with the gravity of my error.

"I'll tell no one," Arcturus said. "Especially none of the cratties you've been mixing with."

"Thank you," I breathed, not knowing what else to say. I'd let my guard down too much these past weeks. I was letting my desperation to quell the loneliness inside me win. It had changed me, having friends. I fought silently with myself. None of the voices within me sounded like me anymore.

The door to the bedroom opened. "Wilhelmina," Muse said from the doorway. "You are thinking so loud you drowned *These Ivy Halls* out."

"I'm sorry," I said, apologizing in a completely uncharacteristic way. But I *was* sorry to have disturbed the seer. "To you both. It has been a strange time."

Arcturus nodded. "That is what Morpheus tells us."

"You've seen him?" I asked, surprised. Though the cat did disappear quite often, he never mentioned where he was going or where he'd been.

Arcturus glanced at Muse, who laughed, gesturing to the fountain that bubbled in the bay window of the flat. It was surrounded by soft cushions, all of which were covered in silver fur. An odd question popped up in my mind. "Does Morpheus live here too?"

Arcturus and Muse stared at each other for the longest time, their faces both incredulous. "He really is gone too much to assume we were his only roommates," Muse said finally.

Arcturus shook his head. "I am truly stunned…though," he said laughing, "I'm not sure why. It is so very like him to let all of us think we were his only family."

I found myself giggling along with the seer and his partner. It was the first time I'd ever laughed this way with people who were so new to me. But if Morpheus lived here as well, if these two were also his family, then there was absolutely no way they were unsafe for me. It was a refreshing thought to trust someone that way, and no surprise that I'd put my trust in a cat.

There came the sound of footsteps rushing up the stairs, and the door to the flat flew open. Ash breathed hard. "Thank the Lady," he breathed. "You're safe."

"Yes," I said with a smile. "Arcturus is almost done with the sketch."

Ash closed the door. "Good."

"Was it Niall?" I asked, wondering if that's why he looked so worried.

"No," he said, shaking his head. Muse stared hard at him. Something seemed to pass between them, though what it might be, I couldn't say. Ash opened his mouth, then closed it, before finishing, "I didn't recognize them."

I frowned, but Muse was already putting the kettle on for more tea. The peculiar tension that had transferred between the seer and Ash had gone, disappearing so quickly I thought I must have imagined it.

Ash came into the flat, watching the moth finish the sketch for a brief moment. "There were two of them," he explained. "And it was the oddest thing, they were fighting each other."

"Maybe only one was following us," I reasoned. "And the other was following the person following us."

Ash frowned for a moment, but then he nodded. "You know, I think you might be correct about that. Odd, still. I think we should take a cab home. Shall we call Fulston when you're ready? Or would you prefer Evie?"

So he'd noticed the two Strix were in competition as well. I smiled. "I'll let you choose your contender for fastest getaway driver."

Arcturus held up the image. "Is this him?"

I tilted my head. "I think the eyes were a bit different. Harder somehow? And maybe a little further apart."

Arcturus set the image down and Acraea went back to work. In the kitchen, which was just off the main room in the flat, Muse bustled about making tea.

"Are you all right?" I asked Ash. "You look a little piqued."

"I'm fine," he said, drawing me to him. "I'm just worried about you. When I realized they'd gotten away and you were alone…"

Strange, wistful joy went through me. "And now I'm not."

He followed my gaze around the room and back to himself. "Now you're not."

"Did you know Morpheus lives here too?" I asked, still scandalized by the news.

"He does not!" Ash exclaimed, as shocked as I had been.

"He does," Arcturus replied. "And we're all the fools." The big man's words were free of malice. He grinned, picking up the image as Acraea clung to his shoulder, both of them watching my response.

"That's him," I said, impressed with their skill.

"That is Lord Eccles," Ashbourne said. "Skye and I did a job for him six months ago. He's a professor at the university and a fellow at the Institute for Research on Interstellar Life."

"From the lecture we missed?" I asked.

"Yes," Ash agreed. "The same. He hired us to find out who had been stealing his mail. He seemed sure someone in his department was taking it for some kind of academic retribution. It turned out that the professor with the office across from his had been gone on sabbatical for a month, and the new mail carrier got them confused." Ash shrugged a little, then frowned. "At the time, it all seemed like an honest mistake, but I remember Skye feeling as though there had been more to the case. We'll have to ask her about it when we get home."

"It doesn't seem like a coincidence now, does it?" I asked.

"No," he answered. "It does not."

CHAPTER 39

MINA

When we arrived home, Skye had returned from speaking to Elspeth, but Poe was not yet back from the undercity. Elspeth had confirmed that the mystery man was Lord Eccles, and that he had not been invited to the party.

"Not because he wouldn't be," Skye explained. "He's very well-respected, but he is a known introvert. Aside from teaching and lectures, he rarely socializes."

"What do we know about him?" I asked. "I've never heard his name, but I know that he was both here and at Somerhaven nearly every month when I was a child. He was the most obvious of Maman's special cohort."

Skye sat down. "He didn't grow up in Pravhna, though Mother wasn't sure where he was before. Apparently, he got a job at the university about thirty years ago, and has been the same the whole time. He isn't a recluse, but he isn't very sociable either."

"We're going to need to find out all we can about Vaness' activities," Ash said.

"Yes," I agreed, a thought emerging. The key, I'd

forgotten about the key again. "I think I know how to get into Maman's workshop. Wait here."

I rushed as quickly as I could back upstairs to my vanity, my knees alarmingly weak as my joints screamed with pain. There would be time for a bath later, I promised myself. I rummaged through my drawers until I found the key ring, with only the key to Somershire and the mystery key left on it. I'd put the keys to Orchid House on a jeweled key ring in the shape of an ouroboros that Mme Laquoix's people had brought with them, and forgotten these were here.

There was a knock at the door. Ash entered. "Someone spotted Niall in Halcyon Gate. Edith sent a messenger. I have to go."

"Is Skye going with you?" I asked.

"I asked her to stay here with you." He paused. "I don't want her to have to bring him in. It's too much to ask of her."

I was impressed with how considerate he was of Skye. It bode well for any future we might have together. "Go find Niall."

He narrowed his eyes. "I asked Skye to give you a little time to take a bath before you tackle Vaness' workroom."

I wanted to protest, but he put a hand on my arm. "Please, take care of yourself. We have time."

"All right," I agreed.

Ash disappeared into the bathing chamber. I heard the sound of water running. He was drawing me a bath.

When he came out, he appeared to be torn about leaving. "Bath's filling. I'm going now." He brushed a kiss to my lips and shook his head. "I wish I could stay and bathe you."

"I can do it myself," I replied, a little grumpy that he thought I couldn't manage on my own.

"I know you *can*," he said as he strode to the door. "But it's less enjoyable, isn't it?"

Now I understood. Innuendo was occasionally difficult for me to detect. I would have to adjust my expectations now. I couldn't keep the smile off my face, as exactly what he meant sunk in.

"There's my girl," he said, casting a lingering look at me. "Do me a favor and spend a little extra time thinking about everything you enjoyed last night while you're in the tub."

I nodded, my skin flushing.

"I'll expect a detailed account of your audit when I return," he said as he closed the door.

His words stole my breath, and I wondered how I would focus until he came back.

CHAPTER 40

ASHBOURNE

Evie's car sped away, leaving me a block from the alley where a baker's assistant claimed to have seen Niall. I bought a mug of tea at a street cafe and sat down to watch the alley. Buskers, a string quartet, played music on the corner, though I couldn't remember the name of the song. I watched the alley for a while, not expecting to see Niall.

Something about the report was off. The baker was one of Herself's oldest friends, but the assistant was new. The description the young Oscarovi had provided of Niall was a bit too specific. No one remembered such details unless they were rehearsed.

Still, it didn't hurt to sit here for a bit and simply watch the neighborhood goings-on. I was deep in the Halcyon Gate district, closer to the Night's Door district than I liked—the proximity made me uncomfortable. The Night Syndicate was very different from the Halcyon Gate Syndicate. The Halcyon Gate bosses were cultured, deeply interested and invested in the people they protected.

The Night Syndicate was another story altogether. They were still better than the cratties, in my opinion, but they were less principled. Ruthless in ways that Skye did not approve of, and thus neither did I. I finished my tea, watching the movement in Night's Door, a few blocks away. There was no marker indicating the change in management, but I felt the border all the same.

I left a tip for my waiter, and slowly made my way down the street. As I'd expected, there was nothing amiss here. Neither was there any sign of Niall in the alley. This was either an ambush or a setup. My shoulders tensed.

I was about to leave when someone else entered the alley. A familiar tall, slender woman with dark hair and eyes walked in, accompanied by a large orange feline. A greymalkin.

They were the two from before, from the alley, fighting the Strix woman. For a moment, I couldn't believe the luck of it. Then I understood. There was no luck to it. The reason the report about Niall seemed shaky was because it wasn't real. How had they managed this?

Ashbourne, the fey cat said, as it rubbed against my legs. This was not at all what I'd expected. *Have you so easily forgotten me and Morgaine?*

I crouched down to pet the beast. He was soft as silk, and his body was differently built than Morpheus', more like a lynxcat. He was magnificent. His giant head bumped my hand, and I scratched behind his ears. He was certainly more friendly than Morpheus.

"I am sorry, friend," I said. "I wish I remembered you."

"At least he's being nicer than he was last night," the young woman said.

"Last night?" I asked, looking up at her. She was a handsome woman. Surely, I would remember meeting someone as striking as her. I'd certainly never forget what she and the cat had managed earlier. "Was this morning not the first time we've met?"

Last night I had been rather taken with Mina. It would have been easy to overlook anyone. Perhaps I'd been rude to this woman and didn't even know it. "Were you at House Aestra's Orilion party?"

She raised her eyebrows, and the cat looked back at her, alarm in his eyes. "No, Ash. In the garden at the house where you're staying. Remember?"

I stood, taking a step back from them. "You were in the garden at Orchid House last night?" My heart beat faster now, my stomach suddenly roiling. I stumbled a little, as I had on the stairs a few days ago. But that had been vertigo. My feet were on flat, steady ground now. The woman took hold of my arm, steadying me.

She spoke softly to the cat. "Is it like Rakul Kimaris? Has he been bound?"

No, the greymalkin answered. *It's much worse. He is cursed.*

"Cursed?" The word was bitter on my tongue.

Yes, and I'm afraid whoever placed the spell on you was quite talented. There's no undoing it. You will continue to forget your past until you find the loophole.

"Well, shit," the woman swore. "Then he's no good to us. We'll have to find Lumina on our own."

Unless he's found her already, and doesn't even know it.

Their words were confusing, and my head swam. I held up my hands. "Please, slow down. Who are you?"

The young woman stuck her hand out. I shook it and she replied, "Morgaine Yarlo, and this little lyon is Bayun."

She opened her mouth to continue, but the greymalkin growled. *Tell him less. The curse will only tighten if you try to make him remember. In that way, it's exactly like what we saw with Kimaris.*

"Rakul Kimaris," I said, repeating the name. There was no reaction in my body to that. "Do I know them?"

Morgaine shook her head. "No, I don't think the two of

you met. Though I suppose you might have known him *before*."

The way she said "before" was significant. As though we'd known one another only a short time, but I'd lived long before that. I assumed as much, but hearing this stranger say it was disconcerting as her claim that we knew one another.

Hush, Bayun warned. *Nothing so far back as that.*

Morgaine nodded. She looked as though she would speak, but I held up a hand. "Did you ask the baker's assistant to report seeing Niall Aestra?"

The young woman's shoulders sagged a bit. "Yes, I'm sorry we lied. But things didn't go well last night."

I nodded, gathering that we had indeed spoken. I was not inclined to trust Morgaine, nice as she seemed. But greymalkin cannot lie, and Bayun seemed to corroborate all she said. I looked at the golden animal. His topaz eyes were fixed on me. "Do the two of you mean me harm?"

No, the cat answered. *We are your friends, Ashbourne. We mean you no harm and wish you no distress. Once, not long ago, we walked the same path you did. We were at the start of our journey then. Now we only wish to go home. But first we need your help.*

I nodded slowly. Beyond the fact that greymalkin could not lie, I believed the cat wholly. Though I could not remember them, I could understand why I would make such friends. There was something of Skye in the girl, and I always had a soft spot for felines. Perhaps they were the reason I'd trusted Skye and Morpheus so easily. Had I been reminded of these two and not even known it?

My head dipped for a moment, my throat tight with emotion. I was cursed. Little bits of the past few weeks came back to me. Morpheus trying to talk with me about something, something I now could not remember. I didn't struggle against the resistance I felt, not wanting the nausea to return.

Was my reluctance to remember even mine? Or was it the curse?

The thoughts slammed into me like a runaway train. Once articulated, I could not unthink them. I spoke without thinking. "I'll help you whatever way I can."

Morgaine nodded. "We'll go carefully then. We're looking for a woman. One you came here to look for as well. Her name is Lumina, and from what we understand, she would be heavily glamoured, but her sister believes she would be tall, with dark hair and a serious countenance. Her eyes are gray, and she has a bit of trouble relating to others."

Lumina. Mina. My knees buckled, and I crashed to the ground. All went black.

~

WHEN I CAME TO, I couldn't open my eyes. This had to stop happening. There were voices speaking.

He's seen her.

"We can't ask him again, not with the curse."

It is weakening, Morgaine. Ashbourne will remember all he's forgotten soon enough. We should find the last door, before it's too late.

A cool hand pressed to my forehead. "I'm so sorry, friend. We'll see each other again soon." The voice attached to the hand quieted for a moment, then whispered. "We have to tell him."

It could cause him to forget again. I wouldn't.

The hand drew back from my face, but the voice added one last thing. "Beware the Strix woman you saw us fighting, Ash. She means both of you harm."

That much I already knew. So the voices were the people I'd seen the day before. Had we been talking before this? About what? I struggled to remember, finding myself unable to move or think clearly. There was a sound of footsteps and then silence. The cat and the dark-haired woman had gone.

When I could open my eyes, I was alone, and more afraid

than I could remember being. The cloudiness of waking up wore off. Bits and pieces of the conversation I'd had with Morgaine and Bayun came back to me, though others remained blurred. Something was there that I could not reach, even if I wanted to. I wasn't sure if I did, but the one thing that was crystal clear to me scared me. My lost memories were not a result of amnesia. I was cursed—a danger to all I held dear.

CHAPTER 41

MINA

After my bath, I was tempted to go right to the study to try the key, but Ash's plea to take better care of myself came back to me. I had a tendency when an idea took hold of me to forget all else, focusing only on what had caught my interest. It never yielded the best results. I often ended up completely exhausted, unable to finish a task. Maman had called me lazy and useless because of it.

My chest tightened at the thought of her. Memories of her disdain, which had once felt almost neutral in my mind, now soured as I recognized them as painful. It was remarkable what being treated better, and treating myself better, changed about the way I viewed my past. The world had opened up so much in the short time I'd been out of the oubliette.

I stared out the attic windows, wondering if it could last. Outside, the autumn rain had turned to sleet in this part of town. Though looking down the mountain, into the undercity, it was obvious it was only the midcity that was getting the freezing stuff.

Nevertheless, I needed to dress warmly. I found a pair of

sheepskin slippers in the back of my wardrobe and slipped them on. Next was a pair of high-waisted wool trousers in a gray tweed, and a silk blouse with a sheer lace back. Ashbourne would be back soon, after all, and so long as my feet were warm, and I fed myself, I could afford a lighter top. I slipped the key in my pocket and made my way down the back stairs, heading straight for the kitchen.

Tea was needed for this venture. Morpheus waited for me on the worktable, blinking several times at me as I came down the stairs. My left knee buckled slightly, still sore from my nighttime activities. I winced as I took the last few steps.

The cat sat up, narrowing his eyes as I leaned against the table. *Is it a bad one today?*

I shook my head. "No, just the consequences of my happily chosen actions." The cat grumbled softly, but blinked at me slowly as I moved through the kitchen, the kettle filling with water on its own. The stove lit, also on its own, and I spooned tea into a teapot.

"Do you need a fountain here as well?" I asked, remembering the little corner of Muse's flat for Morpheus.

The greymalkin's eyes dilated in surprise. *That would be nice. Thank you.*

He didn't address the fact that he had another home, another family outside Skye and Ash... And now myself and Poe. It was all very catlike of him, which should be no surprise. He was a cat, after all. A fey cat, but still feline.

Have you ever wondered at the coincidence that you and Ashbourne both have problems with your memories? he asked.

"That's an interesting question," I replied as I waited for the water to boil. "I hadn't."

Now that I thought about it, it was strange that I hadn't. "He was attacked, wasn't he? On his way into Pravhna?"

The greymalkin tucked his paws under his bulk, in a position Skye called "roast chicken." It was adorable, but I was not about to show that I thought so. *Yes, Skye and I found him near the river.*

"The Achera?" I asked, referring to the river that ran through the forest at the bottom of the mountain Pravhna was built upon. The cat made a noise I took to be affirmative. "What were you doing down there?"

Skye does not remember this, but she had a dream that morning. When she woke, she felt compelled to visit her family's cabin. We found him nearby.

The kettle whistled. I frowned as I poured water into the teapot. "That is very odd."

Confusion battered my conscious mind. My frown deepened. I stared at the cat, whose gaze was so intense I thought it might become tangible. "Why do I feel like this?" I asked, as dizziness sent me swaying. I held onto the edge of the worktable.

You remember what we are talking about? Morpheus asked, sitting upright now.

"Yes, but something—" I clutched my forehead with one hand, gritting my teeth. "It's like something is smothering my thoughts. It's hard to pay attention."

What is your greatest weakness, Wilhelmina? Morpheus' words were sharp, cutting through my blurred thoughts.

My breath came in labored gasps, a clammy sheen of sweat on my brow. I understood. This was magic, strong magic, and the cat looked for the loophole to the working. It was a familiar idea, though at this moment I could not remember why. "Love... And trust. The ways they intertwine. I don't do either easily." I ground each word out with effort. The pressure in my head began to relent, but only slightly.

And, have you learned to love and trust?

I nodded, then winced as the pressure increased. "I am learning. It's getting easier." The pressure relented once more. I rested my elbows on the worktable, my head next to Morpheus'.

Name them, the cat insisted. *Name the ones you love.*

"Poe," I said easily. "And I trust Skye." The pressure was bearable now, but the cloudiness would not relent. I closed my eyes against my fear. "And someday soon, I will love Ash." I opened my eyes, clear about what we discussed. "And I like you very much, but I do not know if you want my love."

The greymalkin rubbed his head against mine. *I believe I would enjoy being loved by you. But this is not enough. The curse will not be broken so easily.*

I laughed, resting my head on my arms. "It wasn't exactly easy to get to this point."

I do not doubt that, child. You have been very brave. I am afraid you must be braver before this ends.

"What does Ashbourne's memory loss have to do with this?" I asked.

Think, the cat said.

I tried, but the pressure returned almost immediately. I stopped trying so hard. Instead, I moved quickly, focusing on bringing the metal basket out of the tea pot, finding milk in the ice box, and pouring it all into a big pottery mug. Each small task sent the pressure running. Soon, I could think through the entire conversation we'd had without it returning, but I could not press on the issue of Ashbourne's memory loss.

"Do you know why this is happening?" I asked Morpheus, careful not to think about it too hard, focusing on the heat of my tea as I took a long drink.

It appears to be a curse, the cat answered. *Every time I attempt to talk to any of you about it, you all forget immediately.*

"Oh, how terrible," I said, wanting to wrap my arms around the cat.

Yes, he agreed, staring at the table in such a forlorn way that I set my mug down. I wondered if this was why he'd been disappearing so much lately. He needed time with people who didn't forget the things he tried to tell them. I was suddenly very glad he had Muse and Arcturus.

"May I hug you, Morpheus?" I asked.

He looked up at me, eyes solemn. *I believe I would like that.*

I wrapped my arms around the great cat, and he leaned into me, his cheek rubbing against mine. I closed my eyes, savoring the contact. Maman would never let us have pets, and because I had no elemental pair, I'd been denied such things as furry hugs. I tried to imagine hugging one of the hares, and snickered.

What is humorous? Morpheus asked, as I let him go.

We walked up the stairs together, towards the study. "I was thinking about hugging a mountain hare."

That is not an advisable action, he replied.

"No," I agreed as we entered the study. "It's not."

I took the key out of my pocket. As I held it up, a lock appeared. Without so much as thought, I stuck the key inside it, my head still swimming. After all that nonsense with the pressure in my head, I was nauseated. The key fit easily, and then turned, something inside the door hissing.

I would wait a few moments, Morpheus cautioned.

I nodded. "Yes, I expected something like this. There's a toxic gas filling the room right now. It will dissipate shortly." The cat's eyes widened at my feet. "Maman liked to be sure about things."

I leaned against the bookshelves, pressing my ear to the wall. There was still the noise of faint hissing inside the workroom. Footsteps in the hall let me know Skye was approaching.

"I found your stash from the Clotted Calf," she called out

as though it might draw me to her. I smiled. If my stomach wasn't so unpredictable, it would have been the perfect lure.

"We're in the study," I shouted back.

A few moments later, she appeared in the doorway. I felt the need to apologize. "I'm sorry my bath took so long."

"No apology necessary," she said, taking my cup of tea from me without asking, and replacing it with the bag of pastries. "You must take these. I took a little nap, and when I woke I ate four pastries. I might burst."

I fished a croissant out and stuck it in my mouth before my body had the chance to tell me it wasn't ready for food. The taste of flaky, buttery pastry was more than enough to quiet any protests within me. I chewed slowly, then swallowed. The first bite having gone all right, I took another, handing the bag back to Skye.

She took it, setting it on the desk with my mug. "Did you get the door unlocked then?" I nodded. She was wise enough to stay leaned against the desk. "Another of your mother's tricks then? What is it, toxic gas? A loose pyxie?"

I smiled at the mention of the mythical creature. "Gas. No pyxies, as far as I know."

She winked at me, a crooked smile quirking up one side of her lips. "Thank the Lady. I was terrified of them as a child."

"Me too," I confessed. "*Bloodbeard the Terrible* used to make me cry."

Skye laughed. "Me too. Niall used to read it to me, just to see me weep."

I put my hands near my face, curling my fingers like claws, "I'll gnash your flesh..."

"And boil your bones for broth," Skye recited in unison with me. "Ugh. That one is the worst."

I shook my head, thinking of Helene reading stories from

The Violet Book of Tales. "It was Helene's favorite. She insisted on doing the voices as well."

"Ghoulish behavior," Skye said, shaking her head. "We should have known they were rotten to the core, shouldn't we?"

I shrugged. "When you don't know any different, I suppose it seems normal." I pressed my ear to the door harder. It sounded as though the hissing had stopped. Only a few more minutes and the gas would clear.

"What do you think is in there?" Skye asked.

"I don't have expectations. Whatever's inside, if I know Maman, none of it will be straightforward."

Skye nodded, and the three of us sat in companionable silence for a few minutes. Skye stoked the fire in the hearth and I swept up my crumbs off the floor, tossing them into the fire. Though I hadn't spent much time alone with Skye, I saw why Ash enjoyed her company so much. She was easy to be comfortable around.

"I care about him," I said, feeling as though I needed to assure her I was serious about her best friend and partner.

"I know," she responded. "And I am in love with Poe."

A pleased smile lit my face. How nice that she felt she had to do the same with me, as I did her. "Does she know?"

Skye grinned. "I told her last night."

"When this is over, I plan to join you all in the undercity. I want to help her find her family." I motioned at the room. "I want no part in all of this."

Skye crossed her arms, but she didn't appear closed off, only more comfortable in that position. "You don't want to be Lady Somerhaven?"

"No," I said. "And not in the way you left the Chevaliers. I *truly* do not want this. There is no conflict in me."

"There's nothing good in this place." She grinned. "Except us."

I turned from her, but I could not muster a laugh. "I'm not so good either, Skye. This body is a fetch."

I felt her hand on my arm. "I know, Mina. Poe told me a few days ago. I hope you won't be angry with her, but I'd started to suspect and wondered if you knew."

"How did you know?" I asked without turning.

"The intensity of your pain made me wonder, as well as your gait," she said, mentioning something few knew of. I was impressed with her depth of knowledge on the subject. "Though I think it's something you probably experienced in your former body as well. Automatons can exacerbate conditions like yours, making them nearly unbearable."

I opened the door to the study, taking a big step back. It was best to do so, just to make sure. I turned to Skye. "Do you care? About the fetch, I mean."

She shook her head. "Not a bit. My mother worked with many before the ban, trying to help them. Her belief was that they were no more unnatural than the rest of us, but that the Oscarovi's metaphysical mechanics were not good enough to justify their use." Skye paused. "Do you mind?"

No one had asked me that. "There are things I don't like. I'll never have children."

Skye's eyes widened in empathy. "That is hard. Did you want them?"

"I wanted to be able to choose," I said.

Morpheus rubbed his face against my leg. *It is safe to enter now, littlelings.*

The cat often referred to us as children. "How old are you, Morpheus?" I asked as we followed him into the workroom. It was completely dark inside. There were no windows. No way in or out but the door. As a child, this room had terrified me. Maman often worked here, but Helene and I were not permitted to enter and she'd used all manner of threats to keep us away.

I felt for a switch on the wall, trying to banish the mounting anxiety in my chest. My hand hit a metal nub, and I pushed it upwards. Aetheric lights buzzed, then glowed dimly at first, brightening by the second.

One thousand, three hundred and forty-three, the cat replied to my question as the lights came on.

"Middle-aged, then," Skye quipped as the lights became bright enough to allow us to look around.

The walls were lined with bookshelves stuffed with leather-bound tomes, all of their spines in languages I did not recognize. In the center of the room stood a heavy table with a giant silver bowl resting on it. There was a dark, iridescent liquid inside it, viscous, with a life of its own.

The lekanomance. I swallowed hard at the sight of it, trying hard not to physically recoil. Logically, I knew my fear of it was irrational, born of Maman's attempts to scare us away from her study and the workroom. But still, the things she'd said about it haunted me.

"This is going to take a while to get through," Skye said with a sigh. "We're going to need more tea."

CHAPTER 42

MINA

An hour came and went and Skye and I had done little more than drink tea and sort through the books. None were written in any of the languages used on Sirin, which was notable in itself, but completely useless to us. We'd sorted out the few that had copious illustrations to come back to. Morpheus had given up on us entirely and was sleeping on the hearth in the study, his feline snores audible from within the workroom.

There was no secret cache of notes or records that would tell me anything about Maman's projects that I could easily find. Opening the workroom seemed, at first glance, to have been an utter failure. The thought tickled my mind. It was just the kind of thing that would have delighted Maman. It would have pleased her that anyone who was canny enough to break into her workroom would only find the lekanomance and a bunch of books they couldn't read.

"How is this even possible?" Skye asked, draining the last of our tea.

I'd dragged in an ottoman from the Maman's sitting room about fifteen minutes ago, and was now sitting on it, thinking. "It's not," I said, an idea forming. "It's not possible."

I began examining the room itself, looking for even the slightest anomaly. Skye watched me for a moment, then shook her head. "I give up. What are you doing?"

"It's a kind of magical encryption." I kept looking, running my fingers across every surface. Skye did not appear to be convinced. Perhaps she needed proof. "Try to take one of the books out of the workshop."

Skye raised an eyebrow, but did as I asked. I stopped my search and positioned myself, just in case. Sure enough, as she attempted to walk out of the workroom and back into the study, an invisible force propelled her backwards. As she was far more athletic than me, she needed little help, but I caught her anyway.

"Thanks," she said as she righted herself, setting the book she carried down on the table at the center of the room. She did not appear any worse for having the spell's power demonstrated in such a fashion. "So, the books have to stay in the room. Why is that significant?"

I leaned on the table, careful to keep away from the lekanomance. "Because if they have to stay, it means the encryption is a part of the room itself. If the spell was on the books, you'd be able to remove them."

Skye hummed a little, nodding as she looked around the windowless room. "So we're looking for something to do what? Turn the encryption off, like an aetheric light?"

I nodded. "Exactly. Of course, it could be a word or phrase, which might be impossible to discern. Maman liked puzzles."

Skye's eyes widened, then she began doing as I did, running her hands over the inside of the bookshelves. Just as I did, she pulled each book out individually, waiting for a response that never came. "What was your childhood like?" she asked.

I let out a dry laugh. Was this small talk? I hadn't spent much time alone with Skye, and I was never sure how to respond to these kinds of questions in ways that satisfied others. Vague answers, bordering on lies, for questions regarding family were probably best. "It felt uneventful, but I learned a great deal."

When I looked up, Skye stared at me, frowning. I wondered if I'd answered the question she was actually asking. Or had she not been making idle conversation? I tried again. "Maman was most interested in things like this," I gestured around the room. "She had little use for children, though she saw Helene as her protégé. I am not sure what I was made for, or why she wanted me if I was not her child."

Skye's expression shifted, her eyes widening further, her mouth twisting into a knot. "I am so sorry you had to go through that."

"Thank you," I murmured as I resumed my search. I was still uncertain about the purpose of this line of questions, but I wondered if perhaps I should ask about her childhood. "I assume that Elspeth was a better mother?"

"Yes," Skye answered, though her countenance told me the conversation wasn't going quite as she expected it to. There was a slight friction in her voice and movements, barely perceptible, but strong enough to let me know that I was irritating her. "She and my father made it clear they loved us, but they were a bit like Vaness in some ways. Like her, they were always working."

I hadn't heard much about Skye's father. "Is your father alive?"

Skye didn't answer immediately. I looked up from the shelf I examined, a prickle of heat blooming in my chest. She'd raised an eyebrow at me.

I had the distinct feeling of wanting to disappear. "Was that too blunt?"

Skye's brows knitted together, and then smoothed. It was as though she understood something she already had information about, but was just now seeing for herself. "Perhaps a little, especially if he was not... Alive, that is."

Inwardly, I winced, but I did not apologize. I'd learned long ago that showing remorse for my blunders only drew more attention to them, so if I had not caused harm, I tried to let things go without remark.

"My father is alive, incidentally. He is an airship captain. He travels to Brektos on a regular trade route."

"Oh." I was mildly confused. Most of the high Vilhari did not have true careers, but Skye's mother was a renowned physician and her father an airship captain. "Is that odd for you? That your parents have professions?"

Now Skye smiled. "Oh, yes. My family follows many of the old ways." We'd searched all the bookshelves. Now we moved on to the worktable, Skye on one side, and me on the other.

"The old ways?" I asked, keeping as far from the lekanomance as I could.

Skye nodded. "Before the Vilhari came here, there was a nominal aristocracy amongst our people, a hierarchy used only for determining how decisions were made. But everyone had enough. Everyone worked. What we've devolved into here should be our greatest shame."

I paused. "That's why you are so angry with Niall."

Skye nodded. "That's why I left home. My parents wouldn't reprimand him or stop him from becoming this. And look where it's gotten us. He's obviously wrapped up in something terrible."

I felt sorry for Niall Aestra, in some ways. We'd all been

drawn into something terrible. He'd simply chosen the wrong side.

The table yielded nothing. I was frustrated, but Skye was calm. She leaned on the table, staring at the lekanomance. "It's been a long time since I saw one of those. They're very rare, and rather finicky if they're not maintained."

I calmed my breath. There was no harm in simply *talking* about the thing. "You know what it's used for, then?"

Skye nodded, though she watched me carefully, as though seeing some clue I could not discern. "In essence, anyway. I've never been that interested in magic. You ask for what you want and it gives it to you, right? Forms something out of nothing?"

"Not nothing," I explained, my skin prickling with the sheer anxiety thinking about the lekanomance brought on. "The liquid is pure aether, straight from the heart of the limen. It's the building blocks of all matter."

"Interesting," Skye remarked with a sigh. I was sure she feigned disinterest, but not why. Perhaps she'd sensed my discomfort in discussing the thing. I had no doubt fear was written all over my face. "Do we think it's a spoken command then?"

"It must be," I had to admit, relieved that she did not press me more about the lekanomance. Disappointment filled me. I'd been so sure when I remembered the key that I'd unlocked the answers to many of our questions.

"I'm going to go make more tea," Skye said. "And find something for Morpheus to eat before he wakes and gets angry with me."

I sank onto the ottoman, nodding. "Of course."

Her footsteps died away, and I turned my thoughts to Maman. Though I knew her well enough to predict when she might smack me, or find fault in my actions, I knew little about her as a person. The place in me that might have been sad about that was only angry.

My explanation to Skye rang back in my thoughts. Why had she made the fetch? What had she wanted with me, and how did it connect to Chopard? There was no way around it; if we couldn't unlock the secrets of Maman's workroom, we would have to do this the hard way.

I would have to remember what I'd forgotten, and we would have to hunt down Maman's friends. As I came to this conclusion, the front door opened. Though I heard Poe murmur a few words to Ashbourne, there was no immediate answer. Only the sound of his feet on the stairs, and then a door opening and closing.

I frowned. He'd gone to his own room. I walked into the study, about to go find Poe, but she met me at the door. "Oh, you got it open. Find anything?"

I shook my head. "Not yet. Excuse me, please," I said. Then I stopped, smiling faintly at Poe. "Skye's making tea."

Poe looked as though she might argue, her mouth opening once, but then she nodded, sinking to the floor to sit next to Morpheus on the hearth.

I hurried upstairs to the Oleander Room. I knocked softly, once, but Ash didn't answer. "It's me," I murmured. "Can I come in?"

Beyond the door, I heard him sigh. "All right."

When I opened the door, I found him sitting in the dark, head in his hands. I rushed to examine him, worried he'd been hurt. "What's wrong?" I asked. "Did something happen?" I kneeled on the rug in front of him, wary of touching him without his permission, but longing to do so.

He looked down at me, frowning. "I'm cursed," he replied, as though it explained everything. The pressure that had built in my head when I discussed my own situation with

Morpheus returned, almost instantly. "That's why I can't remember anything."

My head ached, the clouded feeling returning. I attempted to make the connection between the similarities in our situations. I desperately wanted to talk this over with him. To turn the idea over in each of our minds, seeing how the other's perspective could change what we thought about what was happening.

But my mouth would not open. Not even to allow me to breathe. I tried again and again to make a sound, but it was as though I was frozen in place, unable to move or speak. In trying to calm my rising panic, I recalled what Muse had said about the connections between the four of us.

Our mutual loss of memory was connected. That much was clear. Now I could not move any part of me. Stubbornly, I held onto the thought, refusing to let it go, even as the curse's magic tried to strangle me. I took long, even breaths through my nose, steadying myself. If this curse was aggressive, I could be worse.

Curses were not like other spells; they were more like living things that grew and adapted with the cursed. It's what made them unreliable workings. But I refused to give into the pressure. If this spell had followed me all my life, I would become its worst nightmare now. It could not have me. And it could not have this man. I wanted him for myself, and none would take him from me.

My hand moved of its own accord, the pressure in my head relenting. My voice still caught, but I could move. I reached up to brush hair out of Ashbourne's face. His golden eyes met mine, and I inched towards him. Still, I could not speak, but I hoped he saw the question in my eyes. *Can I comfort you?*

He bent towards me, his lips meeting mine. The kiss was tender to begin with, his hands cupping my face. My arms went around his neck and he pulled me to him, my body resting between his legs. As he deepened the kiss, the magic relented, letting go of my voice.

"I don't care about curses," I said, my lips moving against his. "It doesn't matter."

He pulled away from me, eyes searching my face. "You don't, do you?"

I shook my head. "We belong together. I believe that."

"Show me." His words were a plea, dragged up from the depths of him.

Whatever he had been through before he was cursed, he did not want to remember it now. I feared what might happen when he did, when we both knew why we'd been drawn together in this way. I had the feeling there was not much time. That an hourglass had been turned over, and I watched sand slip through it, with no way of stopping what came next.

Every feeling I'd had of being able to control this, of getting my way, dissolved before me. There was no path that belonged to me now. There was only this moment, this man, and Lady Fate's talons closing around us.

"Show me," he pleaded again, pulling me to him.

My mouth met his, my need rising to a fever pitch, one to match Ashbourne's. If all we had was now, then I would spend these precious moments in ecstasy, not pain.

CHAPTER 43

ASHBOURNE

I woke up tangled with Mina, sharing her breath. A glance at the clock told me we'd fallen asleep, missing dinner and the evening hours after our very long encounter. I pushed a strand of hair off her face. In sleep, she was oddly innocent looking. None of her sharp edges showed, and every instinct I had screamed at me to both get away from her and stay by her side.

How was I to protect her if I was a danger to her? If I was cursed, but did not know why, then I had to admit some hard things to myself. Until I knew the exact nature of my past, and why I'd been cursed, I was a danger to all those I loved... Or in her case, all I *could* love, if only it was safe.

It was in her eyes as she made love to me: she was falling hard. I was too, but I had to stop myself. She was giving me all of herself, and taking every bit of me I would give her, but if we continued on, I would disappoint her.

And there was the matter of my celestial power to contend with, and the Strix woman. Mina had been honest with me about so much, and I knew very well how important trust was to her. I was keeping things from her, for reasons I'd deemed good, but she might not. If I didn't go now, I would ruin it all. I needed to hurt her now to help her the most. To try to save the spark of what we had started.

I said a silent prayer to the Lady as I wrote her a note. *Please cushion this blow*, I begged. *Help her understand all she needs to know and show us both the way back to one another.*

As I placed the note by her pillow, my heart ached. I wasn't sure this was right. Walking away from the women in this house would be the hardest thing I'd ever had to do. They were my family. They had all of me that I could give. But until I knew that who I was wouldn't endanger them further, I had to take some space.

I dressed quickly, stealing out of the room with my boots in my hands. Skye sat on the stairs, as though waiting for me. Morpheus sat next to her. I gestured to the door. She nodded, and they followed me outside.

On the steps, she crossed her arms tightly around her body. "Morpheus thinks you're sneaking out on us. Is that true?"

I looked down at the cat, shaking my head. "Were you spying on me?"

I was coming to cuddle her, the fey cat said defensively. *She seemed worried that I might enjoy Arcturus and Muse's company more than hers. I did not want her to fear abandonment.*

I crouched down to stroke the greymalkin's head. "You must continue to do that, friend."

The feline glared at me. *So you are* leaving.

I stood, placing my hands on Skye's shoulders. "Only for a few days. A week at most. My memory loss is not amnesia, Skye. I'm cursed."

She clapped a hand over her mouth in horror. I looked down at the greymalkin. "You didn't tell her?" Greymalkin could see spells more clearly than other creatures. Surely, he'd known.

The great beast sat down hard on the step, his eyes round and wide with sadness. *I tried. She could not remember it, nor could you. If you have this knowledge, then you are remembering as well.* The cat looked as though he might say more, but strangely kept silent.

"I'm going to the cabin for a few days, if you don't mind," I said when I was sure the greymalkin did not have more to say. Skye's family had a little hunting cabin deep in the forest, near the Achera that was hers to use when she liked. "I'll isolate for safety... In case remembering brings on my celestial fire."

Skye had known from the beginning what I was capable of, and we'd worked hard to hide it. It was a rare gift amongst the Vilhari, and a dangerous one. Even those who wielded celestial power could not always summon empyrae. Keeping this fact a secret had been vital to my blending into the landscape of the undercity. Now, to keep them all safe, I needed to go.

The deeper my feelings for Mina became, the more likely I was to emit empyrae during our intimate encounters. And remembering my past could surely do the same.

"Of course you can use the cabin," Skye said. "What should I tell Poe and Mina?"

"Tell them I was called away. That the Syndicate got a lead on Chopard, and I've gone to investigate."

Skye nodded. "We will pursue Lord Eccles in the meantime. Poe says that Vionette has eyes on Viridian at all times. He's been quiet for the past few weeks, rarely socializing outside his small circle of Caralee's friends. We'll keep an eye out for him."

I couldn't argue with any of those points. "Watch for the Strix woman," I warned. "She wants to kill Mina, and if Mina finds out, her path will be altered in ways Muse warns against."

Skye nodded. She knew all this, of course, but I could not help reminding her. But I had not been able to tell her about the woman or the other greymalkin yet. "There's a young woman following her, accompanied by a large golden cat." I looked down at Morpheus. "I believe he is one of your kind."

Morpheus' eyes narrowed to dangerous slits now. *Interesting. I have not met another of my ilk for centuries.*

"They know about the curse," I said. "And while I don't think they are dangerous, we must be careful all the same." I ran my hands through my hair in frustration. "It's not a good time for this, Skye. If I had any other choice, I'd stay—"

She clasped my forearms, shaking me a little. "Brother, I know this."

It was the first time she'd ever referred to me that way. Tears sprung to my eyes, and I grabbed her, hugging her hard. "I'm so sorry," I said as I blinked back tears. "I've brought you nothing but trouble."

She hugged back just as hard, and Morpheus wound around our ankles. "You are my best friend in the world, and the brother of my heart," Skye murmured, her body shaking with tears. "The day I found you was one of the best of my life. The Lady brought us together once and she shall do so again."

When I released her, we both wiped our eyes. "I'll see you in a week," I promised. "No more than that."

She nodded. "If you don't come back, I will find you. Anywhere you go, Ashbourne Claymore. Whatever you remember about yourself, know this for fact: You are more than a friend to me. We have a covenant deeper than blood, and I will not let you go. Whoever you were in the past, you choose your future."

Skye sounded like the Chevalier she was, formal and grand, all the rules of chivalry fresh in her mind. Standing in the moonlight, she was a vision of the Lady's right arm, the picture of valor and camaraderie the Chevaliers aspired to. I was as proud of her as if she were my own sister.

My heart ached with some forgotten hurt, but I would have those answers soon enough. For now, Skye's words meant more to me than I could ever say. All I could manage was, "I love you too."

I turned away before I could change my mind. Mina would be safe with Morpheus and Skye, safer than she'd be with me. I had to go before I made a horrendous mistake. As I walked down the step to Orchid House and into the street, it felt as though my heart would shatter.

It would, I realized when I looked back. It would shatter because I'd left it in that bedroom. And when she woke, she might not understand the way Skye had. Skye's reassurances about my leaving might work for a week, but if this took longer... She would never forgive me.

As I walked down the street, I felt the pressure of eyes watching me. I looked back. Skye and Morpheus were no longer on the steps, nor were they at the window. As I had been for weeks now, I was followed.

Good, I thought to myself. *Let the Strix woman follow me and leave her behind.*

CHAPTER 44

MINA

The next morning dawned bright, golden sunlight streaming in through the open curtains. Curtains we'd forgotten to draw last night. I rolled over to find Ash's bed empty, but another note on my pillow elicited a smile. His little notes were sweet, and I loved that he could steal away from bed without my waking. There was something comforting in knowing that I could rest. I opened the note and immediately frowned.

I have to go away for a few days. Didn't want to wake you. Skye will explain.

-Ash

I sat up, pulling the covers around my shoulders. It was an unfortunate development, but not entirely unexpected. We weren't courting under normal circumstances, after all. Likely, he had some part of our puzzle to piece together. And, if I was honest, it might be easier to sort out this business with our curses if he were not here.

If I couldn't talk to him about it, then maybe his absence might reveal more than if he'd stayed. Under other circumstances, I would not have minded taking our problems to bed to solve. However, unlocking this part of what was wrong would take a bit more maneuvering that I was sure of at this point.

I made my way up to my own bedroom to dress. After some consideration, I threw on a pair of wool pants, the sweater I'd worn the day before, heavy wool socks, and my slippers. With some effort, I yanked my hair into a nest atop my head, stuck a long hairpin in it to secure it, then headed downstairs. I had thoughts about Maman's workshop I wanted to work out.

As I made my way towards the stairs, I heard Poe and Skye talking in the foyer. It was a bad habit to eavesdrop, but one I couldn't help indulging in from time to time.

Poe said, "Vionette says another warehouse in the country was burned. Same as before, everyone was found in a trance, their memories wiped. Things smelled like sulphur."

"He's gone to hunt a lead down, for exactly that reason," Skye responded. "He's staying at my family's cabin."

"I'm afraid she'll be upset. They're getting close. I don't want to see her hurt, Skye."

"He's not going to hurt her, darling. She will understand."

I peeked around the corner. They were hugging, and the way Skye stroked Poe's hair was endearing. My friend was so tiny, and Skye so tall, she was tucked into the crook of the former Chevalier's arm. The scene made me glad they had each other.

Making sure to cause a bit of noise as I went, I made my way downstairs. The two of them looked up. "Ash left a note. Has he gone after Chopard on his own?" I made sure to look appropriately concerned, but not sad. I didn't want them to worry about me.

"Not exactly," Poe answered. "But he has gone to chase down a lead."

Skye smiled a little too brightly. "Shouldn't be gone longer than a week."

I had to stop myself from laughing at their overt concern. It was sweet, after all, and I did appreciate it. But I was fine. He hadn't abandoned *me*, after all. We had goals, things we were trying to achieve. But I understood why they were worried, why he might be worried. It was one of those things another kind of person might be concerned over, but I was not.

This was good for me. I had no interest in a partner who lived only for me, or who would be constantly interfering in my business. It was good that he was gone now, taking care of our mutual interests. We would be together again soon enough.

"Then he'll be back soon," I said. "I have an idea about Maman's workroom. Where is Morpheus?"

"I think he is a little sad about Ashbourne leaving," Poe replied, as she and Skye followed me to the back of the house. "He went to Muse's."

"But he told us he was going!" Skye added, smiling. "So it's an improvement in his behavior."

I laughed softly. "Indeed. We're all learning, aren't we?"

The two of them looked as though they might be bowled over by a wave of relief.

"I am fine," I insisted, as we walked through Maman's study to the workroom. "Ash will be back soon. Will the two of you be all right without him?"

Skye looked as though she was swallowing some big emotion, but as I had no idea what it was and she and Poe both nodded, I moved on. There were times, like this one, that not being able to discern the nuance of what others were thinking or feeling was a blessing. It allowed me to focus on the task at hand.

We had left the door to the workroom unlocked, but closed with the key inside the lock. I opened the door and turned on the aetheric chandelier, the cold brass of the switch frigid on my fingers. The dark bookshelves seemed to loom over us. Why couldn't there have been a window in here?

My fear of the lekanomance returned as soon as I set eyes on it. I didn't bother to resist it. I would do what I had to when the moment came, but for now there was no use in fighting an emotion so native to my being, so perfectly emblazoned on my young mind.

Now I stood behind the table, gesturing at the bowl of dark, viscous liquid. "Maman used to scare me about the lekanomance, warning me that if I so much as looked at it, it might draw ghasts to the house."

Skye and Poe stood across from me. "How awful," Skye said. "That's not what they do, is it?"

I shrugged. "I suppose it's possible that a witch might conjure a ghast from a lekanomance, but they'd have to really want to. The liquid inside the bowl is pure aether. The same stuff at the heart of the limen, where all aethereal power is generated."

"That seems like a rare tool," Poe said, frowning.

"It is," Skye agreed, taking Poe's hand. "I've only seen one other. It's in the wreck of the Avalonne. Do you know where Vaness got this?"

I shook my head. "Not really. She said it was something Papa's family gave to her when he died. But really, anything might be true. I have no doubt she'd have stolen it from the Avalonne itself, if she thought it served her purposes."

Poe's face crumpled. "Mina," she breathed. "I'm so sorry."

"Why?" I asked, curious.

Poe glanced at Skye. I hated it when people did that. A frustrated sigh rattled through me. "I just..." Poe's words sounded jumbled. "You deserved better. You *deserve* better."

I still didn't quite understand. But what I did understand warmed me. It made her sad to know I'd had an unhappy childhood, and that was a kindness I could appreciate.

"I have better now," I said, my voice sounding unimaginably soft and vulnerable. I smiled at them both. "In all of you."

If I had known they were going to cry, I would have chosen my words more carefully. But from what I could tell, these were happy tears, and I knew how healing those could be. I let my friends cry, forcing myself not to apologize to them. When they wiped tears from each other's faces, both giving me watery smiles, I continued.

"I believe the lekanomance may be the key to the workroom." I paused, taking a deep breath. "But I must admit that while my rational mind knows that Maman was trying to scare me away from it for exactly this reason, I am still afraid."

Poe came around the table to stand next to me. "Do you want to hold hands?"

"No," I said with a small smile. "I have to stick both of mine into the lekanomance, I'm afraid. But please stay near me."

She looked up at me, nodding. "I won't move a muscle."

I smiled at her, then at Skye, just to show them I was feeling brave. Both of them grimaced. "So, that was not my most successful smile?"

"No, darling," Poe said. "Please do not ever do that again."

I laughed now, but for real. Poe smiled back at me. "There's our girl."

It was a reminder that they saw me for my true self and liked that best. That I didn't have to falsify my emotions for them. The knowledge made me brave. Without another thought, I stuck my hands into the silver bowl. The liquid inside, pure aether, was cool to the touch.

It whispered to me, voices both familiar and strange inside my head. I thought I heard my name, but could not be certain; it sounded odd. Before I could think on it further, I whispered words I'd heard Maman say many times over the years, "*Per aspera ad astra.*"

Through hardships, to the stars. I'd tried saying it in the room a few times, but it had had no effect. Now it did. It was as though a veil fell away from the room itself. Skye and Poe stared at the bookshelves, their backs turned to me.

"I can read them," Skye said. "Most of them, anyway."

But I was transfixed by the image that seemed to be projected from the pool of pure aether. It was a map of the stars and planets, which rotated slowly above my head. Some constellations I recognized. Others I did not. The planets that popped out from time to time as the image rotated were labeled in golden lettering. The first was Sirin, which I recognized immediately.

The next was a planet called Okairos, then another named Elysium, another called Earth, and the last, the one that stole my breath from my lungs, was named Interra. I watched it rotate, its land masses as familiar to me as my own face, with a growing sense of horror. Every piece of memory that lived inside me rearranged, sharpening to a clarity I had not imagined possible.

Lumina and Ashbourne.

The useless princess and the general prince.

Not the Mina and Ashbourne of today, but two winged immortals, like the statues Papa had been obsessed with. Both Ventyr, but from warring houses. Sworn to seduce and kill the other, we had been enemies—until we were not. Then enemies once more when torn asunder.

Ashbourne Thuellos, his true name, was the reason I'd been discarded here. The reason my wings were ripped from me. The reason I would never fly again. He was the reason for every sorrow within that could never be mended. I'd spent hundreds of years walking this cursed planet alone, unknown, in pain. Only to fall *in love* with him. Now.

Before, back then, I hadn't known if I'd been in love or not. It was too hard to separate the animosity between our families from the feelings we developed for one another. I pushed these thoughts away as hard as I could. Remembering the past this way… it was too much. I could not be Lumina and Wilhelmina at once. My jaw clenched with the effort it took not to break apart.

But nothing could stop my mind from its unrelenting churn once it got started. Every muscle in my body tightened, bracing against the overwhelming flow of information. It was both inconceivable and utterly predictable that this could happen. That this could be the end to the curse. That loving *him* would break it.

Cruel as it was, it made a horrible kind of sense. My aunts, my mother's sisters, were the ones who laid the curse. They were the only ones with enough skill to do so, and enough knowledge of me to craft such a cunning loophole, such a bitter blessing.

They thought they did me a favor; that if we could find our way back to one another, I might be mended by his love. But nothing could or ever would heal the ways his betrayal broke me. If only he had trusted me when it counted. If only he'd stayed away. But he'd thought he knew better than me, that he and his seventeen generals, and all their armies, could save me.

All he'd done was damn me to eternal pain and loneliness. And now, I would be expected to forgive all that, to love him and work together to keep this little shred of happiness that had been gifted to me in another lifetime of eternal pain. Fury rose in me at the unfairness of it all, of being expected to be the one who forgave and forgot yet again. It was always me who was expected to grant absolution. I tamped the storm of rage that brewed within me down as hard as I could.

Poe and Skye were still distracted by the books. They had not seen the map of the stars. Only a moment had passed, though to me, it felt like an eon. I pulled my hands from the lekanomance, my heart a hollow plane.

There was no doubt in my mind that I loved Ashbourne Claymore and hated Ashbourne Thuellos. The two horrible truths collided with the knowledge that if love was the loophole, I was doubly betrayed. *My* Ashbourne did not remember who he was, who *I* was. He did not love me. A feral cry overtook my consciousness, spooling out from my empty heart in a symphony of anguish.

I tried to shut it off, to focus only on the notes of warning and rage, and to reject the sorrow. But I could not turn it down or ignore the knowledge that beyond any other betrayal, I had cruelly forsaken myself. The man I loved was the reason I would spend an eternity in pain.

CHAPTER 45

MINA

Poe's voice shook me from whatever dark place I had traveled to. I blinked a few times, my vision clearing. Poe stood in front of me, shaking my shoulders gently, her face twisted with worry.

"I'm all right," I said as soon as I realized she had been asking what was wrong. "Just a bad reaction to the lekanomance."

It was not wholly a lie. And the present moment, the now I'd left before all had been made clear, was strangely comforting. Though I was utterly changed, this world was still here. Poe, who loved me, and Skye, who would not when I did what must be done.

My breath caught on the thought, as Poe led me out of the workroom, through Maman's study and into the sitting room. *What did that mean?*

"Sit here," Poe said. "I'll fetch you a bit of tea and a snack."

Absently, I nodded, already lost in thought. Fury and revenge had been the undercurrent of my thoughts for nearly all my life, though I had not understood that so well as

I did now. I'd always believed what Maman had told me about myself, that I was a wretched child, ungrateful and unworthy of more than I got from her. But my anger had been justified. *I'd been betrayed.* The words played over and over in my mind until I shook my head, trying to loosen their grip on me.

Now was not the time to get lost in emotion. Logic must reign. I'd let my feelings carry me away these past weeks. I could not yet say if I was sorry for it, but it could not stand now that I'd remembered myself. The memory of the day I'd confronted Maman was still not accessible to me, and I could not immediately see why.

If the curse had broken, why could I not remember that day?

All I knew now was that it was more important than ever that I understand why this had happened. Why had the fetch been necessary? It would take me days, at minimum, to untangle my thoughts and feelings about Ashbourne. As much as I wanted to hunt him down and dismantle him piece by piece, my feelings for him were real. The man I'd fallen in love with hadn't acted a bit like the spoiled prince I'd seduced in my youth.

I couldn't see how he, or our past, connected to Maman, or what she might have wanted, so I set that aside as collateral. It did not occur to me that I was pacing, having left the chair, until Poe and Skye returned with trays of tea and toasted cheese sandwiches.

As I watched them arrange their trays on the low table at the center of the room, I knew it was not in me to break them apart. If one of us had to leave, it would be me. If I told Poe the truth, she would side with me. I knew that, without a doubt in my heart. She was steadfast and true in a way no lover ever could be. As I was to her.

I watched as Skye touched the small of her back, pressing a kiss to her temple. Poe had lost so much already, was already so brave and strong. I could push all my feelings aside for now and get us to the end of this. I had to uncover why Maman had put me in the fetch.

A plan formed in my mind. I sat down across from the two of them, taking the cup of tea Skye offered me. One deep breath and all my anger faded into the depths of me. I had no illusions that it was gone for good. But I was good at this. I'd spent the last twenty-eight years learning, and I was now an expert at forgetting.

"I've remembered a bit more about my past," I explained. "How much have you told her?" I asked Poe.

"Not much," Poe assured me. "It is your story to tell."

Skye nodded. "I would be honored to carry your tale."

My eyes crinkled with affection, loving the formal way she spoke. Skye was so very special, and I was glad she would take care of Poe, if ever I was unable. "Long before the Ventyr came to conquer Sirin, I was a princess on a planet far, far from here called Interra. Have you ever heard of it?"

Skye shook her head. "I don't believe so."

Poe took her hand, and they shared a look I could not discern meaning from. Perhaps they'd already talked about this part of things? No matter.

"My mother was the leader of a band of Ventyr called the Larae, a matriarchal lineage of warrior queens. On Interra, they were unconquerable. Our people were always at war, Houses forever locked in conflict. My father's House, House Anemos, was the victor for centuries, amassing land and alliances. When only the Larae remained, my mother knew she would have to give in to him.

"There was no other way to protect her people, and with the whole world united against them, she knew they could not hold out against my father much longer. So she married him, leaving her people in the hands of her sisters, Orynthia, Penthe, and Faedra. Soon after my parents' marriage, I was born, and then there was no other child. My mother could not conceive another after me, and I was not a son."

"Was that so important?" Skye asked, frowning.

It warmed me to hear her say such a thing, to be so innocent. Sirin was not a perfect world by any means, but it was so much better than Interra had been. "Yes," I said softly. "In our society, sons were valued above all else. Not within the Larae, you understand, but Interra at large believed this, while my mother's people still followed the old ways."

Poe smiled then, though her eyes were wet with tears. "The Ventyr are fey, as we are. The word Vilhar is not the name of our people, but the place we are from."

Skye's eyes went wide with wonder. "But how?"

Poe shook her head. "I've searched the Avalonne's records for that knowledge, but I cannot find it. If it was known when we came here, it is lost now." She nodded to me, urging me to continue.

"My father spent so many years looking for ways to conceive an heir by my mother. There were... experiments. I watched her grow frail and fade. Strong as she was, she could not withstand his methods, which were dark and dangerous. My father was not only a tyrant, but also a magician of great strength. Eventually, he killed her."

"Oh, Mina," Skye breathed, her face drawn with sorrow. "I am so sorry."

Her sympathy was fresh, but this was a wound I'd carried for so long it hardly stung. "Thank you. She endured his machinations so none of her sisters would have to. It was her greatest regret that she failed. He replaced her with the eldest of her remaining sisters, my aunt, Orynthia."

I paused, wondering exactly how to tell this part without revealing anything about Ashbourne and myself. The easiest way might be to spin the tale without planning, to keep things as close to the truth as I could. "In his efforts to secure an heir, my father lost control over Interra. These experiments he became obsessed with—they took years from my parents, you must understand. So when he married Orynthia, she brought along her generals and her military prowess. Together, they retook the planet, bit by bit, though Orynthia hated every moment of it."

Skye glanced at Poe before she spoke. "Then why did she help him?"

I swallowed hard, not knowing how to explain this to someone who had not lived through it. "You must understand, our people are as long-lived as yours. There had been centuries of wars. Thousands lost, and millions of lives ruined. Orynthia believed as my mother did—that if my father got his way, if he conquered the planet—that there might finally be peace."

"And was there?" Skye asked, her voice choked with emotion.

I shook my head, understanding that she knew how this story ended for her people, with the Ventyr coming here to conquer a whole other planet. But my mother, my aunts, they hadn't known that at the time. They hadn't even known that was possible.

"They were doing the best they could with the knowledge they had, Skye," Poe said.

Skye sighed. "I'm sorry. What happened when they retook the planet?"

I sighed, frustrated that the only story I had to tell would confirm what she already thought of my people: that we were evil. Even now, as much as I hated my father and all that he'd done, I wanted to believe the Ventyr had good in them. "The wars restarted, and in the midst of them arose a new threat. Creatures we called the Ravagers, with the power to feed off of and influence emotions, to render whole cities listless, void of life. They fed mostly on anguish and pain, which they cultivated like grapes for fine wine. My father believed their power could be harnessed for a time, but his Lords begged him to turn his attention to destroying them."

Poe and Skye both looked as though they might be sick. Poe had turned a shade of gray I didn't like, and Skye wrapped her arms around her waist, hugging herself tightly.

I had to finish this story quickly. "They could not be destroyed. We had to make an alliance with our greatest enemies, House Thuellos, to stop them. Eventually, we did. They were imprisoned in the limen, where they sleep, to this day."

It was a struggle not to explain who Ashbourne was, that he was the youngest son of House Thuellos. That my father, looking for a way for me to be useful, had ordered me to seduce him—to gain access to all his secrets, and all those of our rivals. I sucked air through my nose, hoping that if my face showed the distress I felt that they would simply think I was upset by the other memories.

"Mina," Poe breathed. "That is an incredible story. How long ago did this happen?"

It was a logical question to ask, but I had no answer. "I could not tell you. I lost count of my age when I passed a thousand of our years."

"Incredible," Poe said, her eyes wide with wonder. "But—"

"You are wondering why this is important now," I finished for her, wanting to move things along. "Come with me."

I stood, walking as quickly as I could to Papa's library. I pulled several books from the shelf and handed them to Poe. In turn, she handed them to Skye with a smile and a quick kiss on the cheek. I was heartened to see my story had not struck fear into her, or if it had, she was holding up well against it.

We made our way back to the workroom, where Skye set the books down on the table as I pulled more volumes from the shelves. Now that I knew what to look for, they were easy to find. "All of these are, in one way or another, about harnessing great elemental energies."

I waited for them to catch up, for them to understand what I saw so clearly now. It was hard not to jump in with the answer, but this was not how people learned best.

Poe's eyes lit with understanding first. "Surely Vaness did not believe that..." She shook her head. "No. No one could be so cruel."

Skye looked lost. "I told you, I'm not a scholar of magics. You're going to have to explain it to me."

I nodded, happy to do so—anything not to get lost in my memories of Ashbourne Thuellos and all the ways he'd torn me apart. "My supposed Oscarovi father, Alastair Wildfang, was obsessed with the Ventyr before his death. These are all stories he collected about them," I explained, gesturing to the novels and volumes of poetry I'd pulled from his library. "I believe if we search in these, we will find stories about the Ventyr, my true father in particular, looking for a way to channel enormous amounts of elemental energy.

"Before his Lords talked him out of it, my father wanted to use a magically gifted person to channel the Ravagers. He wanted to use their power for himself, for more war."

Now Skye's eyes widened. She looked to Poe, who shook her head as I continued on. This was a lot for them. For me as well, but I had to get it out. They had to know. "The Oscarovi had independently found the means to channel elemental spirits. I believe Maman and her cohort thought they'd found a way to do the same, but with the Ravagers. Their intent was to set the Ravagers loose, and use me as the conduit for their power."

"Why..." Skye asked, her mouth hanging open in pure horror. "Why would they have believed that would work?"

My face was smooth, wan with exhaustion. This was all so much to tell, and I had not even told the worst of it, the ways I'd been used to manipulate House Thuellos, then betrayed by my own people. I took a deep breath. Then I lit one hand with empyrae and with the other summoned aether.

Both Poe and Skye stood frozen, their eyes wide with shock. I sent the two opposing forces into a spiraling column above our heads, fire and shadow twisting together. "I can use both."

"Did you burn Somerhaven down?" Skye asked, the moment she found words. "Was it you?"

"No," I said, shaking my head. "It wasn't me. I don't remember it yet, but I believe this is why I was imprisoned. I believe I uncovered Maman's plans for me."

"What did Vaness want?" Poe asked. "What did she think she could do if she turned you into a conduit for such a creature?"

They still didn't understand. It was a testament to them having grown up in this place, free from the kinds of power mongering that had been my bread and butter for centuries. "To rule this world," I explained. "To conquer it for herself, with me as her enforcer, inspirited by the Ravager."

CHAPTER 46

ASHBOURNE

The cabbie dropped me off at the end of the long gravel driveway that led to the cabin. They'd asked if I wanted to be taken all the way, but I refused. I wanted to walk—to be alone with my thoughts. I'd been followed all through the undercity, and through some of the outer ring suburbs, but once I'd reached the mountain villages, my tail disappeared. I figured I had a few hours at least, maybe a day, before the Strix woman found me.

No matter how much time I had, I meant to make the most of it. The mountain air was crisp and cold, and clouds hung low in the sky, the dim light intensifying the golden glow of the birch trees that lined the drive. I felt as though I could breathe again, free of responsibility and worry, even if just for a short time.

My boots crunched on the crushed gravel of the driveway as a gust of wind kicked up, sending a shower of birch leaves raining down on me. It was magical to be surrounded by them. Dizzying, but beautiful. As they swirled around me, the movement distracted me, familiar somehow.

I tried to focus on the feeling, grasping at it, though it seemed to slip out of my mind's grip.

The moment I relaxed, I slipped into my second sight, memory taking over as though it were a vision. The curse loosened its grip on my mind, even if only a little.

They had been rose petals. Hundreds of thousands of rose petals floating down from the sky. A celebration. Or at least it was for everyone else. But not for me. For some reason, I had been sad as I'd walked through the crowds of winged people. I'd ducked into an alley, hoping to avoid being seen by anyone I knew, and there she found me.

The next few moments were a blur in my mind. A soft body pressed against mine, the pleasure of her kiss, the sting of her knife at my neck. The gasp of betrayal as mine pressed against her ribs. The fury in her eyes as we both realized the truth of the moment, of the lies we'd told one another for months. The clatter of the knives on the stone street. The heat of her kiss, of our renewed passion.

The fervor, brought on by our mutual betrayal and a thousand stolen glances and brushed fingertips. The sting of her fangs piercing me was nothing in comparison to the pleasure I'd felt as mine entered her. To claim her was the height of fulfilled desire, of divine providence. And it was also my undoing.

The vision ended abruptly, my corporeal sight returning in a tumble of senses. The chill air, the smell of winter approaching, and the leaves that carpeted the ground. Despair barreled into me, nearly knocking me over with its force. That woman, whoever she was, she'd meant something to me. Something horribly important. And I didn't know what had happened between us, but I knew I'd betrayed her, hurt her in ways I couldn't be forgiven for.

I gritted my teeth and kept walking. This was why I was here, to figure all of this out. To know the truth of myself so I wouldn't repeat the past with Mina. The only way to keep her safe now and in the future was to know what I'd done to that other woman. I had to be sure I'd changed enough from the man I was in my vision. And if I hadn't, I would work on it harder; I would find whatever help I needed to be the kind of person who deserved someone like Mina Wildfang. Someone worthy of being permitted to love her.

Clouds moved overhead, and I drew a long breath in as I rounded a corner in the driveway. I don't know what made me so sure of myself, but I knew I was capable of figuring this all out. The cabin came into view, and I had to smile. This was where it all began with me, Skye, and Morpheus. Skye had found me by the river, beaten and unconscious, and we'd spent much of the first month of my recovery here, before I'd agreed to come back to Pravhna with her.

There was wood by the door, but not much. I gathered up an armful of what was left and pressed my hand to the door. While this was technically House Aestra's retreat, only Skye used the cabin, and she'd added me to the house wards long ago. The door swung open.

Inside, the cabin still smelled like summer-fresh wildflowers. I unburdened myself of my armful of wood and placed my bag on the bed in the tiny guest room just off the kitchen. All of the bedrooms were small in the cabin, which was luxuriously furnished, but still rather rustic.

I lit the stove first, setting the kettle on to boil, then went to work lighting a fire. It was easy to feel comfortable here. This was the first place I'd known after waking from my coma. Skye and Morpheus had made me feel safe, in a time when it was disorienting not to know myself. As I looked around the cabin, there were only good memories here, which I'd known since I first opened my eyes wasn't the case with my former life.

Despite my amnesia, I'd been left with the unrelenting sense that my life before had been fraught with pain, both others' and my own, and that I was the cause of most of it. Guilt had wracked me for months, but Skye was the one to convince me that if I had sins to repent for, the best way to do that was to live a better life. Be a better man.

The kettle whistled, and I went about making tea in a large pottery mug as quickly as I could, before going to sit by the fire. The quicker I got about this remembering, the better off I would be. I closed my eyes, and tried to return to the memory of the falling rose petals, the woman's body pressed against mine. Some part of me knew things had gone further in that encounter than a passionate kiss, but I didn't want to remember that.

I wasn't the kind of person who could focus on more than one lover at once. At least I wasn't *now*. Thinking of another while my heart was still with Mina felt wrong. Perhaps I should start with a different part of the memory. I tried to take myself back to the walk—the falling rose petals. What had I seen around me?

A city, very different from Pravhna, with tall stone buildings. But in the memory, I'd been on a hill. There were huge evergreen trees in the distance, and a view of a lake—the Nameless Lake. My heart beat faster as I remembered. What was the city called? Kilm. Yes. That was it.

Kilm, the Emperor's city. But I was not from there. No, I was from somewhere further north. A citadel by the sea... Lyonesse. I could see the promontory in my mind's eye, the rocky shore jutting out into angry water. The citadel, rising out of the stony outcropping of land. House Thuellos.

Outside, a gust of wind blew one of the shutters loose from its fastening. It banged loudly against the house, drawing me out of my exploration of the past. I got up, stretched my muscles, and looked at the clock that sat on the heavy stone mantel. I'd been here for over an hour.

I was making excellent progress. At this rate, I might be able to make it back to Pravhna in a week. It would be slow going at times, I was certain, but if I had a bit of luck and the Strix woman didn't find and distract me, I would be fine. Relief flooded me as I walked outside. This had been a good choice.

The wood pile needed replenishing, and moving my body would no doubt trigger more memories if the curse was weakening, as Morgaine and Bayun had suggested. I found the axe and set up my first log. With every subsequent hack into a log, my body warmed and my mind cleared. I let it empty out, removing my shirt, as my skin was clammy with sweat. One log after another, my muscles burned with the pleasurable effort.

In my mind's eye, an image of a great labyrinth emerged, the strange girl, Morgaine, and the cat appearing. *They had been lost, and I walked the labyrinth daily. I was unable to leave my post for long, but the labyrinth offered relief from the creatures imprisoned within Nihil, and was close enough that I could return quickly if something went wrong.*

When Morgaine and Bayun appeared, they came bearing a familiar power, starfire. And they had spoken names I knew. The names of my family, my enemies—my lover. Though that name was one and the same with my enemy. I tried harder to focus on that moment and Morgaine's actual words, but I remained just outside the range of hearing. I knew the broad strokes of what she'd said, but could not hear the specifics.

Lost in the memory, I did not hear my attackers approach until it was almost too late. My sight moved back into my body and I spun with the axe, meeting the masked figures from the day of the fire. This time, there were only two, and rather than the slow approach they'd used to test me, this time they attacked in earnest.

They were fast, seemingly flying at me at once. My mind was still cloudy from the memory, but I ducked their lighting quick kicks and hits, taking a wide swing with my axe, which they both sprang away from with no trouble. One rose into the air, lifted not by wings, but seemingly by power alone, though I could not read its source.

They kicked at me, their legs moving at preternatural speed. I tossed the axe aside in favor of grabbing onto their leg, swinging them around hard as I could, and tossing them towards the river. The other was on me the moment I turned, moving so quickly I could not see the hits coming to block them. All I could make out was their masked head, so I butted it with mine, as hard as I dared.

They went down, but the other leapt back at me, now holding my discarded axe. Inwardly, I swore. I'd made a novice's mistake—my head still hazy with remembering. They swung and I ducked, once, twice, thrice, before summoning my fire. This was not going to end the way our first fight had. They were no longer testing me, but were here to kill me. My empyrae sliced through the axe, but my opponent leapt backwards before it could strike them.

They came back in concert now, and it was all I could do to fend them off as the hits kept coming. I blocked as many as I could, but one got me in my right flank before I landed a kick in their gut. They struck me more than I managed to get them, moving so quickly I was unable to track them.

They were wearing me out. The first fight had been about assessing my style. This was about killing me. They were Chopard's people, that much was certain, but why were they so invested in me? Had we gotten too close to finding out Chopard's identity?

Skye. Mina. Poe. They must have uncovered something in the city. Had they already killed them? Even Skye would not be able to fight foes this fast, and I was uncertain what Mina's powers might be able to accomplish. They would wear me out long before I could beat them, unless I ended this now. Empyrae boiled within me as I mustered up the strength to let it flow, my celestial fire fueled by my rage at Mina's possible harm.

It flowed out of my hands, so hot it was blue. Using empyrae would end my ability to question them, but it didn't seem I had another choice. When the fire hit them, it was imbued with my will, wrapping around them to prevent escape. The air filled with their screams and the smell of sulphur. It had been so long since I loosed my empyrae from within.

I fell to my knees, unable to stop the flow of celestial flame, though both of Chopard's fighters had fallen. The bodies still burned with the fire that would not stop flowing out of me. This is what I had feared—I couldn't stop. The empyrae was feeding on my life force now. It had been too long since I used it.

The day I was captured came back to me as I swayed. Not the burning fires on the battlefield, though those were clear enough in my mind. Now that I'd remembered them, I would never forget the sight of so many dead, and for what? My folly. No, what I remembered was her face. The woman from the alley, with the rose petals.

Her wide gray eyes peered in at me, through the bars that separated us. "I sent word," she said, her voice full of anger and pain. "I told you not to come."

She had. Nothing she said was wrong. She'd given me good reasons to stay away, but pride and guilt had made me think I knew better. The moment happened over and over, in a seemingly endless loop. *I sent word. I told you not to come. I sent word. I told you not to come. I sent word. I told you not to come.*

My second sight threatened to keep me in this moment forever, but my corporeal body caught wind of another presence. It was enough to startle me, my empyrae dying as I slumped over, onto the ground.

I'd almost burned out, lost in the memory of her. Of

Lumina, who I had thought I wanted to save. Who I came here to find. *Lumina*. All I'd wanted when I came to Sirin was to find her, to apologize. To tell her that I knew better now, and that after centuries of imprisonment, I knew that I had been wrong to ignore her warning, that I understood I was the cause of so much trouble, so much pain. And to warn her —I'd known something she needed to know. But what had it been?

A shadow fell over me. I looked up, into the scarred face of the Strix woman. "He's still alive," she called out. "He just burned himself out."

She disappeared for a moment. I struggled to right myself, but I had no strength and only managed to flip onto my back. Try as I might, I could not get up. I'd killed Chopard's people, only to make myself vulnerable to this Strix that wanted to kill Mina. A quiet cry of frustration fell from my lips.

Cool fingers cupped my chin, and a beautiful face appeared over me. It smiled, the full lips sensual, but the blue eyes that looked down on me were cruel. "Hello, Ashbourne," the face said.

The woman's blonde hair was pulled back into a tight chignon, accentuating the finely boned structure of her face. Like Poe, this woman possessed the kind of beauty that could be used as a weapon. Her face was so familiar, and yet I'd never met this woman before. I was sure of it. Where had I seen her face?

"Do you know me?" she asked.

I frowned, unable to form words.

"They're dead," the Strix called out. "He killed them."

The woman nodded, crouching low over me, her long fingers caressing my face. "Have you been enjoying living in my house, Ashbourne? Fucking my sister?"

Her sister? *Helene Wildfang.* That was where I recognized

her face from: the paintings in Orchid House. Mina's sister hadn't died in the fire. She was alive, and could likely answer all our questions. I struggled to speak, as I knew I couldn't rise.

"Hush," Helene soothed, stroking my cheek again and again. "Don't try to speak. You've worn yourself out."

I glanced at the Strix as she came to stand behind Helene. Why were they together? I remembered then what she had said the first time we met, that Mina had wronged her employer. Helene Wildfang was alive, and she wanted her sister dead. Again, I struggled to rise. I had to get away from them. Reach Mina before they could.

"Brigitte," Helene whined. "He's struggling."

The Strix stepped forward, a large dagger in her grip. Before I could so much as cry out, she hit me on the head with it, and all went dark.

CHAPTER 47

MINA

The moments after I finished explaining that Maman had wanted to rule the world were pure chaos. Poe and Skye both talked at the same time, shouting above one another in their attempts to be heard. It was difficult not to clap my hands over my ears to block them out, but I tried to follow what they were saying.

All I could make out was that neither of them could understand what all this had to do with Chopard. When trying to focus on their voices didn't work, I tried counting all the blue leather-bound volumes on the surrounding shelves. The aetheric power in the crystal chandelier flickered a bit, hurting my eyes. If only there was a window in here. Though I wasn't exactly claustrophobic, the workroom suddenly felt too small, too closed in.

The various ephemera on the shelves—skulls, apothecary jars filled with sharp teeth and shed skin from various reptiles—all began to seem macabre, menacing. Overwhelmed, and desperately wanting them to stop raising their voices, I held up a hand, but neither of them noticed. The noise and the pressure of my memory coming back together were all too much. Something had to stop.

"House Montclair is obviously involved," I shouted, unable to listen to the cacophony of their voices for a moment longer.

Both of them stopped, shutting their mouths. Blessed silence filled the air, calming me as my thoughts and the threads of the pattern began to emerge, clearer now than they'd been before. I needed a moment to think this through, and a bit more information.

I held up a finger, signaling that something was coming to me, but my mind was slow and cloudy still. I needed their help. "Tell me, Poe. Where are Viridian Montclair's parents?"

She frowned. "His parents? They've lived in Brektos for years."

I nodded. "But not always…"

She shook her head, obviously trying to follow my train of thought. "No, you're right. When my people were attacked, they lived here, at the estate near Somerhaven."

Again, I nodded. "Do you see a connection? It seems as though there *is* one…"

Both she and Skye shook their heads. They hadn't watched Maman's cohort gather every month, or overheard snippets of conversation over years and years. Fragments of information that never formed into anything truly meaningful, until now.

I paced along the worktable as it all came together, staying clear of the lekanomance. The Montclair choice of country property finally made sense. It was not their ancestral home, as ours was. No, the Montclairs were *from* Brektos; House Montclair was firmly established in Novo Mala, from everything I knew.

They purchased the estate outside Kyovka, short miles

from our own, when Helene and I were girls. And they were friendlier with us than any other family in the area, which, in retrospect, should have been suspicious. While many in Pravhna passed Maman's behaviors off as eccentric, with the disguise of Orchid House's obvious wealth to shield her, country families were different. They'd shied away from us, as though by instinct, though it was probably more a feature of the fact that Maman never participated in country life.

Poe caught my hand, trying to slow my movement. I hadn't noticed her moving, I was so lost in thought. "Come back to us," she whispered. "Tell us what you're thinking."

I frowned. She'd interrupted my stream of thoughts and now I was distracted, discombobulated. Poe seemed to understand, and smiled gently at me. "Take your time. I'm sorry I interrupted."

What had I been thinking? That it was odd that the Montclairs had overlooked our social standing in the country. Why hadn't I thought that was odd as a child, when I'd keenly observed so much else? The faintest of memories materialized at the back of my mind: Viridian Montclair, at ten, sword fighting shadows with sticks, alone by a creek. Letting me play with him when he'd caught me watching, then running away when Helene called me for dinner.

There was a time I'd wanted Viridian to like me. To be friends. Before Helene had seen his value to her social status. I pushed that out of my mind, hard. It had no bearing on what happened here now.

I struggled to return to the present moment, but Poe squeezed my hand again. Her patience with me and her understanding that she'd interrupted my thought process, slowing me down, gave me a boost of clarity. "I think the Montclairs were a part of Maman's cohort, the group that planned to use me as a conduit for the Ravager."

Getting the words out was a relief. I clasped Poe's hand in both of mine. "Thank you," I whispered.

She smiled, pulling my shoulder against hers, our hands still wrapped around one another. I felt no need to pull away. The tenderness I felt for Poe was changing me. *Safety, friendship, love.* These were all things I'd never known, and now I was greedy for them.

Skye leaned against a bookshelf, running a hand through her moonlight hair. "That makes sense." She glanced at me, her face shifting slightly into something I'd begun to recognize as concern. "I don't mean to be insulting, Mina, but Viridian's engagement to Helene was a bit odd."

I waved Skye's worry away, my free hand fluttering in dismissal. "It was. Most explained it away with her beauty… but that's not the point. What they were planning for me, it amounts to a coup. The destruction of everything the Oscarovi and Vilhari built after the Ventyr."

Poe let go of my hand, moving to the workroom doorway. "Thought I heard someone at the door," she murmured, frowning. When she turned back, she shrugged. "Must've been the wind."

I glanced at her, hoping my question wouldn't hurt her to answer. "Would your mother have come out of hiding to stop them from making me into an infernal weapon?"

Her eyes widened, then filled with tears. "Yes, she would have united the courts against Vaness, and likely the Oscarovi as a whole."

The thin veneer of society made it seem as though we had moved beyond the days of brawling for prominence. But those battles had only moved to other outlets—social status, capital, *echelon*.

Skye straightened. "It would have meant war, but the Vilhari would have won if they'd gotten to Vaness before she set the Ravager free—which perhaps someone did."

That was an interesting theory. Had someone killed Helene and Maman because they'd found them out? Skye's eyes went to Poe, who bit her bottom lip so hard I was afraid she might draw blood. Skye's thought had hit her quite differently than it had me.

"The Montclairs eliminated the risk of House Feriant trying to stop them," Poe said, her expression hardening again. "They removed the threat before it could hinder their plans to make you the Ravager's puppet."

My heart ached for her. I had never felt such empathy for another person, such concern for their wellbeing. I wanted to hug her, but feared that I might disturb her equilibrium.

Instead, I nodded. "I think Viridian became Chopard to form an army of his own. While his parents hold your family prisoner somewhere, or have killed them already, Viridian was left here to gain as much power as possible so that when Maman managed to inspirit me with the Ravager, they would have a foothold in the undercity."

"Why all the fires then—and why imprison you?" Skye asked.

"I'm not sure yet about the fires," I admitted. "But confronting Maman about the fetch has to be the reason they imprisoned me. They must have been worried I would escape them before they could enact their plan."

Poe's jaw clenched, her fists balled, her arms tight at her sides. "There's still so much of this we're not seeing." I understood her frustration; I was as impatient as she was to know more. Poe's eyes narrowed with determination. "But we can find out more if we confront Lord Eccles."

"That's dangerous," I said. "We don't know what he might be capable of."

"We need the information, though," Skye reasoned. "Before Chopard... Viridian... makes another move. If he was willing to imprison Mina to keep her safe for the

Ravager, we've got to find out what this is all about before he can get to her."

Poe's jaw twitched. "He's likely had eyes on us all along," she breathed. "He knows Ash is gone. Which means he knows we're at our weakest right now."

I nodded. "And that Ash is in danger as well." I looked to Poe, panic rising in me.

"I'll send for Rue," she said, closing her eyes. "He can get a message to Ash quicker than any other howler."

"Thank you," I murmured.

Skye nodded, gratitude in her eyes before she continued speaking, her voice faraway, as though she were speaking to herself. "If whatever Viridian is doing, burning all these places down, if it's all to get the Ravager here, we need to move quickly. We'll have to go to my mother. The high Vilhari can help us."

Poe's facial muscles tensed as she opened her eyes. "Rue is on his way to Ash," she explained. "We can consider whether or not to tell Elspeth when we find out more from Lord Eccles."

Skye frowned. "Why don't you trust my mother?"

Poe looked down at her hands. "It's not just your mother, Skye… Your grandmother and whatever little group they've gathered…"

Poe was so rarely at a loss for words, her hesitation surprised me. Another part of the pattern flickered in my mind.

"Do you suspect them of something?" Skye asked, her tone chill as a winter wind.

"No," Poe said quickly. "Of course not. I just wish we'd learned more about what they're up to."

Poe was lying. I didn't know how I knew, but I was sure. She suspected them of something else entirely. I had to wonder if she thought what I thought—that if by some chance Viridian Montclair was *not* Chopard, perhaps House Aestra was. They could be working together to achieve some other end, one we couldn't fathom yet. But Mirabelle's attitude had bothered me since the Avalonne. Something more was going on there. I was glad Poe had picked up on that as well.

Skye didn't seem to notice Poe's lie; she sighed with relief. "We'll ask Elspeth what's going on as soon as we can, all right?"

Poe nodded, her smile tight and conciliatory. I had no idea how Skye did not see what I did, but I moved my eyes to my ring, letting the flares of fire within the black opal distract me. This was something for them to work out. When the tension dissipated a touch, I looked up.

"It's settled then," I said, glancing at the clock. "We should get to the university. Perhaps we can catch Lord Eccles before he leaves for the day."

CHAPTER 48

MINA

An hour later, the three of us were on campus, dressed in the casual clothing of Aervale students. Ancient trees loomed overhead, mixing with the gloomy dark spires of the university buildings. Here, in the university district, the buildings were older, feeling almost ancient with their intricately carved arched doorways, every tower capped with stone sentinels, the great gryphon of Vilhari lore.

Some said this was the best example of architecture from the fey's original world, which they called Vilhar. It was not dissimilar in some ways from the more organic ornamentation the Oscarovi preferred, but the university had a feel of liminality, as though doors *between* might open at any moment. Likely, it was all the aether being used here. At any given time, there were dozens of magical experiments happening.

Before we left, Skye had tracked down where Lord Eccles' office was located. Poe and I stood outside the round Heathcliffe Camera building while she went inside to confirm. We were to watch each of the separate exits to make sure he didn't somehow leave without us knowing. Poe was seated on a bench under a stand of maples, ostensibly reading a book.

Students stared at her as they passed. They were right to—she made a beautiful picture, red leaves falling around her as a gentle breeze floated through campus. The day was mild up here, the sun's light golden and low in the sky. I was around the curve of the building, but sat far enough away that I could still see her. I tried to catch her eye, but realized quickly that the rose garden I sat in was likely obscuring her view.

Bells rang over the campus, signifying the end of the last class of the day. I glanced up at the astronomical clock that graced the front of the Lady's temple. A shiver ran through me as I noted, for the first time, that there were statues of large mountain hares scattered through the rose garden, peeking out of the foliage. All stared at the clock.

My breath caught. The statues were obviously quite old, and I'd been to campus plenty of times when in Pravhna. The Vercault Library was one of my favorite places. Why had I never noticed the hares?

The last bell rang. Office hours would begin shortly. Moments later, students came streaming out of the building. A flash of silver hair, moving against the flow of the crowd, caught my eye. Viridian Montclair.

I stood, surreptitiously trying to get Poe's attention, but again, she did not look my way. I would have to follow him without her. As quickly as I could, I merged into the crowd that was entering the building. As I walked through the doors, surrounded by students, I wondered what it would have been like to come here, merely for the purpose of learning things. It was a life I could hardly imagine.

I broke away from the group of people moving purposefully. I didn't know where to go from here. The inside of the Heathcliffe building was stunning. A marble staircase swept up the round walls, spiraling upwards. Light streamed in through the windows on the ground floor and near the domed roof, which was painted with a vivid scene of the Elemental War. Various fey, Oscarovi, and elementals were portrayed as victors, while my true people, the Ventyr, were depicted as wounded and weak.

For the first time, I noticed that when Vilhari artists portrayed the Ventyr, they did not do so accurately. None of the Ventyr had wings, nor had any in any other art I'd ever seen of the War. Only the statues at Orchid House portrayed us as we truly were. I wasn't sure what to make of that.

A fresh faced Vilhar with russet curls and round cheeks flushed pink with the cold bumped into me. "So sorry," she said with a smile.

"Oh, please don't worry," I replied, using the soft rasp I'd cultivated all these weeks in my social visits. This was the perfect opportunity. "Could you tell me where Lord Eccles' has his office?"

"First semester?" she asked.

I nodded. "I keep getting lost."

"This campus is a bit of a maze. It will get easier in a few weeks, you'll see." She pointed to the grand marble staircase. "Up two flights, then it's just to your right. 317, I think."

I thanked her, then joined the people heading up the stairs. My knees protested, but I had a purpose that kept me going: stopping Viridian from catching Skye unaware. He had to be here to see Lord Eccles. It was too much of a coincidence, especially after seeing them together at the Orilion party. I broke from the stream of students on the third floor. It was quieter here. I found 317 easily, and tried the door. I had no plans to knock, especially if Viridian was already inside.

The office was quite typical of what one might expect from a university professor, but for the blood that spattered the room, pooling on the floor in glossy crimson sheets. My stomach dropped within me and I stumbled, woozy, not at the sight of all that blood, but the scent of it. Memories of a battlefield filled my mind, my sisters hacked to pieces around me. I'd fought with the Larae once, just before the Ravagers came. I'd gone home to my true family.

I was lost in a swirl of memory and sorrow. Trauma kept me still when I should move, my ancient past devouring me whole. I felt the grimace of disgust stretch my face. Heard the screams of the dying in my head.

"Damn it all," Viridian growled from the other side of the door. His hand went around my arm and he yanked me inside, shutting the door firmly behind me.

I controlled myself, keeping my empyrae down while I assessed the scene. I had to calm down, push the memories back. Keeping my wits about me was of utmost importance now. There wasn't a body anywhere, and Skye was nowhere to be found. Neither was Lord Eccles, but I feared this might be his blood.

"What did you do?" I hissed as Viridian shut the door.

"What did I—" Viridian let go of me, pinching the bridge of his nose. "Lady take you. Mina, you are the absolute *worst*."

I frowned. His entire demeanor was off. This was not the Viridian I was used to at all. There was no bravado in him, only a kind of exhaustion I recognized. The kind that came from keeping too much in, too many secrets. Perhaps he saw it in me too because he pulled me away from the pool of blood on the floor that crept slowly towards us.

"Come away from that, *please*," he cautioned. "Someone has murdered Lord Eccles, and we don't need you caught up in such nonsense. We must go before Niall Aestra gets here. He'll have you in prison in the blink of an eye."

"You'd like that, wouldn't you?" I asked, but the question

came out more earnestly than I'd expected. Less accusatory, more genuinely searching. Viridian's usually neat and tidy clothes looked rumpled, his cerulean jacket the same he'd worn at Armande's. It looked as though he'd pulled it off the floor, wrinkled and slightly stained. Something was most definitely wrong with him.

"No!" Viridian said, eyes wild with frustration. He looked around the office. On the other side of the pool of blood, there was another door. "We have to get over there. That door goes to a private study."

I glared at Viridian, who was now bolting the door shut. "Touch nothing," he warned, showing me his gloved hands.

"You're not wearing gloves."

"I'm not going anywhere with you," I insisted.

"You must," he hissed, pulling on my arm again.

"No," I argued, angry with his overconfidence. Was he such a fool that he thought I would just meekly go along with him? "You're Chopard. You imprisoned me in an oubliette. Why would I go *anywhere* with you?"

Viridian covered his face with one hand, and I thought he might be crying for half a moment. His shoulders shook. But then his hand fell away, and I realized he was laughing, not with villainous mirth, but nearly hysterical. It was as though everything had gone wrong for him, and I was the thing that might break him. I could empathize all too well. I didn't like the feeling.

Again, he pinched the bridge of his nose, clearly exasperated with me. "I am not Chopard, you silly girl. I'm trying to *find* Chopard and stop you from becoming the conduit for an infernal beast."

"The Ravager?" I asked, hardly believing what I heard. "You want to stop that from happening?"

"Of course I do," he insisted, his voice raising an octave. "That is why I'm engaged to Caralee. Her family is in on your mother's horrendous plans. It's why I was engaged to Helene." He grabbed me by the arms, shaking me. "It's why I helped Helene put you in the oubliette, where you'd be safe—monstrous as it was to do that to someone. Even someone as infuriating as you." His voice has raised to a nearly shrill octave. He really was upset with me. "But you had to escape, didn't you?"

My mind swam. If what he said was true... but how could it be? "But your family was a part of Maman's cohort, were they not?"

Viridian sighed, the noise edged with another shriek of frustration. "No, Mina. House Montclair has always protected Sirin."

"Your people attacked the Court of Aether, though." Let him explain that.

"*Attacked* them?" Viridian tore at his hair. "We don't have time for this, Mina. Niall is never far from Eccles. He will be here in moments."

I crossed my arms. "I can deal with him."

Viridian closed his eyes. "Would you kill Skye's brother so easily?" He had a point. I would not. "I know what you're capable of. The empyrae. You can kill me later, if it pleases you. But for now, could we escape before things become even more complicated?"

"If you promise to explain everything," I said, hating that I followed his logic. "Now, show me how to get beyond the blood."

Viridian Montclair sighed again, this time with relief. "Finally, you see reason."

I gritted my teeth. Reason had nothing to do with it. Viridian was correct; I could kill him later. What I needed now was answers.

Nearly as soon as we'd made it out of Lord Eccles' private study and back into the hallway, there were sounds from within his public office. It was good we hadn't gone out the door we went in; we would have run straight into whoever was in there now.

"Niall," Viridian whispered. The hallway was full of students. "Keep your head down and follow me."

He led us around a corner, to a set of back stairs. They were narrower than the grand staircase and completely empty. I started to ask him for information, but he shook his head. Of course, anyone could be hiding in the staircase. He was right again. It was uncomfortable, Viridian being right so much.

The stairs were quiet but for a stray ghast or two. I kept my eyes deliberately averted. Ghasts had the nasty habit of showing you the way they died if you looked directly at them, and I was in enough pain going down the stairs. When we exited the building, we ran right into Poe and Skye.

Poe rushed towards me, grabbing me, throwing her body between me and Viridian. "You won't take her, you fiend."

I was grateful for her support, both in the emotional sense and the physical. For a moment, I leaned on her, catching my breath as the pain from navigating the many stairs slowly receded.

"You again," he growled, stepping forward, a menacing threat in his eyes. "What do you want with her? I won't let you charlatans turn her into a monster." He lunged for Poe, but Skye drew her rapier, lightning fast.

I looked around. There was a hedge of cedar growing around the back door to the building. We were hidden from sight.

"*Me* turn her into a monster? What about *you*?" Poe screeched.

"Poe," I said softly, regaining some of my strength.

"Viridian claims *not* to be Chopard, or a part of Maman's cohort."

She sneered. "He can claim whatever he pleases. He is a lying sack of shit." Skye kept the rapier against Viridian's throat, allowing Poe to ask whatever she wanted. "Where is my family, Montclair? What have you done with House Feriant?"

So we were doing this now. I was fine with that. I leaned against the back door to the building, fusing it shut with a tiny bit of empyrae, then moved my fingers quickly, drawing a muffling spell around us. It would give us a bit more privacy, and enough time to figure out what to do next.

"I'll never tell you where they are, you imposter," he growled.

Poe's mouth fell open in shock.

"Oh yes, I know what you planned to do, Hippolyta. You've been trying to use me to build your credibility for over a year now. Did you think I hadn't guessed your plans?"

Skye tilted her head to the side, a dangerous glint in her silver eyes. "Just exactly who do you think Poe is pretending to be, Viridian?"

This was not at all what I'd expected when we escaped Lord Eccles' office. Carefully manicured lies and excuses, yes. Some weak explanation for what Viridian had done, of course. But him accusing Poe of... whatever this was? This had not been on my list of things to expect from Viridian Montclair.

He shook his head, steadfast in some resolve. "Do whatever you want to me. Kill me, if you have to. House Montclair is loyal to House Feriant, and nothing you do to me will change that."

Skye glanced at Poe, as all our breath drew in. What was Viridian *saying*? My eyebrows raised as I pushed away from the door. Poe's mouth still hung open in shock.

"Do you mean to tell us that you're trying to protect House Feriant?" I asked, as Poe was too stunned to speak.

"Obviously," he spat out. "House Montclair came with the princess on the Avalonne. We took holy vows to protect her, and nothing any of you do will change that. Torture me, if you want to. I'll never tell where they are, and *you* will never claim her title, Poe."

A tear slipped down Viridian's cheek. It was the most vulnerable I'd ever seen him, but then I wondered if I'd ever seen the real Viridian Montclair. His chin quivered. "I'm surprised you'd be involved in this, Aestra. Do you know what this woman wants?"

Poe and Skye exchanged another look. Some invisible conversation passed between them. Poe nodded, and Skye lowered her rapier, sheathing it. "She wants to find her family, Viridian."

His eyes widened, as though Skye's words confirmed just how wrong he'd been about Poe. Poe straightened her spine, the glamour on her dark wings falling away. She looked Viridian straight in the eye, her shocked expression turning defiant and regal.

Viridian fell to his knees. "You're the *real* Hippolyta?"

The name fell from his lips in a cry of despair, as though he realized every mistake he'd made in one moment of horrifying clarity. If anyone had told me a week prior that I would understand Viridian Montclair so intimately, I'd have called them a liar.

"Your royal highness," he breathed. " I have made a grave mistake and will accept punishment. I thought you were trying to assume the princess' identity."

In a moment I could not quite comprehend, Poe bent down, placing a hand on Viridian's shoulder. "Do you know where my family is? My mother?"

He looked up, deep sorrow in his eyes. "Your mother was

killed in the raid." He glanced towards me. "The people who want Mina. The one you call Chopard—it's his operation, and they killed her on sight. But the rest of your people are safe. The descendants of House Feriant, the princess' retinue, are safe. My parents guard them, even now in Brektos. We thought you and Euryale had been killed."

"We almost were. She died on the Avalonne." Poe drew her glamour around her again, looking at both me and Poe. "I don't think he's lying. But how can this be?"

Skye offered Viridian a hand, pulling him up. He brushed off his pants, then wiped his eyes. Without his usual mask of bad temper and bravado, the lines of his face were sensitive, noble even. If my sister had known this version of him, she would have hated him.

"Chopard, whoever they are, is the one pulling all the strings." Viridian looked at me. "I believe they were the one manipulating your parents, Mina. I've been tracking their movements for years. It's why I offered marriage to Helene. I thought if I got closer to your family, I might be able to discern who Chopard was, and what their aims were. I didn't want to imprison you when Helene asked for my help, but in the oubliette, at least I knew you were safe."

"Did she tell you why I was being imprisoned?" I asked.

Viridian shook his head. "I'm sorry, no. Helping her was some kind of test. I still don't know if I passed it, but she never told me *why* we did it."

I wondered if he knew I was not the Wildfangs' actual child. I was not about to enlighten him, if he didn't. While I leaned towards believing what he said, it was better to keep some things secret and safe. "Did my sister know about this plan to make me the Ravager's conduit?"

Viridian shook his head. "Not that she told me. But I believe Chopard killed your mother and sister. Like you, he wields empyrae, and I fear they'd outlived their usefulness to him."

It was hard not to be frustrated. We'd solved part of the mystery, only to have more questions opened. I wasn't sure what to say to Viridian. His face was so earnest it was hard to comprehend that the other side of him existed. It was as though he was two people.

"Who do you think is Chopard?" Skye asked.

Viridian stared at the building, his eyes traveling around the round outer walls, as he thought. I wondered if he sensed something I didn't; his eyes kept traveling back to the windows in the staircase. "I thought perhaps Lord Eccles might be Chopard, but that seems unlikely now. He came to find me at the Orilion party to tell me to back off..." Viridian frowned, as though he were trying to work something out.

"Back off what?" I asked.

"You," he answered. "He told me to leave you alone."

The door rattled behind me. Someone on the other side was trying to get out.

"We should go," Viridian said. "It wouldn't be good to be caught here. I will call this afternoon though, and we can discuss this further."

Poe nodded. "We can find you, Viridian. If this is some ruse, know that I have eyes everywhere."

CHAPTER 49

ASHBOURNE

My vision blurred, and I was woozy, but my eyes opened. I lay on the floor of the cabin, near the fireplace. I glanced out the window. Not much time had passed, maybe an hour. The clock was too far away on the mantel, my vision still too fuzzy. I didn't want to risk drawing attention to myself before I got my bearings, so I didn't move, but I could tell I was not bound.

It wasn't necessary to move to know that I was still too weak to do anything but lay here like a lump. There was movement near the kitchen. Helene and Brigitte, the Strix woman. I tried to summon a little bit of aether, anything to help me, but I had no energy. I'd burned myself out fighting Chopard's people.

"Brigitte. He's coming around," Helene said, from the other side of the room. "Look."

The Strix woman, Brigitte, nodded. "That he is. Get on with it then."

Her voice was brusque, almost annoyed. It was an odd way for the Strix to talk to Helene, who was supposedly her mistress. Almost as though Helene were an unruly child.

Helene nodded as she came into focus, pulling a chair over to where I lay.

"Do you remember me?" Helene asked.

I figured it was better to play along. Of course, I recognized her from the portraits in Orchid House. She was unmistakable. "You are Helene Wildfang."

"Yes," she answered. "You tried and failed to kill me. I don't appreciate that. My sister isn't in Pravhna. Where is she?"

My breath snagged in my lungs, my heart nearly stopping. I couldn't remember ever having met Helene Wildfang before. I certainly did not remember trying to kill her. What was happening here?

Fear gripped me as I realized the gravity of what she'd said. If Mina wasn't in Pravhna, where was she? I had come here to keep her safe, and now it seemed that I'd left her vulnerable. I longed to ask Helene what had happened to Skye and Poe, but that wasn't wise. Even in my weakened state, I knew better.

I would have to buy some time, let my power rejuvenate. It had been a long time since I used so much, but I had to do whatever I could to draw this out. Making Helene angry would likely work for a little while. She seemed like the type who was used to getting her way. Outright refusal was probably my best bet.

I managed to struggle into a seated position, my back against the heavy, flannel-covered settee, with Helene watching me carefully. Brigitte stood in the kitchen, glaring at me. That was all fine; my strength was coming back, little by little. All I had to do was buy myself a bit of time. "I won't tell you where Mina is."

Helene sighed, standing up so she could look down on me. She was a delicate thing, with rail thin limbs and elegant features. I didn't know what kind of magical power she wielded, but physically I'd have no trouble overpowering her in... a half hour or so, I gauged from the feeling in my muscles. I was sore still, but moving again, a sure sign that my body would recover shortly, if not my magic.

"I was sure she'd come here with him, what with all the fucking you reported, Brigitte," Helene said with a vicious sneer.

She was a beautiful woman, no one could deny that—her hair was like spun gold, her eyes sparkling sapphires—but that *look*. It was pure ugliness. Helene Wildfang had let her mother poison her, ruining whatever physical beauty she might possess.

The Strix shrugged. "And apparently, you were wrong. Again. He won't be happy with you. This isn't what we were sent here to do. We came for Wilhelmina."

Helene sighed. "I thought he would happily kill her. He seemed so bent on it when he burned the house down."

When I burned the house down. The house. Mina's ancestral estate had been burned—that was how Helene, and this Brigitte if I remembered correctly—were supposed to have died.

Brigitte rolled her eyes. "If you say so."

"He was," Helene said. "Weren't you? You were so angry when you arrived looking for her."

Had *I* burned Somerhaven? Dizziness gripped me as I tried to recall, but I could barely think. Why had I been allowed to remember Lumina, but not this? Inwardly, I fought the feeling back.

I had to remember this. Something about this was important. Had I burned Somerhaven? Was I the one to kill Mina's mother? My eyes squeezed closed, the room spinning. Now, more than ever, I had the instinct that it was best to play along. I had no idea what the two of them were after and I needed time to think.

Helene waited for an answer. I had to say something to keep the conversation going. I steeled myself, willing my voice to come out cold and calm. What would happen if I agreed with her? Would she let me live long enough to regain some strength? The words tumbled out of me, a jumble of truth and lies, as I opened my eyes. "Yes, I wanted to kill her. That is why I came to Sirin. But you got to her first."

Helene smiled a victor's smile. What had I said that elicited that look? "Yes. And then the curse got you, didn't it? The closer you got to her, the more you forgot. But you remember now, which means you broke it. What was the loophole?"

She knew about the curse. My stomach clenched with worry. Helene seemed a bit unbalanced, but she knew more than she should. She was more than a few steps ahead of me. I needed more from her, so I shrugged. At least this much I could be completely honest about. "I have no idea."

"Well," Helene said, sitting back in her chair. "I'd rather see my sister dead than what *he's* got planned for her. Do you still want to kill her? You always did before, from what I understand."

My heart beat faster. What did she mean? Had I really gone to Somerhaven to kill Mina? Why would I have done such a thing? Something stirred in the back of my mind— the leaves falling in the driveway to the cabin. What had I remembered earlier, before Chopard's men came? I'd made progress.

Helene placed her elbows on her bony knees, resting her chin in her hands as she looked down on me. "That was what made her hate you so much in the end, wasn't it? That you'd always planned to kill her."

Some part of me remembered what she said, but it was unclear. Wrong... But also, I realized with a sickening lurch, some of it was right. What kind of monster was I? My jaw clenched with the pain of this newly realized knowledge.

I knew I'd been right to leave when I did. These two knew more about the man I'd been than I did. I *had* planned to kill Mina. I choked back a sob, realizing the near miss, the way I'd just barely gotten away in time. If I'd remembered all this when we were in the house together, might I have harmed her? I couldn't bear the thought of it.

"Helene," Brigitte cautioned. "I still don't think this is wise. He'll be angry with you when he finds out."

Helene smiled. "For a little while, perhaps, but then he'll see that *I* am the better choice for his plans."

Brigitte shook her head. "You have lost all good sense, girl."

Helene stood, her hand flying out towards the Strix. It made contact with a loud thud and an explosion of feathers. Brigitte hissed and clutched her face. "He will punish you for this, Helene, and I will enjoy it."

"I won't kill her," I said, interrupting them.

I had to stop them. I could not risk what might come next. The more they talked about killing her, the more deeply I cared for Mina. I could not allow myself to remember how I knew her, or the reasons I wanted her dead. She was my chance for happiness, and I was hers. I could never be the one who ended her life.

"I will never kill her," I said again, struggling to rise. "I will kill you both before I let you at her."

I couldn't do it. I knew that. But maybe they didn't. If they killed me first, I knew Mina could handle them. And if she couldn't, Skye could protect her. My only regret was that I wouldn't be able to say goodbye. But this was the only way to keep them all safe from the monster I knew myself to be, deep down. I had just enough strength for this—I pushed myself off the ground, lunging for Helene.

Brigitte was on me in a second, but I flung her off. She hit her head against the heavy dining room table. It was unfortunate. They'd have killed me faster together. I would have to put up enough of a fight to keep Helene going. This ended tonight.

I gathered my strength as she whispered words I could not understand. The pendant around her neck glowed and an elemental firedrake flew from it, its sharp claws aimed directly at me. It ripped at the skin on my chest as Helene called upon aether, a whip forming in her hands. She struck me again and again, as her elemental spirit clawed at me to keep me from getting up.

This is it, I thought as I surrendered to the pain. *Soon she'll be safe.*

Whatever I'd done to Mina before, something in me was sure that I deserved this now. If she'd hated me, then this was earned. I bowed my head and let the lashes come, only struggling for show.

The door to the cabin flew open. I raised my head, distraught to find the woman I fought to protect standing in the doorway, in a blaze of empyrae and aether. No, she couldn't be here now. Not when I couldn't fight to protect her. Not when I was still a danger to her if I lived.

"Get away from him," Mina said, her voice low and calm.

Helene loosed the lash upon me again, but her elemental rose to protect her. I slumped to the floor, defeated. A hot tear slid down my face. This was not how things should end.

"Come and get him, if you want him so much, *sister,*" Helene sneered.

I watched, helpless from the floor as the woman I loved stepped into the cabin. My heart thumped faster at the thought, panic and desire rising in me, twisting together as Lady Fate's talons wound around my heart.

THE HOLLOW PLANE

The woman I loved.

I did, I loved her, and I was so glad to know it in these last moments. To see that she loved me too—that much I could see in her eyes, though there was fury there as well. Frustration and confusion mingled on her face, and they were a familiar sight. *I sent word. I told you not to come.* The words were familiar, but I did not know why I thought of them now.

"You are no sister of mine," Mina said, taking another step forward.

Something in me changed as she moved, shifting. The pressure in my head lessened. Memories rushed back to me, overwhelming in their magnitude. *I sent word. I told you not to come.* An enemy princess. The woman I'd claimed, who'd claimed me, for all eternity. A bond so strong it had brought me through a portal to this world that no one else could reach.

Helene laughed, breaking my concentration, the flow of logic that had almost reached its conclusion. Her words tore the memories away, confusing me.

"You have always been so slow, Mina. Even now, you're just blundering through life." She raised her arm as though to send the whip forward again, this time in Mina's direction.

I could not let her harm Mina. I reached out, using my last bit of strength to grab hold of her ankle, and pulled hard, just as she cracked the whip. Helene stumbled, and Mina's arm caught the whip. My girl, my beautiful menace, smiled then, a stunning, feral thing to witness.

I had seen such a smile before, but not on her face. What did it mean?

In a flash, her aether wrapped around Helene, snapping her neck. "You should have died in that fire, Helene," she said as her sister slid to the ground. The elemental firedrake disappeared, dissolving into smoke.

Mina rushed to me, lifting my head into her lap. "Don't you fucking dare die on me," she growled.

There was fury in her voice, a fire I would not escape. The memories inside me, the ones I struggled to understand? She already knew the truth of them, whatever it was I'd done, whoever I'd been before. I'd meant to hurt her, and now I would pay. As it should be. The last thing I wanted now was to harm her, to regain some part of myself that would be capable of such a thing. I looked beyond her, worried Brigitte might regain consciousness.

But the Strix was gone—I'd killed her, though, I was sure of it. How had she disappeared? As my vision went dark, I whispered the only words that mattered. "I love you, Mina."

CHAPTER 50

MINA

SIX HOURS EARLIER - PRAVHNA

Viridian Montclair sat in the parlor at Orchid House, explaining the way he'd narrowed in on Eccles as someone who either reported directly to Chopard, or Chopard himself. "I followed him to some of the worst brothels in the upper city," Viridian said, revulsion obvious in the twitch near his eye and the way he wrinkled his nose. "And I tried everything I could to bribe the people he met with. But they would not speak about him for anything."

Well, that explained his trips to the brothels, at least. Viridian's story was growing more plausible by the moment. It pained me, in some ways, to believe him. He had, after all, locked me in a hole beneath the sea. But given what he'd suspected, what he feared, it was hard for me to argue with his logic.

"And now someone has killed Lord Eccles," I replied, thinking of the amount of blood on the floor. "Do you still think he's Chopard?"

Viridian shook his head. "Someone killed *someone* in Lord Eccles' office. There was no body. The cityguard will assume it was Eccles, because they are fools and like things to be tidy.

But we have no evidence that it was actually Eccles who died there."

I was already tired of this conversation and becoming distracted. Now that we knew at least some of Poe's family was still alive, I needed to talk to Ashbourne. If he did not remember me, I could force him to remember. He need not love me, but we had to resolve things between us. The curse was weakening, and I needed closure on this part of things before I could move on.

Curses were fickle things, and it was impossible to curse more than one person at once. Even my mother's sisters, Penthe and Faedra, talented as they were, could not forge a curse strong enough for two Ventyr adults. More likely, the curse was laid upon me, and me alone.

The memories I had of Penthe and Faedra speaking over me seemed to confirm my suspicions. The curse was on me, but applied to Ashbourne as well, and likely anyone who realized what was happening between us. But the spell radiated from me, triggered by my proximity to him. The amnestic effect, the gagging of anyone who tried to talk about the curse—those were all typical of such workings. Measures to ensure that the cursed would not escape their punishment until they'd found their loophole.

Before Ash met me in this life, I was almost certain he had been able to think of Lumina, of my former self. It was only when he reached Sirin that he forgot me. I had questions about how he'd gotten here, and I had no doubt that Skye had answers I needed. But would she give them to me?

I stared at her for a long moment. No. She would not betray him to me. Nor should she. Nor did I actually want her to. More than anything else, what I wanted was for him to explain himself to me. To tell me why he'd done what he'd done. And, if I was honest, I wanted him to let me punish him. To let out all my rage and make him pay the same way I had for the choices *he'd* made.

There was only one way that was going to happen. I had to go to the cabin and speak with him. The trouble was, I didn't have any idea where it was located. I needed a moment to myself.

I stood. "Please excuse me for a moment."

Skye and Viridian nodded, continuing to discuss the way the cityguard would handle things. Apparently, he suspected Detective Brenton and her partner of being in Chopard's pay. That did not surprise me. Poe watched me carefully, obviously suspicious. She was going to follow me, that much was certain.

It wasn't as though I could sneak out in broad daylight. I had no idea where to go. Instead, I went to the library and stared at Papa's books, remembering that as a child I had been foolish enough to think we would have been friends. That he would have liked me at all was a laughable idea now, given the fact that before he died, the man had helped Maman kidnap me and imprison me in this body.

I ran my fingers over the spines of the books. My memory of arriving on Sirin was still fuzzy, as many things were, and would continue to be. A curse that persisted for so long would take time to wear off, especially as it had been enhanced by the oubliette's magic. I paused when my fingers traced the spine of a romance. It was the story of a siren and her Oscarovi lover.

The sirens. The reason I still felt so comfortable with them was because they had been kind to me. For years, I'd wandered Sirin alone, trying to stay as far from the cities and the Oscarovi as I could. Why, I could not remember, but I had a reason, I knew that much. I lived among the sirens though, in an aerie across the sea. In Brektos. We grew fruit, apricoft and pairns, in enormous, terraced orchards, high above the clouds.

Sadness had followed me, a constant companion in those days, but I had finally been at peace. I had been slow to trust the sirens, but they had been patient with me—they gave me all the space I needed. A tiny cottage to myself, amongst their unwinged, humanoid children. Those like Muse. They were not happy times, exactly, but they had offered me something I had not expected when I came here. Peace.

Papa, Alastair Wildfang, was the one that found me. I remembered the day, though not much of what happened. I remembered him calling me Lumina in a market, on a sun-drenched mountain I can hardly remember now. All was confusion after that. He and Maman must have killed me, the first me anyway, Lumina.

I blinked away tears, happy enough not to remember that. The memories of my wings being butchered from my body were too much. If I had to remember dying as well, I didn't know if I could survive. My earliest memories after that were of Maman and Helene. Being a child. I had been an adult, ancient to the children of this planet. Then reduced to a mere babe again.

Was it even fair to consider Lumina my true self? I had her memories, but was I actually her? The question was philosophical in a way I had little patience for. A feline head bumped my ankle as Morpheus materialized.

Ashbourne needs you, he said, alarm in his voice. *Muse had a vision. You must go to him. Now.*

"I don't know where the cabin is," I replied. "Tell Skye. We'll all go."

No, the cat insisted. *It must be you and only you.*

I narrowed my eyes at the fey cat, speaking to him from inside my head. *I don't like to be manipulated. Not even by the servants of the Lady.*

It cannot be helped. Will you go?

I nodded. "Show me where."

I saw the trains I would need to take, the roads to travel down, the curve in the road, and the cabin by the river. It was all very clear. I whispered, "Distract them then. I must get my coat."

Morpheus nodded, and left the room. I headed straight back to the housekeeper's office. I threw a coat on, then scribbled a note for Poe, hoping she would understand what it meant.

"Where do you think you're going?" I turned to find her, hands on her hips, glaring at me. "How dare you think to leave without so much as an explanation. Have you any idea—"

I covered her mouth with one hand, pressing my finger to my lips with the other. With a flick of my free hand, I brought a muffling spell down on us, praying Morpheus could keep Viridian and Skye away for enough time to let me leave.

Bringing my lips to her ear, I breathed in her floral scent. It was comforting as a warm blanket. "It has to be me. I have to go alone. I can't ask you to leave what chance you have for happiness…but—" I slipped the note I'd written her into her hand, then kissed her cheek. "Know I would have followed you to the ends of the cosmos, my queen. We will meet again."

Her eyes were wide and serious as she clung to my hand. "We will meet again. I promise it."

I pulled my hand from hers before I could change my mind. Leaving her was the hardest thing I could remember ever choosing to do. In my long, long life there had been so many things I'd done because I had to. Because I was forced, tricked, or backed into a corner. But this, this was by my own choice. That did not stop the ache of knowing that I might not be able to come back.

That if I had to kill him, Poe might not be able to forgive me. That she might choose Skye above me, and that I couldn't ask her not to. "I love you, Poe," I said as I opened the back door. "You are everything I could have hoped for in a queen, a sister, a friend. Please don't forget that."

"I won't," she murmured as she took the door, tears welling in her eyes as she shut it softly behind me.

I paused there, feeling both our hearts breaking as we stood on opposite sides of the door. Then I turned swiftly, rushing through the garden as fast as I could. Only when I reached the street did I realize that Miranda Willsworth was watching me from her back window, an eerie darkness in her eyes. I hadn't the time to stop to think about it. If I slowed down for even a moment I would go back into the house and beg them to come with me. I'd abandon Muse's mandate, and all my plans to stay with the only friends I'd ever had.

On the train, I realized what the darkness in Miranda's eyes was. They had gone completely black, just like the eyes of the people who'd witnessed Chopard's attacks. There was no way to send a message on the train. I hadn't brought even so much as a calling card with me. Though I didn't know what it meant, I knew it could not be good.

THE TRAIN RIDE was a blur of anxiety, fear of what I left behind, and what was left ahead. I repeated my next moves to myself again and again. Send a message to Poe about Miranda Willsworth at the train station. Hire a car to take me to the cabin. Interrogate Ashbourne, by whatever means necessary, until he remembered what he'd done. Until he explained himself to me, once and for all.

If he was in some kind of trouble, as Muse's urgent message had suggested, I supposed I'd deal with that as well. It was easier to focus on my goals than unknowns. When the train stopped, I hurried off. The little country station was tiny. There was only one clerk at the ticket counter, and no customers in the lobby. When the Vilhari clerk turned to face me, their eyes were black, just as Miranda's had been.

I panicked, running from the station, before I could send a message back to Poe. My body ached with the effort, but I could not stop. I hazarded a look behind me, but the clerk did not follow. There were a couple of cabs waiting outside. I checked each driver in turn. All their eyes were normal.

With relief, I chose a Strix driver that reminded me a little of Evie, though the tweeds she wore were regular. She was not one of Edith's. I gave the address of the cabin and sank into the back seat of the cab.

"It's about an hour, Miss," the cabbie said, her accent a lilting one. She was from north of here, then. "You should rest. Forgive me for saying it, but you look awful."

"Yes," I agreed. "Thank you."

I didn't think I could sleep, but before I knew it, the cabbie's delicate voice woke me. "We're here, Miss."

"Shit," I swore, realizing I hadn't any money left to pay her. I'd used the last of what was in my coat pocket at the train station. I pulled a diamond hairpin from my mess of hair. "I'm sorry. Take this. If you don't want to sell it in town, take it to Orchid House in Pravhna. The women there will make sure you get paid. Ask for Poe."

The cabbie took the pin, her dark eyes serious. "All right, Miss. But this is more than your fare. Should I wait for you?"

"That's your choice," I said, thinking hard about what lie to tell, how to hedge against what might happen next. "If I return, it will be with a very sick man. He may not be conscious."

"Oh dear," the cabbie replied. "Is it the poppy or the bottle?"

For a moment, I was confused. Then I understood. "Both," I said. Why not go all out with the lie? If I had to knock Ashbourne out, she might as well believe he was in a bad way. "He needs a great deal of help. I don't know what state I may find him in. He's gotten himself into some trouble, you see."

The cabbie nodded, sympathy in her eyes. Clearly, she had experience with men who'd given over their lives to wantonness. "I'll wait for an hour. If you don't make it back, I never saw you."

"Thank you," I said, getting out of the cab. I felt a little guilty for playing on the obvious harm that had been done to her, but I would more than make up for it with money, if given the opportunity. "I appreciate the discretion."

She nodded, turned the autocar off, and leaned back in her seat, clearly prepared to take a nap.

CHAPTER 51

MINA

I crept down the long driveway to the Aestra's cabin. In truth, I expected a country manor built by the river, but was surprised to find out that it was, indeed, a rustic little cabin. It wasn't tiny, by any means, but nor was it a sprawling estate.

A window was cracked open at the front of the house. Voices inside let me know Ash was not alone. Silently, I made my way closer to the house, keeping well out of sight. A familiar voice was speaking inside the house, one I'd known my whole life. "...were wrong. Again. He won't be happy with you. This isn't what we were here to do."

I did not have to look inside to know who spoke. It was Brigitte, Helene's governess and lady's maid. What was she doing here? My heart shattered when the next person spoke.

"I thought he would happily kill her. He seemed so bent on it when he burned the house down."

Helene? This could not be. And what she said—did she mean that Ash was the one who burned the house down? When Morpheus said he was in trouble, I assumed he meant that Muse had seen him in anguish, that his memories tormented him, or that he'd been attacked in his pursuit of Chopard.

But this? He'd killed Maman? My heart nearly beat out of my chest, my breath stalling. I could not find air. Somewhere in the haze of my panic, I had the wherewithal to wonder *why* he'd done that. Why had he burned the house?

Inside the cabin, Brigitte said, "If you say so."

"He was," Helene replied. "Weren't you? You were so angry when you arrived looking for her."

And then I understood. Ashbourne Thuellos had come for me. This time he had come for the right reasons—even after all he'd likely endured, being imprisoned with the Ravagers, his heart hadn't hardened against me. He had found his way to Sirin to find me, to set me free from this prison, and when he found that someone had harmed me, he'd lashed out.

I didn't have to know the particulars of what had happened to know that the Ashbourne of my past would have killed anyone who'd harmed me, without thinking twice. Our bond was complicated, but it was nothing if not eternal. For a moment, my heart sang with joy. The Emperor had been wrong. My true father's last words to me had haunted me for so long, and now perhaps I might be free.

No one can love you, Lumina, he had said as he pushed me through the portal. *Not when they know the truth of you. No one is coming. You will be alone here, unknown and unloved, forever.*

His words had been the true curse. They were all I'd feared my entire life, living on the outside of everything. They were the reason I'd done as he asked so many times before Ash. So much harm had been done because I believed no one could ever love someone like me.

But despite his mistakes, despite all we'd been through, Ashbourne had changed. Proven everyone wrong. He had come for me, killed for me. *Did he love me now?*

"Yes," Ashbourne replied, voice calm and collected. He sounded nothing like the Ash I knew now, but exactly like the prince who betrayed me. My hope died, shriveling inside me like rotten fruit. "I wanted to kill her. That is why I came. But you got to her first."

He was the same as the rest of them then. He hadn't changed a bit. I tried to shrug it off, but the knife cut deep. I couldn't let this matter now, not with Helene's return. My sister wasn't dead. And she was meeting with Ashbourne out here in the woods, in secret. Had he been plotting against me this whole time? My heart felt as though it would shatter into a thousand pieces. I curled into myself, staying still as I could. I needed more information.

Helene spoke again. "Yes. And then the curse got you, didn't it? The closer you got to her, the more you forgot. But you remember now, which means you broke it. What was the loophole?"

At least they hadn't been working together. But they might be soon. Perhaps that was what this meeting was about.

"I have no idea," Ash said, casual as could be. But I knew better. Helene might not, but that was a lie. What was happening here?

"Well," Helene said. "I'd rather see my sister dead than what *he's* got planned for her. Do you still want to kill her?"

There was a long pause. I couldn't see what went on inside, but it seemed as though Helene waited for some kind of response. I wished I could peek in and see what was happening. Finally, she spoke again. "You always did before, from what I understand. That was what made her hate you so much in the end, wasn't it? That you'd always planned to kill her."

She wasn't wrong, but how had she known all that? It wasn't possible for Helene to have known these things. Panic had me in its grip, but I wasn't giving in so easily. I had to get the information I needed and then retreat somewhere safe to sort this out.

"Helene," Brigitte cautioned. "I still don't think this is wise. He'll be angry."

Helene answered. "For a little while, perhaps, but then he'll see that I am a better choice."

Who were they talking about? It had to be Chopard. But if that were true, why would Helene want me dead? Did it even matter? Was Ash going to agree to kill me?

I clutched at my head. Memories of the first time I'd discovered that Ashbourne had orders to kill me rushed back, the scent of rose petals in the air lingering in my mind. It had been nothing like whatever this disaster was. I had my orders as well. Once we'd solved the problem with the Ravagers, the Thuellos prince had to die. My father had seen no use for furthering the alliance between our houses. My mission had been to seduce him, gain his secrets, and then, eventually, kill him.

And apparently, he had been mandated to do the same. We'd discovered one another at nearly the same moment. It had devolved into frenzied lovemaking, fuel for a fire that had been building between us for months. But this was something else. He actually sounded as though he might kill me now. Despair filled me. The man I loved yesterday was gone.

Brigitte spoke, breaking the hold memory had on me. "You have lost all good sense, girl."

A loud thud came from inside the cabin, followed by the unmistakable sound of a Strix hissing. "He will punish you for this, Helene, and I will enjoy it."

My sister had hit Brigitte. It wasn't as though it was an uncommon thing. I'd seen her do it dozens of times growing up. But now that I'd lived another way, it was shocking to me. My sister was a *monster*.

She, Maman, Papa. They were all monsters. People didn't live the way we had. Not average people. I'd known no better as a child, but I did now. I'd had an inkling when I grew old enough to understand the world better, but now I was sure of it.

My thoughts were interrupted by Ashbourne's soft voice, deep and clear. "I won't kill her," he said, interrupting them. What was he doing? A moment ago, he'd said he wanted to kill me. Now he wouldn't?

"I will never kill her," he said, the sound of a struggle following his words. Was he hurt? "I will kill you both before I let you at her."

He sounded like the man I knew now, not the prince of before. Sounds of a scuffle ensued. I expected it to be over quickly. Ashbourne was bigger than these two, faster and a warrior. He could easily overpower them. But the sounds of the fight went on. And what did I expect would happen when he'd fought them off?

What part of what he said had been the truth? Did he want to kill me or protect me? There had to be some place else to hide and think over my next move. I could no longer be sure that I could trust him. I moved as quickly as I could, heading towards the river. There had to be somewhere near the riverbank I could tuck myself away in and watch what happened next.

It was odd how little I felt about the possibility that Ash might kill my sister and Brigitte. But I'd never had any trouble remembering who Helene was. It was only that my perspective on her had changed. When I'd been so little loved and respected, even her toxic love had seemed better than Maman's obvious hatred for me.

But now, I wished she had stayed dead. There was no relief in me that she hadn't died in the fire. I had no curiosity whatsoever about how she'd escaped or where she'd been these last months. I would rather not kill her myself, but I would if I had to. When I rose out of the sea I had been willing to kill her, but now it seemed a bit distasteful. I had loved her once, but if she wanted to kill me, I would happily kill her first.

Ahead of me, a tendril of smoke rose from the ground. I scurried to it, finding two bodies, smelling of sulphur, still burning. Someone had used empyrae to kill these people.

I remembered what Helene said. He'd burned Somerhaven. Certainty grew in me. I'd been right the first time. He'd come for me, and my sister had believed it was to kill me. But I *knew* Ashbourne. Both the Ashbourne of before, and the one I'd fallen in love with.

He came to save me, as he had before. It didn't excuse all he'd done. I still wanted him to answer for the ways he'd ruined me. If he had the power to burn all of Somerhaven to the ground, he could certainly kill two people. I looked carefully at the deep gouges in the ground next to the bodies. He'd burned them, and then kept loosing his empyrae on them.

He'd lost control of himself. The threads pulled tight in my mind. The curse had taken him at Somershire. His proximity to me had driven him out of his senses, and there was no doubt in my mind that Maman had tried to fight him. If she thought he might take me from her, take her chance to use me as the Ravager's vessel, she would have tried to kill him. And he would have fought back, with much, much more power than she could ever have expected.

Perhaps he hadn't been attacked, as Skye and Morpheus had assumed. It was possible he'd been caught in the wreckage of the house he burned, collapsing. After that, the curse must have taken him, causing him to forget everything he'd known. I had no idea how he'd made his way here, but the rest made sense. If he'd burned himself out at Somerhaven, the amnestic effect of the curse would have been strengthened.

And he'd used his empyrae again today, burning himself out again, if those marks in the ground were any indication. My heart raced at the realization. My sister was powerful—more powerful than Maman had ever been. If he was weak, burned out, she might kill him.

I turned back to the cabin, my body moving too slow, too tired to run. As I drew nearer, slow as I was, I heard the sound of a lash. Of Ashbourne crying out in pain. She was hurting him, and he was not resisting. Why wasn't he fighting her?

He believes he deserves this fate, a voice said as I struggled forward. Each step was more painful than the last. I hadn't been taking good care of myself. The voice came from everywhere. *Do you?*

"No," I whimpered, limping forward as best I could. My knees burned with more than their usual pain. I was too tired. If I could make it to the cabin, I could stop Helene and Brigitte with empyrae, but I was too slow. I would hear him die as I dragged this body towards him, unable to help him. What was all this power for if I could not do this?

What would you exchange to save him, little one? the voice asked. *Would you choose our side? Would you choose Sirin over all else?*

"Who are you?" I begged, though I knew the answer. The eldritch god I'd called on at the standing stones sounded just like this. She of the Still Places had found me. The warnings the hares had given me were all coming true.

His time runs out.

There was no other choice then. To save Ashbourne, I must agree to be the puppet once again, rather than the mistress of my own life. I had never been allowed sovereignty over myself. My whole life had been one manipulation after another. Saying no to this nameless god wouldn't stop her from coming for me again. It would only prolong the inevitable.

But I wanted one thing for myself. One choice that was mine alone to make. I wanted to decide Ashbourne's fate. "I will agree to whatever you ask. But he must live to answer for what he did to me."

Granted, the voice said, full of wry amusement. *I am sure you're quite capable of making Ashbourne Thuellos pay for his sins.*

Dark blue light, the light of elementals, surrounded me, lifting me. My body floated to the cabin with ease, and some of my strength returned, though the pain did not abate. Apparently, even a god could not, or would not, remove it from this body. I shook my head, a sneer of disgust crossing my face.

I had agreed to this, but I did not have to like it. There was nothing in our agreement that said I had to be grateful. The god's voice laughed in my mind, as though she heard my every treacherous thought. That was just fine with me. Let her know the truth of the bargain we'd made. I was no willing supplicant to her cause.

When you are done with him, I will see you at the standing stones, the voice said. *You belong to me now.*

"Fine," I gritted out as my feet met the ground, pain shooting through my metatarsals. "But I warn you, you'll likely regret this."

The god's laughter filled my mind. *How wonderful you are, Mina.*

I rolled my eyes, flicking my hand at the door to the cabin, my power renewed and strengthened in some way I could not yet understand. The door flew open, revealing a horrific scene. Rage mounted in me.

Brigitte was sprawled on the floor. She wasn't breathing, and I hadn't the time or inclination to check for a heartbeat.

Ashbourne lay near her, bloody and battered as my sister lashed at him, her firedrake elemental keeping him pinned to the ground. He raised his head as my power sprang to my hands.

"Get away from him," I commanded my sister.

Helene loosed the lash upon him again, but her elemental rose to protect her. Ash slumped to the floor, defeated.

"Come and get him, if you want him so much, *sister*," Helene sneered, her cold blue eyes alight with pleasure.

She was enjoying this. Just as she had enjoyed inflicting pain on me her entire life. I had no idea how she'd escaped the fire, or falsified her death. It didn't matter now. She had harmed the man I loved, and I *did* love him, no matter how angry I was with him now. He was mine, and she'd harmed him.

And now she would pay. "You are no sister of mine."

Helene laughed. "You have always been so slow, Mina. Even now, you're just blundering through life."

She raised her arm, as though to send the whip forward again, this time in my direction. Ash reached out, grabbing hold of her ankle. He pulled hard, just as she cracked the whip. Helene stumbled, and I caught the whip round my arm. The aether she wielded melted into the power that I controlled, becoming mine long before Helen could hurt me.

I smiled then, a wicked grin that was wholly my own, born out of every moment Helene had tormented me. Out of every hurt she and Maman had wrought over the longest twenty-eight years of my life. There was no need to draw this out, or to make big speeches. I was done with this part of my life.

A snake of my aether formed a cord of its own, whipping out at Helene and strangling her without a second thought from me. It snapped her neck with no effort at all, and I did not feel even so much as a whit of remorse. "You should have died in that fire, Helene," I said as she slid to the ground.

The elemental firedrake disappeared, dissolving into a puff of aether. This was the price for tying a life to a life for more power. The firedrake could not exist without Helene's lifeforce.

I rushed to Ash, lifting his head into my lap. "Don't you fucking dare die on me," I growled.

His eyes went soft. He wasn't the prince of our youth. He was only Ashbourne Claymore, private investigator. The man that, a day ago, I had thought held my future in his hands. As his eyes fell closed, he spoke the only words I wanted to hear.

"I love you, Mina."

If only it was not far too little, and far, far too late.

CHAPTER 52

ASHBOURNE

I woke at the bottom of a deep hole, something in me fundamentally changed. Dark stone walls curved around me, the sound of water echoing. Memories of who I'd been mixed with who I thought I was. The dim light of the hole did nothing to relieve the looming feeling that everything had gone terribly wrong.

Or had the scene in the cabin been a nightmare? It seemed impossible that everything had changed so much in just a few short days. In search of hope, I raised my head upward, toward the light. The woman I loved had been stuck in a place much like this for a year, and now she sat above me, her pretty legs dangling over the edge.

Somewhere far beyond, waves crashed angrily, and rain fell on us both. "Good," Mina said. "You're awake. Do you remember what happened?"

I nodded, glancing down at my body. My wounds were healed. I frowned. My clothes had been changed as well. I was warm and dry enough, despite the rain. "Did you heal me?"

I didn't bother yelling. Both of us could hear just fine without the volume.

Apparently, Mina had come to the same conclusion. She shrugged. "You got the medical attention you needed. I wanted you awake and clear-headed for this."

I was mostly dry, but her hair was wet from the rain. She wore a long white gown, but no coat. I worried she might catch cold, with the rain falling on her, revealing every curve of her body. It was a beautiful picture, if melancholy, but I worried for her health.

I was at the bottom of the oubliette, and if she was sitting at the top, then nothing I remembered was a nightmare. That was most unfortunate.

"I am clear-headed," I agreed, then tried for a lighter tone. "I don't suppose you'd let me out so we could talk this over somewhere a bit more comfortable?"

"I think not," she said, matching the light tenor of my voice. "I think what we need now is some time apart."

Hadn't we had enough of that? It seemed that in the thousands of years we'd known one another all we'd done was stay apart. Things were different now; why continue with the same old mistakes? Looking up at her, at the steel in her eyes, at the sheer will written all over her face, I knew she was the same as she'd ever been, stubborn and convinced her way was the only way.

I sighed, feeling eternally exhausted. "What good will that do us, love? All we've ever done is fuck and fight." The words slid out of me before I could consider them. I grimaced as soon as they hit her.

She peered over the edge of the oubliette, unadulterated fury on her face. A terrible thought crossed my mind; *she was somehow even more beautiful sinister and angry than she was calm.* Why would I think such a thing? But then, I had remembered, hadn't I? The man I was before. And now, I was no longer Ashbourne Claymore. Or at least, I was no longer just that man.

Now I was someone else as well. Trying to reconcile the two parts of me was unsettling, and likely dangerous. Perhaps she was right to have stuffed me down here. That other part of me took over, the prince that had bedded the princess the moment he knew she was out to kill him. The man who was aroused by violence and cruelty.

I stopped fighting it for a moment. Stopped fighting the memories that threatened to overtake all I'd done, not only in the past year but the centuries of imprisonment I'd endured, to become a better man. Now though—it was as though that moment on Interra, eons ago, was merely a day ago. The ghost of her knife at my throat sent my heart racing, the memory of her fangs impaled in my skin lit every nerve in me aflame. I leaned against the wall, letting the wicked grin of a young prince spread over my face.

"Oh good," she sneered, looking down on me. "I hoped this side of you would show up. I was afraid you didn't remember yourself. That you were stuck inside the narrow little tunnel you built for yourself as Claymore."

Mina pulled her legs up with some effort, wrapping her arms around her knees. The sight of her struggle brought me back to myself, back to the present. She was cold, and I ached to wrap myself around her, warm her shivering body with mine. It was as though I was being dragged in and out of the past, moment by moment, the two halves of myself unable to exist at once. I couldn't find the words to say that to her though, not after all I'd done, and all that she'd endured.

"All that Thuellos charm is still in you, isn't it?" Her voice was sad now, but her words still held a bite. My girl was a fighter. And I was willing to take my punishment. But I feared what she was up against. What might happen to her while I was paying for my trespasses.

She had to keep fighting, even if it took making her hate me even more. "As I recall, Lumina, my Thuellos charm is in you, too. Has been in you from that first fuck." My words were coarse, meant to inflame her. She needed to be angry at me now. Needed to hone herself into the weapon I knew she could be.

She scoffed. "Have you forgotten the fetch?"

I laughed, low and cocky. "Do you think my claim was on your Ventyr body? I claimed your soul, and you mine. We are bound forever, my girl. Unless you'd like to come down here and kill me."

She stood, her face distorting with pain. When she spoke, her voice was soft. "I know what you're trying to do."

I looked up at her. She was the most beautiful thing in the world. In all worlds. I had searched for her, even in Nihil deep in the limen, even imprisoned, I had looked for her. I found her once, I could find her again. But if she didn't want me—then none of it mattered.

"Did you know they cut my wings off?"

My eyes fell to the ground. I had not known that. Her wings. The space between my shoulders ached just thinking of it. I would need to remove my glamour now that I remembered myself. Now that I remembered my true form. If I did, I could shift now, toss off my glamour and fly out of here. But I would not insult her in such a way.

But her beautiful wings—severed from her body. It was unthinkable, a betrayal that no Ventyr could forgive. And I was the cause of her pain, of that most grievous mutilation. My breath caught in a sob.

"No," I choked out.

"They kept me awake. Forced my eyes open and made

me watch in a mirror. Each time I passed out, they revived me."

Every word was a knife to my soul, as it should be. When they cut her, they knew that someday I would learn of it. That she would hate me for it forever. It was the last thing her father, the Emperor, had said to me before he locked me in Nihil. "If you ever see my daughter again, she will hate you more than any person she has ever known."

I had not believed it at the time. Now I knew what he meant. Years had taught me my mistakes. I'd come here to make things right. To find out if the woman I'd known on Interra was still my mate, still my claimed partner, or if we would have to go through the painful ritual of unwinding our bond. I dreaded the moment she would ask for the reversal.

Her voice was quiet when she spoke again, almost drowned out by the howling wind. "I walked this world, abandoned and alone. Spellbound to my glamour for centuries. When I was finally at peace, the Wildfangs found me, killed me, and turned me into this."

Her voice was softer still, so vulnerable and young. "And it is all your fault, Ashbourne. Because you would not listen. You would not believe the prophecy Alcyone gave to me. Why could you not trust me?"

Tears slid down my face. Honesty was the only way now. Truth would not set me free, but it was my only choice. "Because I could not stand for you to be imprisoned when I walked free."

"I told you," she shrieked, her voice ravaged with the pain of over a thousand years of loneliness and betrayal. "I told you what she said. That if you came for me, it would end like this. In eternal war, with the Ravagers free. All lives forfeit—the cost for what *we* have done."

My shoulders shook with the sobs spilling out of me. She *had* told me. Nothing she said was an exaggeration or lie. I had known when I gathered my generals that the siren prophetess had spoken, and I did not believe her.

I did this. I was the reason for all of this.

"And still I love you," she said, her tears falling into the oubliette. "But love is not enough, Ashbourne. This kind of love is nothing but pain. Do not look for me."

Before I could say another word, before I could beg her to listen, the sea came crashing in, flowing over the invisible seal on the oubliette. I waited for the forgetting to begin, welcomed it even. It would be a blessing to forget this—and, I realized as the hours went by, that was exactly why it would never come.

Mina had not left me here to forget. She had left me to remember.

~

THANK you for reading THE HOLLOW PLANE. The duology will conclude with THE RAVAGED DARK.

If you would like to know more about the story of the Ravagers, and Ashbourne's life before Sirin, part of his tale is in THE IMMORTAL ORDERS TRILOGY. The first book in that series is DARK NIGHT GOLDEN DAWN.

EXTRA CONTENT

Are you looking for a glossary or a full color version of the world map in this book? Perhaps you'd like to read deleted scenes or see all the wonderful character art I've commissioned.

Please visit my website at www.allisoncarrwaechter.com to learn more about Sirin and the worlds I've dreamed up.

THANK YOU FOR READING

Thank you for reading this copy of *The Hollow Plane*. Reviews are the lifeblood of publishing. They tell other readers what you enjoyed about the book, as well as telling retailers that folks are reading. If you would not mind leaving a review for this book before you go, that would mean the world to me.

ACKNOWLEDGMENTS

This book was written in one of the hardest years of my life. When I first wrote these acknowledgments, I was in a dark place. I truly felt like my career might be over, like I might be ready to give up. That the indie gig was just too hard, and that I might not be cut out to do this work.

But some wonderful people with a lot of good ideas and fresher brains than mine stepped in and changed the course of things so quickly that I am reminded of how lucky I am. Sometimes, when things are at their darkest, our friends come and pull us into the sunlight. We feel warmth on our faces, and we can go on.

If you were a part of that, please know that I know how fortunate I am to have you with me. Lady Fate has blessed me with hard paths to walk in this life, and also with wonderful traveling partners. This does not go unnoticed.

My husband is the first person I need to thank. Thank you, my love, for staying. For hanging in. For giving me the kind of love that I learned all too acutely this summer how devastating it would be to lose. There is so much of you in Ash, but I'm really going to need you to get on this mushroom tart business, ASAP.

And next, my mom, who always let me read what I wanted and watch soap operas. I write good friendships and great family relationships because you showed me how it's done. I know just how lucky I am to have been your kid. This year has just been more evidence of that.

HUGE THANK YOUS:

To the people who inspired the friendships in this book: Annie, Victoria, and Holly, thank you for being my backbone when I needed it, my hand to hold, the loves of my life. Every book gets better because of your advice, and I get better because you love me. I can't write each of you an individual note here, because printing is already too expensive and I'd write whole chapters devoted to how much I love you.

To the bookish besties who keep me going on a day to day basis: The Rogue Order, my Old Guard, the Steadies. I. ADORE. YOU. Right when I was about to give up, y'all stepped in and said "not today." I will literally never forget that.

Charlotte. You will scoff, because you always do when I tell you this, but you're the sunshine to my slightly grumpy, the ray of light when I need one. Your friendship means so much to me, and I am so lucky to send and receive several unhinged voice notes a week with you.

Chels. Thank you for always, always getting it. For dreaming big dreams with me, for talking about the hard stuff and for letting me share every big moment. You mean the world to me.

Ali. Your belief that I've got this and your willingness to step in when I need an extra hand or brain blows me away. Love you, friend.

To my sweet Ash, who always has an ear and an encouraging word, who always sees right where I'm going with things. Thank you, love.

To Kenna for cleaning me up and dusting me off and letting me use as many em dashes as I like (that's not true at all, *but what if it were????*). Thank you for doing the part that most people hate the most.

To Christin for bringing yet another cover to life in a way that blows both my and readers' minds. I am so lucky to have you in my life.

To Rachael Ward for making the interior of this book prettier than I ever imagined it could be, I'm clinking my teacup to yours and I can't wait for readers to see what we're dreaming up next.

To the Coven as a whole, but especially to Lisette Marshall, who answers every silly question I ever have with such patience and grace. I literally would not be hanging in here without you.

***To all my readers.* I say this every time, but every book you read, every review you leave, every time you talk to friends about my books, you are making a dream I never thought possible come true. I love you. This is literally all for you. You changed the course of my life and I will forever believe that I have the best readers ever. This is my hill, and I'll stay right here.**

MEDIUM SIZE THANK YOUS FOR MONSTER ATTITUDES:

Neville and Tibby, thanks for napping for at least part of this. You both are lucky you're so effing cute.

ALSO BY ALLISON CARR WAECHTER

THE IMMORTAL ORDERS

COMPLETE SERIES

Dark Night Golden Dawn

Beneath the Alabaster Spire

Awaken the Fifth Order

OUTLAWS OF INTERRA

REVISED SECOND EDITIONS COMING 2024

Vessel of Starfire

Sea Smoke

The Last Witch Queen

Gods Walk the Earth (2025)